BAND OF GYPSYS

BAND OF GYPSYS

GWYNETH JONES

GOLLANCZ

LONDON

Copyright © Gwyneth Jones 2005
Frontispiece © Bryan Talbot
All rights reserved

The right of Gwyneth Jones to be identified as the author
of this work has been asserted by her in accordance
with the Copyright, Designs and Patents Act 1988.

First published in Great Britain in 2005 by
Gollancz
An imprint of the Orion Publishing Group
Orion House, 5 Upper St Martin's Lane,
London WC2H 9EA

A CIP catalogue record for this book
is available from the British Library

ISBN 0575070439 (cased)
ISBN 0575070447 (trade paperback)

1 3 5 7 9 10 8 6 4 2

Typeset by Deltatype Ltd, Birkenhead, Merseyside

Printed in Great Britain by
Clays Ltd, St Ives plc

www.orionbooks.co.uk

Acknowledgements

Thanks, as always, to my editor, Jo Fletcher, my agent, Anthony Goff, my illustrator Bryan Talbot, and my home team, Peter Gwilliam and Gabriel Jones, for invaluable support. Special thanks to Gabriel Jones for helping me with my guitar masterclass, and to Peter Gwilliam and the insiders for research assistance on the Montmartre, Parliamentary and Metropolitan Police fronts. Thanks to the Insane Stupid Behaviour Crew, (Newman chapter) for the loan of their name, and Skin Candy of Baker Street for advice. There's an account of Paul Thompson's 2001 study of the "forest fire effect" in early onset schizophrenia at http://www.loni.ucla.edu/~thompson/thompson.html: needless to say my use of this clinical study is entirely fictional. 50 Berkeley Square has the reputation of being "the most haunted house in London", and was the house that inspired Bulwer-Lytton's classic story 'The Haunters and the Haunted', "Wallingham", although entirely a fictional creation and used fictionally, bears some debt to Waddesdon Manor, Buckinghamshire: many thanks to the Rothschild Archive for their assistance. 'Ruin is the devil's work' from Emily Dickinson, 997 'Crumbling is not an instant's act'; 'Is My Team Ploughing?' AE Housman, from *A Shropshire Lad*. 'For I dipt into the future . . .' from 'Some Day', Alfred, Lord Tennyson; 'Out of this nettle, danger . . .' Wm Shakespeare, Henry IV Pt One. The curious cardgame described in Chapter 7 is called poo-head, and was devised by Jon and Pat Mayes; used with permission. More sources, bibliography, discography, picture archive, in the Band of Gypsys scrapbook, www.boldaslove.co.uk

The location for the frontispiece is the Oscar Wilde Memorial, Père Lachaise cemetery, Paris: Lachaise cemetery, Paris: original photo, Bryan Talbot

Band of Gypsys

of

Gypsys

by

Gwyneth

Jones

PROLOGUE

Along The Watchtower

In a bar in Washington DC, not far from Capitol Hill, two smart young fellows met one evening and spent a while impressing one another; covertly checking the tailoring and the accessories while the snow fell thick and fast outdoors, turning all the mighty public buildings into bridal confectionery. They had a few drinks, conversation became pleasantly indiscreet. They were both in positions to be indiscreet about great affairs, but Frank could see that tonight the other guy had the good story. Without haste, he drew his friend to speak. Businessmen came and went, beautiful women sashayed by; the neat, discreet waitresses plied refills, and in due course it came out. Lavoisier. Something about that awful secret bubo on the body politic, which the Pres had been revealing to the select behind closed doors: audiences from which Fred Eiffrich's friends and enemies both emerged grey in the face and shaken.

These two, along with a few other smart folks around the citadel by now were savvy on Lavoisier, without benefit of one of those solemn need-to-know sessions: a desert nest of terrorists, Manson family on the edge of going critical with the weird occult superweapon. And the raid, how about that raid . . . ! The FBI and the National Guard were going in with a division of infantry, in their chemical suits and their breathing apparatus, deep stealth, full metal jacket, you betcha Bob—

'—meanwhile these two English guys dress up as cowboys, ride over there on *horseback*, and shoot up the town—'

'It's hilarious,' agreed Frank: waiting to be told something he didn't know.

'It's a scream. It gets better, bro. We have live coverage.'

At this Frank stared, truly impressed. 'You're *kidding*.'

'I'm not kidding.' The man with the story leaned forward, into the dead space that every one who talks in bars believes can be found, directly above the mid-point between their two drinks on the polished mahogany tabletop. 'There is footage. This Baal, the Black Dragon: the town was wired, hidden cameras everywhere, and he has the true-life movie of what went down that night. He's dickering with our acquisitions guys right now, from his undisclosed place of detention.'

'Protective custody, mister.'

'Whatever, he's open for business. Detainees' rights are a wonderful thing.'

'What, he had the stuff *with* him? On an eyesocket chip or what? And our great Homeland Security experts let him *keep* it?'

'Naw ... He knows where it is, though. This is the real deal, Frankismo. I can't tell you how, but I've personally seen the trailer. You want to see Mr Ax Preston *garrotting* a poor misguided Gaia-loving martyr? You want to see the expression on our rockstar peacemaker's pretty face when the kid's windpipe cracks?'

'Jesus.'

'You want to see holier-than-God reformed bad boy Sage Pender dealing with the soft-bellied little geeks at the hideout's back gate? Some of them women?'

'You have to be shitting me—!'

They contemplated the potential mayhem. It was *nice*.

'You know, Jude,' said Frank at last, measuring his words, 'joking apart, this could be a serious bummer for that Kill The Evil Research, Ban The Neurobomb route. This sounds like bad doody for Mr Fred Eiffrich altogether.'

'Yeah, well. Don't know about you Frankie, but I voted for the other ticket.'

They laughed, immoderately. Then they had one more drink and went their separate ways, as the hour was getting late.

PART ONE

ONE

Rue Morgue Avenue

Sage had fallen asleep with Fiorinda tucked against him, his chin on her shoulder, his arm around them both, a safe and good place to be: in many ways, the best place the world can hold – but they'd moved away from him in the night. Had to have their fucking personal space; he couldn't cure them of the habit. It hurt his feelings. Slighted, and also *cold*, he lay with the morning light seeping through his lashes, frosting his eyeballs. He was thinking about his greatcoat, which was on the floor on the other side of the room. Weigh the cost of making the trip against the reward of increased comfort: seal a few of these gaps, body heat soon builds up . . . In the end it was the pressure of a full bladder, slowly becoming insistent, that forced him to make a move.

'Was' matter—?' mumbled Ax.

'Need a piss.'

'Me too.'

The chemical toilet was behind a screen in one of the garret room's slope-ceilinged corners. They hunkered down on either side of the pot, grinning at each other. They liked pissing together.

'We could make tea with that much,' said Sage proudly.

It would be quite a coup to wake her with a cup of hot tea, which they could not otherwise provide until somebody went to fetch the drinking water. Ten minutes in the treatment jug would do it. But Ax was secretly squeamish. Spaceship earth austerity, okay, no problem with that, but he preferred a little distance from the details. Let the arondissement do the recycling.

'Yeah, except it could be read as cheating, unless we knock it off someone's five litres.'

'Oooh, we can't have that.'

The cold in the room was intense, but somehow pleasurable once you were out in it. It had been storage space; the conversion for human occupation was minimal. They moved to the window, which had a sheet of solar insulation taped over it but no curtain, and sat on dusty boards. Slate roofs and gables, pigeon-breast shades all crusted in frozen white, rose into the grey, laden sky above Montmartre.

'Looks like more snow coming.'

'Nah, it's too cold.'

Like London, Paris was shrinking: the centre collapsing in on itself as the sprawl fell apart. The artists' hill was crowded. Though no traffic murmur reached them, only stillness like a doubtful blessing, and the rumble of a single car traversing the cobbles of the rue des Dames, Ax could feel the weight of numbers out there. The world's energy economy plunged into chaos, all the indicators of recovery crashed back to zero ... So many people, in Europe and in all the world beyond, unthinkable numbers of people, crouched like mice in stubble under the beating of monstrous wings, waiting and wondering, *what's going to happen to us now?* And only begging for a little more of this respite, this long strange winter.

He turned from their roofscape – for which they'd developed a profound affection – to the more mysterious beauty beside him. The indigo shadows that lie between muscle and bone on white skin in the wintertime; Sage's yellow curls, not so Boot Camp cropped as they used to be, clustered over his skull in a helmet of coiled-gold coins. Ax had always loved human bodies, never had the time, or the peace of mind, for an idyll like this before. The more you look, the more you see. He reached out – asking permission with a glance, he liked to have permission – and slipped his hand under Sage's shabby T-shirt to trace the ropes of scar, where the magician had torn out his friend's liver, nearly two years ago now; Sage smiling, accepting the caress with the forbearance of a kindly pet tiger. He didn't like those scars, but he'd come to like the way Ax touched them

They hold your life inside, thought Ax. They tell me we came through.

'This is a *good* time.'

'Hahaha. You do realise, babe, that our brilliant careers are in ruins, we are starving in a fereezing foreign garret, in daily danger of being deported—'

'Details. We're in excellent shape.'

'—I *hate* trying to talk French, an' our girlfriend is pregnant?'

Ax stopped laughing, suddenly focused. 'You think she's pregnant?'

'Yes. Forty-five days: no, forty-six. I think she could well be pregnant.'

They looked to the bed, where their girl was fast asleep.

'We need to think about how we're going to make a living,' said Ax. 'It's on my mind. One day we'll be free, but I don't see us making a comeback as rockstars.'

'Fuck that, no.'

'Living like this is good for us, I love it, but kids needs security.'

'I veto white collar applications.'

'Don't worry. I am not going to try and make you work for your dad.'

'Tha's a relief.' Sage stretched and refolded himself, leaning back against the wall. 'Okay, lemmee see, what are our skills? We could be drug dealers, but we'd need start-up capital. We could be mercenaries, how about that? We're not bad at killing people, an' God knows there's plenty of openings—'

'*No thanks.*'

'Ssh, all right, don't panic. Well, then, sex. We're good at sex, I do b'lieve.'

'You're not taking this seriously.'

'Yes I am. I was a crowd-fucking entertainment industry whore for years, why not get honest about it?'

'You were never that . . .' But now Ax was intrigued. 'Do you think you could do that, sex for money? Really?'

Sage considered (a glitter of blue mischief through thick stubby blond lashes downcast). 'Hm. You would be there? With me the whole time?'

Ax shook his head. 'Not on the face of it, big cat, no. I'd take the money and wait round the corner. I think that's the more usual arrangement.'

'Oh. Well, in that case I'm not sure. I was imagining you'd be there. I could do it if you was right there watching, Sah. Dunno about otherwise.'

9

Silence, while they mused on this scenario, letting it grow. It had merits, but there were doors that opened onto ugly memory—

'Maybe we'd better stick to me busking,' decided Ax, at last. 'Busking's fine, I like it: except, this weather, my hands get so fucking cold.'

The narrow casement. The white-capped quilt of roofs, the frozen silence.

'Is there any way we could *sneakily* get her to take a test?'

Sage shook his head. 'Don't see how, if she doesn't want.'

'Couldn't we, er, slip it into her food or something?'

'You have to piss on them, Ax.'

Fiorinda sat up, rubbing her eyes. 'What are you two sniggering about?'

'We were discussing my new career.'

They leapt across the room, bringing Sage's coat (Ax and Fiorinda's coats were already enhancing the bedding.) 'He's going to sell his arse under the bridges of Paris,' explained Ax, burrowing into the warmth. 'It could work, he has ex-celebrity cachêt. But I have to be there, holding his hand throughout. God knows what the punters will think. They'll think we've gone nuts.'

'They already know that,' said Fiorinda. 'Don't be stupid. If we're going to start selling sex, obviously it's my job. I'm the girl.'

'Oh no!' Sage wrapped himself around her back, kissing the nape of her neck through silky tendrils of red curls. 'Not you. Never, never, never.'

'Not even in jest, sweetheart.' Fiorinda had done her share of that kind of hard labour, and worse. Ax took her face between his hands, and gazed. He wanted to tell her, nothing's ever going to hurt you again, but he didn't dare. Say something like that and there's demons listening, ready to make you eat your words. All he could do was this, drink her up, fill himself with her eyes, the curve of her mouth—

Sage and Fiorinda had realised they'd never, either of them, felt the weight of Ax Preston's undivided attention before this winter. There'd always been some little task like saving the world, to take the pressure off . . . They were agreed it was quite a rush; a little scary. 'I know you were ganging up on me,' said Fiorinda. 'Don't pretend you weren't.'

'Hm.'

Both the men withdrew. 'Fiorinda,' began Sage, propped on one elbow, cautiously addressing his remarks mainly to their shabby pillows, 'we don't want to crowd you, nothing further from our thoughts, but we've noticed . . . Today it's forty-six days. Could we, er, talk about that?'

'It's your business, woman business, we just – we can't help it—'

Fiorinda sat up, and folded her arms tight around her knees.

'My period's about two weeks late, big deal. Can't I have *any* private life?'

'Sorry.'

'Okay, let's look at this. I was de-sterilised four months ago. You two have been shooting live ammunition for how long?'

'We tested good in London. Six weeks, at least.'

'You see, barely any time at all. Be reasonable.'

'We're sure you're *not* pregnant,' agreed Ax, hurriedly. 'We're not stupid. We're not saying you should go to the whitecoats with this, nothing like that.'

'But what if . . . what if we quietly bought you an old-fashioned pregnancy test, from a neighbourhood pharmacist, and brought it back here?'

'Just for the hell of it, nothing serious.'

'Oh yeah? What about p-protecting my identity? Mr ex-dictator virtuoso busker, with the media popping up wherever he goes, and his Zen Master bodyguard, six-foot-six blond bombshell with the very weird accent, ooh who the hell could *that* be? Oh, we're just a couple of English tourists (there aren't any), making this intriguing purchase for a friend—'

'Ax would do the talking, he looks normal. I would hide around the corner.'

'I wouldn't take a guitar into the *shop*, Fiorinda.'

'I see you have it all worked out.' She sighed and lay down again, disarmed in spite of herself. 'Listen, idiots. You know how people say you can't be a little bit pregnant? It's bullshit. People get a little bit pregnant all the time, and it fades because something or other goes wrong. Now is not the time to get excited: three months, that would be worth talking about. Oh, okay. Let me think about it.'

The topic of Fiorinda's child was too vital. They fled, into the whispering and giggling, the blind urgency and sweetness of sex in this winter bed.

Ax had thought he'd known what he was taking on when he'd agreed to return to England. He would complete his term of office, no longer as dictator but as the figurehead President of Countercultural England, and he'd be working with a hostile government. The green nazis had been driven out, but the Moderate Celtics, in the form of a junta known as the Second Chamber, were secure in power. It was the way things were going over much of Europe. The extremists had been defeated, but 'moderate' neo-feudalists were applying brutal solutions to the problems of the Crisis. But Ax would have plenty of leverage of the kind that can't be measured easily, and he had the mandate of the leader of the free world – which counted for something. He would be able to claw back some civil rights for the people, at least; it would be tough but it could be done.

There's always another turn of the screw. They'd arrived in England to find that Ax's brother Jordan – substitute candidate for the Presidency, after Ax had resigned – had not, after all, accepted the gift of a stately home from the government out of crass greed. He'd been told that there was a security issue: the Prestons could not be adequately protected if they stayed in the old homestead. So Jordan had meekly quit Bridge House in Taunton, sacred headquarters of the original Chosen Few, and allowed himself to be installed in luxury in an isolated country house, hundreds of miles from Somerset: behind razor-wire and dog handlers, surrounded by minders and armed guards over whom he had no control. The deal included all of Ax's immediate family: his mother, his five-year-old nephew, and Milly Kettle, the Chosen Few's drummer, formerly Ax's girlfriend, now Jordan's wife and heavily pregnant with their second child. The Triumvirate were expected to move into the lovely new house too. Poor Jor, doomed as so often in the past to *infuriate* his brilliant brother, hadn't explained the situation when he'd had the chance, because it had taken him a while to spot there was something dodgy about this set up (it had taken Milly a while too, which was more surprising: Ax had thought Mil would have had more sense). Don't all top celebrities live so?

Ax had taken a look at the situation and realised he could do nothing in a hurry. After the reinstatement celebrations (part traditional, part invented), the Triumvirate had taken off on an impromptu tour of the provinces with their closest friends, the bands of the inner circle, during which they'd visited some of the agricultural labour camps that were the secret envy of less hard-headed neo-feudal régimes. It had been November when they returned to England. In February, running short of excuses to stay out of the gilded cage, the three had picked a fight over an unrelated issue and decamped to Paris – without announcing their travel plans. They'd been in Montmartre for a month (co-incidentally through the deepest freeze of all the frigid 'global warming' winters of the European Crisis): staging a show-off, rockstar protest about conditions in the camps, while Ax entertained approaches from a variety of lunatic émigrés.

Ax was confident that he could come to reasonable terms with the Second Chamber, and he knew that the Prestons weren't in immediate danger. No hurry. He was happy to go on embarrassing the suits for as long as they liked.

At two in the afternoon, when Ax and Sage arrived on the Île St Louis, the ironbound sky had given up none of its burden. They had tramped down from the 18me by way of a meeting of the Restore The Thames party (main platform, some massive landscape engineering to return the Thames to its pre-Ice Age route, thus persuading Gaia to reverse climate change); and a fascinating presentation from a Devon couple who'd devised a way to make wind turbines invisible. They were met in the street by Alain de Corlay's *physiognomistes* and escorted through an archway flanked by frosty stone satyrs, between the shells of bijou foodie boutiques, into the courtyard of the seventeenth century mansion which had for years been the stronghold of the Paris techno-greens. M. de Corlay, formerly the front man of a Eurotrash intellectual band called *Movie Sucré*, was waiting, with an entourage of hardnut *absurdistes*, in a morgue-cold conference room on the first floor. The delegates from the Plantagenet Society had been sent off to get nervous in the brown and gold salon next door.

These were the idiots who favoured a Wars of the Roses scenario. They'd been holed-up in Paris since Ax's dictatorship – a period when the French, out of sheer cussedness, had provided asylum for a hotbed of disgraceful United Kingdom loyalists. They were now thrilled to be negotiating with their arch-enemy, the former rockstar warlord. Mr Red, a thin, sallow middle-aged gent, and Mr White, young and hearty *rosbif*, wore velvet robes over business suits, and velvet caps adorned with sprigs of flowering broom. *There goes your project*, thought Ax, with mordant amusement. Hothouse wild-flowers are so naff, and did you forget we are soldiers of the queen?

Everyone knows Fiorinda hates cut flowers.

Nah, the neo-Plantagenets knew nothing.

The Reds and the Whites had made it clear that they'd buried their differences, and were ready to share power. They'd agreed to abandon the plan whereby Ax – purely for legitimacy – would marry the Yorkist heir, a young Greek woman. They had insisted that Ax's Islamic faith was no obstacle. Hopes for the face-to-face meeting were high ... They had documents, ancient and modern, including what they called a 'writ of perpetual abdication' from the Hastings family, surviving Plantagenets on the public record, who didn't want anything to do with these nuts. They had maps of the familiar headless chicken (in this case mainly the pregnant headless chicken representing England-and-Wales). They had fanfold genealogies in oak-gall, scarlet and gilt; they had a recorded video message from the elderly Canadian who was their senior, Lancastrian heir-male. They had plans for the ceremony where Ax would simultaneously be adopted by the Canadian by video-proxy and consecrated king; taking the dynastic name Richard Henry the First.

The meeting was conducted in French, without any record being kept: Mr Red and Mr White were fluent in the language. The Mediaevalists doffed their velvet robes and caps. The former dictator and his Minister did not remove their coats. Mr Preston wore Dickensian, fingerless dark mittens that looked none too clean. He smoked one of the expensive cigarettes that were proffered (but declined the carton); showed an interest in the ornate paperwork, and asked only a few, tactful questions about the dirty business of actually taking over a country. Tall Mr Pender, with the intimidating good looks, kept his hands in his pockets and his collar turned up. He rarely spoke, except in an undertone to his chief – murmured asides that brought out Mr Preston's flashing smile, and made the negotiators envious. Alain sat sideways at the end of the table, chain-smoking green bidis that stank of marijuana, and watched over the proceedings with exasperated disbelief.

Mr Red and Mr White were keen on their ceremony. They knew what everyone would be wearing, they had speeches prepared and place-cards designed. There were several possible venues, indoors and outdoors, historically significant and non-denominational, all with points for and against . . . Sage gazed at the curling satellite print-outs of London and the south coast of England that were pinned to the panelled walls. When England had been in the hellish hands of the green nazis, this room had been the nerve centre of Ax's velvet invasion. But why does Alain keep the relics? Strange taste. A phalanx of defunct landline phones stood on a side table, gathering dust. A modern trash-eater stove, placed where it could send its heat straight up a cavernous seventeenth century chimney, hissed in the background.

At last Ax squared the documents in front of him, slipped an ancient vellum into its silk-lined folder, and swept the lot – not ungraciously – across the board.

'Mr Red, Mr White, thank you. That's all I have time for: you may go.'

The delegates looked at each other, nonplussed.

'You *could* move that stove out into the room,' said Sage to Alain. 'It would be slightly more fuckin' use than where it is.'

'Certainly not. It would mark the parquet.'

'Welsh sovereignty wouldn't be a deal-breaker,' announced Mr Red, after a sub-vocal consultation with confederates elsewhere. The Plantagenets were not ultra-green; they had tech support. 'We believe that political union between England and Wales is natural and right, but separation wouldn't be a deal-breaker.'

'Well, that's *good*,' said Ax, smiling; and raised an eyebrow.

They didn't take the hint. Mr Red, the pinch-faced older man, steepled his thin hands and leaned forward. His street name was Woodville, he had straightforward criminal provenance apart from this show, a background of which Ax was well aware.

'Mr Preston, Sir, before we leave, having come this far, ah, at the risk of being indiscreet, can we assume that we have Fred Eiffrich on board? Or are we, er, hm, is Your Majesty waiting for that assurance?'

Mr White (aka Henry Lovell, of the British Resistance Movement, which used to be known as the BNP) glowed like a rose, overwhelmed by visions of glory.

Ax had no idea what Fred Eiffrich thought of his present course of action, and he didn't plan to try and find out. The US President had worked hard to get Ax to come back to England, but the rest was up to Ax: this had been understood when they parted. He grinned. The friendship of the mighty is a fickle thing, the kind of high card that does more work if you never try to lay it down.

'I could be. Or I could be mulling over my chances of waking up one morning in some draughty Norman tower, with a red hot plumber's mate up my bum . . . or else starving to death in chains because you folks got tired of your new toy.'

The Plantagenets looked shocked, the stove hissed: Ax smiled like a wolf, leaned forward in his turn, and became affably confidential.

'I don't have to tell you this, but the fact is we're getting headhunted all over the shop. We've been looking at a rather nice package from the Sealed Knot.'

Mr Red and Mr White bristled like scalded cats at the hated name. 'They're lying!' cried Mr White. 'Whatever they told you. Those bastards have no money!'

'Yeah, they speak highly of you, too . . . And the Irish are putting out discreet feelers,' continued Mr Preston, 'about Fiorinda for High Queen. They're getting interested in having a decorative head of state, and she's an O'Niall, you know. Apparently the Tyrone branch, the legitimate family, are cool about the idea. We're thinking that might suit us very well.'

Sage nodded in confirmation. 'Nice mild climate in Ireland.'

'So, what can I say? It's all up in the air. If you want to be looking at alternatives you might try the Mountbatten-Windsors. They've a posse of children, they might let you have one, for the right offer. Just as long as you don't try to get any member of my family involved in your games. Or any other connection of mine.'

Briefly, the smile vanished from Mr Preston's pretty brown eyes.

M. de Corlay sighed, and pressed a banana-shaped yellow buzzer. At its merry, discordant summons the door of the salon opened and some techno-green muscle appeared, bizarrely costumed and visibly armed, or *carrying heat*, as they preferred to put it. The pressure suits were fake, but the ray-guns were functional sidearms. The delegates stood, with dignity, and donned their velvet.

'Edward II wasn't killed like that because he was a homosexual,' exclaimed Mr White, suddenly. 'The homophobic element in the case has been unfairly exaggerated.' ('*Unbelievably absurd*,' muttered Alain, lighting another bidi.) 'The primary issue with the poker method is to leave an unmarked corpse—'

'Tha's a meme,' said beautiful Mr Pender, in English: grinning with such tigerish affection that the White Rose took a step backwards. 'You must be one of us.'

*

'You clowns are abusing my hospitality,' said Alain, when the other clowns had been shown out and he had delivered a small item of secure mail to Mr Preston. 'This hôtel is a serious centre of excellence for utopian radical thought and action.'

His friends cackled like fools.

'Oh yes, very amusing. And useful. Mr Preston, who needs nobody to crown him, gets the rabid dogs to come to *him*, so he knows exactly who they are, and can deal with them at leisure once he's whipped his bureaucrats into line.'

'Nah,' said Ax. 'Nothing like that. I'm just pissing around.'

'You're a *madman*. Sage, I almost pity you for being tied to him. My God, why didn't you both get out of this while you could?'

'There is no "out of this".' Ax retrieved a guitar case from under his chair and shrugged it onto his shoulders. 'Not for any of us, not any more. C'mon, Sage. It's late. Got to get the beer-money in before dark.'

'Thanks fer the room, and the heavies,' called Sage, over his shoulder.

Grinning, they clattered down to the courtyard. Under the naked chestnut trees that stood gleaming in the frost like giant, funereal candelabra, Ax stopped dead, transfixed.

'What's up, babe?'

'Sage. Could she be pregnant? Tell me, truly ... so quickly?'

Fiorinda had been sterilised when she was thirteen, after her occult monster of a father had seduced her and abandoned her pregnant with his baby, the little boy who had died. As long as he'd loved his best girl, Ax had lived with the knowledge that she would never have his child. Of course he had *hoped*, when she'd decided she could bear to have the treatment. No promises: but non-surgical sterilisation can often be undone. But he'd been expecting to live on that hope for years, a gentle letdown; and nothing would ever happen. It was dizzying. Fiorinda's child!

'I don't know,' said Sage, with equal urgency. 'But it works like that, it does, sometimes, straight off. There's reasons why—'

'Yeah, yeah, lutenising bodies—'

Naturally they'd been researching the topic, on the quiet.

Alain lingered a few moments in the small salon, which was for him a shrine, a time capsule of the last days of rational materialism. This is where we were, laying our desperate plans, when that lanky, blue-eyed alchemist who just left was turning himself into the New Prometheus, breaking the barrier between Mind and Matter. And how little we understood, then, exactly what Sage had done to the world.

What annoyed him most was that the sober guitar-man, *Ax Preston*, of all people, had become a perfect character in this farce. While he, 'Alain Jupette' (Alain Miniskirt had been Alain's stage name), found himself unable to mock a world that was beyond ludicrous. Who would laugh, when nobody retained the slightest memory of the world of reason. When *European government* was a bland, toothless, comedy of corruption, and *magic* a debased metaphor—

All the amnesiacs, except for Fiorinda. Thank God for Fiorinda.

In the freezing conference room a knot of people stood by the windows. He joined them and saw Ax and Sage: stalled in earnest conversation under the sweeping branches of the chestnuts and the first difficult flakes of snow. You would stare at those two if you knew nothing. You would follow them down the street. They shone as if clothed in golden armour, invincible, untouchable. Ha. God protects (not that Alain was a believer, he detested the supernatural, new and old) drunks and lovers.

'What can they be talking about?' muttered someone beside him.

'Obviously, the exquisite shape of Fiorinda's left earlobe,' said Alain sourly.

'Is it true they're on the oxy again?' asked somebody else, hopefully.

The speaker was a government spook, here by agreement. The techno-greens fully accepted that the bureaucrats (a government a whole three-months-old must command respect!) should be keeping an eye on the Plantagenet Society. And on Ax Preston. Everyone wants to know how Ax is going to jump.

There had been a time when Ax and Sage had been addicts of oxytocin, the intimacy drug: shoring up the three-way love affair with brain-wrecking quantities of synthetic tender devotion. But they were clean now – as Alain was glad to know, because he was genuinely fond of the three. There was nothing fake about their trefoil infatuation. Fiorinda (who never touched modern drugs) behaved equally sottishly, if she ever deigned to appear.

'Drowning in it. But it won't help you to nail him.'

All megastars must have crap sex lives, thought Fiorinda, left alone in the nest. No matter how often they get 'happily married', hohoho. Because which of us rockstars, hardwired from birth to be continually starving for love and pleasure, forced by the working conditions to be addicts of excess . . . ? Which of us would strut on stage, or fret in a recording studio, a moment longer than we had to, if we were getting what we needed at home? It would be: make the money, take your bow and quit. And how often does that happen? How often does anyone get clean away?

But it was time for this rockstar to go to work for manager Ax. She dressed, on camera, briskly and chastely as if she was in a communal changing room (me concentration camp inmate here, not Top Shelf Girl). Checked the stats, which were gratifying, as usual, and here we go. Cribs of the certifiably insane. Hi everybody, and special hi to anyone who's logging on for the first time. This is our very green chemical toilet, which I'm going to empty downstairs. Sage doesn't think we need the chemicals, but I insist. Do I always get landed with this job? Nah, not always. Just often. (*Oh, hi, M. Jouffroy, Il fait encore froid, eh?*) That's the concierge, he thinks we are evil English spies. Sloosh, sploosh. There, that wasn't too bad. I don't mind the smell of disinfected shit when it's fresh. I'm used to it, after about a million post-civilised rock festivals, where believe me, sanitation is also an issue in the VIP nettle patch . . . They don't have organised drainage in the camps, and they aren't allowed GM gut bacteria, so the brown stuff is a real health problem. The cold this winter has helped. It kills the elderly inmates and the babies quite a lot, but it does keep the epidemics down.

Okay, back to our lovely garret, acres of spacious living, which is not exactly realistic, but hey, we're dilettantes, what do you expect? This is our bed, with my luxurious personalised coat-bedspread. We do have heat. Our building has power, from the French National Renewables grid, and we're allowing ourselves the same wattage as you get per person in a camp. But it's Thursday and we're on a three-day week here in Paris . . . We have no personal vermin, which is great. The lice powder is just in case. These are my clothes, all hung up on *my* piece of string. These are my boots. These are Ax's clothes; and Ax's other hat, his Ned Kelly hat. I love this old hat, as long as he doesn't wear it. The mess is Sage's stuff, I kick it out of the way, oh, I trod on his board, it's okay, they're tough; and *voilà* the kitchenette, our tasty tins, the ATP battery micro-ondes and that's the drinking water. My boyfriends fetch the water. Isn't that sweet of them.

No, we don't wash a great deal. Yeah, we have digital devices and telecoms, obviously, it'd be a bit of a dumb protest otherwise. But we don't use our phones for personal calls, and we make our own entertainment. No, you can't watch. Don't be so pitiful, what did Gaia give you imaginations for?

Press? Anyone awake in the press room today?

. . .

'But what *is* the solution?' asked Fiona Ward, a well-groomed lady from the premier government-sponsored English newsite. 'There were agricultural camps in the dictatorship, weren't there, Fiorinda? Human labour must take the place of the machines, or how can we feed ourselves? And the elective-nomads must be cared for somehow, we can't just let them wander. Wasn't it Ax himself who said that we're social animals, and it's our nature to look after each other?'

Elective nomads was the currently approved term for the drop-out hordes, the millions who had taken to the roads in the economic crash and afterwards ... who were now digging potatoes, disenfranchised and under armed guard.

'Yes, there were camps in the dictatorship,' agreed the nation's sweetheart: Titania in exile, upright and graceful on the frowsty bed, grey eyes clear and bright. 'But they weren't locked, Fiona, and in those days everybody took their turn. Picking peas, cleaning hospital floors, whatever was going ... Didn't you ever join the Volunteer Initiative? You should try it. It's great physical exercise, excellent for bodytone, and bonding experience, which is very good for de-stress, and that would help your skin; and a lot of fun. A kind of extreme sport, without the horrible failure-factor, because everybody wins. I can send you the application form—'

Oh, outrageous! Oh, what a way to address a problem Fiorinda knew to be complex and intractable as all hell. She could hear the Second Chamber spooks grinding their teeth. Serve them right, hahaha. Who started the dirty tricks?

More questions, more or less idiotic and/or disingenuous, until the press was dealt with. And so to her desk, remote-accessed at the Volunteer Initiative Office in London (housed in the building once known as Buckingham Palace). Here we trade in surpluses, scraping the barrels of over-production, tracking down strange customers for strange lost wares, view to ending up with the food and water that we need (yeah, we trade in water, we know it's dodgy, grey area, but we have no choice). Five clean litres and fifteen hundred calories a day for every man, woman and child, or near as we can make it. Yes, this means the Rock and Roll Reich is helping to keep the evil camp system functional, until it can be dismantled. Your point is?

Sanitaryware mountain in Bulgaria, ha, I have a customer, powdered porcelain is a soil-cleanser, powdering can be done by hand, doesn't need machines. More Libyan military apricot jam? Ooh, I'll have some of that ... Oh NO, it's already gone!

Being ahead of the game is a bust, complained Fiorinda, cheerfully. The game only catches up, and do they respect you for showing them the way? Do they fuck (excuse my rockstar language). They resent you for making them feel slow, they insult you while copying all your moves, and they rob you blind any chance they get. Only we should be doing this, it was our idea: but now everybody wants to play. And I can't really object to the Aid Agencies, but the private brokers going after futures in grey-bloomed chocolate bars, have they no fucking shame? Trouble is, demand increases supply, so the more people come scrabbling round, the more scrapings they seem to find. But it's not true you know. It doesn't mean there's more of the actual resource, it just means the resource is getting used up faster—

Sometimes as she worked like this: assembling her packages, skymining the condensing clouds of information (and not infrequently coming second in the bid battles) the spectre of a terrifying future would rise before Fiorinda. Once she had believed that the end of the world was an event. A spray of bullets at a political reception, red flowers blooming on swanky evening clothes, the smoke of cordite: the Hyde Park Massacre, which she had survived. For a long time she had looked back on that night, eight years ago, when legal government in England had been blown away, as the final fall. Death was instantaneous. Oh no, not at all.

Ruin is the devil's work, consecutive and slow.

Fail in a moment no man did—

We can just go on falling, on and on, through loss after loss, through shock after shock: go on swimming across this dark river, into which the modern world stumbled, way back then: getting weaker, getting chilled, long ago lost our footing; tasting the salt on our lips, guessing the awful truth but keeping on, as if we believe in the other shore, because what else is there to do?

Europe is going to starve. Not this year, but soon.

Today she smiled as she kept up her merry, acerbic commentary: the greater part of her mind at ease, bathed in delicious thoughts of this morning, of last night; and all the way back to that deep bowl, walled in hills and roofed with stars, where they had made their camp, out in the desert after the Lavoisier raid.

The chill of the air, the red rocks breathing out the furnace heat of the day. The charged, miraculous sex that had overwhelmed them, sweeping them up into an immensity in which the death-dealing in the ghost town (such a pall of death over that place, the whole time she'd been there: the martyrs all consigned, waiting for their rapture), was neither excused nor denied. No answers, no limit, no duration, only the whiteout, luminous complexity that opens and opens, and draws you into itself—

She needed that abyss, it was her only shelter. But you can't live in a state of non-being, and Fiorinda wanted very much to live, so she rationed herself. Think about the sex instead; which is safe and fun. So this is what I do, while the tiger and the wolf are patrolling their territory. Shopping and fucking, how suitable.

At the end of the live session 'Sparrow Child' played her out: Fiorinda making a dance of her exit, keeping to the beat from memory, with the sound turned down on her earbead. She'd have preferred 'Stonecold', one of the few songs she'd written as a kid-diva that she still liked. But a punk homeless anthem would be too aggressive, mustn't alienate the middle of the road, must make the drop-outs sound *nice*. Oh my darling Ax, have you finally turned me? Stonecold for years to the vision of techno-green utopia, when it's a case of *screw the bastards*, Fiorinda gets interested.

Hey-ho, know thyself.

Now how shall I spend the afternoon? Well, it's very cold in here, and I don't want to go out. I do b'lieve I'll go back to bed. You're supposed to rest.

Fiorinda knew she was pregnant. One of the luxuries they'd allowed themselves was Sage's first-aid kit. Her lovers wouldn't have dared to suggest she avail herself of the futuristic resources of the white box; they believed Fiorinda hated whitecoat medicine. They were behind the times (I got myself de-sterilised, didn't I?). She'd secretly given herself a blood and urine test a week ago; and she was pregnant. She'd had a look at the DNA, too, just out of curiosity.

She'd have known she was pregnant anyway. She could feel the changes in her body and mind, subtle but commanding. This dreamy lethargy, this curious unwillingness to leave the den ... She'd intended to stay in denial a while longer (denial is safer). But of course they were onto it, and now the secret was burning a hole in her belly, a tiny wormhole to another universe. How long were you planning for us to keep up the protest, Ax? Weeks? Months? It could become more of a statement than we planned.

Maybe she would tell them this evening.

She retired under the covers with her camp-ration lunch, a small lump of cheese and two aged, sticky, dried bananas. Plus Peter Straub's *Koko*, from a box of storybooks donated by a thoughtful Parisian secondhand bookseller. The gruesome maybe-supernatural plot was all too familiar; right up Fiorinda's street. The setting was so alien and entrancing that she lost the thread, and started to imagine an alternate reality for herself. Where the world had not ended and she was someone with *a loft in SoHo*. With two boyfriends (call them Richard and Stephen, hahaha). They were dating her separately, except that occasionally they would turn up together, as if by accident. Then they'd all end up in bed, but nobody would say anything about it afterwards . . . So that Fiorinda (no, Frances) was never sure what was going on, and tormented herself over the relationship between the two men. They pretended not to know each other, but did they have a complete life together, that she knew nothing about? Was it all a cruel game? Or were they as confused as she was? She would not dare to ask. She'd try to find out, playing detective, uncovering sinister disquieting secrets, but saying nothing; and still fucking them both, separately and together, mmm—

Nah. Forget it. Nothing mysterious or complex is ever going to happen to my sex life. I'm stuck with this awkward, ordinary trefoil knot, clear as print, set in stone, until the day I die . . . But how different from the sexual fantasies of her loved ones! Once it had been handcuffs. They'd liked the idea of being handcuffed together in bed (as indeed they were, in a sense), a scenario that seemed to have permanently retired, since Ax's real-life experience as a hostage. Then it had been the galley-slaves; still a favourite. But what's this about Ax the pimp, Sage the rent boy? Now that is *creepy*. Although she could see where it was coming from in their present situation.

Perhaps fortunately, they never seemed to want to act out their ideas. (Advice to rockstars: never do any sex that you wouldn't be happy to meet on public tv one night. You will get caught on camera somehow, it's Sod's Law.) They just liked to talk, mulling over the details, elaborating the scenario, and keeping score, of course, on who's the first to break and make an actual move. The tiger and the wolf, they always keep score.

If I ever *find* that little black book—

The endless conversation of those two soft, West Country voices, reeling out for years, the ground under her feet, right back to a water meadow by the Thames at Reading, in Dissolution Summer. Bruised grass, black bin bags, the smell of rain, and a stubborn, self-obsessed, oblivious little girl: looking for her father, finding instead these brothers, these lovers—

Someday, she thought, I'm going to want to go back on stage. Not now. *Now,* I'm the national sweetheart taking a career break to have my baby. Or babies ... But later. No more industrial arenas, no thanks, but I haven't finished with being a rockstar. I'm only twenty-three! I've hardly even started. She wondered how she would break the news to her lovers, and her friends. How would she convince them it was safe? The room was very still. There was ice in the air, a deadly cramping chill. *Koko* slipped from Fiorinda's hands. She sat up and drew her knees to her chin, her eyes wide and wary: as if listening, intently listening, to a whispered threat—

Outside the pharmacist on the avenue de Clichy, Sage bent over Ax's hands, blowing warmth onto the busker's fingers. 'Good luck—'

'You're really not coming into the shop with me?'

'N-no,' said Sage. 'I don't need to. Gimme the guitar, I'll be out here.'

He walked away, immediately bewildered and bereft without Ax by his side, but that's the price you pay, and he didn't want to lose this feeling. The beaten copper of Ax's naked shoulders, the sweet column of her throat ... And even now, the electric shock whenever he reaches out to touch me. What's that? The thrill of transgression? Fuck no, *boring.* It's the thrill of permission. The moment when the world says *yes!* to something they told you was impossible, was forbidden: more of that, always more of that. Will I ever get used to him? I don't think so. He almost walked into the first little bar, but remembered he had no money, not a cent. Ax was holding the beer-money. Besides, sitting in a bar could be regarded as cheating, and we can't have that. He stood in a shop doorway, watching the snow clear the foot-traffic, thinking of the mysterious way Fiorinda's grey eyes change colour as her skin turns winter-pale. Shattered gold and green striations; the ads on a shuttered kiosk. *Re-ignite the Nuclear Power Stations!* Not a bad idea, except for the political suicide aspect. But nobody would dare. He tried to remember what Paris had been like before, when he was young. There were cars, cars stacked every-where, and the air was poison. He couldn't picture it. Is it snowing today in Cornwall? Is my river frozen between its granite boulders, except for that deep pool under the holly trees?

Sometimes he felt like a little boy, pining for home. But they would be back in England soon, he had no doubt. What worried him was the effect of all this on Ax. There's a brittle, aggressive Mr Preston – oh yes, those Lennonisms – never far from the surface now. Never will be far, until he quits the struggle, but how can he ever quit? They won't let him. The dancing flakes and the shadowed air said, you will never be free, you're in this for the cold and dark duration.

He smiled, Ax's guitar on his shoulder, thinking of her eyes. I knew that.

Ax had to wait, lurking around the shelves with his woolly cap pulled well down, while other people were served. The closer you get to someone, the more you know the child in them. Sage is scared, and so am I . . . this is *intense.* I feel about twelve years old. Shampoo, soap, herbal extracts, food supplements. All claiming to have been hand-milled by virgins with the moon in Aries, or some such nonsense: but only the packaging had changed. All else was reassuringly the same.

It would have been more discreet to look further afield, but this was Thursday; only one duty chemist open for miles. And the place seemed more friendly, given that they'd often walked past the door. He fingered the coin in his pocket: slim pickings, hope it's enough. Trouble is, the punters don't believe it. They think we're making a video. Or so he told himself . . . He was on. Something for the weekend? He swallowed laughter, fright gripping his belly, and advanced. The woman wore a proper white coat, which he liked; not young, dark hair pulled smoothly back into a twist. Touched by his errand, she tried to convince him he wanted a greener, more spiritual product. Ax stood firm. He wanted something from the old world.

'There are better ways to divine a pregnancy now,' she told him, fetching the goods from a drawer. 'Your girlfriend might prefer something more harmonious.'

'No, thanks. This'll do.'

She was looking over his shoulder, frowning. He turned to see Sage outside the glass, his face beautifully framed in the turned-up collar of his coat. The pharmacist looked from rockstar-features out there to Ax: from Ax to Sage, strangely amazed. In a flash he understood that she'd seen them around, maybe they were the subject of neighbourhood gossip. But what she'd recognised was not the notorious former dictator of England, it was that foreign busker guy-couple, the tall blond and the one with the guitar—

'But, excuse me, this is for you two?'

'Miracles of modern medicine,' said Ax; and fled.

They came into the garret laughing, brushing snow from each other. Fiorinda was waiting for them. There was a covered dish in the microwave, their bowls and spoons were laid out on the plastic pallet they used for a table. They were in public, it was the evening live session. What are we eating? It's tomato soup, the genuine Heinz, how about that, and only a decade or so past its best-by date. For dessert, steamed jam pudding with powdered-milk custard; er, not quite so fresh.

Is this really what they eat in the farm camps?

Yes it is, ironically enough. The fresh produce goes straight out the gates.

The custard's so old the yellow has worn out, but hey, it's genuine Birds—

Hm. The jam's kind of jellified glue, a solid layer on top of a shrunken thing like a chunk of old loofah. Not much of it either, between three. But it's sugar and other quick-release carbs, which is the right stuff for manual labour.

These quality foods are sent to us in the green diplomatic bag, are they?

Nah, would you believe there's a *black market* in our slave-camp supplies—

And what's the collection plate looking like today?

Their stunt was generating some very useful and generous donations, none of which came to this address, but there was a daily print-out; the gems which they shared over their meal. They kept up the banter: Fiorinda laughing and joking, a deadly blankness in the back of her eyes. The men were paralysed, unable to say *switch the fucking cam off, tell us what's wrong*. They had no idea what had happened. Was she in fugue again, with horrors crawling out of the walls?

When they'd said goodnight to the world she went to kneel by the window, looking out. The snow was falling fast, you could hear big flakes tapping on the glass, though all you could see out there was the room reflected, lit by their ATP battery lamp; dimly painted on the blackness. 'I was pregnant,' said Fiorinda, baldly. 'I *was* pregnant. I did a test last week, with the first-aid kit, and it— the baby was his.' She jerked her chin at Sage. 'I'm not pregnant any more. I started to bleed this afternoon. You see. I told you so.'

Fiorinda stayed where she was. Sage went and sat on the floor by his belongings, staring at nothing. Ax decided he might as well look at the *courriel* Alain de Corlay had given to him; there was nothing else useful he could do. Try to kiss it better when her voice sounds like that, you'll just get ripped to shreds.

The envelope looked like a half-inch tube of liquorice, or a scrap of 10mm cable sheathing. It was a shape-memory polymer. You could pulverise this, reduce it to its component atoms: it would reveal no secrets. Match it with the right partner, it would remember its former state and the molecules would rearrange themselves into a datastick. Alain hadn't said, but no secret where this missive came from. The over-specified gadgetry had Internet Commission written all over it, which probably meant it was something unpleasant. Ever since the data quarantine, one of the momentous features of the early Crisis – when Europe had been cut off from the digital world for years, to contain a killer virus – the Commissioners had made sure Ax knew anything that was going to depress him.

Oh well, it can't spoil the mood.

He dug out a tiny baggie of cypher-jacks from the toolbox in the base of his phone, screwed a pair into the tube and jacked the stick into a port. Who needs magic, when we have high tech? Cold-paired with its complex-chemical mate, the liquorice transmuted, visibly, in seconds. Only good for one use, but cryptographers love that kind of thing. His password went to work, decoding.

Sometimes, he thought, tucking a soundbead into his ear and staring at the blank, virtual screen that blossomed on the air, I understand my babe better than Sage does. No matter how wise he is, our bodhisattva. She said *now is not the time to get excited*, and she's usually right. It's okay ... It's horrible right now, but it's okay.

When they calm down they'll see this means Fee can get pregnant, and one of us can do it, which is great news, and something we didn't know before. He would have to get rid of the stupid pregnancy test, before she saw it—

—though he'd almost have liked to keep it as a souvenir, today had been so intense, and when he looked within his hope was brighter than ever—

The message was a big fucker, and heavily encrypted: what could it be? Oh, here it comes. A letter, presented as if on paper; and a movie clip. He read the letter, without taking it in: watched a little of the clip, and froze.

So this is it, he thought, intuition working faster than his understanding—

This is what they did.

Last summer, when the A-team came on stream—

Just a year after Sage Pender's brief success in breaking the mind/matter barrier, a team of US military neuronauts had reached fusion consciousness by a different route. The project had involved a tank of raw petroleum buried under the desert. They'd been supposed to try to disrupt its chemistry by mind-power. Instead, having achieved, it appeared, a state perilously far beyond the experiment's limits, they had willed the destruction of the world's crude oil reserves, incidentally rendering other carbon-fossil fuels useless. They had died in the act. A suicide note had been found explaining they'd given their lives to secure World Peace, and declaring that all further development of the so-called Neurobomb should be abandoned.

Fat chance of World Peace. The Oil Wars had been on their way out anyway, Water Wars were far more fashionable. For weeks afterwards, and then for months, nobody had been sure exactly *what* the A-team had done. Hospital lights had gone out, industries had foundered, millions had died when the fuel vanished: but still it had been as if the billions were holding their breath, the few on the inside track, the masses who had no idea what was going on; all through this long strange winter of frozen calm.

Ax had a feeling like talons thumping, *bang*, into the back of his neck.

This is it, he thought, while the bodies of the Gaian martyrs tumbled in the ghost-glow of his screen. This is our destruction. What Fred Eiffrich foresaw, and why he fought the Pentagon's project, tooth and nail. Losing the oil was nothing, this is what the A-team did. Black magic has become a player. We had a chance that there would be no proliferation, now it's unstoppable. Those grisly lunatics in Lavoisier have joined hands with the mainstream, and God help us all.

And he remembered, now when it was far too late, how part of him had leapt for joy when he'd heard that the black gold was gone. He'd been appalled, of course, and scared. But part of him had cried *Yay! Death to the Evil Empire! The Living World strikes back . . . !* So that now, in this cold room, with Fiorinda staring into the night and Sage looking gutshot, he knew he shared the blame. He saw the world as a palimpsest of minds, and knew what he'd done, all the times when he had taken up the blunt instrument of violence: because he was desperate, because it would work—

He'd broken eye-contact for too long. Lavoisier vanished, replaced by a picture snagged from his own files. It was a still from the cover art for 'Heart On My Sleeve', the Heads' stupendous dance-track from the summer of the Floods Conference. There stood Sage in a white singlet and tight white jeans, the gymnast Mr Muscle he used to be; but without the living skull mask. Smiling sweetly, crippled hands open by his sides, and shall we say, clearly very pleased to see someone?

Ah, glory days. The fun we had!

Fiorinda heaved a sigh, crossed the room and tugged at Sage's shoulder. *I'm sorry*, she muttered, and they hugged each other.

Reassured, Ax turned back to the covering letter. Yes, the implications are appalling, but enough with the metaphysical nausea, let's get practical. His family were still being held hostage. He had to get them out, and he had just lost a couple of major advantages. Who knows about this? With luck, nobody else in Europe, yet. Time for a spot of insider trading. But the text was breaking up—

'Hey, Sage? Could you give me a hand? I need to fix something that wants to be ephemeral.'

TWO

The Doors of Perception

The Triumvirate returned to England. Ax told the press conference at Dover, at length and soberly, that the protest had served its purpose. They had collected an impressive list of supporters, and he could now do more for the camp inmates by working closely with the government, on the spot . . . The mediafolk adjusted this according to what they imagined to be public taste (TIRED OF DRINKING FRENCH PISS, SAYS AX!); ah well, at least it made the front pages.

In hospital rooms when Sage was at death's door, on a cold beach in Mexico, and in the alien glitz of Hollywood, they had dreamed of a sweet hereafter: a country life in Cornwall, in Sage's cottage at Tyller Pystri. But Cornwall was an impossible commute, and with the awful fate of Bridge House as a warning, better the suits had no reason to *think* of Tyller Pystri. They announced their intention of returning to Matthew Arnold Mansions, Brixton Hill, where they'd lived during the dictatorship, 'for the time being'. The place had been redecorated and Allie Marlowe, admin-queen of the Rock and Roll Reich, had arranged for their furniture to come out of store. It was surprisingly okay to be back there. There were ghosts, and painful memories of tragedy and disaster, but the past that haunted the freshly painted rooms was a defeated foe, and they don't make bad company.

Things could never be the same. The Ballroom at the Insanitude, in the State Apartments at Buckingham Palace, would never again host those wild brain-burning club nights of the Dissolution. The Palace of Rivermead, at Reading, was now the property of the official Countercultural Government, an institution that hadn't existed in Ax's day. Times had changed, the revolution had grown up, and the mighty Rock and Roll Reich survived as a celeb-sponsored charity foundation, fundraising for the drop-out hordes and running a few free concerts. Some might wonder why Ax had accepted the President job at all when he hardly seemed relevant any more. Yet still, the Triumvirate's return from Paris set a golden seal on the new era. There was a feeling, irrational and general, that Ax had *really* come home this time, and therefore all would be well. Tough, pragmatic commonsense would rule at Westminster, but Brixton Hill would be the centre of an invisible republic, where the romantic moral protests would be made, the wild ideas would fly, just the way it was supposed to be.

The Prime Minister, Greg Mursal, and his colleagues in the Second Chamber Cabinet were particularly delighted. There'd been some hitches, but they'd snagged Ax Preston, internationally famous do-gooder. They had him on the payroll. That's worth a few Lennon-isms. We are going to be re-elected! And what next? The Nobel Peace Prize? Why not!

Fiorinda and Sage had a rehearsal in Collette House on Piccadilly. They'd agreed to be soloists in some kind of arty *son et lumière*, which would debut as the finalé of the Reading Mayday concert. Mayday at Reading was one of the big events of Countercultural England's calendar, and the finalé, a tradition started by Sage at Ax's inauguration, was a prize commission. It had been won this year by Toby Starborn, the figurative/digital artist who'd done a famous portrait of Fiorinda during the dictatorship.

His design space was an office floor 'torn out' to look as if it had been subjected to green revolutionary violence. A copy of the portrait 'She Feeds And Clothes Her Demons' stood in an alcove: a free-standing hologram, glowing with colour in its faux Pre-Raphaelite frame. Behind a floor-to-ceiling beet-plastic screen, rows of code monkeys sat at their desks. The artist and his favoured assistants greeted the demigods of the old guard solemnly. Toby wore a green velvet cutaway coat over a yellow waistcoat and slick, cellymide breeches with a moulded crotch – giving the impression he was naked from the waist down, the way the wild lads used to dance in the mosh in the days of Dissolution. His hair was combed back, Mr Preston style, and tied with a black ribbon; he had faun's eyes, amber-yellow, tip-tilted. He looked (he wasn't very tall) like a dissolute hobbit with Winnie the Pooh's dress sense. Fiorinda remembered meeting him at the art show opening where his work had attracted such crowds. He hadn't had a lot to say to the raw material that time, either. Well, it must be difficult having your vision walk around, looking at you, thinking it is a real person …

Toby warned them that *The World Turned Upside Down* was an oratorio, which meant no, er, *moves,* and asked if Fiorinda could read sheet-music, as he knew she had no implants or eyesocket tech. Fiorinda agreed to give it a try. They stood on a flatbed stage, orchestral and chorus tracks rough-cut in their ears, while the immix effects cascaded invisibly around them. The code-monkeys made adjustments, the assistants chivvied. The technical run-through proved difficult and rewarding. The soloists came out of it bright-eyed, aroused and sated, two hours later. Nobody in the long room cracked a smile. Toby muttered that *he thought that had gone all right.*

Sage and Fiorinda grinned at each other. Anyone who stays the course long enough has to face moments like this, so take it with a good grace.

Accept that the young bloods don't like you!

Fiorinda looked at the portrait in its shrine. She still didn't care for it. Do I really look like that? The sallow, beleaguered redhead in her ragged green dress stared out into the room, while the goblins she was feeding crept closer. Too many, too hungry, the nursemaid herself will be torn to pieces, trying to keep them alive—

Hm. If that was a prediction of my future, it turned out true enough.

'Would you like to see the new, uh, canvas?'

She started, caught out. 'Er, okay, I sup— Yes, please, that would be great.'

'She Feeds And Clothes Her Demons' disappeared. It was replaced by another hologram: at first a struggle to resolve, then, oh, a blue woman. With swirls of white and splashes of green, curled over so she's almost a sphere, and something bursting out of her side, as if taking flight … Was that a child? It had the oversized eyes and naked head of a baby, and it was clutching something, an electric guitar.

'Very impressive,' said Sage.

'Knock-out,' agreed Fiorinda, taking care not to catch her boyfriend's eye.

Toby seemed satisfied with these comments. 'It needs work,' he muttered, shrugging, head down. The earth giving birth vanished, the goblin nursemaid by the fallen oak returned.

Fiorinda smiled brightly. 'Do you know Flora Morris? Can we meet her?'

Flora Morris was the composer of the oratorio, and the next big thing on the choral music scene, which was high fashion and cool these days, apparently.

'She's uh, done stuff with Tim Bowery.'

Tim was a theatre director, fearless Reich fan, one of their few artsworld friends to have prospered in the post-Ax era. They nodded encouragingly and the dissolute hobbit unbent at last, his faun's eyes coming to life. 'And there's *Sacrificial*, of course. I saw *Sacrificial* live at Wethamcote last summer, at the Festival of the Ponds. They put it on in Spitalls Farm Wood. The singers were in tiger cages, hanging over the site of the pit itself. Immense, immense. I knew I had to work with her after that, so I got Tim to introduce me. What did you think of *Sacrificial*, Sage? I found it very, very moving—'

So it goes. The most appalling scandals have a short half-life, a much longer glow of fame. Wethamcote, in South Derbyshire, was one of the places where the Extreme Celtics had held their rites, when things first started to go downhill. Ax and Sage had busted a human sacrifice rave network there.

Sage shook his head. 'I missed that one. Think I was in the US.'

'Me too,' said Fiorinda. 'But I'm going to *love* doing this.'

'We better leave you to it,' decided Sage. 'Fancy a quick pint, Fee?'

'Sage, you're incapable of having "a quick pint".'

'All right, a quick six, then.'

They took their leave, bestowing grins of sunny goodwill.

It was the beginning of April: Fiorinda had just had a birthday, she was twenty-four. Outdoors, they entered a hell's kitchen of dust. Everything unbeautiful in the centre of London was being torn down, to leave a mosaic of new green spaces, a lo-tech but fantastically harsh and noisy process, in the cold, dry spring that had followed the freeze. This was the way it would be for every city in England, once the recovery got going again. The ancient centres cleansed and beautified, then a ring of garden suburbs for concentrated housing and amenities, interspersed with intensive (but green!) market gardening. Transport pollution would not be a problem. There'd be H-power and the renewables, with improved mobile sourcing, strict laws limiting private car ownership, and *no* proliferation of horse-drawn vehicles. Industry wouldn't be a problem either. It would have decentralised power and live alongside the people. If it wanted to make a profit it would have to be clean, sustainable and energy-audited first, all enforced by lucrative government licensing. What happens beyond the garden suburbs? What about the millions who gave up and took to the roads, in the great crash and after? Ah, well, that's the difficult area, let's not go there—

Thank God for the sacred immunity of licensed premises. They found a pub, where they were, of course, recognised: but nobody molested them, and so far they had escaped the ignominy of minders in constant attendance. Fiorinda downed most of her first pint at speed.

'The blue woman representing Planet Earth had my face?'

'Yeah.'

'And she was giving birth, by Caesarian section, to an alien with guitar?'

''Fraid so.'

'*Fuck* him. *Stuff* him. Did he ever stop to think I might have human feelings?' Fiorinda glowered defiantly. 'I don't care. I'll take the Small Grey if I have to. Any kind of baby's better than none.'

'You can't blame the kid,' Sage was magnanimous. 'He's trying to be avant garde, and we are in the way. Tha's bound to lead to dumb, pompous affectation.'

'D'you think he sacrifices to that portrait? I didn't see any bloodstains.'

'Nah. Don't worry about it. He just likes to have his number on show.'

You are my rock, she thought. A big calm warm rock, and I remember when everyone thought you were a complete lout, except me and the Heads. And I'm very glad you didn't punch Toby out, there would have been no excuse for that, I'm being an idiot . . . but *I'm glad you thought about it.* Sage laughed, and went to get another round in, just brushing her cheek with his fingertips as he passed. 'My brat.'

They drank in near-silence, pondering the dreadful aftermath of being pop-culture icons, *corpses in the mouths of the bourgeoisie*: thinking of the appalling shadow that was hanging over all these happy neo-feudalists with their style-victim souls. What's this about Wethamcote? They knew the Festival of the Ponds, a sterling rural-desert regeneration enterprise, no problem there; a human-sacrifice musical didn't bother them. Artists will make art out of any fucking thing they like. They hadn't realised that *the site of the death pit* had become a venue . . . This struck them as a spooky lack of revulsion, and a straw in the wind. Who dictates decisions like that? Or hints at what is acceptable? Exactly how much of the evil régime survives, behind this 'Moderate' façade?

Their eyes met, telepathy artefacts.

'Sage—'

'Mm?'

'It's not going to work. We can't be a gracious elder presence and let the next generation take over. They're just not the right next generation.'

'Hahaha. They never are, sweetheart. But you're true, I was thinking the same. We're going to have to rule the school a little. Are you ready for that?'

'I'll be all right.'

'I know you will.'

'The immersion effects are going to drown us in that finalé.'

'Yeah.' Sage looked into his beer. 'You know, I take his point, oratorio, dignified, no one jumps around. But when I get out there, front of a big crowd, in spite of my advanced age . . . Dunno what might come over me.'

In the old days, when Sage had been the skull-masked king of the lads, Aoxomoxoa and the Heads had had a spectacularly brainless live act: full of stunt-dives, circus tricks, and the thrill of unscheduled, blood-splattered disaster.

'You have been known to drive your poor band nuts. But, okay, thinking about it. If you had Toby's immix code live, on your mask button, it could be a *constructive* stage coup. D'you suppose he'd give you a copy?'

'Not if he has any sense. But I think he might—'

They were white-water fishes, alight with the joy of battle.

A burst of laughter from that table (at which they did not stare), startled the pub's clientele, and sent a flurry of secret smiles around the room.

There were snow flurries in the week before the great holiday, but Mayday itself dawned bright and fair. President Ax's inner circle, the radical rockstars who had once ruled England, converged on Brixton. Rob Nelson and the Powerbabes came from Lambeth in the Snake Eyes' Big Band's minibus, bringing with them Anne-Marie Wing and Smelly Hugh, and the junior half of AM's brood. The Wing family had come up from Reading by train the day before. Ironically, considering the country was now being run by hardline greens, there was no public transport available today. Allie Marlowe and Dilip Krishnachandran, who were still living, separately but amicably, at the Insanitude, came by taxi; Chip Desmond and Kevin Verlaine cycled from their virtually furnished rooms in Notting Hill. The great city, silent and enchanted, let them pass like a scattered drift of ghosts: over the river, along the wide roads that had once ached with teeming traffic.

By nine a.m. they were in Fiorinda's music room, watching State Occasion prelims with the helpless fascination that strikes on these occasions: chairs and tables being set out for countless street parties; crowds in sleeping bags waking up at the Big Screen locations up and down the country; church bells being rung, the ropes pumped by hearty and broadminded Christian-Pagans. Hawthorn blossoms, rose and white, unfurling in English hedgerows (this was CGI, because the flowers were being sulky, but you could hardly tell) ... Maypole ribbons whirled and wove, organic bunting fluttered. In Reading Town the route of the motorcade was thronged with shining faces, on which the flying cameras swooped for soundbites: from humble folk who had tramped for weeks, and families with humorous, safely anodyne, tales of how travel restrictions had been subverted ... And all to see the rockstar king and his courtiers come home. Back to where it all began! To the Festival Site by the Thames, where thirty thousand or so staybehinds were still encamped, faithful to the heart-warming ideals of Dissolution summer—

The rockstar courtiers exchanged uneasy glances, or else tried not to meet each other's eyes. Oh, this was strange ... The children were downstairs, with a posse of Snake Eyes youth-team babysitters. Only Marlon Williams, Sage's sixteen-year-old son from a long defunct relationship, with his father for the holiday weekend, had been allowed to stay. The technicians were setting up: talking digitised-world arcanities with Sage; and communing with George Merrick, Sage's second-in-command, at the remote site. 'I hope the Stonehenge bit comes on again,' said Anne-Marie. 'I kept missing it. I was up at five, but it was already over.'

'Don't worry,' said Felice, senior Powerbabe. 'It'll be back.'

A feature on 'Ax's Rock and Roll Cabinet' provided some distraction. They watched themselves, quaintly clad in pre-Dissolution fashions, in clips from ancient news and music programmes – *known as the Few, to discriminate them from Ax's original group, the Chosen Few, they followed his star to fame and fortune, as the social leaders of the revolution's youth culture* – Well, my God. Is that what we were doing? Fame and fucking fortune. Now that is a JOKE. Not that we care, but ...

Misrepresentation, street fighting; ancient cities in flames, flood devastation, vapid rockstars singing and playing, apparently nowhere near the heat ...

Indignant jeers and groans fell silent when the cameras returned to Reading. The lost heartland, *trompe-l'oeil* lifesize on Fiorinda's wall, was so real it seemed you could step into the frame. Say this for the Second Chamber, they don't let their hard green agenda get in the way of the tech. And the stats, which they were following in a sidebar, were impressive. We have a government that has achieved ninety-three per cent penetration, of the people who can get to a screen. That's very solid, even if only partly true.

We shouldn't have come back, thought Dora, the middle Babe, struck by horrible certainty. We should have stayed in California and made a new life.

'The old home town looks the same,' intoned Chip. 'As they step down from the train—'

His friends advised him to shut up.

'Time is a helix of semi-precious stones,' announced Kevin

Verlaine. 'Here we are, coming round again, everything changed, everything the same, inescapable—'

'It'll take a lot to break us out of this attractor.'

Smelly Hugh frowned. 'But it oughter be July, shouldn't it?'

It had been a wet and muddy July, in the last year of the United Kingdom's existence, when the festival that ignited a revolution had gathered by the riverside, and a handful of idealist young Indie hopefuls had stumbled into the maw of history.

'Ah, now tha's the fifteen-dimensional tachyon shift, Hugh.'

'You have to watch out for those.'

'It's the rock-sidereal precession.'

Hugh joined the laughter, pleased that he'd said something funny. He'd been trying for *clever*, but you could never tell with this lot. Funny was good, anyway.

'Of course,' offered Rob Nelson, coming to terms with the situation a little, 'this is bass-ackwards. We should be physically in Reading for the gig, and bi-locating back here to hang out. So we'd be working with the muscle-power, and having fun at home at the same time. Isn't that the idea, Ax?'

'Dunno about the fun,' muttered Felice, rolling her eyes.

They were to appear at Reading by b-loc. This was the deal that Ax had made, when he accepted the Presidency. No flesh and blood on State Occasions until the Second Chamber released the Few's professional earnings from the knots tied by that gang of savages known as the green nazi régime. Human sacrifice had been their entertainment, genocide their aim, but they hadn't been above malicious accounting on the side. The present administration fully admitted that the deal was illegal, but they were still dragging their feet: hence the shutdown. Rob and the two senior Babes agreed in principle, but they didn't like weird science. They could accept b-loc as a futuristic kind of mobile phone, one to one. It had taken a lot of persuading to convince them that today's stunt would work.

'Not this time, Rob,' said Ax firmly. 'This time we're making a point. We're also showing what's possible, and it's good advertising. It's the way you do it with novel tech: toys for the rich, crowd-pleasing stunts, the industrial applications follow.'

The b-loc techs, who were crew, members of the sprawling tech-circus that supported Sage and the Heads, grinned at each other, ɔreciating Ax Preston's famous bloody-mindedness. But they'd ɹve appreciated any excuse to do something weird and cutting-edge spectacular again. The boss had been away too fucking long.

'Except who needs mass b-loc,' mused Fiorinda, 'when labour camps are so much more organic? I'm with Felice. I hate modern drugs. Didn't getting out of your head used to mean having fun? Now it's how we commute to Berkshire on a public holiday.'

'Not a *drug*, Fee,' corrected Sage, his attention on the 10^{28} closure figures for the superposition: freestyle, outdoors, my God, this is impossible— 'Wash your mouth. Absolutely no drugs, genes, or anythen' mind-altering involved.'

Bi-location had been a spin-off from the Zen Self project, the Anglo-Welsh experiment that had taken Sage through the mind/ matter barrier. In the early stages it'd needed nasty spinal injections, and heavy neurosteroids. The set-up they were using today was Scottish, which was galling, but too bad, the Scots had done the development while England was busy flirting with occult cannibals, ah well, at least it's in the family—

'Nyah, pedant. Are you trying to tell me b-loc isn't psychotropic?'

'Anorak gene, anorak gene,' crowed Marlon. 'He can't help it.'

This pallid, sullen youth, barely recognisable as the teenage form of a sweet little boy called Marlon Williams, wanted to quit boarding school, come and live at Brixton Hill, and continue his education (if his estranged parents absolutely insisted) in London. He didn't seem to realise that needling his dad incessantly was not the way forward: it's the hormones. Sage was amazingly patient with him.

Fiorinda demolished Marlon with a glance. The tech set-up continued in its mysterious way, the caterers arrived. A murmur like headphone-leak came from Smelly Hugh, *hair of gold and lips like cherries . . .* Dilip sighed and stretched. Last summer, in California, he'd been ready to bring his long struggle with HIV to an end. But you quit the drugs, and you get better. He knew it couldn't last. He felt the fragility of a golden Indian Summer . . . Will I have the courage to keep off the medication when the virus catches up? Ah, there's a fascination in living like this, poised on the brink . . . Allie looked across the room, and looked away. The Few's tactful, silent curiosity plagued her: *what happened between Allie and DK?* Nothing happened, nothing to do with the disease. DK's a lover of the world, a good friend, but he lives alone. That's all. She was falling into a pattern she hated, the kind of well-groomed efficient woman who gives her life to an organisation. I don't want that, I want to be loved, normal, how can I escape?

She reviewed everything that could go wrong with this day, and shuddered.

Chip reviewed the naked room. He missed Fiorinda's trademark party frocks that used to be displayed on the walls. The scruffy secondhand Martin, her other guitars, her red boots: all the totems that used to be company for overnighters, when this was Brixton Hill's spare bedroom. There was nothing left of that fellowship except the grand piano: and even that was shrouded, in a great sheet of midnight velvet. He sighed. Triumvirate lore ought to be richer than this—

'Fiorinda space has stripped down and gone public.'

'But we're not allowed to touch her secret keys,' said Cherry Dawkins, junior Babe. 'The message is conflicted. She lets us common folk in, yet she shuts us out.'

'Idiots. I'll change the semiotics when I unpack,' said Fiorinda.

Rob, Felice and Dora exchanged a sad, furtive grin. Things were easier in Lambeth. The brothers and their white desperanto allies had calmed down now that Ax was back: Felice was no longer desperate to move out. But they could be losing Chez. The little sister gravitated more and more towards Chip and Verlaine, and Fiorinda. She gets their jokes, she plays their games ... The grin expressed a fledgling state of mind, beyond hurt and confusion. It said, *let the girl go home*, wherever home may be. We won't hold her back, we love her.

Ax sat on the floor, on a rug that belonged elsewhere; the music room carpet hadn't come out of storage. He'd been rolling a new blend of Bristol Bud, supplied by Ksendziuks of Clifton – cannabis suppliers to the President, and very proud of the fact. He couldn't get used to paying tax on his drugs, but the Pres can't support contraband, got to set an example. He lined up the neat spliffs in his smokes tin, and decided it was time to make a move.

'Shall we go next door for a while?' He glanced at the techs. 'Is that okay?'

'Yeah, Ax. That's fine. We won't need you folks for about another two hours.'

They never do. They just like to make you get out of bed.

Everyone stood up, including Marlon.

'No,' said Sage. 'Not you, Mar. You keep an eye on the fest tv for us.'

'But Dad—'

'*Stay.*'

There were tones of that voice with which the boy did not argue. He subsided, muttering *don't talk to me as if I was a fucking pet animal*. But he said this in Welsh, a language of which his father (allegedly) understood not a word.

Marlon cruised. The old 'alternative' channel favoured by his elders had gone walkabout at the Reading site: prowling the morning arena, accosting sluggish hippies. Boring. A history item on EBC, premier English fragment of the great BBC empire, fascinated him for a while. Apparently nothing much had happened in the last few years, except that the Reformed House of Lords, aka the Second Chamber, had grown in power and wisdom. Some bad guys called *the green nazis* had been defeated, in the last gasp of *the chaotic years of transition*, and now the lords and ladies, natural leaders of the native English Counterculture, had chosen *the so-called rockstar warlord* Ax Preston, for President, because they were in touch with the somewhat mindless grassroots—

Unbelievable, muttered the boy, who had seen a little of those *chaotic years*.

The two minor state tv channels were at Glastonbury, the last stronghold of the Extreme Celtics, which was now totally respectable and had begun to host a rival Mayday event with all the Pagan bonfires and things that weren't allowed at Reading. But he couldn't find any live sex ... Or else you could have Reading permanent campground's public tv, and watch hippy councillors having a meeting about litter. That was it. Every other number bounced you back to the ridiculous fake history show. The caterers had departed, the techs were in their own world. Marlon ate some buffet (but it was all ugly, nothing tasted Welsh) and finally managed to hack through to the viewing of choice among the gilded youth of the London

Reich: a public tv station which he'd heard about from a friend. He got an error message and a Happy Beltane smiley. *Diawl y' myto i.*

Sheep in human clothing, that's what the English are.

Across the hall the Few were also watching tv, crowded round the little screen of a pre-Dissolution black box set. They'd been told about the content of Alain's *courriel*, but this would be their first viewing of the movie clip. Ax had been waiting for the right opportunity. They lived with a high degree of surveillance: the Insanitude was hopelessly compromised and their houses were monitored. All open and acknowledged, of course, for their protection. But that only meant you couldn't take counter-measures without looking guilty. Ax was working on getting the 'security' stepped down, but it was a slow dance.

The legacy of a terror régime is enduring: so many features that ought to be dismantled linger on, because they're so useful.

Here it comes. Twilight in the desert, in the red waste between the Inyo and the Panamint ranges, some two hundred miles northeast of LA. Two men in dusty range clothes hunkered down in the opening of a tunnel to check their weapons, and discuss mass-murder. 'I never thought that violence was going to be phased out,' said the tall, skinny blond. 'I was just surprised when *I* got a chance to play.'

'The killing makes me feel real,' said the other, with a flashing smile—

They slipped from their lair and set off, bent double, towards a huddle that looked like some quake-struck Third World village: frequent close-ups lit to catch the flat eyes, the tight, blunt muzzles of two animal predators. Next shot, they'd penetrated a humble shanty school. They spoke coldly of the numbers they would have to 'reduce' as they rifled the children's copybooks: then whirled and fired, without a moment's hesitation, on a group of wide-eyed goth and hippy types who seemed to be unarmed.

Events were mainly left to speak for themselves in a silence broken only by gunshot, crunching boot-heels, choking breath: but there was a sporadic commentary. Over a brisk search of the bodies outside the school, the mature, female voice came up. 'Do you see any heroes here, Dan?'

'No Ma'am,' replied the male voice, sober and kindly, of a highly

43

respected US national anchorperson (uncredited). 'I see a couple of burned-out young men, far from home, running around like psychopaths.'

'This shouldn't have been allowed to happen,' declared his partner.

'I think we can all agree on that, whatever our politics.'

'The Lavoisier kids were misguided, sure, and they had strange beliefs, but they were trying to save the world. They didn't deserve to be slaughtered!'

The Few watched, without comment, until the picture faded to grey.

'And that's why you came home?' said Rob after a pause.

'Yep,' said Ax.

'Apparently it's the trailer,' said Fiorinda. 'There's a lot more.'

'But – but it'll be easy to prove it's been edited and tampered to shit!' exclaimed Rob. 'Who's going to believe in that shit? You could never get that kind of quality from outdoor secret cameras!' He sounded shaken.

'We think it's real,' said Ax, evenly. 'Yeah, tampered, but not by much.'

'Don' see why not,' said Sage. 'The tech's available, and the Lavoisiens were part-geeks with money to burn. We just never thought of this, it never crossed our tiny minds. Okay, you probably need a second look.'

'*No!*' cried Allie, horrified. She was on the floor, in the front row, and felt she'd been sandblasted by hateful images. 'We *do not*! My God, that was *awful*—'

'You think? Ooh, I dunno. I like the bit where he says "young".'

Sage's laddish flippancy in the face of horrors had never failed to infuriate Allie, *especially* because she knew it was pure affectation. But she looked up, caught the bleak set of his beautiful mouth, and changed her tone. 'I'm sorry. I was just shocked.'

''S' okay.'

'It's shocking,' agreed Ax. 'Can't fault them on that.'

'*Did* you fire on anybody that was unarmed?' asked Anne-Marie, seriously.

Thanks, AM. That's an excellent illustration of the problem.

Ax shrugged. 'It was a combat situation, Ammy, and we were insanely outnumbered. I wouldn't swear we always stopped to ask.'

'Imagine,' remarked Verlaine, in awe. 'Imagine it's the year 2000, and two international rockstars, British international rockstars, have been videoed live on an intensive *Natural Born Killas* murder spree. Words can't express the dynamite.'

'Ideally it would be Bono and the Edge,' added Chip, getting into the idea. 'For the moral dimension. And maybe they should desecrate a church—'

'The tampering won't matter, Robbo,' Fiorinda broke in. 'They get those very powerful moving pictures in front of the public, presenting the footage as pristine. Howls of protest, they bow to expert opinion and admit there's been enhancement: when the damage is done and the impression has been made. Oldest trick in the book.'

The Few stared at the blank screen of the little tv, lost for words. The tiger and the wolf glanced at each other. Yeah, brother; what we thought. If truth be known, they'd been making excuses not to show the Black Dragon's trailer. They had not been eager to see this reaction, which had the weight of professional experience behind it. We live and die by the images that are put out there—

'Does Harry know?' wondered DK. 'Does this explain his silence?'

Allegedly, the English radical rockstars had gone to California to do the promotion for a virtual movie about the Reich. Under cover of this project, President Fred Eiffrich had been consulting the Triumvirate about a problem with rogue 'fusion' weapons developers, at the Pentagon. It had turned out that the bloodthirsty ritual route to creating a human superweapon was really being pursued by terrorists, Countercultural suicide warriors. Rescuing Fiorinda from their desert training camp had been the occasion of the Lavoisier Raid.

But the movie had been maybe just as significant as the superweapon, in the President's view. Fred Eiffrich had seen Ax Preston and his Rock and Roll Reich as the model for recovery, in Europe and beyond. The biopic on Ax's futuristic utopia, created by golden boy producer Harry Lopez, was supposed to be a key element in Fred's fight to pull the world out of the frightening tailspin of the last decade. The last anyone had heard of *Rivermead,* Harry had been negotiating the terms of the global release, hampered by moneymen who did not understand conditions in Crisis Europe. But the golden boy had gone very quiet recently—

'Oh, I'm sure Harry knows,' said Sage. 'Poor kid, what a bust.

I think you can safely say our brief career as Fred's peace and love poster boys is over.'

'B-but those bastards were insane!' Chip burst out, recovering from the glorious vision of Bono plus AK47. 'Seriously, *seriously* insane! They were disembowelling each other in the hope of creating a magic psychopath like Fiorinda's dad! They'd *cupboards full* of chopped-off heads in jars! They were going to chop *Fiorinda's* head off! The US government was so scared that the National Guard was about to turn Lavoisier into a glassy hole in the ground! How can a video of Ax and Sage, er, okay, killing some of them, be used in a smear campaign? They're the psychotic evil monsters, dabbling in dark forces!'

'It wouldn't have worked last season,' Fiorinda agreed, reasonably. 'But then the A-team did what they did, and ended the oil wars at a stroke, with zero casualties. All right, you know different: but to a lot of US voters that's a very positive image, and no matter how he feels about the Neurobomb, it's been impossible for Fred not to go along with it. So black magic is now a *good* thing, in Middle America, and the Lavoisiens can be presented as good guys. *They* didn't murder anyone. Their victims were volunteers. And in the end they were proved to be harmless, remember. It turned out they had no magic, they were just innocent, self-mutilating fantasists . . . Stop spluttering, Chip. That's the story we told, and we can't change it now. Anything else is either too complex, or involves explaining things I would rather we don't explain; as I would like to stay alive.'

Her calm was a little chilling.

'The letter we can't show you,' said Sage, after a short silence, 'because we failed to haul it back out of the shredder, said something like this had been long planned. The US media barons don't like Fred Eiffrich. They built Ax up, when we were over there, with a view to knocking him down at the most damaging moment; then Baal the Black Dragon contacted them with this. What a gift, eh?'

Baal the Black Dragon had been one of the Lavoisien leaders.

'This means the shock, horror, how appalling, machine is all in place, whenever the opposition decides to let fly. Fred's campaign manager thinks they'll wait until October, which seems like a long time to hang around, but it's traditional. At least Fred's team gets a good chance to prepare their defence.'

Everyone nodded, looking bemused.

'So both sides know all about it,' said Felice, 'am I right? And it's a huge scandal, but the story won't break for six months. Americans are weird.'

'No,' said Ax, softly, his eyes on the blank grey screen. 'They're not weird. They're experts. They know how this thing called democracy works, and how to work it. The unfortunate thing is the bad guys tend to have the edge, be more intuitive, when it comes to handling the mob—'

'Not *always*,' declared Verlaine, loyally.

A muscle tightened, at the corner of Ax's jaw. 'Well, that's the situation. We could have six months, but there's been a leak. Which is why we were warned, and why we decided to quit Paris. We probably won't hear anything more from the Commissioners, so we have to be prepared to deal with the fallout at any time.'

'But I don't get this. What are we supposed to do?' demanded Dora.

'Nothing,' said Ax. 'There's nothing we can do. Stay out of it, and hope Sage and I don't get extradited. Okay, probably not that bad, but . . . Fred authorised the official raid, the one that didn't happen. They'll claim he knew about our stunt and let it go ahead, and I wouldn't like to stand up with my hand on the Qu'ran, and say he didn't. That'll be the issue, and it doesn't have to make sense.' He sighed. 'It's the way things work. You do what seems necessary, in an emergency, then later you have to answer for it, and all the rules you ignored are back in place.'

The living room at Matthew Arnold was like Fiorinda's music room: a sketch of its old self. The same old-fashioned gas stove in the cast-iron fireplace, same rust-red couches. A couple of pictures had been returned to the walls, but there were no books, no details. The Falmouth Jade, the ancient stone axe the Second Chamber had sent to Ax to prove they wanted him for President, stood propped on a stand on the mantelpiece. It looked lonely.

The Few were indifferent to the fate of *Rivermead*. They had seen it, they would be happy not to see it again. They did not feel that losing the personal support of the US President was a crippling blow either. There goes Hollywood stardom, there goes our career on the world stage, see it falling away from us, spinning off into the dark.

We're back to making a difference on this little offshore island . . .
That was fine. It was all they'd ever hoped to do.

But Fred Eiffrich stood between the world and the proliferation of
the new superweapon. If Fred was blown away, and the US started
up the experiments again, there wasn't a hope. For sure, global
recovery had been knocked back by the A-team event, but there were
still great powers . . . China? The Russian Federation? Japan; who
couldn't possibly leave fusion consciousness alone if the USA was
building Neurobombs? The horror that had struck Ax the moment
he saw the Lavoisier video was in the room. This could be it. Our
protection has been stripped away—

'Do you think they know?' began Dora, trying not to sound as
spooked as she felt. She cleared her throat. 'The Black Dragon,
I mean, uh, the people behind this?'

'Hey,' said Ax. 'Fred's not even damaged yet.'

'I don't think so, Dora,' said Fiorinda.

All her friends looked to the rock and roll princess, who sat
between her bodyguards as always, on one of the rust-red couches;
her bare feet tucked up. 'Listen,' she said, calmly. 'I'm Rufus
O'Niall's daughter, which makes me potentially, possibly, the only
human weapon of mass destruction left alive. I'm going to be looking
over my shoulder for the rest of my life, and I accept that. One day
someone's going to come up to me and say, I know you can commit
magic, and I will have to stand and fight, one way or another . . . I
know it might happen, I hope it won't, and I'm not going to let it get
me down. But there's no reason to believe we're in that kind of
trouble, yet. We don't even know that the Black Dragon's backers
would start the research again. We *do* know that anyone who
understands the science will tell them to *forget it*. Most likely they
just want their bloke in the White House, and as they are living in the
past they see no harm in playing good old-fashioned dirty—'

'Are you going to be all right, going on stage today, pet?' asked
Anne-Marie. 'I'm just a bit psychic, and this has really upset me,
that's why I ask.'

Ax and Sage set their teeth.

'I'll be fine, thanks.'

'What about the home front?' asked Chip, changing the subject.

'Have we any idea what'll happen over here when the video gets aired?'

Ax shook his head. 'I haven't a clue. It could have very little impact. News from the US might as well be from Mars, these days. It could do us good, if Fred publicly disowns us, which I think he must. At least the US-haters in the House will have to stop calling us dupes of Babylon—'

'Shame,' sighed Verlaine. 'I like *dupes of Babylon.*'

The Few had a sense that they'd missed some vital meaning. There was something they had not been told, something they were supposed to guess. Not the *Rivermead* aspect, nothing to do with the Bomb; or Fiorinda. What was it?

'Ax,' began Rob, uneasily, 'you guys are not *buying* this shit, are you? You didn't do anything wrong. You had to do what you did.'

But Rob had never picked up a lethal weapon in his life.

The entryphone chimed. Ax reached for the house remote: a security crew voice announced Roxane Smith, the veteran post-gendered music critic. Soon s/he was at the living room door, which had to be unlocked for hir, by hand. S/he entered, deploying a splendid ebony and silver cane and raising hir eyebrows at the paranoia. Rox had aged in the last year. S/he'd left the last of youth behind as s/he bravely put it. But hir trademark Dante-robes were as gorgeous, and hir make-up as superbly over-the-top as ever. S/he took a seat, carefully, beside Verlaine, on the red couch across from the Triumvirate.

'Sorry I'm late, my dears. It takes me such a time to make myself decent these days. Well, is it safe? Am I to view the *corpus delicti?*'

So Sage got his wish: it was twilight in the desert again, and the two predators were hunting ... Fiorinda watched her lovers. What were they looking for, when they studied this tampered record so intently, over and over; frame by frame?

The trailer reached its final image, and was gone.

'Hm. It has a brash, synthetic, Sergio Leone appeal,' boomed Rox, 'but I believe I prefer the Harry Lopez cartoon. Let me see ... I gather we need to discredit the cultists, who have somehow become sympathetic. Wasn't there one "volunteer" human sacrifice you know to have been an innocent bystander? Might hard evidence of that be produced?' S/he looked around, seeming puzzled by the depth of the gloom. Roxane had stayed at home, for health reasons, when the rest of them went to California; s/he had had not shared their brush with global politics. This had opened a slight distance that didn't seem to be growing less.

"Fraid not, Rox,' said Sage, politely. 'We won't be asked, an' anyway, it's not that kind of movie. I don't think there's going to be a courtroom scene.'

'One measly murder?' muttered Verlaine. 'Sounds like nailing Al Capone for tax fraud.' He still woke, sweating and blubbing, from dreams where the Lavoisiens had succeeded in their noble scheme for saving the world—

Ax reached for the remote again. 'Well, you've seen it. Now I'm going to destroy this charming artefact, before it gets us into any more trouble. I hope you've memorised your favourite moments, Sage.'

'Right.'

'*Le jeu est fait.* We'll have to play it the way it lays.'

They did not step down from the train, but it was supposed to look as though they did. The arrival happened in a VIP lounge inside Reading Station, out of sight. They met the public on the forecourt, where rainbow-bedecked open cars were waiting. At Richfield Avenue Gate they disembarked and strolled through the crush, under arches twined with living vines of rose and honeysuckle. There were banners flying and drummers drumming, and a cordon of minders to gather the gifts and messages; and obscure the fact that the leaders of the Reich could not be touched.

Soon all celebrities will make personal appearances this way!

'Hey Ax, hey, hey, Ax! What d'you think of Glasto pre-empting you?'

The Mayday festival at Glastonbury had started at sunset on Beltane eve.

'Glasto always used to be a slick machine for taking money out of hippies. I'm glad they're getting back to their roots.'

'Hey, hey Sage! Fio! How about leaking some details of Toby's Masque?'

Traditionally, the secrecy of the prize finalé was fiercely protected—

'Not as many jokes as mine use' ter have,' allowed Sage.

'I'm appearing as a concept,' confided Fiorinda, capriciously awarding this questioner her most fabulous smile. 'It's very, very moving.'

When they reached the Palace of Rivermead, the screamed questions and demands ceased. The crowd, mostly veteran Dissolution mediafolk at this point, grew quiet. Ax stood on the forecourt, looking up at the fantastical, multi-coloured Gaudi cathedral: built for him by the Counterculture's chief architect in the glory days. This palace, which had fallen to the enemy, which had been Fiorinda's prison, and place of torture, through the terrible green nazi winter . . . His Triumvirate partners moved in on either side and they walked up the steps by the Dead Cars sculpture together, the Few following close behind.

It seemed as if there should have been applause, or a fanfare. There was none, only the sober accolade of silence.

Ax and his friends passed through the flower-wreathed doors, masked by minders. They had disappeared before they reached the lobby. The guests at the VIP reception, upstairs in the grand solar, with those beautiful great windows looking to the west, had been told that there was a technical hitch. Topsy the architect's recycled walls were full of metallic paint fibres from mulched car bodies, which interfered with b-loc reception. That was why the President couldn't join them. Ax had made no objection to the face-saving. If truth be known, he'd have been at the reception if the suits had pushed just a little harder. He could have walked into Rivermead smiling: because his girl was beside him, and she had *won* that lonely battle.

He'd been tempted to ditch the whole b-loc idea, in fact, because he *needed* this day. But when you're engaged in insider trading, the last thing you want is to leave a trail of suspicious concessions.

Consciousness is a point, not a line. They had been in Reading, they had been in Brixton, with no noticeable lag, no blanks, no lapses. Still there was a collective sigh of relief as they lost the remote site. Rob and Felice reached to tug off their headsets.

'Sorry,' came Sage's voice in their ears. 'No pass-outs.'

They were in the music room.

51

They were in Reading Arena.

They were standing on uncannily green grass, in the central piazza of a pocket metropolis of some fairground, Bohemian land; the bright sun overhead. The air smelled of spilled beer and burned beet-sugar plastic, and roiled with conflicting musics. Fx, masks and costumes glowed in the cool sunshine. Hordes of campers, plus further hordes of ticketed punters, filled the scene. In the distance there was Red Stage with its towers, and the tiny figures of some hapless early band. There was Orange Stage, and Yellow Stage (also known as Scary Stage, because of its accident record); and the cobalt cone of the Blue Lagoon. There's Violet Alley with a new crop of rides, the Green Room and the Mood Indigo tent; where things get smoky and jazzy and slow. Here are the sheets of hardy wildflowers, ladysmock and hawksbit and dog violets, planted by some inspired unknown, in the first spring of the permanent camp—

The eau-de-Nil geodesic dome of the Zen Self tent, which should have been right beside them, was gone, its absence dispelling a fleeting, intense impression that they'd died, and this was their eternal home. Or else they'd fallen foul of that tricky rock-sidereal precession, and landed in some Mayday of the past, with the worst of their struggle to do again . . . Those who hadn't been absolutely sure that Chip and Sage were joking about the risk of slipping back in time laughed in relief.

The virtual self of bi-location was really present, and visible to any observer. But unless you had immense powers of concentration, or took some vicious steroids, your appearance at the remote site would swiftly revert to the self-image held in the somatosensory cortex: a goblin form, all hands and mouth and genitals. Hence commercial b-loc piggybacked on an older technology. The Few were clothed, so to speak, in stagecraft hologram 'shadows' of themselves; each in characteristic finery. Sage wore his sand-coloured suit, with the glitter of gold in it (in reality, long defunct), and Aoxomoxoa's living skull mask. He felt the ethereal tug of the mask's presence and saw beside him a sixteen-year-old boy, not very tall, Celtic tattooing around his left eye, slightly transparent, and making a touching, futile effort to look like he did this all the time . . . Joy rushed upon him: the sheer delight of seeing those mountains of crunched numbers turned inside out, the information revealed to be *all this* . . . Did I say my rockstar career was over? Musta been on drugs. Take England back from the bad guys? Got to be a piece of piss. Three Hallowe'en skulls were grinning at him from the press of people around the mark (the Heads did not wear avatar masks, they preferred simpler fx). He spotted them at once, and pretended not to; plunging gladly into the forgotten mode.

'Now, where's my band?' Hands in his pockets, the skull doing insouciant arrogance, with a touch of show me the fun. 'I *know* I left them round here somewhere.'

Mr Preston's family (barring Ax's mother and the new baby, who had to stay behind for security reasons) had agreed to come to Reading in the flesh. They were the stars of the reception in the Rivermead solar, where the great and the good and the A-listers were doomed to chat over canapés and English champagne, through an interminable State Occasion afternoon. This had been a risk. Jordan, even when sober, had an unerring talent for locating exactly the person he should not speak to, and saying exactly what he should not say. And it would have been cruel, not to say pointless, to tell him he couldn't drink. But it was important for the family to be co-operative. Fortunately Sayyid Mohammad Zayid Barlewi, premier leader of English Islam, and Ax's patron in the Faith, was also at the party. He could be trusted to steer Ax's brother away from trouble, and maybe even moderate the alcohol intake: Jordan was scared of Mohammad.

No use worrying, there's a crowd to be worked.

They were not free agents. A shimmer in the air, on either side of their field of view, warned them of their limits: anyone who strayed was liable to vanish. But it looked as if they were. They had a live path winding through the arena, another through the graded corrals backstage of Main Stage, and a location inside the Blue Lagoon. Their touch was thistledown, they could neither eat nor drink, nor smoke; their voices had a tendency to break up like a bad phone signal. But they leant on Aoxomoxoa's exuberant energy, just like long ago, until the confidence and ease they affected became genuine. The backstage B-Z-listers were very touched that Ax and the Few were socialising with them instead of the grandees, *and* making a stand for creative rights. The camp councillors in the Blue Lagoon were thrilled, and talked of having the whole site live for next year. Ax enlightened them about the cost, and was taken aback by the mad, starry-eyed glaze that came over a certain hairy hack—

'What's up with you, Joffrey—?'

'You sound *just like Ax*,' exclaimed the editor of *Weal*, overcome by sentiment. The proud-to-be-annoying hippyzine must have missed Ax terribly: the Second Chamber simply ignored opposition media, except when destroying an issue or arresting a few journalists.

'Well, thanks. Oh, yeah, and while I remember. That thing you did, "Ax is back and he has a little (hit) list"? With the border of SA8os and the coffins? Just fucking cut that out. I have no hitlist. And don't give me any arse about the "freedom of the press". Not until you grow up and know what to do with it.'

'JUST like Ax,' sighed Joffrey, grinning like a kid meeting Santa.

It was intoxicating. They were lucid dreamers, they were messengers from a better world, further along ... They'd been looking forward to the freestyle walkabout with varying degrees of terror. By the time they'd been on the loose for ten minutes they were sure the evening performance would be the disaster, a huge let-down, probably get canned. Everything pre-recorded, every 'impromptu aside' scripted, hologram shadows playing virtual instruments: awful, terrible, big name behaviour. Still, it had to be done. Be professional, get through it—

The Few and their leaders took to the stage just before the oratorio, for what was supposed to be a reprise of their Hollywood Bowl 'supergroup' set. It was liquid night, the cold spring stars washed out by the stage lights, that sea of dark, round eyes and mouths swirling, beyond the gulf of the security cordon. The mosh yelled Ax's name insanely, until they realised he was waiting for them to shut up. 'You know,' he said, in a conversational tone, head bent over the neck of his Fender so a sleek wing of hair fell forward; the sleeves of his red suit jacket pushed up, Keef Richard style, [back in Brixton, Ax looked over the shoulders of the techs at the mixing desk, yeah, that's it, hold all the values there ... and wondered why he did not feel spooked. Two places at once, two voices instead of the monologue, it was exhilarating.] 'A week or two ago, I thought I was done with this. Almost cut my hair, if you know what I mean. I thought, tonight, I'd be going through the motions, and you'd be nice, for old time's sake.

But then I realised, maybe what I need is not less rock and roll in my life. Maybe what I need is … *more.*'

The guitar screamed. Ax swung around to face Fiorinda, who came leaping to the front of stage with a banshee howl, and they fell on the music with utter savagery, such a fury of naked brilliance, such a *pas de deux* between punk diva and guitar-man, as no one had seen in their lives before—

The oratorio struck the crowd as a little slow, after the Reich's set: which was a shame, because in its way it was incredible. Ax, watching from the shadows, felt that his lovers were divinities, *djinns* commanded directly by God, reaching peaks of harmony and counterpoint that he'd never known were possible. He turned his head (the gesture a useful adjuvant) to see what they were doing in Brixton, and found their corporeal bodies motionless, not touching but very close, eyes open and tranquil, lips slightly parted. He thought he saw their living souls, in passionate congress, no kidding angels in paradise; and had to look away, disturbed and wildly aroused in equal measure. *The World* ended, and there was a sea-roar of relieved approval as everyone came trooping on again, crews and all, until the stage was full. The punters remembered this part. Joyful roars continued through Ax's Hendrixed-solo of 'I Vow To Thee My Country'; but a hush fell when it was time to sing. Then sixty thousand or so voices, augmented by millions more at the Big Screen locations, were raised in the national anthem: word perfect and as tuneful as the English are ever going to get.

> *Her fortress is a faithful heart, her pride is suffering …*
> *And soul by soul and silently her shining bounds increase,*
> *And her ways are ways of gentleness, and all her paths are peace.*

Dora lunged for the baby-alarm, which had been flashing for some time, listened and held the plastic brick out to Anne-Marie.

'It's for you, Ammy.'

The babysitters were losing it. Felice's daughter, Ferdelice, was a treasure; Dora's baby boy Mamba was a reliable sleeper. Anne-Marie's bender-rats did not know the meaning of the word bedtime.

They just got more and more tired and hateful, until they fell over. AM believed this was the natural way.

'Hey, *Ammy*—!'

Ammy blinked, and gazed at the brick. 'I don't like to be with my babies when I'm on drugs. I'm too sensitive, I lose the plot. You better go.'

'I went the last three times. You aren't on drugs!'

'Sage says b-loc is *like* a drug. I know my limits, Dor.'

Dora's co-parents were pretending they couldn't hear this. Smelly Hugh was nodding, eyes shut and a beatific smile: no doubt jammin' with old Tom again. Meanwhile, thought Ax, marvelling at the selfishness, it's my office the little darlings are trashing. He felt he ought to practise fatherhood, and get good at it—

He moved, and realised he was soaked in sweat, his hair clinging to the back of his neck: glanced at his watch, and found it was past midnight.

Where the fuck was I? Where did the time go?

'Don't worry, Dor. I'll sort them out.'

'No, no. It's okay.' Dora gave AM a smouldering glare (entirely useless) and touched Ax's shoulder as she passed, for a moment bewildered at the solidity of her own smooth brown hand, the feel of Ax's muscle and bone; seeing the sheeny-red of his best suit, which was what the Ax hologram had been wearing on stage, imposed on a brown KEEP THINGS COMPLICATED T-shirt, dark with sweat.

Am I real here? Or was I real there? What does b-loc *mean*—

She left the room. 'Dora has left the room,' announced Kevin Verlaine, softly. Chip winked at him, and everyone started laughing. It worked! It *more* than worked! They'd forgotten what it was like to play the Reading crowd, to feel that whoosh of history coming back at you. The b-loc sets were tugged off and heaped in a victorious pyramid among the tired buffet plates. Wine was poured and food attacked, they were ravenous, hey it's very quiet, let's have some music—

Fiorinda stayed where she was while Ax and the Few, and the Heads techs, jabbered around the food; and Sage debriefed the remote site on a conference-line, grinning fit to split his beautiful face. She touched her skirts, surprised to find that she was wearing the same dress as her b-loc shadow: the smoky-opal party frock Sage and Ax had bought for her in Hollywood. Where was the silver and blue and green of the costume she'd been wearing for *The World* ... ? But of course, that had never been real. They'd decided against the stage coup: having realised it would be much cooler to pump up their own set, wipe the floor with everyone heheheheh. She wondered what she'd been doing back here, while she was singing the oratorio. She would have liked to know, because that had turned out to be an amazing experience, but too late, forgot to check, short-term memory waits for no man. The bright face of Reeka Aziz, the young singer they're calling the new Fiorinda (we'll see about that). All those eyes gazing up at you, colours burning, but already the mad intensity was fading—

Oh yes, b-loc is a drug. You don't notice the effect with a phone call, but it's definitely a drug. I suppose people will get used to it, if we develop those industrial applications. Or maybe there is a lite version, for everyday.

'Tastes and smells, Fiorinda.'

Roxane, who didn't leave a comfortable chair lightly, was watching her with acute, sympathetic interest. Tuh, critics. They think they know everything.

'Huh?'

'Tastes and smells: the ethereal diet of the gods. Is it going to be enough?'

'It's better than feeding on human flesh, Rox.'

Sage came over with Ax, both of them bearing plates of spring veg and cold meats. They sat on either side of the babe, plying her with tidbits, in loveplay that was distinctly sexual (if you hang out with rockstars, you get used to being bathed in post-performance pheromones). A dressed cutlet? Rocket and nettle salad? 'Fiorinda doesn't like to eat too many green things,' said Ax, tucking in. 'She thinks it's disrespectful. Try her with the Moroccan-style carrots.'

'I hate to interrupt,' said Roxane, 'but I'm sober, remember. May I say, another triumph ... Yet some might say you delivered a dangerous double snub to the Second Chamber. Ax Preston comes to Reading, but he won't touch his guitar; *and* he forces an ultra-green government to embrace his beloved futuristic tech.'

'We've done b-loc on stage before. We did it in California.'

'Ax, don't be obtuse. That was the Chosen Few, bi-locating briefly to the Hollywood Bowl, controlled by I-Systems, a very different kettle of fx.'

The Preston family band had been known as the Chosen for years, to avoid confusion, but Rox was a pedant over these things. Ax ate a forkful of chicken. 'What are you after, Rox? You know why we did it.'

'I know the cover story. But the many observers who analyse Mayday won't be dwelling on that rather obscure financial dispute. Some will say this is your Presidency. You've come back as an insubstantial figurehead, with no hands-on power: literally, no muscle. Is that really what you wanted to say?'

'Am I supposed to practise the answer I'd give in public? Okay, I'd say ... damn right I want to be insubstantial. It's my intention to leave government to the government, encourage good practice in social welfare by gentle persuasion, and put my influence behind techno-green lifestyle choices.'

'Very good. And in private?'

Ax looked up: a gleam of grim amusement. 'But not straight off.'

Marlon had dropped out of b-loc during *The World*, felled by slumber. His father carried him off to bed, an unexpected privilege; came back and sat down by Ax.

'How was that?'

'Excellent,' Sage grinned, sheepishly. 'I even tucked him under the duvet. Well, it's a little chilly in there ...' For years he had barely seen his son, a deserved punishment. His happiness at the détente was good to see, an inner glow, impervious to teenage obnoxiousness. He took Ax's hand, measuring the long fingers against his own. 'That went very well. Don't you think?'

'Oh, yeah. Weird and ... I'm older, but I still love it.'

They turned to face each other.

'You still got the horrors over that video?'

'Yes.'

'Me too.'

When Fiorinda reappeared after showing the last of the guests to the door, they were sitting quietly, hands clasped, heads tipped back, enjoying the silence. Sage knew she would make straight for Ax, and she did: her whole body, even that smoky *dress*, it seemed, alive with single-minded hunger. Ah, female choice. It's a fabulous thing to watch. Even better when you know you're next.

Before they left for Paris the Triumvirate had begun talking to some people, under the useful heading of charity foundation business. Some of the people were permanent Civil Servants, like minds who had served Ax Preston's cause for a long time; some were Countercultural MPs. The Party was not monolithic, it had its rebels, defiant anti-feudalist techno-utopians. All of them knew that Ax had not come back to England to be the Second Chamber's figurehead.

These people were not told about the video. They were, however, warned to be prepared for trouble. Most of the discussion at the meetings was about Fiorinda's cold equations. The camps must go, no question of that, but there has to be an alternative in place. This is the monstrous question, for all the world. How are we to feed a modern-sized population, without fossil fuel, without environmental costs we can't afford; and without slave labour?

The scale of the problem must not daunt us.

In another discreet venture, Ax and Sage had rejoined the netheads of Europe in trying to get a handle on the vast unknown of Africa, and Australasia, South Asia, the Pacrim and the Russian Federation and bridge the knowledge-gap created by years of data quarantine and global crisis. Suddenly the Chinese had sprouted a huge 'sphere of influence' that Xinhau.net journos were calling the 'Great Peace'. Was that a political force, or just advertising? The Pan-Asian Utopians Ax knew, whose patch he had once visited – busting data quarantine to make a remote-presence call on Hiroshima – had a sinisterly positive attitude to the new China. Indian, Pakistani and Australian sources also seemed compromised . . . It was strange work. Suddenly it's brought home to you that the datasphere has become your only access to places that were just a plane-ride away. You have no idea what's really out there, no idea what might be hidden. The world has exploded to enormous size, and become very small, at the same time.

The Second Chamber's Neurobomb Working Party had been asking for a meeting with the Triumvirate for months. They got their wish in the week after that triumphant Mayday at Reading. They came to the

Insanitude and were escorted into the maze of the North Wing by a young man with floppy paintbox-red hair who wore the dress-uniform of the barmy army. Ax's militarised hippies had been disbanded when legitimate government was restored, but the Insanitude retained a token force as guardsmen. The barmies weren't allowed military-gauge weapons but the young man was armed with a holstered pistol: a precaution that the visitors were glad to see: this part of the old Palace was mainly a sink estate for London's most recalcitrant, gun-crazy Boat People. When he opened the doors of a room on an upper floor they were taken aback to see Fiorinda there, alone except for the most puzzling members of the inner circle, Chip Desmond and Kevin Verlaine; otherwise known as the 'techno duo', the Adjuvants.

The room was not generously proportioned. The oval hardwood table, polished but shabby, and a random assortment of chairs barely fitted in. Oltech slates and earbeads were laid out, with water jugs and glasses, and small plates of macrobiotic ginger nuts. At the head of the table stood a white smartboard, lab-quality imaging hardware beside it on a trolley. The walls were hung in faded blue paper, with a narrow stripe. Naked windows looked out on the cool sky, yellow copingstones and grey corners of roof slope.

Chip Desmond, the black boy from inner Manchester, his hair a golly-forest of little tails, wore a crumpled metallic-grey flying suit with a red silk scarf. Verlaine, aka Kevin Hanlon, sported a skull-and-crossbones bandana wrapped tightly over his choirboy curls, purple linen knee breeches and a ragged *My Favourite Molecule* tee. They looked like quirky undergraduates: Fiorinda, between them, was the good-girl model student, demure in a grey tailored jacket and a long narrow plum-coloured skirt. The working party had plenty of time to take in the full picture. They'd frozen in the doorway, like dogs wary of crossing a strange threshold.

A voice rose, self-betraying. 'Are the President and Mr Pender delayed?'

'No,' said Fiorinda, in that crystalline, old-fashioned accent. 'They're not going to be here. Do come in, everybody.'

She rose and came to greet them, each by name: Wendy Carter, media-star conservative neurologist. Ardhal Fitzgerald, expatriate academic computer scientist, and probably a spy for Dublin. (*Cead mile failte* little brother; and mind you take good notes.) Boris Ananthaswamy, high-energy physicist from Culham; guilty by association, presumably. An official Countercultural Party contingent headed by Mairead Culper of Glastonbury Council. Jack Vries, the Wiccan Scholar, consultant to the Home Office. Consultants from the conventional weapons industry; ethical watchdogs. Not a single fusion consciousness specialist, naturally. But that wasn't entirely the Second Chamber's fault. There weren't many experts in the new science anywhere in the world, and Olwen Devi, the genius who had run the Zen Self project, had returned to her company's headquarters in her native Wales, taking most of her people with her. There was probably no one available for the suits to recruit.

Polite greetings were exchanged: no one liked to ask what had gone wrong. Fiorinda was patroness of the Reich's charity work, as far as the Working Party was aware. She had been the innocent victim of her father's terrible magicks: nobody expected her to be able to deal with the implications for National Security—

Fiorinda returned to her place. 'I can give you half an hour,' she said. 'It should be enough.' She steadied herself. Be careful!

The extremist junta is cast out by force of arms. A couple of years later you look around and faces you recognise have sneaked right back into office. Jack Vries, the leader of this Working Party, had once been a visitor at Rivermead in the months when Fiorinda was captive there, on display as 'Fergal Kearney's' whore. The second time she'd seen him had been in the Command Tent of the Extreme Celtics: when she took their surrender, before the Battle of Glastonbury that never happened. Lord Vries had been exonerated: a mistaken patriot who had never known the horrific truth about 'Fergal Kearney'; never guessed what the green nazis were really doing.

It's the way of the world. You can't touch these people, it's too costly, too much of a can of worms. You work around them. The best revenge is to live well.

Fiorinda didn't seem to do anything, but the smartboard behind her was suddenly flooded with colour and movement. Psychedelic roses blossomed, the same images appearing, in smaller scale, on the slates at each place. The Working Party stared, most of them with

61

poorly concealed alarm, as if it hadn't occurred to them that they might need to know something about the human brain.

'Bear with me. The images are relevant. For those who need it, there's full annotation on your earbeads.'

A pause for them to insert the beads, hardliners frowning with distaste.

'My father,' began Fiorinda coolly, 'Rufus O'Niall, could commit magic, because magic is a real force. This is now very generally accepted, in Europe and the USA at least; and I know I don't have to convince anyone here today.'

There was a silent, helpless stir of recoil. The last time Fiorinda's relationship with Rufus O'Niall had been an issue with the English government, it had been a reason to burn her alive ... She let them have a moment to recover.

'The world is made of information, a concept we express digitally. We see the state of all states, everything that is, as a mass of noughts and ones: which inevitably implies a fundamental level where the noughts and ones outside our heads are the same stuff as the noughts and ones of the information in our minds. That's the great secret, expressed in different ways in a thousand occult traditions, which has become the basis of a new science, where neurology meets physics. Every one of us has a vestigial interaction with the whole vast ocean of information space, and a vestigial ability to affect its whole arrangement—'

'Up to the whole fifteen-dimensional kaleidoscope,' put in Chip, gravely.

'Some people, including many scientists, find the implications of this model for the physical universe perceived "out there" with all its stars and galaxies, very disturbing; but we don't have to worry about that today.'

Some of the Working Party looked confused. Kaleidoscope? What kaleidoscope? Most remained blank, waiting for keywords to emerge.

'Tiny "fusion events", that tunnel through the barrier between mind and matter, happen all the time; as a feature of big number behaviour. We may perceive them as random "psychic experiences". If you have above-average interaction with the great ocean of noughts and ones, a leaky mind; you'll notice more of these. You may decide that you are psychic; or be recognised as a potential shaman, according to the customs of your culture. Then rarely, *rarely*, someone like my father comes along, with a mind so "leaky" that the traffic flow pulls contiguous vestigial interactions in the same direction ... "Contiguous" in this case means the people who are paying attention – it's a specific brainstate – to the shaman, or psychic. They are therefore linked with him in information space, however near or far they may be from him in our world and they involuntarily donate to him their own vestigial ability. It's a positive loop. The more you steal, the more you *can* steal. You learn, intuitively, that your power over other minds is greater if your followers are in a state of arousal. You may become a stage magician, or the leader of an occult group. You may be able to shift small material objects, or perform other pointless tricks, with results measurably better than chance. In nature, that's as far as it goes ... Magic is a weak force. It takes millions, even billions, of little thefts, to make a true magician. My father may well have been the first in the world, because he was the first of the rare few extreme cases to command a global audience.'

'Synchronicity,' announced Verlaine. 'The population explosion gave us the number-crunching machines that could model cognition, and they powered the Zen Self quest. Population gave us global entertainment, Rufus O'Niall, immersion code and the Vireo Lake experiment, all in the same generation!'

'It's been inevitable since time began!' added Chip.

Vireo Lake: the laboratory where the A-team had been trained.

Fiorinda smiled, indulgently, and went on, 'Now, the scans. What you see on your slates, and on the board, is a time-lapse sequence showing the course of early-onset schizophrenia. Clinicians call this the forest fire effect. You can see where the destruction starts, in the parietal cortex, and how it speeds, down and around the sides, and all through the frontal lobes. After five years there's a loss of up to twenty-five per cent of the grey matter, crucially in areas called the loci of convergence, where it is currently believed that what we call the "binding" of consciousness is organised.'

The Working Party went on waiting for keywords. Bomb. Weapon.

'Classically there's an onset of unmistakable symptoms in late adolescence, but by then the damage is done. Even today, once things have gone as far as you see here, a one-way ticket to catatonia is probably the patient's best hope.'

'Extensive neuronal tissue seeding,' muttered Wendy Carter, studying the forest fire with a clinical eye. 'Might help her, it would be worth—'

'I doubt if you'd have got close enough to try that on my father. But the disruption caused by magic isn't strictly physical, Wendy, though it shows up in the material loci. It's the shift of intentionality to information space that does the mischief, and you can't fix that by surgery. Tissue grafts would vanish.'

Dr Carter nodded, cautiously.

'As I'm sure you all know, schizophrenia – disintegration of the palimpsest of consciousness – can have many causes: infective disease, drug abuse, prolonged psychological stress; torture. Any or all of these: plus there's a whole suite of genetic accidents that can make people more vulnerable. The psychological experience is equally varied. It may be complex and baroque.' Fiorinda glanced around the room, smiling faintly as if struck by some private joke. 'I'm showing you the developmental version, because it most closely resembles what happens to someone who commits magic. There is the same rapid pattern of destruction, in the same locii.'

They didn't get it, not yet.

'I don't know if my father heard voices in his head. Or if he had lurid hallucinations, or if the world seemed like paper. If it did—' A note of reluctant respect crept into her voice. 'He didn't let it get to him. But he was certainly insane. Anyone close to him knew it. He lived in the state we call paranoid delusion, surrounded by plots, malice and hatred. No one thought anything of it, because that's hardly unusual, for a megastar. He passed for normal.' She paused. 'But the damage starts at once, it gets worse every time, and the use of magic is extremely addictive. He must have been in appalling, constant, mental agony, long before the end.'

No response. They frowned, listening to the earbeads.

'The idea that using black magic drives people crazy is well attested in tradition. Until recently we assumed the effect was psychological: the evil magician deranged by the horror of his acts. No we know otherwise. Morality doesn't come into it. If you commit magic, for any reason, *this* is what will happen to your brain.'

The colourful wreckage shuddered and squirmed.

Mairead Culper gathered herself. She was a small woman, simply dressed in a long brown homespun tunic, a double line of tension, or possibly eyestrain, ploughed deep between her brows, every visible inch of her pale skin tattooed.

'Fiorinda! With the greatest respect, magic is *proud* to be a black art. The powers we summon are beyond our understanding, we give ourselves blindly into their hands, *and we fear them*. But Rufus O'Niall was the hellish personification of the global village, and he is gone. *Our* unknowing is not evil, nor insane, and none of your—your *lab science* will convince me—'

'*Mairead*,' said Fiorinda, 'don't upset yourself. I'm not talking about hippy fortune-tellers, I'm talking about the Neurobomb. Perhaps you need someone to bring you up to speed on how fusion consciousness theory relates to mystical and occult tradition. I could arrange that.'

One of the industry consultants found his voice. 'I, er, I thought Rufus O'Niall's brain was never examined.'

The young lecturer nodded, pleased that someone had been listening. 'That's right ... So we can't be a hundred per cent sure about him. But we have scans of the A-team's brains, taken automatically at the moment of their deaths. They show just what the theorists' model predicts. You can see the "forest fire" damage clearly; and how fresh it is. They became very magic, and instantly they were crazy as bedbugs.'

The man from the conventional arms trade snapped to attention. 'You've *seen* those scans, ma'am?'

Fiorinda raised her eyebrows. 'Anyone with a public library PIN can see them, Mr Townsend—' she glanced at her own slate, '—Eddie ... They're on the open access section of the international investigation site. Along with the last routine scans from before the fatal experiment, for comparison.'

A pause for embarrassment. The Adjuvants grinned at each other. Stick it to 'em, Fio. The weapons trade consultant scribbled a note and passed it to Jack Vries: *is she saying we don't have a Neurobomb?* Jack nodded, put the slip of paper in his pocket, and raised his voice—

'Ms Slater, ma'am. We're all aware that the Vireo Lake subjects were chosen for psychic ability, the same kind of power that Rufus possessed to such an extreme degree. Most of us are aware of the "international investigation site", though, hm, some may say its usefulness is limited as it will reveal only what the US military wish to reveal. We were hoping, we believed it was understood, to talk about our own, English, Neurobomb. I mean Sage Pender, of course. The first, ah, neuronaut to breach the great barrier between the Seen and the Unseen; and who went on to defeat Rufus, in the magical duel at Drumbeg. The Zen Self route works with clean, healthy brains, does it not? And the use of neurosteroids leaves no permanent damage? Naturally, we'll want Sage to take a brainscan, to assure ourselves of that.'

Fiorinda shook her head. 'I'm sorry, that won't be possible. Sage has retired from being a lab rat.'

Jack Vries was a tall man, blonder than Sage, his hair and brows bleached straw. His skin had a painful, ruddy delicacy, as if several outer layers had been peeled away. His light eyes gazed at Fiorinda intently, on the edge of rudeness: and yet she felt that their previous meetings had been erased from his mind. Political survivors have selective memories. But he's not a fool. Don't start thinking that.

Be careful!

'I see,' said Jack, at last. 'Well, Sage is the star of the show, and he writes his own er, rider, is it? We will have to find the right inducement—'

The Working Party stirred and murmured. This was going too far. You don't sneer at the Zen Self Champion, not even nowadays.

'I detect a misunderstanding,' said Fiorinda placidly, taking no offence. 'The Zen Self route uses heroic doses of neurosteroids to reconfigure a normal brain to the state of fusion: without hijacked increments of connection from other minds.' (The Adjuvants looked modest, they'd been among the heroic lab rats. No one noticed.) 'But breaking the barrier between mind and matter that way is a brief explosion. Either you quickly return to perfectly normal consciousness—'

The Buddhist rep, a prim-looking middle-aged white woman, acknowledged this description with a faint smile; and resumed her air of distant disapproval.

'Or you remain permanently – so to speak, where there is no

duration – in the state of non-being, non-intent. Which is not useful in a weapon ... "No permanent damage", Jack, means no magic either. The Vireo Lake scientists were aware of the downside of the Zen Self route. That's why they set out to weaponise natural psychic ability, although such experiments had already been outlawed in Europe.'

Lord Vries accepted defeat, by means of a slight bow.

'But you wanted to know about the English "event"—'

The Working Party perked up. This was worth something. The tale of that mighty duel, from before the dawn of their world; and told by Fiorinda!

'When my father held me hostage, disguised as a dead man called Fergal Kearney, I found out that the Extreme Celtics had enlisted him to reduce the population of Europe, dramatically, by an act of magic. I believed he could do it, but I was helpless until Sage came back from Caer Siddi—'

'Having achieved the Grail,' murmured Verlaine.

'I had been condemned to death for witchcraft by then, by the people we call "green nazis", though of course they were as English as any of us.'

Another of those silent recoils: I have closed the account, she thought, I have moved on. But I'm not going to let you pretend it didn't happen.

'He rescued me from the fire, and we went together to Ireland.' She propped her chin on her hand, and looked into the past. 'They fought with swords, in the courtyard of Drumbeg Castle: my father liked archaic things. Sage knew he had to challenge Rufus, and Rufus had to accept, so that the two assaults on the fabric of reality would be cancelling each other out, and we would only have to worry about the margin of difference. Which was not great. Really, they were competing to see which of them had more power over the information. But the fight was part of it, the physicality ... They say that when "fusion" is reached, when a coherent, *solved*, human self – or selves, in the case of the A-team – is aligned with the state of all states, of which the human reservoir Rufus drew on is a subset, the mapping discovers, or imposes (it's not clear which) a virtual self there. The whole fifteen-dimensional kaleidoscope becomes a mind, for an instant, maybe—'

'They were battling for the right to meet God on equal terms,' breathed a slim, elderly gentleman who wore his collar on backwards, over a little fuchsia bib.

'Mm. Well, anyway, if Rufus had won, eighty or ninety per cent of the people of Europe were supposed to die, and human information space, our consensus reality, would have been mapped onto a mind/brain as wrecked as the one up there.'

She glanced behind her, at the smartboard. 'The brain in the images is female, by the way, but there are no significant differences, in this context.'

'Put it another way,' suggested Chip, 'Rufus would have become the Fat Boy, and we'd all be living in a Hieronymous Bosch nightmare-dimension right now.'

'Fat Boy' was the runaway chain reaction of fusion consciousness, a magic psychopath with limitless powers. The Lavoisiens had been trying to create one.

'They say Rufus could put his enemies living into hell,' ventured Dr Jones, at last; the fellow in the fuchsia bib. 'Is it true, Ms Slater? Could that be *allowed*?'

The Islamic consultant smiled, enigmatically, into his beard.

'I don't know about allowed,' said Fiorinda. 'He could do it . . . It's an Aleister Crowley spell that my father liked so he made it work for real. You die, but you stay in your body, conscious, while it rots; for all eternity, as far as you can tell. That's where the real Fergal was when Rufus inhabited his body. It's the threat my mother lived under. I think there were a couple of others, too. I hope they're all right now. I hope, I believe, that we freed them, that night.'

The abyss between what she and Sage had done at Drumbeg and these disconcerted suits was threatening to unhinge her. 'I'm not Rufus,' she added, limpidly. 'But I could try to help your lordship to— to understand the idea?'

One of Fiorinda's beardless counsellors kicked her under the table. Okay, okay.

She glanced at her slate, and then around the group. Any questions?

There didn't seem to be any questions.

'My lords, ladies and gentlemen: you will now understand why the US Neurobomb research was abandoned, and why it's unlikely to be

68

resumed by any future administration. The term "Fat Boy" is a reference to the early nuclear devices, and the analogy seems apt. The weapon of all weapons has twice been demonstrated in anger. We know it works; I predict it will now sink into a long, uneasy retirement. Perhaps the risks are not so appalling as they seem ... Perhaps global thermonuclear war wouldn't be so bad after all, but who would like to try? The cost in devastating pollution, to both sides, is too high; the risk of even more awful consequences too impressive. I'm sure people will go on trying to devise safe, tactical occult weapons, but a schizophrenic human weapon of mass destruction is simply untenable. My recommendation, and I speak for the Triumvirate, is that we join our sister nations and support President Eiffrich's call for a total ban.'

Wales, Ireland and Scotland had made their position clear, as had the Nordic countries. The EU as a body had as yet no official opinion.

'Ms Slater.' Jack Vries stood out in the subdued shades of the other faces, as if he drew the light. 'With respect, isn't there, in everything you've recounted, an equally strong argument for a deterrent? Though we all deeply admire—'

'There's an argument,' said Fiorinda. 'I don't think it's strong enough.'

'Get a grip,' cried Chip, bouncing in his seat. 'What are you thinking of, man? *The oil's gone.* Doesn't that scare you? The hell dimension scenario isn't bleeding heart loony tunes. It's a threat with teeth and hair!'

Discussion broke out. Predictably, Mairead's faction was repelled by the *lab science* and the references to nuclear power; while the technologists hankered after a Neurobomb in a black box with a chrome trim, and hated having to talk about the occult. Equally predictably the token Doves barely cheeped, and no Hawk had been swayed by Fiorinda's deposition. Fiorinda and the Adjuvants let it run, adding to the confusion where they could, until Fiorinda pointed out that the half hour was up.

Boris Ananthaswamy, the Culham physicist, had been making notes (a fogey, no implants, he used a pda and stylus), during the free discussion. 'Ms Slater, last couple of questions, would that be okay?'

'That would be okay.'

'The Reich collected data on an explosion of reports of, er, paranormal activity, during the dictatorship. Is it possible to have access?'

'I'm afraid not. The records were destroyed in one of the police raids.'

'I understand the incidence of paranormal ability, "leaky minds", is likely to have been constant, a normal Bell curve, since soon after consciousness emerged. Rufus was an anomaly, the A-team a construction, impossible in nature . . .' Fiorinda nodded. 'The nuclear device analogy. Do you believe the explosion you tracked could indicate a "fall-out" effect, dating from before the two fusion events, but caused by their presence in the simultaneity, and possibly still growing?'

Not just a pretty face. 'You mean, are we heading for the Fat Boy state right now, and it's too late to stop it? No, Boris, I don't think so. I think cultural change accounts for most of the reportage. The world hasn't changed, people just see things differently. Plus there are a lot of people out there in clinical delusional states who've stopped taking the medication because visions and voices have become acceptable. But if there's anything in that bad idea—'

The physicist nodded, waiting.

They noticed how tired she looked, suddenly: this young woman who had been addressing them with such cool insolence; whose past sufferings made her so difficult to face. Was she less striking, without that wild cascade of hair? Her grey eyes were remarkable, but was she beautiful? Or barely pretty? She was Fiorinda: an icon, a legend, and they felt the effect.

'I went to Ireland because I felt I must. I was close to the event. I can tell you that for a long time, afterwards, I saw people dead. Not ghosts, I mean people walking around dead, who would have died in another outcome.' Her gaze passed over them, one by one. 'Ooh, I saw them dead. I still do, sometimes . . . I'm Rufus's daughter. Perhaps that made me vulnerable, though I don't have his powers. But *believe me*, we don't want to get any closer to that fire.'

Fear touched them, for the first time. It made the hair on their napes rise: fear not of magic but of chaos, the world of sense falling away, nothing to trust in—

'But this could . . . could be the end of it?' suggested Wendy

Carter, slowly. 'A self-correcting mechanism? Aberrant minds with potential for "effective magic"—' (Mairead glared) '—are vanishingly rare, and can't reach critical mass without the global audience? Which no longer exists, and may never recover in the same form?'

'That's our best hope,' said the arms trade man. 'But frankly, I don't know why anyone's worrying about "a new Rufus". The A-team died and that's given the US something to think about, but now everyone knows what can be done. With the greatest respect to Ms Slater, how far behind do you think China is, right now?'

Another pause. Fiorinda was about to dismiss them, and they weren't sure they'd learned anything at all. There must be something they could say, some key question she would have to answer. The doors of the room opened. Zip Crimson, the barmy dress guard, stood waiting. The Working Party rose. Maybe they should regard this as a preliminary bout.

'The catch-up you spoke of, ma'am, on fusion-consciousness theory?' said Dr Jones, the Anglican bishop. 'I don't think Mairead's the only one of us who would greatly welcome that. Would . . . could Mr Pender himself to talk to us?'

'He could,' said Chip. 'But I think you'll find he won't.'

'He'd only advise you to chop wood and draw water,' warned Verlaine.

'Or tell you to eat your hat.'

'Should you be wearing a hat.'

Fiorinda propped her head on her hands. The brain in the scans was not her own, it was a textbook simulation: but it could well have been, the state she'd been in last spring. It was grim irony, but she owed a great deal to those lunatics at Lavoisier. I want to be a rockstar, she thought. That's what I want to do with my life, but there's this angel with a fiery sword, damn it. Was that the right image? Have to ask the Bishop.

Chip and Verlaine watched her, and waited, until at last she looked up.

'They could have asked *us* for a briefing on fusion theory,' complained Chip.

'Nah,' said Fiorinda. 'I mean, look at you. You're not even grown-ups. D'you think they got the message at all?'

71

'About the Black Hole nibbling at our toes?' said Chip. 'Wendy Carter bloody did, and maybe Boris. But they won't be making the decisions.'

They had been feasting with panthers, and they were shaken.

'What if they want *you* to take a scan?' wondered Verlaine

'They won't ask, but it wouldn't matter. They'd see nothing weird.'

Fiorinda sat back, pulled out a red curl and picked at the end of it.

Chip surveyed the empty table. 'This Crisis. We thought we knew what a Crisis was, but then you get magic psychopaths, you get trees talking, ghosts walking, concentration camps in Norfolk, Paranormal Thermonuclear war, you get ... Well, you see what I mean?'

'There'll be no Paranormal Thermonuclear war,' said Verlaine, gloomily. 'And no techno-magical utopia either. The bad guys will find a way to make the weirdness into field-guns and nerve gas, and the Middle of the Road will suppress people like us again, the way they always do. The doors of perception opened a chink, but it won't last. They will be slammed shut.'

'Hahaha.' Fiorinda pushed her fingers through her hair, still missing the warm weight she'd lost when the Lavoisiens shaved her for their scanner. 'You're probably right. We won't get no hell dimension, magic is so last season. Something much worse and totally unexpected will come along instead.'

THREE

Small Ax

The stately home was quite a pile. It stretched, interminable, crusted with artistic fortifications, along the base of a low green hill: a redbrick Gormenghast. From the south terrace the lawns of a formal garden fell, with a drop like a tank trap, to a tree-scattered park. In the distance, where another hill closed the horizon, the turrets of a gatehouse could be glimpsed through fresh young foliage. The village, Wallingham Camp, was a mile or so off to the west. A drive, or private road, crossed the park dead straight, between deer fences so tall they were an eyesore. Must be some well-hard three-day-eventer stags around these parts. A few sheep, rare breed pet animals, were grazing.

Make a list.

Forget Bridge House, it's gone, it has a blue plaque and a car park.

(A minor issue: that car park has to go. It's an outrage to local feeling and it makes Green President Ax, even if he likes a good car, look a hypocritical fool.)

'I always thought of Kent as flat,' he remarked.

'It's flatter by the sea,' said his companion, stiffly. He was a fleshy man, in Islamic dress but bareheaded, about Ax's own age: his red mouth like fruit in the middle of a full set beard, waves of thick dark hair crowding round his face.

They were on the terrace together because Ramadan had begun, and the rest of the party was eating lunch. A quartet of minders – barmy squaddies from the Insanitude – sat on the low wall a few yards away, armed but placid. They were a compromise. Ax liked to drive his car alone, walk down the street alone, and in England, who had ever been able to stop him? But you provide your own security, or you need your own security anyway, to keep an eye on the spooks.

The barmies had a Shakespearian look: sitting there patiently idle.

'When are you three planning to move in here?'

'Not immediately.' Ax left the balustrade and strolled.

Faud kept pace beside the President, maintaining a slightly surly air while observing protocol. 'This place isn't quite big enough?' he enquired. 'You're holding out for a private Triumvirate castle?'

'Nah. We just prefer the bright lights.'

In the days of Dissolution, Faud Hassim had been the front-man of an Islamic guitar band from Bridgwater called The Assassins. They'd been vocal, politically engaged, and very encouraging company for a mixed race outfit from Taunton called the Chosen Few – a year or so behind them on the trail. It had all gone sour, of course, after Ax's meteoric rise. Especially when he'd committed the appalling gaffe of converting to Islam. Faz had been a sore, rancorous loser, hanging around the Reich and finding ways to make trouble. Ax remembered a night at Reading that had ended in a planned and ugly free-for-all; and other times, several times, when he'd found The Assassins' prints on acts of deliberate, dirty, political sabotage.

Yet it was Ax Preston who'd paved the way for Faud's present success. He was the *other* Islamic rock musician from Somerset, eager to be noticed and a genuine Countercultural Movement activist (which Ax had never been). How could he not be in demand? He'd gone into politics and risen steadily, leaving the music biz behind. Now he was the Second Chamber government's Adviser on Countercultural Affairs, filling the same post as the unlamented Benny Preminder, and making more sense of the job than Benny ever had. He still wasn't a big fan of Ax Preston; and made no secret what he thought about the fact that President Ax was officially the leader of the CCM. But Ax had more tolerance for the resentment these days. He could see that from Faz's point of view fate had simply been damned unfair.

The terrace was a lengthy stroll. The kind of house that you might never leave, thought Ax, as he kept up his side of the stilted conversation. The women, of course, would rarely get further than that tank-trap; indoors there would be long expeditions for little serving girls with coals. Well, scratch the coals ... He glanced at his watch, another antique, *fogey* wristwatch, replacing his sun and moon Seiko that the kidnappers had nicked; which he still missed. He never felt hunger pangs in Ramadan; he just started to get that running-on-empty feeling that Sage found so addictive. Sharp-set, as the old phrase goes. The fasting gives you an edge.

'Maybe we should be praying, loudly, outside the dining room windows.'

'Testifying our witness,' agreed Faz.

They were alone in their observance, as they'd been alone for midday prayer; a sad change from a couple of years ago. The shock of having no oil in the bank had cooled a lot of Muslim ardour in the diaspora. Attendance at Friday prayer had plunged, the Haj – already battered by decades of unrest – had dwindled. Converts had melted away. As much as you wish it could, no religion can thrive on spirituality alone. Faz Hassim, far from conventionally devout in the old days, had the air of sticking to his ethnic garb with gloomy resignation.

'We'll soon be as dickless as the Christians,' he said. 'Can it be God's will?'

They would never agree on matters of religion. Faud refused to acknowledge the human rights disasters of the Islamic world; Ax found the hypocrisy of that attitude *disgusting*. But they laughed together, human warmth suddenly uniting them: because it was the fasting month, and because they both cared about such things.

'How difficult is it, living with non-Muslim partners?'

'It's not a popular topic. I keep my observance to myself.'

'Where are they today, Sage and Fiorinda? Don't they respect your family?'

'They couldn't make it. Sage may turn up later.'

'None of the Few could make it either?'

'It wouldn't have been appropriate.'

Ax looked at the front of the house, the first storey laden with lavender-blue torrents of wisteria in flower. A south face. The red and white roses in the bed below were opening, undamaged by the long winter. It reminded him of Bridge House, his lost *Heimat*. Bridge House inflated in a disquieting dream.

Nearly time to go in—

Faz was peering at him with earnest curiosity. Well, now what?

75

'Do you ever feel left out? On the sidelines, watching Fiorinda and Sage do their hot, romantic Cathy and Heathcliff thang?'

'All the time,' said the President, who had long been resigned to cross-questioning about the Hot Couple. (He was pining like a lost child for Sage's presence at his side, in place of the bearded Assassin, but that was his own business.) 'There's always something like that. Feeling left out is the essential threesome experience. Our relationship is like democracy, you know: a terrible idea, except for the alternatives.'

'I'm sorry,' said Faz, embarrassed.

'That's okay.' Ax glanced at his watch again, and at last came the deferential summons in his ear. 'Time to go in. C'mon, let's get into character—'

'What?'

'Nothing. Listen, Faz, could you do something for me?'

'What is it?'

'This afternoon, could you talk to my mum? I'll be occupied, and I don't like her to get ignored. Just stay by her, could you?'

'Okay. I'll do that.'

Wallingham, built in 1906 for a newspaper millionaire, an erudite, oversized imitation of an Elizabethan fortified house, was supposed to be a national treasure. Ax didn't see it. From outdoors the place was horrible, like a secure hospital thinly disguised as Hampton Court. The indoors was undeniably beautiful, but not to his taste: Art Nouveau in full *grande horizontale* spate, obsessively restored (there were records: you don't blow a fortune on a place this size and forget to keep a scrapbook). It was a sumptuous period stage-set that they walked into, complete with black-and-white uniformed servants everywhere you looked. They were directed to the clouded yellow drawing room, the one with the Klimt wall hangings, to join the infidel.

Back to that list—

Find out where Jor and Milly would *like* to live. Let's face it, those two are the ones who have to be satisfied. Identify a suitable piece of real estate.

Ax waved aside a flurry of respects (maliciously, he knew this set loved to play at courtiers), and took the opportunity to get next to

Milly. She'd lost weight again, she was looking very stylish. The old Milly, down-dressing drummer Milly with the don't-care haircut and the gardener's hands, had finally vanished. It was an obscure blow. He sat on the arm of her clouded-yellow satin armchair.

'Okay, Mil?'

There was nothing sexual left between them, not a twinge. But there was something . . . There were times, such as today, when Ax hated to be touched: a legacy of the hostage experience. She had not touched him, in the kiss-and-hug obligatory greetings. She did not touch him now as she looked up, her locked hands in her lap. The new baby wasn't here. He'd been taken off on a visit by his Kettle grandparents. Ax had discovered this only when he arrived, and he had not been pleased.

'I'm okay. Ax, there's something I meant tell you—'

'Go ahead.'

'Don't be pissed off with Jor. It was my idea to send Troy away.'

'Well, congratulations. Listen, could I use that? You didn't want me and the baby and Jordan together at the same tea party, something on those lines?'

She stared at him. 'You're a bastard.'

'Yeah, and I'm sorry. It's your call. But may I?'

'Anything that helps, Ax.'

He gripped her clasped hands briefly, and moved on.

His brothers were standing together in front of the summer fireplace, where a huge jardinière of cut flowers stood under elven swirls and swathes of beaten pewter.

'Y'all right, Jor? All right, Shay?'

They talked a little. None of them had heard from Tot (Torquil) for a while. The fourth Preston brother, who came between Jordan and Shane, lived in Canada. He had an engineering degree and a proper job, he'd never been into music.

'Lucky bastard,' said Jordan. 'Me, all I ever wanted was to be a famous rockstar. I knew I had it in me. But it had to turn into something else, didn't it?'

Trust Jordan: he'd win prizes for Most Inappropriate Time To Pick A Fight. But Ax was not going to bite back. Not today, when his heart was full of the knowledge that what he'd done to his family was *terrible*. You follow the light of destiny, you think you know the price. Then the real price comes and smacks you, from the direction you least expected, and you see it was obvious all along.

'D'you remember when we learned to play together, Jor? You and me and Mil, in her mum's garage, and then the four of us in the basement at Bridge House? How we'd talk all night, about being stone-free futuristic artisans, first born of the new?'

'No,' said Jordan. 'I remember how *you* used to talk, and it was crap.'

'Don't be like that,' pleaded Shane, the peacemaker. 'Did you see the ON AIR signs, Ax? They're giving us a tv show, in here. Live at Wallingham, it's going to be a music showcase.' He jerked his chin at Jordan. 'He'll be the host.'

Ax looked, and saw the violence that had been done to the distant, watered-silk yellow walls. There were several big, boxed, retro studio signs, knocked up in the gaps between fabulously valuable pictures.

'My God. When's this going to happen?'

'Dunno. Soon.'

'Bet you're jealous,' said Jordan, with a smouldering glare.

'I'm consumed with envy.'

Then the Prime Minister came to join them with his willowy Anglo wife. Greg Mursal was medium height, broad in the chest, with a bruiser's thickened features and vigorous hair cut *en brosse*. He had a discreet Celtic tattoo job on his cheeks and chin, which to Ax combined strangely with his sleek business suit. His wife, Hilary Sallet, was in finance of some kind.

The first time Ax had heard this man's name he'd been getting ready to fight a bloody, mediaeval battle with the Celtics at Glasto, the one that hadn't happened, due to Fiorinda's intervention. He remembered a tent on a flowery hillside, Allie trying to brief him on the changes at Westminster. Greg Mursal, who he? Never heard of him. How can he suddenly be Prime Minister? He knew it was dangerous, but he still couldn't shake an inner conviction that the Second Chamber Cabinet was composed of insignificant upstarts. He had to keep reminding himself that these men and women were the experts. They hadn't been seduced by the utopian Reich. They had taken 'Feargal Kearney's' measure and stayed out of the monster's way. They'd been waiting in the wings when the chaos died down. And how did they see Ax? A captured legend ... A youth-culture celebrity, boosted into power by extraordinary times, who had failed to hang onto that power and was now their property.

'I hear Fiorinda says Fred's going to kill the Neurobomb stone dead,' said the PM, 'if he gets his second term. Do you believe that, Ax?'

'I did until I heard it was an election promise.'

'Hahaha, okay! Now, can we talk about you three moving in here?'

'Maybe this afternoon isn't quite the moment,' murmured Hilary.

'You know it's what the country wants,' Greg plunged onwards. 'They want their nouveau royal family – you don't mind me calling the Prestons that? – living together in a beautiful landmark palace. C'mon, Jordan, tell the man. You'll love it, Ax. You have your top recording studio, your immix theatre, your pool, your sports courts, wonderful gardens, the most gorgeous countryside in England all around, and you don't have to lift a finger because Lady Anne takes care of everything.'

Lady Anne was an old lady with a long record on the right and occult wing of the Green movement. She was Principal Speaker, but her Cabinet role was vague. She wasn't here today. Although she managed their palace, she stayed tactfully out of the way when the Prestons entertained; and you didn't tend to see her in the same room as Greg. Ax wondered if they were the same person: in some mystic, organic way.

'Security's good, too—' put in Jordan, glumly.

'I wasn't going to mention that: but it's true. We all love funky old Brixton, but I admit I'll be happier when you're safely installed.' A thought struck the Prime Minister, or he made out it had struck him, widening his eyes and gripping Jordan's upper arm. 'Have you told Ax about "Wallingham Live", Jor? You'll love this, Ax. A showcase for the country's best, er, new popular music. Recorded live, with a VIP audience, in here. And you're to be the host. Between er, sets, you get a prime-time forum to talk to the people. Any topics you like, absolutely no holds barred—'

Oh, the perfidy of management. Ax and Jordan, fully interchangeable, looked at each other, for once in reasonable accord. Can you *believe* this arse?

Ax laughed. 'We'll talk about it in office time, Greg. When we go over a few of those disputed clauses in the contract. Excuse me.'

Hilary was muttering to her husband as Ax walked away: probably telling him he'd fucked up, and she was right, but it was a saving grace in the man. He's clumsy, he makes ridiculous gaffes, these are forgivable, human faults—

When the President moved, the focus of the room changed. These were the green lords and ladies, the high society of Countercultural England: they had Hollywood minds. Ax was the money, because he was called 'President', and because they believed (not that they would know a good guitar riff if it jumped up and bit them) he'd recently been the star of the show at Reading, a big event. Therefore, though they knew he was powerless, they watched him and they wanted to be near him.

It was quite a gathering. Twenty-five covers at lunch, and the afternoon guests were still arriving. Cabinet Ministers, celebrity media folk, fashionable scholars and artists. . . . Ax strolled and smiled, exchanging words here and there; musing on the ironies of history. When David Sale, visionary Prime Minister of Dissolution, had packed his reformed House of Lords with newly made green peers, he'd meant to weaken the Countercultural Movement; while seeming to appease them. (Ax knew this, because David had told him.) Divide the leaders from their popular support, cripple their access to the mob, using the ju-jitsu of those great English vices, greed and snobbery. The joke was on David – who was dead, a casualty of 'Fergal Kearney's' reign. The new ruling caste loved their titles, and the mob did not vote any more.

The guests whispered about Ax's private life. *Could* he be the second child's father, do the dates fit? Does that explain why Jordan is sullen and Milly so nervous; and why Fiorinda and Sage aren't here? Next to his brother Ax looks older, lean and worn in his shabby best suit (the President's austerity is an example to the nation). Next to the President, heart-throb Jordan looks soft. If you were Milly – the big question of the day – which would you choose? If you were Jordan, how would you feel about Milly's sexy President-exy moving into Wallingham?

Mr Preston reached the far side of the crowd and stood for a moment looking back. Men and women both in colours; as fashion decreed. Ax in his dark-red suit was one of the more subdued male figures. Any Utopian revolution that requires discipline and self-denial will be corrupt in about six weeks; here is the living proof. Ruthless idealists morphed into fat cats, the next generation just enjoying the sweet life, no idea there's anything wrong. Straight from green to rotten, yeah.

But that's okay. All I need you to do, my lords, ladies and gentlemen, is stand by and let it happen, the way you stood by and let my girl end up on the bonfire. Can you handle that? I think you can.

He spoke to his mother and crossed back again, deriving malign amusement from the way he could tug their eyes to and fro. A bold young fashionista touched his arm and asked how did he like the décor.

Ax shook his head. 'I don't care for aspic, it's like eating dolls' house food.'

She gasped, *Oh!*, round-eyed; reminding him of Allie, when Allie used to be a fashionista. Maybe that's where this babe had picked up the mannerism, Allie Marlowe on the tv; in a magazine. 'You would revision it? What an *immense* idea! But Wallingham is, like, sacred! *How* would you revision this?'

You can tear it down for all I care.

He didn't say it. By the windows to the terrace his sister Maya was surrounded by admirers (she had to be the belle of this ball). She flashed him a smile. Maya is solid, she's a legend . . . Ax nodded, and gave his attention to a table display of art *objets*, which placed him beside the Wiccan scholar, Jack Vries.

'That's very beautiful,' said Jack. 'Could I see it?'

This was Greg's *eminence grise*, according to some the most powerful man in England. One of the 'mistaken patriots', but rumoured to be up for a Cabinet post in the next reshuffle. Devout Pagan, independently wealthy (family money from an old Belgian electronics firm). A bit of a mystery man, otherwise. Ax handed over the piece he'd been examining. It was a small bronze: a hunting dog, seated, full of life; her narrow, graceful head turned to groom her flank, her tail arched over her back. Obviously Celtic, and if not a copy, probably about two thousand years old.

'*Very* fine,' said the scholar. He was more sombre than Ax, in a suit of deep, rich midnight-blue. 'A lovely example of La Tene, isn't it?'

'I wouldn't know,' said Ax. 'I thought it was found at Wallingham Camp?'

'Oh yes. In the nineteen twenties, I believe: in a back-filled pit at the threshold of the sanctuary. It's rare to find a votive offering so well preserved.'

'I only recently found out we have a ritual site next door. I'd thought "Wallingham Camp" was a minor hill fort. You know the place well, Jack?'

'Not well,' said Jack Vries. He handed the statuette back.

'Nor me. We must pay our respects some time.'

Faud Hassim, obedient to the bond of the fasting month, was sitting with Sunny Preston. He had thought Ax's request strange; this was supposed to be Ax's mother's birthday celebration (infidel habit). But it was true, the old lady had been sidelined, left to look after her grandson. He wondered at the President's behaviour. How could he neglect his mother like this? What had all these showy people to do with a family celebration? Every time you try to admire Ax Preston, he disappoints.

He knew Ax's mother by sight: a woman in her mid-fifties, a Christian from the Sudan, with dark skin and crisp grey hair; who rarely appeared in public. He had never spoken to her. Her face was smooth, her hands coarse, with thickened joints. He knew her husband was dead. At a loss for topics he asked about the problems of running such a huge place? He was surprised to be told she had no part in the housekeeping. It was like living in a hotel, she said. But she didn't mind, she was fully occupied preparing for her university course.

Ah, studying what?

'I intend to qualify as a lawyer,' said Ax's mother, sifting pasteboard pieces. She and the child had a jigsaw beside them, spread on a scallop-rimmed drum table. 'Though my eldest son threatens he will never speak to me again.'

Faud recognised that sudden smile.

'*Ax* will never speak to you?'

'No! Son-in-law, maybe. I mean Sage. I hope it was only to frighten me. He has the sweetest nature of any man I ever met, but he's full of mischief, isn't he?'

For Faz, this was a new view of Aoxomoxoa.

The grandmother worked on the jigsaw. The five-year-old piled towers of pieces, flicked them over with his thumbnail, and watched – furtively, intently – the burly servants, in their formal black-and-white, who stood in pairs at the doors of the room and along the windows that led to the terrace. Faud followed the child's eyes, and experienced a moment of revelation, a *Gestalt* shift. Mrs Preston glanced across the throng to where her actual eldest son was talking to Jack Vries. 'Tell me, Faud. How do you get on with this new method of calculating the *Zakat*? It's a torturous work of the devil, according to my Ax.'

Faud recovered himself, and plunged into a detailed explanation; it was a subject dear to his heart.

Greg got up a party to visit the newly restored Edwardian Real Tennis court. Maya Preston, the handsome young woman who'd taken over from Ax as the Chosen's lead guitarist, was observed *flirting* with Jack Vries; which raised eyebrows. Jack's sexual tastes were unknown, even to his intimates. At four they moved outdoors. Tea and birthday cake and champagne were served under the lime trees, by the croquet lawn (it was almost warm enough). The younger crowd set up a game while the older crowd discussed the success of neofeudalism.

'The people want a conservative society,' declared Greg. 'With a small "c", of course!' (His audience chuckled obediently.) 'They're not afraid of inequality, Ax. Or even a spot of hard work. And they're not afraid of Paganism, it's our natural religion, anyone'll tell you that, Monotheism is culture, Pantheons are nature ... But nothing against Allah, it's your futuristic tech that scares them.'

'My husband believes in an *organic* Counterculture,' explained Hilary. A well-worn aphorism. 'It's the English way.'

Ax took out a pack of tobacco cigarettes. A flunkey (the kind of flunkey who wears a shoulder-holster under his jacket) swooped with a lighter; the President shook his head. 'Ooh, I don't know, Greg. In the old days, the money men in the music biz used to say: look, the people like to buy crap records, it's their choice. But the people didn't choose the playlist on the radio. They didn't decide who had the promotion budget, or which bands got the sound turned up on the festival stage. The record company made those decisions, and commercial success went to those who knew how to play the system more often than to those who could play their instruments.'

Greg Mursal grinned. 'This is an analogy, Ax? One of your Lennonisms?'

'Oh, maybe. Well, there will always be scores being settled, favours paid off and all of that. But then criminal corruption moves in because the system is ready for corruption. At the gloves-off end it was rough, even in England, when I was coming up. The punters were making their "choice" among the bands who were prepared to take a cut from organised crime. So we talked it over, and we decided we'd do without a record company. We'd take the music straight to the customers.'

'And the rest is history—' murmured someone.

'I *love* that!' exclaimed the young woman who dreamed of a commission to remodel Wallingham interiors. 'That's *such* a great idea!'

'Mm. Yet we couldn't have done it without that futuristic tech, which would never have got off the ground without venture capital. We'll always need the money men, it's just that we don't need them deciding our lives for us.'

'It all goes around!' gasped the hopeful fashionista. 'How clever!'

A breeze shivered the bright silk of the linden leaves, a mallet struck a wooden ball with a resounding *Pock!*; above shouts of laughter and indignation the sound of motor engines became audible. A convoy was coming slowly up the drive. A long, pale-grey van was followed by several squat, chunky vehicles that would have looked military, except for the bright paint and the circus balloons. The guests stared, like cattle, at a novelty. At a glance from Ax the barmy minders, who'd been hanging around in the background, quietly moved over to where Sunny Preston and the child (and Faud Hassim) formed a group on their own. Frowning, the PM pressed his finger to his ear, one of modern life's odd, commonplace gestures. His face changed.

Sage was driving the van, wearing hippy-dippy battledress, which took him back. George Merrick sat beside him, similarly attired. The uniform didn't mean much but it was a sop to appearances, invoking our right to behave like this—

'You know what this stunt reminds me of, boss?' remarked big George.

'What?'

'Remember the gig in Manchester, on the Rock the Boat tour, Boat People summer? Heaton Park, and it rained like fuck ...When we was in that folkies' talking-shop tent?' George smiled fondly. Boat People Summer had been a frantic time: riots in the ports, refugee reception camps burned out; and some of the worst English weather in living memory. But distance lends enchantment.

'No. I don't remember. I don't think I was there.'

'You never remember anything.' George tipped his head back. 'Hey, Cack, Bill? *You* remember the boggart story? In that park with all the mud?'

'It wasn't Heaton Park,' called Bill Trevor, from the measureless caverns of the van's back quarters. 'I reckon it was the other park.'

'With the more mud,' agreed Peter (Cack) Stannen's serious little voice.

'Yeah,' George recalled, 'but in Manchester the grass grows back faster, it's the toughest grass in the world. It's the best place in England for rock festivals.'

'They kept saying that,' yelled Bill.

'Anyway, there was a boggart, troublesome house-pixie they have, driving a farmer's household up the wall. They decided to quit. The family's out in the yard, their stuff piled onto carts, and another farmer drops by, says, what, are you flitting? An' the voice of the boggart pipes up, from deep down in one of the carts—'

'*Aye, neighbour, we're flittin!*' shouted Bill and Peter, and started cackling.

'I don't get it,' growled Sage. 'What's that supposed to mean?'

'This isn't going to cure anything, boss.'

'It's not meant to. It's more clearing the ground.'

Where the south drive of Wallingham House met the tank-trap at the bottom of the garden there was a ramp, which would have been winched into place by hand in the media-baron's day. The mechanism was now controlled from the gatehouse: it didn't shift as the convoy approached. Nor did the formidable gates at the end of the deer-fenced corridor; also electronically controlled. The van stopped. Four figures, one of them notably tall and slender, emerged from the cab. They jumped up and down, waving, apparently trying to attract the attention of the CCTV cameras. Some guests began to laugh and clap. The men in the skull masks were obviously the Heads, Sage's band, and this must be a planned entertainment. Other figures in Bohemian military dress tumbled from one of the trucks like circus clowns and proffered a folding stepladder. The big, broad skull-masked fellow climbed it. He waved (grinning, naturally) to the company on the lawn: applied a circuit breaker, and set to work with bolt-cutters.

'*What* is going on?' demanded the PM.

He was on his feet, as was Jack Vries. Applause faltered. The armed servants looked to Greg Mursal: Ax hadn't stirred from his Edwardian-repro deckchair.

Faud Hassim, primed by a little boy's betraying eyes, had come to his own conclusions. His heart thudded. The perimeter guards must have been dealt with. How many Wallingham servants? Six here, but an army of them indoors ... My God! Was this going to end in blood? Was this party *meant to* end in blood? An afternoon of long knives, the wicked and the parasites gathered here to be slaughtered?

Albi tugged his sleeve. 'I mustn't touch the fence. Sage says don't even think about it. A big deer is much bigger than me.'

Faud stared at the child in horror. My God, the man is reckless. Or ruthless. He recalled that the baby (rumoured to be Ax's own son) was not here today.

Sunny patted his arm. 'Don't worry. It's going to be fine.'

Ax rolled the cigarette he couldn't smoke until sundown between his fingers and gathered Milly, his brothers and his sister, with a glance. Be calm. He thought of Fiorinda. The spectre of leaving her all alone, if this went badly wrong, went through his head as he grinned for the audience.

'It's a Happening, Greg. Sorry about your fence—'

The deer fence was flattened, the convoy was up the ramp and onto the lawn. The tall ringleader came strolling over, an army rifle slung on his back, and now everyone knew the beautiful, fearsome mask of the living skull. Sage bowed extravagantly to Sunny Preston, the skull doing loutish charm with a dash of tough reassurance: and proffered a slim briefcase.

'Happy Birthday, Sunny. You havin' a large one?'

'I'm having a *lovely* birthday,' said Sunny.

'Well, here's the deeds, ma'am. Your new residence awaits.'

The barmies raised a cheer, waving their rifles, but thankfully refraining from an Afghan salute. The Prime Minister repeated Sage's words, pop-eyed in dawning comprehension; and then everyone heard the *taktaktak* of the helicopter rotors. Who can this be? What immensely rich rockgod friend of the family can run to a fuel-cell helicopter? Ax kept smiling. Jordan (never the acting star) stood with his arm clamped round Milly's shoulders, wearing a frantic grin. Nice one, Jor. If you end up having to convince your masters you had nothing to do with this, you'll be cool.

'You *broke* the fence,' remarked Albi, looking up at Sage with worship.

The rattling grew. A splendid old blue-black personnel-carrying machine hove into view, the chequered hatband speedily announcing its provenance. Who had called the police? What the hell's going to happen? Some of the high-ranking guests (it was written on their faces) took a good hard look at the idea of running for cover; but no one stirred. The Prestons and their allies, the Prime Minister and his, seemed held in the same suspense as the big machine descended and the rotors slowed.

Two spruce young uniformed officers got down, a man and a woman. They stood to attention as a very senior and very well-known policeman appeared, also in uniform. It was Commissioner Kieran Matthews, who had worked with Ax Preston since the Islamic Campaign in Yorkshire. He came over the lawn with his heralds, acknowledged the Prime Minister and his wife with a nod, looked indulgently askance at the paramilitary display; took off his cap, tucked it under his arm and saluted.

'Everything all right, sir?'

'Everything's good, Kieran,' said Ax. 'Thanks for turning up.'

'Not at all, sir. I'm delighted to pay my respects.' A grin cracked the Commissioner's sober features. 'Birthday cake on the lawn. No need to call in the regulars for that, eh?'

'Hahaha. I don't think so.'

The Prime Minister looked at Jack Vries for an unguarded moment, and gave a bark of laughter. 'You don't mess about, do you, Ax?'

'No,' said Ax. 'I don't mess about.'

This exchange was instantly forgotten, as if it had never been. The senior policeman went to offer his birthday greetings and Ax turned to his family's guests.

'Sorry about that. I'm afraid things got a little out of hand.' He shook his head at Sage. 'You couldn't have called ahead to get the gates opened?'

The skull-masked one saluted smartly. 'Tried that, Sah. Cock-up, Sah. Somethen' wrong with the security coms. Service should be back to normal soon.'

At this moment, reinforcements arrived. Guards and armed servants poured from the house, brandishing firearms, and attempted to ambush the party guests. The barmies held them off, good-humouredly, shooing the phalanx of black-and-whites like sheep. Under cover of the confusion Sage took off the mask and Ax took off his smile.

'Hi, soldier. How's the perimeter?'

'Hi, other soldier. The perimeter is ours.'

'No misunderstandings, no scuffles, no casualties?'

'None, zero. Never in doubt, not a shot fired.'

Breaking the hostages out by force had not been Ax's original plan, not even after he'd discovered that Wallingham was a fucking *fortress* and that his family were never allowed to leave the grounds all at the same time. But he'd had no choice, with the Lavoisier scandal hanging over him. He dared not leave them as prisoners. A daylight raid, in public, had looked like the safest option; but it wasn't done yet. My mother, Milly; a five-year-old child. My God—

The skull reappeared and morphed into a cheery and convivial grimace. Sage turned away, to work the crowd.

'Greg,' said Ax. 'Jack? Could I speak to you?'

The Prime Minister and Jack Vries walked with Ax towards the Elizabethan knot garden. 'I'm sorry,' Ax said, 'about the circus. But I'm afraid my family has to leave Wallingham: this place doesn't suit my mother. I've found them a smaller house. It's further from town, but they genuinely prefer my arrangements. Don't worry, I promise security won't be a problem.'

They had seen the military-gauge weapons, supposedly forbidden to barmies, which had been acquired with ease. They understood that if Commissioner Matthews was with Ax, that meant Mr Preston controlled most of the police forces of England. They must realise, also, that many of the party guests were on Ax's side right now. The great and the good will accept a lot, if they are well looked-after. Even hostage-taking, as long as it doesn't happen to them. But they don't like the practice much. The message had been delivered. How were these two going to take it?

Ax waited, gravely smiling.

Greg Mursal nodded. 'If you're sure, Sir.'

'Oh, I am. And there's Wallingham Camp. When I found out we had a Celtic ritual site on the doorstep, I felt the association was not ideal. Although, of course, I'm sure the blood ritual hasn't been practised there.'

Ritual animal sacrifice had always been illegal, but there'd been a time when the right wing of the official Countercultural Movement had defended the practice and demanded a change in the law. They'd had to change their tune after the blood ritual became tainted by association with human sacrifice: but the occasional horse was still getting disembowelled in country places. There were rumours, vigorously denied, that perpetrators were protected.

Greg looked shocked. 'Ax, that site has *never* been active in modern times!'

'I should hope not. Nevertheless—'

'The President is right,' cried Jack. 'The association gives entirely the wrong message. This should have been raised when Wallingham was proposed as the Royal Residence! I'm a believer, but I share your feelings, Sir. Especially since there are, hm, excuse me, very important personal and dynastic considerations. Milly and her, er, children must leave at once. Immediately! As the Wiccan consultant to the government, I have been shockingly at fault. You have my abject apology, Sir!'

How about your resignation? thought Ax. No . . . ? I didn't think so.

He nodded. *Dynastic* considerations. You can't complain about colourful gossip you have encouraged, but he was chilled. He had a vision of these charmers keeping a little prince on a leash, the inconvenient adults having succumbed to mysterious diseases. Ax had considered rehabilitating the Second Chamber gang. Why replace them? Can they be so much worse than any other suits who might take over? Keep the bastards in sight and work around them; it had looked like the simplest plan. But he was changing his mind.

'Well, that's the explanation. I wanted to make a happy occasion of the move rather than a scandal. I couldn't consult without spoiling the surprise; I was sure you'd be sports about it. I hope that was okay.'

'Of course!' declared Greg, looking dangerously flushed. 'Of course!'

'Good, that's good. Thank you, both of you.'

(They have to go. By legal process, but they have to go.)

Greg, Jack and the President returned to the party in complete accord, having agreed that immediate departure would be a little extreme. Before the guests departed there was a gypsy encampment all over Wallingham lawns. The barmies were staying on, with Sage's brother Heads in charge, until the Prestons were ready to leave: they would have a barmy army honour escort to their new address

Ax would have liked to stay, at least until the crowd thinned and he'd had the chance to talk to his mum without a hundred eyes boring into his back. But better not. He had to get away from Jordan. He was old enough to recognise, in himself and in his brother, the signs that meant a screaming match had become inevitable. You know the buttons and how they get pushed, but you can't do anything about it.

He had driven himself down from London in his beloved vintage black Volvo coupé, with the barmy minders in another car. He and Sage headed back alone: up the remains of the M20, the old grey highway potholed and ragged at the edges, and almost stone-empty. The motorways were a refuge for people who liked to drive (and who had a President's privileges). Most traffic, such as it was, avoided them because they were lonely and dangerous, and full of hijackers. Sage called Fiorinda from the car, as soon as he could get coverage, to confirm that all was well. Fiorinda was frosty: she had been left out. Two sentences and she was gone. He sighed and turned his wrist so the time-function figures flickered; from the tanned side to the white side. He'd lost an implant in Lavoisier, this one was Californian.

'I knew it would be okay.'

'I just hope it sticks,' said Ax.

Make a List, revisited.

Find a house near Taunton. Get Jordan and Milly to approve (figure out how to show them pictures; they can't be taken to see it). Acquire house. No money? No problem, Joss Pender will stake us (however much it hurts to take money from Sage's dad). While buying house, without appearing in the transaction, plan the Wallingham assault. Secure plans of fortress, hack the security systems. Set up the barmies, get hold of the weapons, recruit Keiran. Prepare the family (never talk to anyone but Mum; don't trust the others to handle a conversation that is not secure). Keep Jordan sweet. Convince Fiorinda she has to stay away, needed as outside man, sorry woman, there to pull the irons out of the fire if they get too hot—

He thought of the reality tv, with his brother as smiling host.

'We'll have to keep the new place garrisoned, indefinitely ... Jordan hates my guts. What's his life like? A choice of captivities.'

Sage watched the road, and the rearview mirror on his side. Ax was in the mood where he'd be *delighted* to meet some hijackers and put that charmed life of his to the test again. But someone has to worry, my reckless friend.

'Fuck Jor. Don't all top celebrities live like so?'

'Well, it had to be done. I cannot work while somebody holds a gun to my mother's head. It was a fucking insult. I called their bluff and we're all pals. For now.'

'What about the Extreme Celtic connection?'

'I don't think so. Jack and Greg are rational villains. In another era they'd have been normal slightly dodgy right-wing politicians. They've just been around riff-raff like you and me for too long. Gun-crazy paramilitaries.'

'Mad dogs.'

'You know what, Sage? I bought my parents a house with my first rockstar earnings. I was incredibly proud of that. But my dad mortgaged it, remortgaged it, spent the cash and got behind on the payments. I had to sort that out, in the middle of a blood-daubed revolution, and I didn't have any money. Ten fucking years on, well, nearly, and I'm just where I was. I'm even driving the same car.'

'What's wrong with that? I *like* this car.'

'It's a bit small for you, my big cat.'

'Oooh, I don't mind. It's cosy.'

They glanced at each other, and grinned. The distant green banks, awash with speedwell and daisies, bluebells and feathery chervil, flew by. After the shame and distress of that video, it felt very good to be going back to her with clean hands. So we made it, one more time. All you can ever do is hope the luck lasts.

'It's a job,' said Sage. 'We can do it.'

Ax laughed. 'Yeah. Live for the weekend.'

The barmies invested Wallingham for four days, and Ax knew he was winning when the popular media reported the Happening with merry approval. Let's face it, not much of a free press survives ... Joss Pender, software baron, one of England's few really successful survivors of the Crash, had missed that remarkable birthday tea due to a diary clash. The evening after the Prestons had been safely delivered to their new home in Somerset, he held a dinner party at his Holland Park mansion. Greg Mursal and his wife were among the guests, all smiles; and everyone knew they were celebrating a shift in the balance of power.

The night after that, the Triumvirate had to have dinner with Sage's mother, the novelist Beth Loern. She was in London visiting her daughter Kay, the younger of Sage's two big sisters (the bourgeois matron: not to be confused with the brainy one Sage likes, who lives in Cambridge and has no social life). Beth had not been invited to Holland Park and had therefore missed a chance to refuse the invitation, with menaces. Her resentment of Joss and his high life was thick in the air. Then Kay unfortunately served farmed salmon, the food of the poor, as a compliment to Ax's green austerity. Sage will not eat farmed salmon. He likes fish. Anywhere else he'd have pushed the pink carpet flesh around his plate, but not at Kay's ... How did it go from there? Something about Sage's childhood eating habits, and Sage's mother pitched in, deliberating stirring (she's not the sweetheart Sage would have you believe). Impossible to follow, but it was hateful.

At least the torture ended early, due to austerity curfew. They took the newly H-powered Victoria Line back to Brixton, *sans* minders, because they weren't on official business, and stopped at The Monkey's Paw for the first unpoisoned drink of the evening. Or partly unpoisoned: Sage was still glowering.

'You know,' began Ax, 'I'm not going to defend Kay, but—'

'Leave it,' advised Fiorinda, bored.

'It can't be easy. Okay, they have food on the table, but were you fooled by that "oh, we're doing this as a fashion statement"? It's *hard,* for people like your sister and her husband. They never thought the Crisis could reach them.'

'So don't defend her,' said Sage. 'Pints?' He got the drinks in, and set them off the tray with a glare. '*Yes,* Citizen Ax, I *know* they're brim glasses, and *no* I'm not going to ask her to top them up. Ask her yourself if you are so fucking stingy.'

Fiorinda picked up an ancient copy of *Weal* and retired from view.

When they got home Fiorinda said she would have a bath. Ax followed her into the bathroom and sat and teased her, while she turned an alarming scarlet under the bubbles. Fiorinda likes her bathwater scalding. He carried her into the bedroom wrapped in a big towel. Sage was lying on the bed, naked, propped on one elbow: smiling like he'd found his temper.

'What' you got there?'

'I'm not sure,' said Ax. 'But they scrub up very rosy and juicy-looking.'

'I've heard they're edible.'

'Yeah, me too. I'm gonna give it a try.'

'You want me to look after the front end, while you do that?'

'If you would.'

He laid his sweet burden down and unwound her clinging arms, kissing each fingertip; and the delicate skin on the inside of each elbow. Took a gentle bite at the firm, yielding muscle below the curve of her ribs, each side; then the hipbones need some biting, each side, then we nuzzle into this tough, silky mat of hair, but every step on the way is worth a pause. He pressed his cheeks, his lips, his brow, to the fresh, damp living warmth of her inner thighs. Fiorinda lay in her towel with Sage bending over her; taking his kisses.

'If I let you go, will you try to escape, strange creature?'

'You'd better hold me down. Just a little bit, to be on the safe side.'

When Ax was let know he had finished eating he sat back on his heels and wiped his mouth, every fibre of his body thrumming, keen to get indoors, hard and quickly now, not fussy which of them he took: but he could hold on. It's good to have someone on watch. It feels safe.

'All yours, brother.'

'Hey,' said Fiorinda, equably, 'I think Ax gets held so I can eat him now.'

'She's right, you know. Fair's fair.'

'Well, okay. I can see how that would work.'

He woke many hours later, rising from a blank of oblivion that was a rare treat for Ax. The impact of what he had done at Wallingham had come home to him in his sleep. The hostages were free. The weeks of plotting, all the tricky preparations, all done. He had proved he could still use his Mr Dictator network, and the Prestons were safe. Under a different armed guard ... A jolt of terrible panic went through him, oh God, can this be my life? He calmed himself. Uneasy lies the head that wears the crown, eh? We'll weather the Lavoisier scandal (if it ever hits). I'll do my three years, we'll establish something like a civilised situation, *then* we'll quit.

It won't be so bad. Sometimes you'll be allowed to play guitar.

He rolled over and took Fiorinda's warm, sleep-softened body in his arms.

'*No more* relatives,' she mumbled. 'Not for at least twenty years.'

'Yeah.' He kissed her closed eyelids. 'Fiorinda, would you marry me?'

Fiorinda opened her eyes, nose to nose with him: she seemed to think it over.

'Yes,' she said, 'I don't mind, if you like.'

'What about you, big cat? Sage ... ? Are you awake?'

'I think you should have asked me first,' said Sage. 'I'm the oldest.'

'Sorry, I've never done this before.' Ax sat up. 'Okay, I didn't mean to do it like that, it slipped out. But I've been thinking about it. We love each other, we're going to stay together, and have children if possible, and children want their parents to be married. The way I see it ... I'm not asking you to marry a man, Sage.'

'Good, because I don't like the idea.'

'Me neither. It's too fucking New Agey. What I see is, it would be we two would both marry Fiorinda, and you would marry both of us, Fee. How does that sound?'

'Fine,' said Fiorinda, thinking she could sort out this weird notion later.

Sage turned on his back, hands behind his head. He understood that this was one of those lightning decisions you don't hear about until Ax has been brooding over it for weeks. Marriage is a religious ceremony. Guitar-man must have consulted his patron in the Faith, and between them Ax and Mohammad have tracked down a precedent: some funky Mughal Caliph and his beloved Vizier, sharing a bride. So now we can go ahead. Great. Can't I have *any* private life? Ah well, that's what you get for shagging the king of England and what the fuck, why not?

'Yeah, okay. I'm in.'

'Oh.' Another aspect came to mind. 'But I won't convert.'

'Oh,' said Fiorinda. 'Nor will I. Sorry, Ax. I didn't think of that.'

'I'm sorry. Did I *mention* Islam?'

They did not get the chance to agree he had not. Ax exploded out of bed and grabbed at his clothes, eyes blazing in hurt and fury. 'Did I *say the word* Islam? I know *fucking well* you hate my religion. Okay, forget it.'

'Ax, don't—'

'Ax, Ax. Hey. Calm down, listen—'

No use. Slam, bang, crash. He was gone.

Fiorinda and Sage were left staring at each other.

'That's *your* fault,' said Fiorinda.

Ax breakfasted at the Insanitude, where he picked up his barmy minders, whom he must drag around with him on government business like a collar and tie for the office. Meetings paved the day in slabs of weary words. The ones that furthered the agenda had to be camouflaged with make-work, which was never-ending. Once the Departments know the President is willing to do this, they give you no peace. At the end of the last of them he walked down to Victoria Embankment, trailed by his faithful shadows. He stood staring at the water, his head full of contesting ploys and projects, and aching with sorrow. They hadn't called him.

There were tears in his eyes, which he had to blink away.

Something nudged his elbow. 'Be with you in a minute, lads.'

Fiorinda's left hand appeared on the top of the wall, lining up so the red and white and yellow braided gold of her Triumvirate ring was level with his own. He looked round, and her grey eyes were watching him with such loving understanding of all his faults that he wanted to fall at her feet.

He looked the other way and there was Sage, arms folded on the parapet, gazing dreamily ahead of him. 'How many ceremonies d'you reckon, Sah? One for each region, and one for every major belief system? We're going to need a fuck of a lot of cake. And I think Fee ought to have a different new dress every time.'

'Damn right,' agreed Fiorinda. 'Hm. I've never been inside a working Christian church. I hope I don't turn into something ghastly and fly out of a window.'

Ax's heart rose from the depths into golden light.

'You don't have to be nice,' he croaked. 'It was a s-stupid, crass idea.'

'I *love* you,' said Sage, turning around. 'Will you ever believe that? I would be happy to say so in public, swear it 'til death do us part. I didn't mean to piss you off, I was tactless and I apologise. Let's do it. Why shouldn't we do it?'

He took Ax's face between his hands and kissed him, fuck-the-public-place: an embrace that Fiorinda thought she should not join, but they pulled her in.

Then they drew apart, hands clasped, looking at each other ruefully: all three of them feeling the pull of that cloud of white tulle, the chaste beauty of morning suits, the gold and scarlet and the bride led around the fire. The clamour of bells, the ridiculous presents, the hideous array of scrapping relatives, drunken friends and gatecrashing paparazzi at the show-off feast ... Ax had been right to raise the question. (He's always right.) Marriage is what all lovers do, or plan to do, when they truly mean to stay together, and there is no obstacle; unless they are some kind of cranks. But it was not for them. It was for some other people.

'Let's think it over,' said Fiorinda, diplomatically.

The armed guards followed as they walked by the great river.

The Insanitude was to be refurbished. Apparently the Reich had a budget for this, although the charitable foundation was perennially short of cash, no matter how much money the fees and royalties of the radical rockstars pumped into it. Representatives of the Few households came to collect the last of their effects from the Balcony Room, which had been The Office. It was a strange, sad occasion. Apart from Allie and Dilip, none of them had been back to the Insanitude much, since before the US trip. Not for a long time; they had not realised how long. Everything seemed small, and tired, and old. The room which had been the nerve centre of the Rock and Roll Reich had already been stripped of its office furniture, and looked very naked. The circle of secondhand schoolroom tables, where they had made such momentous decisions, was roped off, untouched.

'It's going to be some kind of shrine,' said Allie. 'The decorators have to take a video and number all the parts, so they get it right when they move it all back.'

'What, with waxworks?' asked Chez, uneasily.

They had been 'immortalised' in Madame Tussaud's, some years before.

'Maybe they'll buy copies of our virtual avatars from California,' suggested Chip. 'So poor old Digital Artists will get some return on their investment.'

'No they won't. Tha's lab science. Carn' have that.'

'I'd like to know where the money comes from,' grumbled Rob. 'Whenever we need funds, they tell us the Reich is flat busted.'

'A cosmetic makeover isn't going to screw neo-feudalism,' said Chez. 'Mystery solved.'

'The Citizen King needs a palace,' said Allie. 'Where the suits won't be embarrassed to bring people. That's what it's about. Our admin will mostly be farmed out. But I get a new office.'

They poked around, unearthing dust-bunnied items of clothing, scraps of food; forgotten mascots from behind the radiators. 'Are we spooked?' wondered Dora, feeling like a redundant yuppie. 'Oooh, Sage, you're on the wrong side of the rope.'

'I'm an exhibit.'

'We are not spooked,' decided Verlaine. 'We're used to shedding copies of ourselves. Let the public worship our old toenail clippings, we don't care. Move your arse, Sage, we have to sanctify those chairs.'

Sage moved his arse, and walked around staring at the pale patches on the dirty candy-pink walls, the Triumvirate's yuppie box under his arm. The Adjuvants were sanctifying the circle by laying a fragment of Few arcana on each seat: a desiccated pondweed cracker here, a fossilised lump of canteen veggie curry there; a venerable hairgrip that may have belonged to Fiorinda. Or possibly to Her Majesty Elizabeth the Queen Mother, as the sub-radiator strata might have become confused.

'I feel nothing,' announced Anne-Marie. 'It was time to move on.'

The Few's token hippy earth mother had decided she had to come up to town, to take a spiritual reading at the end of so much history.

'That's great, Ammy,' said Dora, while others rolled their eyes.

'I'm more worried about us getting through Lúnasa.' Anne-Marie picked up a broom left by the decorators and absentmindedly began to sweep the floor.

'Lúnasa—?' repeated Rob. 'Don't bother, AM. This floor's going to be ripped up and converted into a sacred wall in Tate Modern. They'll want the dirt left on it. What's wrong with Lúnasa?'

'Something around there stinks. Think about it.'

Sage took his box away with him across Green Park under a grey sky, longing for Cornwall and the grey Atlantic. Please tell me we can go to Tyller Pystri. Please tell me we'll be there soon. But May rushes by, and soon it will be June. The festival season will begin, and forget about having a private life until September.

He was to meet a former Reich camp follower at the Royal Academy, where an exhibition of Sage Pender's immersion cells was about to open. He had been interviewed by Dian Buckley many times: she'd written a book about Ax. He didn't expect any surprises. They walked around the august halls together (the galleries closed to visitors for the benefit of this interview), getting videoed.

She asked him how he felt about having his work elevated to such heights.

'It's okay, I suppose.'

'Oh, come on, Sage. That's the kind of thing you'd have said a decade ago. How do you really feel about snagging a show like this now that you're a grown-up?'

No it isn't, he thought. A decade ago my language would have been con-fucking-siderably more colourful. Maybe he should explain that the financial aspect had soured his triumph. The RA had apparently 'acquired for the nation' notebooks that had gone missing in the green nazi occupation. Sage had not been involved, nor seen any money. Nah, waste of time, it would never get onto the screen.

'Well, this is not the way I'd have done it, see. Immix is a live act. It's possible to display notebook cells live: so anyone who looks at it for more than a second or so gets a dose of the code, direct cortical delivery, an' cops some level of the perception I built for them, full sensurround. The way they are here, with the code stripped out, they look stone dead to me. Waste of space.'

'But immix perceptions are fake. Your, er, drawings are real art.'

'Why, thank you . . . Are you using a digital cam?'

Dian's crewperson looked alarmed. 'Uh, yeah, er, Sage—'

'Shame. Those images are totally fake. You aren't storing colours, an' walls, an' the back of Dian's head. Jus' bits of information. But it wouldn't be any better if you was using your bare eyes. We live in a virtual world in a fake universe.'

But it's unsporting to tease the minions. Soon he dropped out, dissatisfied with himself and knowing he was safer on auto: answering nicely while he thought about the promise he'd made to Dilip in California, and how differently it was shaping, thank God . . . Fiorinda, whose period was late again, but barely, and this must not be mentioned. Will I ever do anything new, or is that life over, pinned to the walls here like dead insects? And it's bullshit, Anne-Marie. There is no curse on the moon of the seventh month. Terrible things have happened to us at any time of year they pleased.

He was even thinking of Dian, whose eyes were greener, her tits more peach-perfect and splendid than ever. Wonder what's she had done under her clothes; and what's she going to do when she gets *really* rich? Have the lot chopped off? Still, a woman he could near enough look in the eye, he'd always liked her for that. He had once fucked the lovely Dian, after a tv show, mainly because of the charm of her height. George had taken him to task, he remembered. *Do not* fuck the mediababes, boss. Everybody does it, everybody regrets it. You think she knows she's a sandwich, does she fuck, you're gonna hurt her feelings and that's—

Dangerous?

How can Dian Buckley be dangerous?

She was asking him how he felt about being in an unorthodox sexual relationship, and when had he realised he was gay?

'I'm not.'

'Oooh, of course, I'm not allowed to say that, am I? So when did you realise you were—' Dian smiled indulgently, '—bisexual?'

'I'm not. Dian, if you're gay nation by birth, I b'lieve you know it before you are five. But anyone can have a same-sex lover, why not? I can't believe you've never tried it. You should.'

'Oooh, Sage, I don't know. All those one night stands, the macho posing. You were a textbook case. But okay, how do you feel about being in an unorthodox sexual relationship that's a national obsession? And religious, to many people.'

They'd left the exhibition. They were in the coffee shop, still alone except for the crewperson: facing each other across some very teeny patisserie, a bottle of dry white wine and another of fancy water. What had snapped him to attention? It surely wasn't the questions.

'Religious? What does that mean?'

'It means you three are sacred. Look, I have you on my key-chain.'

'Oh, well that proves it.'

She laughed and showed him. She had one of those silver charms on her chain (no keys) depicting tiny Ax 'n' Sage 'n' Fiorinda engaged in a three-way fuck.

'Will you touch it for me? That'd increase the potency fantastically.'

Damn. Aoxomoxoa never vets interview questions. It's a crime against the Ideology to vet interview questions, like it matters, pah. It never matters ... But maybe Sage Pender ought to, because he could feel his mood spinning away from him. I can't do this. I don't want to chat about my sex life with this idiot, I can't remember how irreverent and outspoken I'm supposed to pitch it, without mortally offending the *nice* Pagans, and there's nothing real I can say. Can we talk about how the government takes every cent I earn, gives me pocket money and spends the rest on razor wire? No, thought not ... But he had never (not since the hell of his own making he'd endured over what he did to Mary Williams) let an interviewer get to him, and he wasn't going to start now. He grinned at the green-eyed babe, took the charm, and handed it back with a smile. 'There, now you can

100

rub that on your struggling petunias, if you think it's going to help. I can't promise anything.'

He was still wondering what had given him that jolt of noradrenaline. And short- term memory gave it up. The silver charm, glinting on Dian's well-turned hip, a smell of ooze and smoke, a slimy tightening net, something heavy—

'Now you're telling me you don't believe in magic? But you're the Zen Self Champion, Sage! You went beyond death and came back and fought a duel with Rufus O'Niall that stopped him becoming the Fat Boy and saved all our lives. For many people, intelligent sceptical people, you're the reason why *we* believe in magic.'

The Zen Self champion poured himself a glass of wine, eyes down: exercising self-control. 'I haven't ever been dead, Dian. Tha's a misconception.'

Dian recalled the physical magnificence of Aoxomoxoa, the fabulous young bull he had been, and the sweet dream she'd once had. The memory of that morning when she'd found out he didn't love her (Sage had told her nothing, she'd just had to find out, in public, that he'd spent the night with Fiorinda), would never lose its sting. He's still got to be one of the most beautiful men in the world, she thought. And his voice is still fantastic. But he'll never be what he was when I had him.

'Hey, wow, when did you start drinking again? Isn't that terribly irresponsible, when you've had a liver transplant?'

'It's not a transplant, it's a regen. Livers are easy, they grow like—'

'It was an intensive care bed. Okay, you won't talk about magic. I suppose that means you won't do any yogi tricks for me, oh Bodhisattva?'

'You'd be right. Well, we've done talking about art, an' rock and roll is beneath our dignity. How about Paris? I could wax lyrical on subsistence living. I love it. I want to live like a refugee, except with a dry place to sleep an' futuristic tech, for the rest of my life. That's where it started, d'you remember? You should, you were there. Treading lightly on the earth, in the mud and blood and beer at Reading?'

Dian shook her head. 'I can't think of anything to ask you about Paris. What's your opinion about other psychic phenomena? The

Grey Lady in Amsterdam, or ooh, werewolves. Do you think humans can really transform into wild beasts?'

'Hahaha, oh yeah. For sure. Now we're talking cocktail hour.'

And he waxed lyrical, relieved to have found a safe subject, on the new drugs that were appearing on the street, sadly forbidden to him, being far more demanding on a regenerate liver than alcohol—

'What was it,' asked Dian, with an impish twinkle, when he paused for breath, 'that happened when you were five, that made you realise you were gay?'

Fiorinda was giving a masterclass course on rock guitar for the Reich's hedgeschool education scheme. Hedgeschool had been invented for the drop-out hordes and illiterate hippy campground kids: but it was open to anyone who was keen enough, and (in the case of masterclasses) could pass the audition. Fucking ridiculous, how can you *teach* rock guitar? Anyone who was worth anything would despise being taught. They'd be practising in their bedroom, with a broom handle and a string if they had nothing else. But hedgeschool students were obliged to learn to read and write and figure, if they wanted to sign up for something more glamorous. And we will need these outdated skills again. So it was worth doing, and it was her turn.

The sessions were being recorded at Battersea Arts Centre, because they sure as hell were not going to be recorded in Fiorinda's music room. She got back to Brixton Hill late in the afternoon and put her head round the door of the guardhouse (was: the little front office downstairs, next to Ax's office). Doug Hutton, supremo of the Reich's personal security, was in there, making an inspection that involved a large jug from the Monkey's Paw; the cubbyhole was wreathed in fragrant smoke. She accepted the fat spliff she was offered.

'Of course you guys would leap up, fully in control, if I needed defending.'

''*Course* we would, Fio.'

Actually, she didn't doubt it.

'Anyway, you don't need us. Sage is up there.'

'Oh, good.'

She climbed the stairs slowly, chasing the tail of a memory. Long gone the days when they had real-people neighbours upstairs; the off-duty security crew slept there now. How can anyone think having armed guards in your house is a status symbol? The naked walls, the echoey feel of a place you've just moved into. She knew the dress she'd been wearing, her blue taffeta with the emerald sparkles, and the sound of Ax's guitar, sad and lonely. Why so sad? It wouldn't take shape.

Sage was sitting cross-legged, quiet and still, on the brick terrace outside the French doors at the back of the living room: where Fiorinda's orange trees had once stood. Absent on Zen Self business. He was probably thinking about Mary.

The Lavoisier video had torn things open in both her boyfriends: she knew that Sage had started visiting places in his life he had never dared to touch before. She sat at the patio table and watched him, feeling a little frightened, because he had gone where she couldn't follow. She could never trespass on another woman's territory.

He knew she was there: and presence returned to his open eyes.

'Hi, sweetheart.'

'Hey, my pilgrim. How did the interview go?'

Sage grinned. 'Badly.'

'Well, fuck her,' said Fiorinda, automatically: but she was taken aback. Sage and Dian Buckley doesn't go badly! Except possibly from Fiorinda's point of view.

'How do you mean, badly?'

'Oh, bog-standard Dian. I just wasn't in the mood. I was pissed off about the notebooks, an' it put me off. Gaugh. I was listening to myself, talking ooh, so seriously about "my work", I sounded like David Bowie.'

'My God, how awful for you.' Fiorinda took alarm. 'Did you hit her?'

'I should have done. That would have been *good* copy: Aoxomoxoa lives! Nah, the violence didn't go beyond mild sarcasm, and I don't think I said anything I shouldn' have. But she's going to tear me to shreds: I'm not invulnerable any more.' He sighed. 'Oh yeah, something else. They know about the video.'

'What?' She stared at him, electrified. 'You mean, Dian told you that?'

'Give me credit, Fiorinda. If Dian had told me something like that, I would not be sitting here calmly whining. I had a snapshot flashback. I could try describing it, but it would make no sense, I just came back knowing the suits know, an' it's bad. We are screwed and they are playing with us.'

'Oh.'

Sage had taken so much snapshot, the neural aligner they had used on the Zen Self quest, that he would never be free of it. He would have lapses into alignment, like tiny epileptic fits, come back with a glimpse of his brainstate at another place and time: and he would know things. Generally bad. So this is what it's like, thought Fiorinda, living in the post-fusion world. The oracle gives you a message from the future, and it does you no bloody good, just makes you scared. Magic is real, same as it always was; and useless as it always was. Great.

'Okay,' she said at last, 'it's a big scandal, Fred loses the election and we get fired.' She sat down on the bricks beside him. 'Would that be such a tragedy?'

'Nah.'

But *we are screwed* didn't sound too good.

'You're going to tell Ax?'

'Of course.'

Sometimes, when they were alone together at the flat, the spectre of what might have happened was almost too much to bear. She took his hand and felt it grip hers, warm and strong. The bogeyman didn't get us. The past is a defeated foe. Sunlight fell through the soft dusty urban air; neighbourhood sounds made a subliminal hum. The industrious afternoon gardeners, in Brixton's vivid backyard strip farms, looked very peaceful.

'You know that thing about if you put a frog in water and then slowly heat the water, it never has the sense to leap out?'

'I've never seen it proved.'

'I'm glad to hear it . . . I used to think the Crisis was like that. We're mad, everyone is mad, the way we don't notice how bad things are, how much we've lost, the way we don't struggle and panic, we just go on. But maybe the frog's not so stupid. It doesn't jump because there's no place to jump.'

He laughed, lifted her hand and kissed the knuckles. 'Trust you, Fiorinda. What's the use in worrying? We're all doomed and this is not your world.'

'Fuck off. I didn't mean that, I meant the opposite. I meant, I realise this is it, there's nothing else, and I'm satisfied. No matter what comes, nobody owes me anything.' She reached up and touched the sickle-shaped indentation at the left corner of his mouth, which had once needed a trick of the light to make it visible.

'It's the only way to live. Here and now.'

'Augh.'

'What?'

'I left our yuppie box at the Royal Academy.'

'What was in it?'

He screwed his face up. 'Can't remember . . . A manky cardie. Old hairgrips.'

'Oh well, never mind. Dian's got them on ebay by now.'

They sat in the afternoon sun, hand in hand: listening for Ax's step.

FOUR

Careless Love

Fiorinda went North, for a reunion with her associates DARK; who were now calling themselves the Charm Dudley Band, because the world had moved on and they were going Country. Rob and the Babes went off to the Midlands for a week, with the Big Band and pro-Reich support. Marlon returned to Brixton, having finished his exams. The plan was that he would stay in London until the full-on festival season began at midsummer. A spurious normality lay over the surface of life: as if they were back in data quarantine and the rest of the world didn't exist.

Fiorinda's lovers worked late in Ax's office, because it was mournful upstairs without her. Schubert on the sound system: one of the recordings she made for her piano teacher to tear to pieces, which they were not usually allowed to use as entertainment. Sage, in his role as the Minister for Gigs, was going over festival season admin (all delegated, he never interfered, but they like you to show an interest). Ax was practising Chinese calligraphy, copying from a book of proverbs. Marlon was out, on a midnight curfew and it was past twelve, but Sage wasn't worried. He knew where his son was; knew where he'd been all evening (and the report didn't accord with what Marlon said on the voicephone).

'Going to have give this woman more money, Ax.'

'Can't. What woman?'

'Road manager, Jennifer Lateef. She does not hump boxes, she does the informatics. We're paying her beer money. She's going to quit, get a real job an' we'll never find anyone else, she's a star.'

'Well, I can't help it.'

'Ah well.'

Sage pushed back, folded his arms on the back of his chair and watched the calligraphy. He read documents on a screen, reams of them, to the amazement of less hardy persons: he was used to it, but now he'd had enough. The brush in Ax's hand paused, the tip swept down again, making a long, curved stroke—

'Is China to be your next theatre of operations, Sah?'

'I'd like to go there,' said Ax. 'It seems like a happening kind of place.'

I'd like to go *anywhere*, thought Sage, resignedly. If I can't have Cornwall, China'll do. Soft winds and rains of a cool night, out there in the streets of London—

'What's that one mean?'

'Qi huo ke ju ... It means a precious treasure worth cherishing. Merchant Lü identified a hostage prince as a precious treasure worth cherishing, and this was very smart, because with Lü's wily support the prince became king of Qin, and his son ... Who was actually Lü's son, it's a long story ... Became the first emperor of China.'

'Was he a good guy? The first emperor?'

'No!'

'What happened to Merchant Lü?'

'It ended badly.'

'Fuckin' inscrutable proverb ... Ax, please don't suddenly run off to save the world from the wicked emperor, an' leave me.'

'I won't. This is a beautiful thing to do, you should try it.'

'Mm. Would you care to come over to my side of the fire, at all?'

Ax set down his brush and tipped the bead out of his ear, losing the Mandarin commentary. They smiled at each other, the sexual pull between them warm and certain. It would be better if Fiorinda never went away, but this life of drudgery has its moments. This shoe-string public service that was our terrifying great adventure, not a bad way for it to end up, considering—

'Shall we go upstairs?'

'Let's go to bed,' countered Sage. 'There are loose teenagers about.'

On cue, his screen chimed and there was Marlon on the doorstep. Marlon and female companion it looked like: a glimmer of long silvery brown hair in the shadows, where she's trying to lurk out of sight. Their iris-recognition hardware had given up, after a chequered career. It had been replaced by a homely PIN and card lock, which meant sneaking strangers into the building was now feasible, in theory. Marlon habitually forgot his father was likely to be spying: in Wales all domestic surveillance, State or private, was completely illegal.

'Don't call him on being in the pub,' advised Ax.

Sage was afraid Mary would snatch her son back, if she knew about the underage drinking. But Brixton's not Mid-Wales. And he's sixteen.

'Wasn't going to. What about Silver? Send her home?'

The female companion was certainly Silver Wing, AM's second oldest rugrat, a scarily independent young woman of thirteen. She was living in the Snake Eyes commune at present, having left Reading after a big fight with her mother.

'I'd say not. We could drive her back, or send her in a car, but the car would be followed and that would piss the brothers off, they don't have our tolerance. I don't want to piss them off. Better let her stay.'

A dissatisfied silence from Sage.

'All right, so make up a bed in the music room. Don't forget a few rolls of razor wire. Teenagers will have sex, Sage. It's a fact of life.'

'She's far too young.'

Marlon and Silver sat on Marlon's bed, having negotiated the front door and the guardhouse without attracting attention. Marlon counted this a success. Silver had other ideas. She combed her damp hair, it had been raining gently out there.

'We should say hello.'

'No. They're busy. You don't barge into Ax's office.'

'Why not?'

'You just don't.'

Silver rolled her eyes. I knew Ax before you did, she thought. But Marlon outranked her in the Reich, she had to accept that. In the old days their paths had hardly crossed. This friendship dated from the Triumvirate's return, when Marlon had started coming to London. They both found it useful. They sat with an ashtray between them: smoking, showing-off to each other; trying out lines. The gig at 69 had been not much, although it was cool to get in free. The kind of thing you do so you'll have something to talk about, boring but needful –

'My dad would like to stop me having sex or taking drugs,' said Marlon. 'He thinks I'm too young. Thank God Ax is different. And Fiorinda's my best mate.'

'When I was eleven,' remarked Silver, 'my parents wanted to give me to Sage, as his junior wife.'

'You're kidding.'

'Nah. My mum and dad are totally decadent, without knowing what the word means. They thought being his concubine would be a great career for me.'

'*Arwan.*'

Maybe he looked like his mum: Silver didn't know. He didn't look anything like Sage. He was no more than Fiorinda's height, with peaky Welsh features. His eyes were gold under thick black brows, naff-o tattooing round the left one. The dressing on his hair smelled like woodsmoke and hemp oil, which she liked. She wondered how it felt to be a boy who had no chance of outdoing his father. Never going to be taller, or stronger. Or more famous, or more beautiful; or equal to his dad in any way. Silver had grown beyond her parents before she had her first period.

'I was Fiorinda's handmaid when Rufus was doing her, as Fergal. We were in and out at Rivermead, Pearl and me. She wouldn't let us near him but—'

'I don't think you should talk about it,' said Marlon.

The thought of Fiorinda's suffering preyed on him. He had sometimes lain awake at night, unable to get the idea of it out his head.

Silver looked at him, a knowing gleam in her black Chinese eyes. 'Okay.'

The two men were coming upstairs. 'Will they look in on you?'

'No.'

Light, powerful footsteps came down the hall. A brisk knock, and Marlon's dad stood in the doorway, filling most of it, rangy and wide-shouldered. 'Hi Silver. There'll be a bed for you in the music room. Don't stay up too late.'

'Yeah,' said Marlon. 'G'night dad.'

'G'night kids.'

The door closed. The teenagers smothered giggles, bowing towards each other. They talked and smoked again, coming no nearer to what they both knew Marlon wanted. At last Silver glanced around the spare room, once full of Sage's junk, now made over lovingly for this little prince. She reached for her sandals.

'I think I'll be off.'

Silver walked around London at all hours. She thought nothing of taking the night trains and buses by herself, when there wasn't an austerity curfew. But he knew she was leaving because he hadn't allowed her to socialise. If he let her talk to his dad for five minutes she would stay, it was understood: no chemistry, a straightforward transaction. He wondered what it would be like to fall in love, with someone his own age ... It wouldn't be this girl. Wanting to have Silver had nothing to do with Silver.

'Okay, Ax'll send you back to Lambeth in a car. Come on, let's ask him.'

The living room was dark and empty. The door to the adults' bedroom stood ajar, a trickle of lamplight spilling out. Silver wrapped her arms around herself and held her breath. She heard Ax's familiar voice, a question, tinged with laughter, so low she couldn't make out the words. Then her heart's darling answered, her rightful owner, with a crooning, roughened softness that dizzied and wounded her—

'*Lissen, Ax-*'

What would you see if you opened that door? The heart of the Reich, the red dragon and the white. She closed her eyes, shivering: wrapped in the heat of that core, but blocked, reversed by personal feelings. When she opened them Marlon was staring at her, through the deep shadow of the hallway. 'I don't want to disturb them,' he whispered. 'It doesn't sound like we should knock.'

'Let's go back to your room.'

They lay down together like children dressing in Mummy and Daddy's clothes. They were Sage and Fiorinda, and the king of England sat on the end of the bed, keeping watch. They did not mention the make-believe to each other, they both felt it was shameful, and wrong. But the enactment of power was irrisistible.

George Merrick, Bill Trevor and Cack Stannen had abandoned their private lives in Bristol and Cornwall. After the Wallingham stunt they returned to London, and took up residence in their old headquarters, the converted warehouse on Battersea Reach, gearing up for the summer season. Ax went to find Sage there, one afternoon in the week when Fiorinda was still away, but Rob and the Babes were back again. He was admitted on the first floor by Marlon (the ground floor of Battersea Reach wasn't living space). Techno noises, couldn't call it music, poured down from the floors above, stray immix effects caught your eye like unattached hallucinations. Assorted strangers were drinking and talking in the hallway.

It was always this way, when the Heads were in town.

'Hi Mar. Is your dad about?'

This was for the bystanders: Ax knew where Sage would be found.

'I haven't seen him for hours,' said Marlon, distantly. 'Bill's upstairs.'

He went back into the room he'd left. Ax glimpsed an illusory glade of shining branches; the river through a long window and Silver Wing, her silvery hair tied up in a complex knot, dressed in green brocade and sitting on a green sofa, beside a red and white chessboard. She looked like something out of a fairytale.

Bill Trevor was playing host to an embassy of non-Reich rock gods. The RA interview had just been aired, and Sage had been ripped to shreds. He'd been sent a preview for approval: naturally he'd been far too proud to do anything about it. The fresh-faced young divinities (neo-feudalist Metal called The Gintrap, well-meaning but hungry; they reminded Ax of that fashionista at Wallingham) thought the whole thing was hilarious. They worshipped Aoxomoxoa. Ax accepted the commiserations, declined the drugs and affected to enjoy the joke. Dian's hatchet job did have some fine moments of unintended humour.

'Hey, Bill? Where's the boss? Is he in his workroom?'

'I dunno where they all got to,' said Bill, looking disgusted. 'I think they went boating. Down the river for a cup of tea at Greenwich.'

Ax took the back stairs to the basement, where he found a detail of burly crew persons idling, ready to fend off wandering strangers. They let him through the secret door to the annexe stairs: graciously disabling the stupid Cornish password routine. Once, 'the annexe' had been a canvas army surplus tent, pitched beside Aoxomoxoa's van in Travellers' Meadow at Reading. The young Fiorinda had spread her sleeping bag there, among the black boxes and the stage props, when the king of the lads was her self-appointed guardian angel. Now it was a suite of concrete rooms under Battersea Reach. They didn't appear on the plans of the building: a useful attribute.

When Olwen Devi had gone back to Wales for good, she had donated two of her Zen Self cognitive scanners to the rockstar neuronauts. The Heads had stored them under Battersea, dismantled, not knowing what else to do with them. Over the last winter the weird science cabal had reformed, and the scanners were up and running. They were not pursuing the Zen Self quest. No one could contemplate that without Olwen: and each of them (except possibly Verlaine) knew they'd have soup for brains if they took any more snapshot. It was an unforgiving drug ... But there were other things that could be tried.

Ax trotted down the narrow whitewashed stairs, frowning. How easy would it be to find this place? Not hard enough. Passwords, fancy locks, Bill 'on guard' upstairs, it was all nonsense. If it came to a search, they'd just need to know there was something to find, and take Battersea Reach apart ... He had been unmoved by Sage's flashback (those snapshot glimpses are fucking useless, bad as telepathy), but he didn't like the Royal Academy interview. Dian Buckley doesn't do that to Sage unless she knows she has a licence. Did she take a hint, or was she given instructions; okay, not new bad news, but a bad sign. The scanners must be moved. There was nothing illicit about them, technically, but it would be so stupid to have a run-in with the anti-science lobby—

People used to say the Zen Self dome in Reading arena was bigger inside than outside: Ax'd felt the effect of an excellently designed geodesic himself. The annexe seemed *smaller* than it ought to be, and smaller every time Ax visited, until it was like squeezing through channels of bone into a skull. At the foot of the stairs he passed through one meagre white chamber into another, and then into the main lab, a square room, brilliantly lit, claustrophobically low-ceilinged, packed with expensive equipment; and just now full of people.

A body lay on a trolley bed, pasted with telltales, a drip in one skinny arm. It was Dilip Krishnachandran, eyes closed, wearing a b-loc headset. The space blanket that covered him rose and fell; his shuttered face was calm. Two paramedics, Zen Selfers who had chosen to stay in England, were in attendance. Chip and Verlaine,

Cherry Dawkins, George Merrick, Cack Stannen and Sage – plus the professionals, two post-docs keen to get into fusion by any means accessible – were occupying the remaining space, perched on stools between the scanners and the coolant towers. Another DK was with them; looking good except for a touch of transparency.

Only the paramedics – both called Gwyn, one male and one female – acknowledged Ax. Everyone else was riveted to the action.

'Hi, anoraks. How's it going?'

'It's going to be fine,' said the virtual DK, looking round. 'Glad you made it, Ax. I wanted you to be here.'

Ax propped himself against a tower beside Chip, there were no spare stools. George Merrick, the centre of attention, appeared to be playing an ancient black and white videogame. Cross-stitch trails moved across a tightly hatched grid, changing almost faster than George could nail them.

Chip glanced round and distractedly offered a spliff.

'No thanks.'

'Oh, sorry, Ramadan.'

'A technicality,' said Ax, 'considering the passive effect in here—'

'Slight screw up,' said Chip urgently. 'We have to re-enter the insertion, George has to key it in, manually, doing it from memory, and there's not much time before we miss the launch window. Could you keep quiet? Please?'

Ax thought of cannabis smoke escaping from a ventilation shaft somewhere on Riverside Walk. Yeah, all kind of idiot possibilities, and then the hidden rooms, guards and passwords, it all looks like guilty conscience. Battersea Reach had major advantages. Crystal cable, a hefty energy budget long established, dish aerials on the roof that nobody questioned. Maybe a short moratorium, after this . . . On the wall above the cot, where DK-in the-flesh could watch it without stirring, someone had taped a plastic tv screen. Fiorinda was up there, playing with the Charm Dudley Band in a clear-walled marquee, whaleback hills visible behind the stage; no sound. The women were dressed in fake animal skins with flirty tails, and painted white-face with blue spots all over; like Hindu cattle dressed for a festival. Ax was not sure if this was an improvement on the torn jeans and safety pins. And somewhere in that crowd on stage was Allie Marlowe, who'd travelled up to the North East with Fee. Was DK looking for her, as he gazed, eyes wide open now?

No one knew what had happened between those two. It seemed like a crying shame they'd had to break up, but who knows what goes on in any relationship, let alone how two people cope with the strain of long term illness? The fact that Allie wasn't here was a statement. Maybe she couldn't stand the idea of DK risking his life, when he had so little left to gamble with. Maybe that was it—

One day, he thought, what's happening between my friends will be all I worry about. I will live by the seasons. When it's the fasting month that will be my main concern, and the door of my house will have a latch, which only gets fastened at night . . . There was a whoop from George, and a burst of relieved applause. But first the camps must be opened, the Bonded Labour Bill must be repealed, the Second Chamber gang must be removed from office. Oh, and got to protect the science base, and keep the hedgeschools going . . . . The space cadets were straight with Goddard again, all systems go. Ax grinned and clapped, along with everyone else.

Sage looked round, at last, with a sweet and dazzling grin.

'Hi there, werewolf—'

'Hi, other werewolf.'

'I didn't know Ax was a werewolf too,' remarked Chip.

'Hahaha. Look at him, blatantly he's a werewolf. He can raise *either* of his eyebrows, independently. Hey, Ax. If immix brings out the beast in people, I'm leading my audience back to a state of primal innocence. Ain't that a good thing?'

'Oh, a Daniel come to judgement!' crowed Gwyn y gwr.

'It's George,' explained Sage. 'He's my moral wrangling coach.'

'You can shoot a rabid dog,' said big George, eyes on the screen in front of him, where the cross-stitching had been replaced by outer-space tv: very clear, 2D movie images. 'Without accusin' it of anythen beyond bein' rabid, boss. It won't be funny if the fucking government makes immix code illegal.'

'Nah, they won't do that. It's their money.'

According to Sage, Dian had asked him about the new cocktail drugs that could give you hallucinations of being an animal. After Dian's cut' n' paste it had come out as immix turning people into alsatians at the full moon, and what's more, the creator of direct cortical code thought this was a great idea. You say one thing, they print what they damn' well please, always, and if you protest they print that, in such a way it makes you look an idiot for whining. It's not worth worrying about.

'– no, Chez, you can't give it to me here—' DK passed his ethereal hands through each other. 'See? Can't hold it.'

'Sorry.'

Sage bounced off his stool, took the spliff from Chez and bore it off to the body on the gurney. Last summer in California DK had decided to quit his drugs. He wanted to go out Aldous Huxley style, making one last attempt to reach fusion, and he'd used emotional blackmail to get Sage to promise he would convince Olwen to go along with this. Sage had hated the idea: Olwen Devi despised assisted suicide.

'D'you still want to stuff yourself full of snap and die under the scanner?'

'*Not yet, my lord,*' whispered DK-in-the-flesh, a ghost of a voice, adamant. '*This is good for now . . . But soon, yes.*' He raised his hand to take the spliff.

Shit. Fucker's going to hold me to it. He's a hard bastard, in his way—

'Hey,' said Gwyn y gwreig, minding the telltales. 'No major muscle effort!'

'*Sorry-*'

'Nearly there,' announced one of the post-docs. 'DK's locked down, a-okay?'

The Zen Selfers confirmed this. Sage returned to his stool. Chez, suddenly scared, darted over to the cot. She wanted to be the one taking the flight, she had a hunger to leap into the dark. But she didn't want Dilip to die. She hadn't realised how much she didn't want Dilip to die. 'Let's have the sound, Chez, ' he breathed, holding her hand. His liquid dark eyes, that looked so huge in his hollowed face, were fixed on the taped-up screen. 'Let her sing me out there, my oceanic Fiorinda-'

'You're sure you won't fuck up something scientific?' Ax was asking. 'And piss off the people who own this space junk?'

The weird scientists looked at him.

'They encourage amateurs,' said Verlaine, slowly and clearly, as to an annoying toddler. 'They're fine with this.'

'It's okay,' said Sage. 'The Goddard AI's in charge, it won't let us screw up. All we're doing is sending out a signal, an' getting some free pictures back.'

A time-displaced Fiorinda (the Hartlepool tent-show had been yesterday) stood up to a mic on a stick at the front of the stage, her guitar slung back on her hip, singing low and tender, close to the ground—

> Heard her
> Whisper
> As he
> Ploughs her-

Then leaning in to belt out the punk-goes-Country catch—

> Let the sun come up tomorrow,
> Let the sun **go down** tonight
> Let the ploughshare and the harrow
> Work and rest,
> Work and rest!

Dilip-in-body, on his narrow bed, was primed and run into the realtime cognitive scanner until the cowl swallowed his head and shoulders. The b-loc DK vanished. The experimental data took off, on its piggyback relay ride. The big old satellite they had importuned, which had been keeping its steady vigil on the X-ray universe for more years than Dissolution could count, opened to their input; generous as the earth to the plough. The massively rich signal that was Dilip Krishnachandran flew, and was there. If he had not been paralysed by amazement he could have danced like thistledown on the six-metre-square counter array, in the microgravity and the cold blazing darkness. Seconds later, in the secret room under Battersea Reach, they could *see* him, standing on the array, snapped by one of the satellite's exterior cameras: fuzzy and blued-out like Neil Armstrong on a ladder.

YES!, howled the professionals, and burst into applause.

Dilip's friends held their breath. If something went wrong with the b-loc, the scanner would have a snapshot of DK's last normal brainstate, and restore at once. If DK suffered major physical collapse, which might happen, no specific reason why, just because he was so fragile, that would be different—

The paramedics ran him out of the scanner. He opened his eyes.

'Oooh, that was high! Oh, the blue earth, the coloured stars—'

The cramped space of the bunker erupted.

We've done it! We can do it!

Hey, hey, what else can we try? Pity the International Space Station is a hulk, can't place a call when there's no one home. There're live installations moping on the moon (no US or EU space programme since God knows when, but all we need is a live transmitter). What about a big old telescope? What about that orbital hotel, abandoned half-built? Hey, the Chinese have stuff on Mars! It's a hell of a long way. For the signal to travel so far, go around corners, uncorrupted, how would we—

I can't stop them, thought Ax, as the babble rose (wondering how he'd explain it to Fiorinda, praying his big cat would not be test-pilot for any of the really mental stunts, the virtual self is not a toy!) This is why the Reich exists, to hold the pass, to make the future possible. I can't stop any of it. I can't get out. Oh God, never?

A shudder went through him: he saw the endless meetings, corridors, papers. Is this my life? This is my life. If it must be, then it must be.

The Food Production Group met in the President's office in the Railham Building, Richmond Terrace, the address for Reich affairs in Whitehall for a very long time. They had established themselves, they had regular b-loc and video conference links with other such groups in the sister nations of Britain, and further afield. This particular day Lucy Wasserman was there: a forty-something Member of Parliament for North Stoke (House of Commons, not the Second Chamber), with an impressive post-Dissolution cv. She was the woman the Permanent Civil Service favoured as Greg Mursal's replacement. She didn't have anything else going for her at the moment: no campaign, no Cabinet-in-waiting, but on the whole, that made her a better bet. The President and the prospective PM checked each other out, while discussion ranged over the application of very high tech to very small mixed-arable farming units; GM crops as a positive concept that needed work; and ethanol-crop/oilseed production. Perhaps there might be many hectares of rape grown in superfluous underground car-parks, with gro-lights? We must not be afraid of quirky small-scale initiatives, partial solutions, the piecemeal of many ideas and techniques—

'We should call this approach Gold Beach,' said a DoE civil servant.

'Oh?' said Sage. 'Why a beach, what's gold?'

'Before D-Day,' explained the speaker, a young white guy with glistening, slicked-back hair, in a retro suit and tie, 'a British Major-General called Hobart invented an array of strange tank accessories, for getting the troops through the Germans' awesome beach defences. The US commanders rejected the lot, because they looked ridiculous. The 50th, using Hobart's funnies, landed 25,000 men, with 400 casualties. The US landing on Omaha was a slaughterhouse. Such is the legend.'

WWII references were a tradition, possibly started by Fred Eiffrich and his 'Fat Boy' coining. They'd come to signal a worldwide network of those who grasped that the Crisis was global war: a war without an enemy, an all-out battle for survival.

'Okay,' said Ax. 'Gold Beach it is.'

Lucy Wasserman nodded.

The meeting ended. Ax and Sage walked a corridor, talking about Fiorinda, who was due home in hours. They would always be uneasy about Fiorinda and Charm Dudley. The relationship between their babe and the queen of Northern Dyke Rock was too stormy, too intimate. Someone you'd scuffle, is someone you'd fuck, Sage maintained (a bizarre sidelight). So, we say *nothing* about Charm? No, no, wrong message, we say a few, casual, normal things. How was she, did you fight—

'I'm afraid of a backlash,' said Sage. 'She's been *clingy* by Fiorinda standards since we got back from Paris. She's going to come home hating me—'

Sage in this nervous, gabbling mood was so touching Ax accidentally broke the rule about public display and hugged him close, just a morale-boosting squeeze. A figure appeared on a crossing passage in front of them. It was Jack Vries. The Wiccan scholar started, averted his eyes, and passed out of sight.

119

'What's he doing, wandering around here?' murmured Sage.

Ax grinned. 'Getting shocked by rock and roll behaviour. Fuck him.'

But they were alarmed. The FP group meetings were not *secret*, but . . . but Jack Vries had no reason to be in this building. One thing you learn in politics is to take notice of a warning shot, take notice of the little accidents. Be careful!

'Reeka Azziz woke up overheated, with a talking-heads tv studio pasted onto her eyeballs. She groped, whimpering, and pressed her fingertips against the wall. A tug of ATP, cell metabolism energy, leaving her fingertips, and the window by her bed turned to shade. But she couldn't switch the tv off because overnight she'd forgotten the nerve-impulse tweak you have to learn. She had to fall out of bed, blunder to the washstand, rinse her fingers in saline and excavate the button.

Fuck, she muttered. *Shit.*

She'd been warned not to sleep with her eyesocket tv/av, but no one had said it would be so comfortable she'd forget. Now her left eye felt as if someone had been gouging at it with a blunt penknife, and she wouldn't be able to wear her new toy for a week: fuck fuck fuck. Her dad had said she should wait 'til she could afford the tiny permanent-wear kind, like Sage's mask button; but he was living in the past. Things don't get cheaper if you wait. Things disappear.

She took some ice out of her heat-ex minifridge, switched on the ordinary tv with another ATP touch, and found a clean sock. She'd been woken by Music Nation Live, the Channel Seven breakfast show, one of her personal settings on the house computer: the computer must have detected the socket gadget, which she had not installed in the system, and wirelessly activated it of its own accord. This fucking house! It was her parents' house, a Tower Hamlets emergency prefab from the dictatorship, futuristic and fucked-up. She loved it, really, but fuck, it has a fucking mind of its own. Fiorinda was there on the screen, talking about the Reich. Areeka knelt, the sock full of ice to her eye. 'We were angry *all the time*,' said Fiorinda. 'I didn't see it in Sage, because I was an oblivious little brat; I just thought, wow, gross, he has such a taste for horrors, but looking back, I know where *Arbeit Macht Frei* came from. Helpless fury and disgust, it's all we wrote about. Then we met Ax and he said, you can do something about it. You can't escape your own hell, but you can do something about the hell that's engulfing the world ... I don't know how he does it, how he makes good things sound *possible*, but it was like breathing without choking, for the first time in my life.'

I want to have my hair like that, thought Areeka.

Her mum said Asian hair would fall out if you heat-treated it into corkscrews. But natural curl gene treatment was expensive, and it made your scalp wrinkly ...

She was about to take to the road. A tight schedule of anti-camp protests, volunteer farmwork, tent-shows, tech fairs, would fill the next weeks. Her parents were terrified she would get arrested, but it was their own fault, they'd brought her up to be an Ax Preston baby. Her friends reproached her for being a half-and-half, because the end of summer brought her home. She felt the pull to go all the way: but there were career considerations. London calls, you can't be the new Fiorinda and live in Norfolk. Downstairs, Mum was haranguing the drinking-water-man, telling him his cans were short measure and the water smelled of sick. Inertia rules the over-thirties. Mum and Dad hated what was happening to England, but the nearest they came to protest was buying dodgy water from the Roms, in futile solidarity.

Areeka sat among her half-packed clothes and camping gear, nursing her eye while Music Nation moved on to a forum, for which the Fiorinda clip had been the intro. Roxane Smith's fruity old voice boomed out, smearing the Paris Protest, making the Triumvirate sound like harmless cranks.

Fucking traitor.

At last she dived into her rucksack and pulled out the battered make-up case that travelled with her everywhere: took out the plaited cord and the knife, and bound the cord around her wrist. The box was lined with green and yellow tissue flames, each flame edged in glitter, a work of patient handicraft. Fiorinda's photograph (on stage, her tiny face a screaming mask in a cloud of hair) was framed in fragments of Traveller's Joy, supposed to come from the wreath she'd worn at the inauguration, and covered with clear sticky paper. Her dad would go berserk if he knew she had Pagan stuff in the house, but he never came in here uninvited.

You don't understand, Dad: this isn't against Ax. Paganism doesn't belong to the bad guys. She stabbed herself in the web between finger and thumb and let a few drops fall. *I wish no evil to my friends' enemies, only the harm that will bring them to peace . . .* She didn't believe the blood ritual achieved anything, any more than Friday Prayers. But it's not like that, Dad. It's not *for* anything, not like praying to Allah. It's just something you do, to express yourself, to be part of what's happening.

Roxane climbed the stairs to hir rooms in Queen Anne Street, making heavy use of the silver-mounted walking stick that s/he used with the swagger of a Regency Buck while in public view. Nobody was waiting for hir, which was still hard, though s/he hadn't lived with Chip and Verlaine for years . . . Ah, I miss my boys. But how good to have them back in London, and do I detect a trace of broodiness?

How late-Roman-empire, s/he thought. How superbly grotesque, for a middle-aged (sixty is the new fifty) sexual neuter to be hoping for grandchildren: from a young man to whom one was once mentor, parent and lover; and this former lover's current boyfriend, with whom one has also had intimate relations—

Yet these days both medically feasible, and almost respectable.

S/he took a glass and a bottle of good port to hir favourite armchair. It was barely eleven in the morning (ooh, I hate morning tv), but s/he trusted the old painkillers best. I need a new hip, and perhaps a new knee, but I'm not *old*. I'll have the operations, and I'll be young again (maybe the boys will travel with me to the Pacific Rim, in search of the miracles of modern medicine). Well, the pack smells blood, but the sacred monster of rock can still cut it. I fear no winds of change, for I am the Vicar of Bray sir. But I will be true to you, Ax, in my fashion.

S/he sipped hir wine with discrimination, thinking sadly of all the little gods, going over the hill into oblivion. Soon nobody on earth will remember that cunning old priest, *The Vicar of Bray*. Or know why the curate's egg was *good in parts,* or how it's on a Monday morning that the gasman comes to call. All things must pass. If Fiorinda would only realise there is no danger whatsoever that she's going to turn into her father: if I could see her burning bright star ascend, I would retire happy.

We have done what we could.

No green field shall be broken, Ax. Not for fifty, or a hundred years. The beauty of this beautiful country will be restored. The birds will sing in the bushes, the sheep may safely graze (a great many of them, but not too many). And every child who gets to school will absorb, and take with them out into the wicked world, that culture of music, recreation and the hard work of compassion which you created. It isn't what you wanted. It's a long way from Utopia. But it's enough, it should be enough for any one man. It's time to let go. The Mountain's too big for you, Mohammad. There is *nothing you can do* about what's happening now, in England; except go down with the ship . . . Roxane caught hirself, a little horrified. With a turn of hir wrist, s/he flicked a few blood-red drops onto the rug. *Absit omen.*

FIVE

The Way It Is

The old mad woman lay dying while Fiorinda waited beside her. In a corner of the room (sunlight reversed by slatted blinds at the windows) a brawny woman in uniform sat doing a crossword. Someone had to be there, it was one of the rules of this place, in case Fiorinda's grandmother leapt up and tried to kill her. Which was not quite ludicrous (though Gran had never been physically violent, not like some of the suffering wrecks). But not now, not anymore.

She watched Gran's withered hands, the hoops of her rings sagging loose, diamonds and sapphires winking as her fingers crept the straight-tucked sheet, as if she were playing a keyboard or plucking strings. It can't be long, she thought: and remembered that Puusi Meera, the virtual movie star, had told her, *don't ever wear a lot of rings*. It makes you look frustrated. What an amazing compendium of useful, practical information Puusi was. Fiorinda wore only one ring, so she was safe from the imputation. Were you frustrated, Gran? What was it you wanted out of life? You can't have wanted what really happened—

You can't have—

My food tastes funny, Gran. I think I'm ill.

'You're not ill. If your food tastes funny, Frances dear, that's the first sign you're pregnant.' The grandmother says this to the twelve-year-old girl with a twinkle in her eye. The little girl thinks Gran can't possibly know that Frances, STOP CALLING ME THAT! I'M FIORINDA! I CHOSE IT, IT'S MY NAME! could be anything like pregnant. She feels superior because she doesn't yet know her grown-up lover has scarpered, and it'll be many more days before she realises *pregnant* is exactly what she is ... But here, in the nursing home, Fiorinda can step back, look through those twelve-year-old eyes as if through peepholes cut in a picture, and see the grandmother's wicked knowledge.

She hated being made to think about what had been done to her. Visiting the nursing home filled her with revulsion, because *here*, where mad old Gran was kept locked up, the story was what it had always been. Not cauterised by heroism, not rinsed clean by great affairs; nothing to do with a scientific revolution. Just a little girl in an ugly suburban fairytale, 'seduced' by a big man she didn't know was her father, with the connivance of her Gran and her Auntie. And of course she blamed herself for the whole fucking thing. What raped woman ever didn't blame herself?

An image of a naked young girl with her arms and legs twisted up, glistening, ready for the oven, on Grandmother's kitchen table—

Oh, no, Frances dear. I can't tell you! Your mother would skin me alive!

I expect you loved him. You worshiped him, of course, he was the Master, but I bet you were in love with him too. She leaned forward, chin on her hands, trying to read the past in that secret little face, already folded in death's mystery. Gran in big skirts with small waists: a young woman with classy connections, no money, no morals, and a taste for high living ... 'I wasn't the sort of girl a man marries', said the grandmother's voice in her mind, smug and salacious. The Wicca covens set, joining hands with the rich-as-fuck rockstar set, and there you found your niche, first you and then your daughters ... Fiorinda's mother had been different, ambitious, a career woman: but rock journalism had been no escape. What was she like when she met him? The only image Fiorinda had was Dian Buckley. She could see Dian, knowing Rufus was a spooky evil bastard, but still thrilled to have landed a megastar—

(Probably *exactly* the way Dian thinks of Sage these days. Her rockstar beau who turned spooky, and how cool yet creepy that she's fucked him.)

Was my Mum like that? I want to believe not, but I'll never know. Everything I never asked is leaving the world with this old woman's last breath.

Frances dear, I have a little present for you—

A dry chuckle came from the bed: sounding so close to her ear it made her jump. The clock on the wall said time had passed, she'd been staring at Gran for an hour and a half. She got up and went to the bathroom. She'd been thinking she felt her period come on, but the pantie-liner was still corn-husk blonde (she didn't like tampons, only used them at night or if she was bleeding hard; which was rarely), not a drop of red. Oh, God, what if I'm pregnant? She was significantly late now, eight days in the North, four days before: that's nearly two weeks. She was twelve again, and *oh God, what if I'm pregnant?* And all the tales, she thought, all the fairytales that say my kind can't stay ... Ploughboys and princes can marry us but it can't last; this is what they mean. I can't have a normal life. I have to go, to the waters and the wild, into the lake, I have to vanish under the hill.

On her way out she stopped at reception.

'I'm leaving. If there should be a change, call me.'

There would only be one change now. 'Of course, Ms Slater.'

One pays for perfect tact. Fiorinda had meant to stay to the end. She'd missed her mother's death, she'd been determined not to miss this one. She was bottling out, but they never judged you. They protected their charges, never commented: and they'd seen everything. Her lovers and friends usually took care that Fiorinda did not visit the nursing home alone. Luckily she'd taken the call this morning herself, fresh from her nice holiday of pretending to be a local-heroine rockstar, so she'd been able to deal with it herself, which meant that she could just walk.

When she was on the train, passing through the leafy, depopulated outer-London end of Surrey, she remembered she had left a car and a driver behind. I'll sort it later, she decided: imagining she was a kid again, and nobody cared where she was. She crossed the maze of overground and underground: the city newly, beautifully riven with drifts of flowering meadow, galaxies of Queen Anne's Lace, buttercups and sorrel; buying tickets with coins from the platform machines, still feeling that she was a child, invisible in the adult world; until she reached a north London cemetery. Her mother's ashes had been forked into a flowerbed here, but somewhere there was an actual grave belonging to her baby (Rufus's baby), who had died when he was three months old. Her friend Mrs Mohanjanee had arranged it, under the bizarre impression that the family of the lonely little girl next door were Christian.

But Fiorinda had never visited before. She didn't know where to start, she didn't know what she was looking for (is there a headstone?). She couldn't face the cemetery office, so she went back, automatically, to the cold house of her childhood. It wasn't far. In through the garden gate, under the overgrown laurels; a tunnel of darkness broken by thick drops of sunlight. The basement door was padlocked, but she had the keys in her bag. She'd been planning to come here when Gran was finally gone, to see what state the house was in.

The basement had been cleared. There was nothing left of the witch's cave where little Frances had fed on spicy gossip while her mother brooded upstairs. She wasn't scared, but she didn't linger. She'd found a dead body in a place like this once, when the Reich was young. Empty basements smell of murdered children. She unlocked another door into the house above, and her feet took her through the dusk of boarded windows to her old room. Under the bed there was a secondhand acoustic guitar. In the mattress she would find the split where she had hidden her music—

There was no furniture left but a dust-coated mirror, propped in a corner. She sat against the wall where her bed used to be. Me and my stupid, fragile, mutant brain, like something that grew under a stone, what use am I to anyone? The curve of her palm still remembered the feel of a downy little skull. She could not wipe her tears, she had to hold him very carefully. Oh, shit, what if you drop them?

I will never forget you, I will *never* forget you.

She woke with an aching head, her face sticky with tear-tracks, curled on her side in the dust. There wasn't a streak of light from the boarded window; it must be late. She sat up, feeling panicked, and realised she'd been woken by the sound of intruders. Shit! What'll I do? She listened, wide-eyed, until the door of her bedroom slowly opened, and who's this looming dark figure? A man, a big powerful man, and he's brought another even bigger, taller man; an accomplice—

They came in and sat down, cross-legged on the floor in front of her: shadowy in the gloom, seeming unsure of their reception.

'How did you know where I was?'

'Masculine intuition,' explained Sage.

'Is she dead?'

'No,' said Ax, with regret. 'Your Gran is still breathing, last we heard.'

'Bugger.'

The thought that today was all to do again defeated her, it was awful.

'I'm sorry I left the car. I just forgot, I'm not going loopy, I just *forgot*—'

'We narrowed it down,' said Ax. 'After we remembered you'd been planning to look at the house. Don't worry about the car. What was loopy about that? You have a fucking right to be distressed. We're here because we love you.'

'D'you want to talk about it?' asked Sage, gently.

She stared at them, her mouth trembling, her dirty face streaked with tears.

'It's . . . I was at the nursing home, waiting for her to die, and I started thinking about my baby. He was such a great baby and no one remembers him but me. He . . . he hardly ever cried, and I *know* he liked me.'

The closer you get to someone, the more you understand the burden of memory that shapes them: what's important and what (amazingly) is not. Ax saw a little girl with a baby in her arms, and all the bewildered, painful love in that child's face. And everything else passes away, the monster, the horrors, leaving only this. Overwhelmed with pity he reached out, too choked to speak, and took her hand.

'Yes,' said Sage, taking the other. 'Ssh, stupid brat, it's okay.'

Fiorinda sighed, and pulled herself together, clinging to those two lifeline hands. 'I never hated her, you know. I hated Mum, because she was so miserable, but I knew Gran was wicked and I didn't care. She was interesting. Even in the really bad time, when she knew Fergal was Rufus, she knew what he was doing to me and she was *on his side*, I still didn't hate her. There was no point. Morality and my Gran don't belong in the same sentence. The expression *beyond good and evil* was made for people like her.'

Ax was choked, terrified of making the wrong gesture: Sage was reckless. He swept the babe into his arms and held her on his knees, rocking her while she shoved her face against his shoulder. 'Oh God, how can I dare have another baby? Sage, I can't have a baby. It's impossible, it wouldn't be safe, God, what might I do to a baby?'

'Oh, leave it out. Tha's bullshit, my brat.'

'It's *not* bullshit.'

'All right,' said Ax, 'not bullshit. Let's say unduly scrupulous. Why shouldn't you have a baby? Heartless selfish bastards who are not fit to be parents have kids all the time, and you are not one of those, protector of the poor. Far from it.'

'Think of my fucking dad,' suggested Sage.

Fiorinda covertly turned her face and glanced at Ax. Not to mention your fucking mother, they thought: but they didn't say it. Ax swallowed, and cleared his throat. For hours they hadn't known where she was. He had been sure that she was okay, but he was more relieved than he dared to show.

'I suppose this, er . . . Does this fear of babies imply you didn't bleed yet?'

'No blood,' she said, raising her head with a tough little shrug. 'The scare continues.'

So-called to confuse the demons. Fiorinda held out her arms to Ax and they shifted until they were sitting in a row, Sage and Ax with their backs to peeling wallpaper, Fiorinda cuddled between them. 'I'm very sorry,' she said, humbly. 'I didn't mean to scare you. Did anything happen? Any more lost boys, space flights, disastrous tv coverage?'

'We don't know,' said Sage. 'We've been off-line all day, looking for you.'

They were not using personal telecoms much; the constant spooking made it ridiculous, no such thing as a private conversation, and if you encrypted it they just shot the message down, the fuckers . . . The Reich's youth were also post-mobile, for their own devious reasons: which explained how Marlon had managed to vanish for eight hours in Central London, presumably with Silver Wing. He'd given the bodyguard he wasn't supposed to know about the slip, he'd found he had no travel card and no money: so he'd walked home from Hyde Park. He could not understand what the fuss was about.

The kids walked everywhere, it was a craze. No adult could understand it. They would wear their leg-bones out.

'We left Marlon tied up in a cupboard,' said Ax. 'With Doug on guard.'

'You can laugh,' said Sage. 'I am *not* overprotective, I just know he's not streetwise, how could he be, he's spent his life in the middle of Welsh nowhere, or at boarding school. And—' He shrugged. 'Obviously, there's risks, we have enemies.'

'What a life for him,' said Ax, unhappily.

'It's not your doing, babe.'

They were silent, thinking about surveillance culture, armed guards in the front hall, the countless small and not so small annoyances: their resentment softened by the fact that right now they were alone together in a secret place, an unexpected haven; and by the tiny doubtful promise of a child.

'I think it was always like this,' decided Fiorinda. 'We're just older.'

'Older, aargh, how I hate that word.' Sage tipped his head back, frowning. 'I don't like the way they never asked for another Neurobomb meeting. They haven't consulted anyone else either . . . an' I would know. I can't believe they've given up the idea of building themselves an A-team. It's not nat'ral.'

'Maybe they've given up asking the pacifists. I did tell them to forget it.'

'Mm, yeah.' Sage withheld judgement.

'I still don't think it was wise for you to talk to them, Fiorinda,' said Ax.

'Nah, no danger. They don't reckon me. I'm under their radar, true.'

They had begged her not to come near the Wallingham stunt because they were afraid it might turn nasty, but they didn't seem to have a clue why she'd insisted that she would deal with the Neurobomb Working Party. They hadn't forgotten about the Lavoisier video, far from it, but – as she had noticed over the years – they didn't see risk in the same way. They didn't think things through. It must be genetic, a male thing. How else would soldiers go off to war so cheerfully? When she'd realised they didn't know they were in danger she hadn't wanted to explain. She'd been forced to appear the pushy brat, determined to make her mark with a government committee.

Ah well, too bad, Fiorinda had been that brat often enough.

Coming back to Brixton Hill in the starry summer night, footsteps sounding in the quiet, through the elven streetlighting of SW2, Ax's private domain, the downturned golden flowers welling open before them, dwindling into candles again behind; unless other late passers-by triggered another wave. They had no premonition. Before Ax could slip his keycard into the lock the door leapt open. Allie was there, in smart work clothes though it was eleven at night: big-eyed, pale and frantic.

'Where the fuck have you been?'

'Neasden,' said Fiorinda. 'It was my fault, I got pissed off waiting for Gran to die so I did a pilgrimage to the old homestead. I'm *sorry*, Allie, I didn't mean to scare anyone, least of all you. Did they call? Is she dead yet?'

'What?' snapped Allie. 'What are you talking about?'

'Is she dead?'

'Who?' Allie recovered her wits, feeling she'd well overstepped a line that certainly existed, if only in her head. 'Oh, you mean your Gran. I don't know, Fio. It hasn't been on my mind. You'd better come upstairs. Faud's here. He's seen it.'

Ax gave her a look of quiet concentration. Sage nodded. They went upstairs. Faud Hassim, in his customary white shalwar kameez, his rich hair rebellious under a close little cap, rose and bowed when the Triumvirate entered the living room. He had seen the Lavoisier video. He'd been asked this morning to join the Prime Minister and his closest advisors for an emergency meeting about the shocking scandal that was just breaking in the US.

They moved to the square oak dinner table and sat around it while Faud told them that the Prime Minister wanted a Parliamentary debate. The venue would be the Lower Chamber, once better known as the House of Commons. Ax and Sage would answer to the House, with Jack Vries, the government's Wiccan expert, as moderator.

Quick work. Ax and Sage and Fiorinda looked at each other. No question, Sage had been right, whatever he'd picked up on at the Royal Academy interview. They have connections we don't know about ... We are screwed, and they've been playing with us.

Faud Hassim had never been inside these rooms before, he had never come close to being a personal friend of the three. So this is how they live, this spare and modest dwelling, just as the legend tells it ... He was impressed. Unable to reach the Triumvirate, he had spent his day consulting the non-government leaders of the Counter-culture, the staybehind councils, the urban communards; and also the rebel Countercultural Movement MPs, techno-greens who hated their official leaders. He had talked to Ax's friends, the ones who'd been warned to be prepared for trouble. He'd talked to others. They all felt the same. They were minded to advise Ax to accept the government's challenge.

'Who was at the briefing in Downing Street?' asked Ax.

Faud hesitated. 'The PM, Jack . . . It was a small meeting.'

'They were alone?' said Ax, acutely.

'Yes.'

Well, that's interesting. That's a telling piece of information.

'What are the issues?' Sage asked. 'What's this debate supposed to be about?'

'It will be about the Lavoisier Raid,' said Faud, slowly. 'Superficially it will be about the raid. The authenticity of that video, and the choice the titular leader of the English Countercultural Movement made when he attacked those people—'

Fiorinda nodded. 'But what are Jack and the PM hoping to get out of it?'

Faud and Allie were drawn to stare at each other, across the table: Allie bit her lip. 'Our national stance on fusion consciousness weapons will be— will be aired,' said Faud, as if he hadn't heard the question from Ax's lady. 'It will be brought into the open. Ultimately, the debate will be about the future of this country. It will be a trial of strength between the Countercultural Movement as it was originally conceived, and neofeudalism at the top.' He leaned forward, passionately earnest. They could see in his eyes the effect that the video had had on him, but he wasn't shaken. 'Ax, we need you to do this. You can't turn them down, it would be a very bad signal. We have to welcome the confrontation. That's the message I've been asked to bring.'

They're looking for impeachment, thought Ax. My God. And we should say no. We should skip the poisoned chalice, resign right now.

But the trap had closed, and he could see no way out.

In the night, Fiorinda woke and went to the bathroom. Her womb had started weeping, a few little bloody tears. She had not tested herself this time: and now she knew it had been nothing, just an irregular period. She felt no distress, only the familiar weight falling back onto her heart, to match the sad cramping in her belly.

I will never have a baby. I knew it couldn't happen.

The 'Lavoisier video' affair exploded in the popular media, proliferating into variants, copied and soundtracked; censored or bloodied, according to taste. The global village – as far as it survived – thrilled to the images of those morally superior rockstars on their killing spree. In the US, political scandal unfolded with moves as formal and long-prepared as the opening of a classic chess game. In Europe the Lavoisier story was not well known: it had been high security, and then lost in the backwash of the A-team event and the LA quake. But the English media soon sorted out that Mr Ex-Dictator and his Minister had been slaughtering Gaian martyrs, on the orders of the US President. Maybe Ax 'n' Sage could explain themselves! But hard questions must be asked, and urgently. It was probably a Constitutional Crisis.

Is Ax Preston fit to be our President?

The opening of the debate was set for June 17: giving the House time to prepare after returning from its archaic Whit Recess, and ensuring that the show would be over before Alban Heruin, the Summer Solstice. The Insanitude Mail Room was swamped with messages of support, and forced off the air. The Countercultural rebels waxed fearless and sarcastic. Facts and fictions about the occult terrorists in the desert were unearthed, the country (that is, everyone who could get satellite or cable) became addicted to the US coverage. Ax went to visit Joss Pender.

Joss's wife (his first wife; he and Beth Loern had not been married) didn't detain them long. They retired to the den. Joss, grim and furious, sat at his oversized Italian car-designer's desk: surrounded by generations of lovingly maintained hardware, dead media, gadgets, digital art.

'Well, I've seen the "video". In several formats; although neither you nor my son thought to provide me with a copy. D'you mind if I say it's appalling?'

'Lavoisier' was looking to be the summer's red-hot underground hit. With Ax Preston on guitar, inevitably. You can't stop that kind of thing. Someone ought to release *Rivermead* so it could hitch a ride.

'We think so too,' said Ax, suppressing a desire to yell what did you all *think* we've been doing, these last years? What did you imagine we were doing when we fought a war with the Islamic separatists in Yorkshire? Making MTV?

'Have you considered IMR, imaging memory retrieval—?'

Ax shook his head. 'I don't see how anything like that is going to help. Why wouldn't we have manipulated the pictures we keep in our heads? Joss, the video isn't the issue, it's the pretext. There's nothing to engage with there.'

'Hm. The country seems to disagree.'

The software baron looked like Marlon Williams grown old: slight and energetic, with the same cocky, wary, golden-hazel eyes; same jet-black hair, in Joss's case thickly powdered with silver. Normally you would never guess the man was nearly eighty. Today the years had fallen on him as he glared from behind his ramparts of tech.

'My son,' he announced, savagely, 'was eighteen months old when he lost the use of his hands. By the time he was four I knew it wouldn't ever slow him down. He could write code such as you couldn't fathom in a lifetime before he could dress himself unaided. *My son* is one of those rare people who could have done *anything he chose* with his life—'

Whereas instead he had to end up the bumboy of an underclass rockstar warlord, starring in a cowboy snuff orgy . . . Ax's relationship with Sage's dad had been fine until Sage insisted Joss had to know they were sexual partners, edgy ever since. A tactless third party (Sage's mother, of course) had told Ax that Joss felt very, very sorry for Fiorinda. Maybe it would be better if Ax just came out with it. Yes, it's true, your son and I do sodomise each other now and then. But! We always use a proper condom! And always will, because I am Captain Sensible. But then Joss would probably just think Ax was boring. No, no. Keep your temper.

He studied the nest – part geek, part bowerbird – that was so disconcertingly familiar. A Perspex paperweight holding a dab of photonic-crystal and bearing the legend *eks: not fade away*. That's a sacred relic, from the start-up days. A framed photo of Stevie, later to be known as Sage, aged about six, mugging at the camera, the hands which had lost several fingers to infant meningitis septicaemia hidden in his pockets. How well Ax remembered that gesture, and the pity that would cut you like a knife, watching Sage's daily struggle, often in pain, to make sure the disability didn't ever slow him down.

'Your son is Leonardo da Vinci, Joss. I know it. I'm not arguing. Is it my fault he never wanted to be king of the hill?'

Joss sighed, hard and long, and gave himself a moment to recover from the outburst, which had been beyond his control. While so many others had been snake-charmed out of their assets over the years, eks photonics had escaped Mr Preston's depredations. He had not flattered himself that he'd been spared because he was Sage's father, he'd understood he was mistrusted as a donor: too powerful, too pushy, too demanding. But he'd sometimes felt Ax was *saving him* for something.

And here it is.

'So, what do you want from me, Mr President? I'm at your disposal, let's have it on the table.'

'I want you to be my Post Office,' said Ax, immediately. 'I'd like to give you my Internet Commission cypher, and for you to take over that connection until the debate is out of the way.'

Joss nodded. He'd been expecting that one. 'And the Open Gates policy?'

From October of this year the agricultural camps run directly by the government would be administered as open shelters. If the pilot scheme worked, the same conditions would become mandatory for the private sector. Ax believed this project was safe. It had very strong public support (who says rockstar protests can't achieve anything?), and though there were fewer voters, they still had to be obeyed.

'No, that's okay, I think that's best left alone. The other thing is the annexe. I was planning to move it, but there won't be time. I need someone, other than Sage's band . . . Someone as safe from reprisals as possible, who will decide when to pull the plug there, should it come to that. Dismantle the scanners, ship them back to Caer Siddi, destroy them, whatever seems best.'

Joss knew about the annexe. The lines around his mouth deepened and tightened. 'I suppose you'll tell me what I need to know.'

'Sage will tell you.'

You're going to kill him, thought Joss. You're going to get my son killed.

The video was a cruel blow. Temporarily, at least, this affair was a wrecking ball to the hopes of the people who had wanted Ax Preston back, the people who had undertaken his return. But he could see no way that Ax or his son could be held to blame for what they had done in Lavoisier. And no way, really, that the Triumvirate could have avoided a vicious twist of fate. The cognitive scanners under Battersea Reach were something else, a wilful, reckless defiance of the times. They don't mess around, this current administration. They're not rocket scientists but they are not the clowns you take them for, Mr Preston—

'You keep thinking I own him,' said Ax, answering the unspoken rage. 'I don't, anymore than you ever did. I'm not the one who set up that lab. But I wouldn't have stopped him if I could. That's what we do, Joss. We keep the doors open, the lights burning, in case civilisation comes home.'

They stared each other down. Joss made an impatient gesture, possibly some kind of apology. 'All right, consider it taken care of . . . My God, Ax. Why the hell did you two have to get into that insane situation? Couldn't you have left it to the professionals, for once in your lives?'

No, because the professionals meant to kill Fiorinda, thought Ax. But he couldn't say that . . . He must not hint at secrets. He kept trying to remember exactly what could be told and what could not, what was known and what was not, and he was afraid he wouldn't be able to keep it straight in his mind. Just answer the question, he told himself. Just answer the question, volunteer nothing.

'We were in Mexico with Fee, and we were losing her, Joss. She was falling apart, after what her father did to her; and then helping to kill him. We couldn't reach her, we hardly dared touch her. Then Fred's emissary arrived, and his story, a new problem, brought our babe back to herself. I don't remember making a decision. I wanted Fiorinda, you see. That's what was on my mind.'

'Is that the line you're going to take in the House? You got yourselves hired as mercenaries, in the grip of a sexual obsession?'

Ax smiled warmly, and nodded. 'Yeah. That's it, spot-on.'

137

Death wish, thought Joss Pender, with a cold shock. Ooh, death wish!

'I'm sorry,' he said, after a moment. 'That was completely uncalled for.'

'It's okay. I'm sure I'll have to field worse.'

In Washington the scandal had resolved into something weirdly mundane about public spending. The cost of the planned raid that didn't happen. Who had authorised the hiring of these rockstar 'foreign mercenaries'; paid in vouchers for Hollywood stardom? At Westminster, the actual event would be avoided, as far as possible, as it entailed extraordinary courage, and saving Fiorinda's life. Their spies had warned them it would be character assassination. It would get personal, and it would get dirty.

Joss frowned, on a different tack. 'You've heard nothing from Fred?'

'Not really.'

'But you've seen him, you've heard his voice?'

'No more than you. On the screen, saying his lines.'

Ax had known, the moment he saw Alain's *courriel,* that he wasn't going get any privileged or personal access to Fred Eiffrich for a while. Compared with the implications closer to home, this hadn't worried him. They'd been friends. Fred was one of those fathers Ax would always look for because he had lost his own. But they'd known, when Ax'd left the US, that they might never meet as friends again. But that had been Paris. By now, Ax was earnestly hoping that Fred's utter silence was a diplomatic snub. He was afraid it meant something worse.

'D'you think he has other trouble besides this affair?'

'I don't know.'

The two men, old and young, faced each other, silently. Their personal differences, the jealousy that would always be between them, slipped aside. They were thinking of the prospect of a Neurobomb arms race, and the threat Joss Pender understood better than most people outside from a handful of esoteric specialists. Ax stared at the photonic crystal sealed in Perspex: fighting a black rose moment, fear in everything. He wanted to tell Joss it would be okay. We'll hold the pass, we'll turn this around, we always have. But he wasn't sure.

'The debate is nothing,' said Joss at last. 'It's a punishment for what you did to Greg and Jack at Wallingham. Anyone who matters in this country knows that; and fuck those two and their cronies, petty self-important bastards. What you did at Lavoisier was heroic ... I haven't said that, I want to say that, and I'll make sure my opinion goes on record. But you have to do more than win, you have to undo the damage. You have to make the people see you as Ax Preston again. Our hero, our saviour. Can you deliver?'

Would I say no? thought Ax.

He reviewed the odds he'd been weighing up night and day. The rebel Countercultural MPs, who had put him up to this; the rest of the elected Members. Greg Mursal's Cabinet, the front benches; the rest of the peers. The secret rulers (I'm looking at one of those right now). The fourth estate, and the callous, wayward English people themselves. A home crowd, spiteful in parts, basically manageable. How many genuine, determined enemies did Ax have, lurking in that woodpile? Very few. Perhaps only two of them.

'I can do it.'

Maybe you'll pull it off, thought Joss, feeling the young man's resolute calm, and the ability that nobody could doubt. Ax Preston has never lost a battle yet. But you still have a death wish. Joss had seen no live action on a battlefield – which had galled him, since the rules of manhood had been changed, without notice. But he'd seen enough blood on the boardroom carpet to recognise certain states of mind.

'Good,' he said ... and moved on. 'Tell me, what do you think about China? Do you and your Utopians admire what's going on there?'

'For what it's worth, a lot of net denizens I trust are worshippers.'

Joss shook his head. 'You can't trust a chat-room.'

'Well, they tell me the Great Peace brings liberty, equality and techno-green solutions to the benighted, they say you don't lose anything by joining the sphere, you retain national and cultural freedoms, and they kind of hero-worship the mysterious person or persons behind it all ... But I have to say, the precedents are lousy.'

So they spoke of the newest superpower, currently busy painting half the globe red. And then Fiorinda's tour of Teesside (Fiorinda was a great favourite with Joss). North Cornwall; sailing; the hope of better weather this summer. Before Ax left Joss was in a better humour (though slightly piqued that he'd not been asked for more largesse), and had accepted the Commissioners' cypher. They parted friends: or at least, more like friends than they had been for a while.

The combatants made their preparations; the people of England formed opinions based on unshakeable prejudice, or else had none. To most of the London Reich's youth culture – a numerous community of crew, admin, rockstar and related offspring – the whole thing was a senseless mystery. But there were exceptions. Silver came to Brixton Hill, where she hadn't visited since that time she'd stayed the night, and argued with Marlon: away from surveillance, out on the warm, dusty street. Passers-by noted the young couple, isn't that Marlon and Silver? – and maybe wondered what it was about. This was SW2: no one turned to stare.

'We have to tell them,' hissed the girl with the silver-brown hair.

Marlon was like a hunted animal. 'You don't know my dad. You don't know what he might do, he'd do something horrible, disastrous and stupid.'

'*Fuck you.* I know Sage fucking better than you *ever* could. Time's running out, Mar, make up your mind. D'you want them to find out in the House?'

The sex had been nothing personal, the friendship self-interest, but there was a bond now all right. She was afraid she might never escape from it. The look in someone's eyes, the fucking stubborn pain in him when he glared at her. It was like touching naked metal when you've only handled the sheath.

'Okay,' said Marlon, staring at the dust, hating her. 'You win.'

'You too, bro,' said Silver, viciously. '*All* of that.'

Ax was in his office, clearing up neglected trivia. He was reading an impassioned handwritten note from William the cleaner, a demarcation dispute with the security crew, when Doug Hutton put his head round the door.

'Can Mar see you for a minute, Ax?'

'Yeah?' said Ax, 'huh? Of course, he can see me anytime.'

It was bad luck that Marlon's visit had been sabotaged. You get preoccupied by adult concerns, and next thing you know, shit, we let that precious time go by. Ax put the note aside, and tried to look inviting. A timid knock, then Marlon walked in, with Silver Wing beside him. They got themselves chairs, without speaking, and sat close together. Oooh boy, thought Ax, immediately. She's pregnant—

'How's it going, Ax?' said Silver, 'you know, the debate?'

'It's going to be okay, Silver.'

'*Really?*'

'Never in doubt.'

A slight exaggeration: the indicators were mixed. Respectable mediafolk (in the three nations, that is, and across the board of Crisis Europe) were dismissing the whole thing as idiotic, which was heartwarming. Close to home it was a mess. But Ax believed what he had told Joss Pender. We'll take our licks, a little public humiliation, the CCM will get their Neurobomb forum, and everything will be fine.

'That's good,' croaked Marlon.

'You two wanted to talk it over? Something you wanted to ask?'

'N-no,' whispered Silver, gripping the folds of her nut-brown homespun skirt in grubby, childish hands. 'It's something we have to tell you.'

She's pregnant. Fuck. Silver Wing was nearly fourteen, a woman according to the customs of her people, the Counterculture. Not in English or Welsh law ... What a moment, and Mary is going to be *livid*. Then Ax was disgusted with himself. This is no time to be thinking about our reputation: the child's going to have a baby.

'Okay,' he said, gently. 'C'mon, you're not in trouble. Tell me.'

Marlon looked to Silver. Silver looked back, hard and long, and then at Ax.

'He's been questioned by the police.'

Chills ran down Ax's spine. 'Oh, yeah? About what?'

'About my dad, mostly,' whispered Marlon. 'I thought it was the police.'

'Wait a moment,' said Ax. 'I'd better get Fiorinda down here, and your dad, Mar. It sounds as if they should hear this.'

The teenagers told their story. The day that Marlon had disappeared for eight hours, he and Silver had been in Hyde Park. They'd been rounded up in a group of Reich youth debauchees and taken to Southampton Row for a severe telling-off about the evils of alcohol, and the wickedness of drinking it in public. So far, good. Sections of the Metropolitan Police had never come back from their 'green nazi occupation' mode; they could be obstructive, possibly they picked on the Reich's youngsters. But the kids had been outside the Park's sanctioned campground, and public drinking is against the law. Quite rightly, in Ax's opinion. Then Marlon had been told he had to see someone about another matter. He'd been driven to a private house, not far, he wasn't sure of the location, and interviewed. He'd been very scared, because he thought the cops had found out that he'd committed underage sex with Silver. Which was statutory rape and he might go to prison, and it would cause a stink.

In the end they'd taken him back to the police station and he'd been allowed to go with the warning that next time he was in trouble his father would hear about it. He'd just been glad to escape. It was only when he talked to Silver, who'd waited for him, that his head had cleared and he'd realised something weird had been going on.

'Why didn't you tell us about this right away?' asked Sage, who had stayed on his feet, propped against Ax's desk, his arms folded.

'Because I knew why they'd done it,' said Marlon, looking up at his father. 'They wanted me to tell you, so you'd g-go berserk about them questioning me. And then you'd be out of control and get f-fucked over in the debate—'

Ouch.

'You should have told us,' said Ax. 'But you're doing fine now . . . What made you think it was about underage sex, Marlon?'

The boy coloured up, and looked at the floor. 'The questions they asked.'

'It's because of what we did,' whispered Silver, twisting her skirt in agony. 'All of this, the debate and everything, is because of what we did.'

Fiorinda had been watching her handmaid with a very *Fiorinda* expression of cool compassion. She got up and went to kneel by Silver's chair and took her hands. 'Silver, little girl, listen to me. If you think it was wrong to fuck Marlon, then you shouldn't have done it. But whatever you have seen, you've only seen it. You haven't changed anything. Trust me, I would know.' She held the girl's eyes until some of the alarming, drained and white-lipped tension left Silver's face.

'All right?'

'All right,' whispered Silver.

'You know what,' Fiorinda decided, 'I'm going to take you home. We'll get the guardhouse to call a car, Doug will drive us to Reading, and I'll talk to your mother. You'll stay with her, on the festival site until the debate is over, all right?'

'All right.'

Fiorinda left with Silver. Ax and Sage cut the rest of the interrogation short, not to put Marlon through the same experience twice. When they were done they were both very angry, but they did not show it, and Marlon – hopefully – was reassured that his dad would not be running amok in the House of Commons. Marlon's travel plans were already made. Sage had decided to send him back to Wales rather than have him in London for the show trial: a decree Mar had accepted, they now realised, with suspicious docility. Sage and his dad went upstairs. A little later Sage came back to the office and sat down, hands clasped between his knees, staring into space.

'You were right,' said Ax. 'We should have given him a 24/7 bodyguard.'

'Bodyguards all round, yeah ... I got through to Cwm Gared.'

Mary Williams, Sage's long-ago ex-girlfriend, was likely to be very angry. She'd always claimed that Sage'd made Marlon a terrorist target by getting himself mixed up with Ax Preston.

'What did she say?'

Sage looked at the strong, shapely artist's hands that had been crippled paws. 'Mary says ... if I need her she'll get on-line to testify for the defence.'

'Wow.'

Sage nodded. Wow indeed. 'I told her it's not that kind of trial.'

They relapsed into silence, each of them lost in thought: images from that video, calling up other images, things that you've lived with for years, and suddenly you can't stand it anymore. No use talking about it. Soon the 'debate' would be over, vanished like the miasma it was, and they would get back to work. Ax felt that the Bodhisattva would be okay. There was that core of peace in Sage which nothing could touch ... He was trying to keep the depth of his own emotional crisis to himself. 'Well,' he said. 'Despite Silver, we're going to win this.'

'Yeah,' Sage agreed, wearily. 'I know.'

On the sixteenth of June Fiorinda was in Liverpool, on Volunteer Initiative business. She saw Alan Cosby, the waste-plastics magnate, at his stark but central offices in Ranleagh Street, and traded a popstar-royal geisha hour for a commitment that Cosby's would support the Open Gates scheme; in practical ways to be determined. They were old friends (that is, Fiorinda had come begging at this doorstep more than once before). She wore the smoky-opal frock from Hollywood, so she looked like the Fiorinda of the dictatorship. The interview was recorded for regional tv, and broadcast live on the net. And it was a damn fine change, in spite of everything, to talk to someone for whom the future looked bright, even if she did have to suppress thoughts about the cold equations of supply and demand.

Mr Cosby shook her hand warmly as they parted. 'Ax Preston took the beggars off my streets,' he announced, 'gave them a life, and gave me back my self-respect, because I don't have to step over the buggers no more. Now, while you're at it, there's young woman who plays the didgeridoo outside St John's—'

The nation's sweetheart laughed. 'Sorry, Alan. She's not a drop-out, she's a working musician, wild and free. We don't clear those away. Offer her a job yourself, if you think she'll take it.'

Fade out to Mr Techno-Green Recycling Magnate of the Year sitting on the footpath, at ease in dusty sunshine: finding out about the different styles of Western and Eastern Arnhem Land from the young woman with the didgeridoo. Business as usual among the citizens of Utopia; thank you Mr Cosby.

The sleeper sabotaged her by breaking down at Crewe, but she was on her way again at dawn the next morning, leaving less hurried passengers placidly waiting to see if their train, which was having H problems, would blow sky-high; along with a portion of Cheshire. A patchwork of power sourcing, including wood-burning steam at one point, slowed her journey. She stood on platforms and watched the crowds as the great casket of the Palace of Westminster was opened, on National Rail tv. They were very quiet. It dawned on her that many of these shabby, ordinary-looking Crisis-years commuters could not have *voted* for Ax (as once they had voted for him) if this had been a referendum. They were debt-casualties, bonded labour, neo-feudal serfs. We will get the Bill repealed, she thought. That is something my prince will do for you. You will be free again.

At Watford Junction she saw the opening salvos; part traditional, part improv. The President and his Minister, Ax in his best red suit, Sage in his blue-dyed leathers from the glory days (altered for a slimline figure) took their seats at the table. The back benchers looked down; the front benchers surrounded the narrow pit like gentlemen-bruisers, plus a few tough, stylish ladies, jostling at a prize fight. The Member for Teddington – let his name be expunged from memory – proposed the motion of censure, and the first speech began, to roars and grumbles.

There was a ban on digital technology on Fiorinda's last train, and problems with live reception on the Underground. At two in the afternoon, having ditched her overnight bag, she walked across St Stephen's Green under a cool and clouded sky. The turf where the bonfire had been looked as if it had been there for always. She made her way through the quiet crowds to the Gallery entrance. Here she was saluted and ushered upstairs into a hushed, avid, VIP crush. There was a roped-off section for Ax's close associates. She snuck in at the end of a row, beside Rob.

'How's it going?'

'It's okay,' said Rob, eyes front, rigid as a gun-dog. 'It's okay.'

'It's been horrible,' whispered Dora, leaning past her lover, showing the whites of her eyes. 'Horrible but *good*. It's going great. You need a bead, here—'

Ax Preston had never used speech-writers in the dictatorship – something people found hard to believe now. He had no tricks of oratory, except the ones carried over from his other profession, such as his sense of rhythm, his effortless timing, his instinctive, peerless feel for an audience. Those who knew had warned Greg and Jack: *don't let Ax speak*. If you let him speak, you're screwed. Work on Aoxomoxoa, who has all that dirty washing, and a famously short fuse . . . Faud Hassim's team, in the other corner, had rehearsed their principals furiously: where the worst questions would come from, who was undecided, the dangerous special interests. They had provided cunning plans and fallback positions to ensure that Ax took the floor while Sage knew when to duck—

All of this had gone by the board. The PM and his allies must have been inwardly rubbing their hands in glee for about the first hour, because it had seemed that the leaders of the Reich had no idea how to protect themselves. Quite right, Ax admitted. We didn't know what we were doing when we agreed to help the President track down those occult terrorists. No more than we did when joined the government's popstar Think Tank, when this whole thing began. We blundered into a situation out of stupidity and vanity, and then we were in too deep to get out.

Yeah, said Sage: we knew the Lavoisiens were sincere in their beliefs. They'd been forced into suicide-warrior terrorism by righteous desperation, and we knew that when we shot them down.

Asked to confirm that the terrorists had been training a 'Fat Boy Candidate', a psychic monster of unimaginable power, Ax said they'd known there was no 'Fat Boy Candidate' among the occultists when they went into Lavoisier. They'd just had to get Fiorinda out, they were afraid she'd get caught in friendly fire when the government raid happened. Implored by a friendly questioner to condemn the faked 'video', Ax responded that it wasn't faked that much. Sage said, and what did you think we were doing up in Yorkshire, that time? We were killing people, it looks nasty: now you've seen us doing it, dunno why it makes such a big difference.

Were they admitting the secret camera footage was substantially accurate?

Yeah, we thought so.

Had they fired on anyone who was unarmed?

We don't honestly know.

Did the President and his Minister take *pleasure* in dealing out death?

'There are people who will not pick up a lethal weapon,' said Ax. 'I wish that was me. As to whether it upsets me to kill someone, that doesn't make them less dead. I'm efficient, I've taken pleasure in that . . . Insh'allah, I'm not going to do it again. Tell the truth, I'm grateful to the Black Dragon for the shove up the arse. You'll never entirely get rid of violence, it's part of life. But our fight for survival is turning into something else, and we all know it. It's time to think hard about which traits we want to encourage in this new thing, and which traits we want to keep down. Initial conditions are crucial: we're the parents, we've got to be careful what kind of a start we give to this baby world.'

This was Mr Preston's longest speech.

Parliamentary convention was not much observed. Most of the Elected Members, tracked down, bussed and bullied here for the occasion by one side or the other, had never been in the building before; they didn't know the protocol. But the chamber grew quiet, sober and concentrated, as on the best occasions in its active career. It became evident that Ax and Sage were not self-destructing; not at all. They had spotted the one straight path and they were sticking to it. The subject was violence, the ultimately futile solution of violence that had haunted England since Dissolution. Ax and Sage, unprofessional soldiers, were the expert witnesses Parliament had called to offer their experience.

By the time Fiorinda arrived the bad guys were on the ropes. Jack Vries had launched a blatant cross-examination of the former Aoxomoxoa, and nobody had tried to stop him because it looked like desperate tactics. Does Mr Pender agree he has a history of uncontrolled aggression? That as 'Aoxomoxoa', the king of the lads, before Dissolution, public outrage was his trademark?

'Yes.'

'Rapine and pillage are the signs of the berserker,' mused Jack, consulting his notes. 'Have you ever raped anyone, Sage?'

'Yes.'

'Did she prosecute?'

Sage shook his head. 'No.'

'Well, we shan't accuse you either,' said Jack, with a courtroom flourish, 'nor count that a confession of a serious crime. You're wise not to deny it, considering the media reportage of your liaison with Mary Williams. Rape with grievous assault was quite a hobby of yours, wasn't it? Could you explain how a rapist, and, may I add, a former heroin addict, came to achieve the Zen Self?'

The House stirred and muttered. Mr President Ax sat back, mysteriously passive, and let his friend take the punches—

'*Achieve* is technical, Jack. It means you're there because you reached a point where you will be there, an' fusion is outside time. I don't know what would happen to someone else: the science is neutral. What happened to me is ongoing. I would say it's hardly begun an' I don't know if it has an end.'

Whoever told you you could make me take a swing at you was mistaken, sunshine. The sad truth is, half the time when I was nineteen I wasn't out of control. I was worse than that. I used to hit people cool as ice: because I felt like it.

Jack nodded. 'Ongoing. A process that might be reversed, and isn't that what happened in the desert? You invaded a place of power, in a state of unwisdom and unpreparedness, as you have confessed. We have been told there was no occult evil at Lavoisier, it was all mere delusion. But I don't believe I'll take my opinion on these affairs from US internal security sources. The forces of magic are beyond their understanding, and I can show that in fact you and Ax became—'

Jack opened his notes, and commenced to explain what a *werewolf* is, very cogently: dismissing the common errors, and referring to learned sources. Might he draw the House's attention to their slates, where they would see a certified copy of the relevant passage from that notorious 'Royal Academy' interview, including damning details excluded from the broadcast version—

Uproar.

Consternation. Suddenly, out of nowhere, they were dealing with an accusation that could put Ax and Sage out of here, and on trial for their lives: because magic is real, and witchcraft, the hard stuff, is a capital crime.

Faud Hassim, who had a seat in the Second Chamber in his role as Countercultural Adviser, leapt up, demanded to be recognised (which Jack didn't deny him) and urged that both Houses affirm that any attempt to weaponise natural magic by any means, by state, opposition group or private persons, was anathema: thus turning the censure against Ax and Sage on its head. There was loud and prolonged applause, almost drowning the boos and hisses—

The session closed at six in the evening. The debate was to run for three days, like a test match. Tomorrow it would start later and finish later; but not too late. The suits had been warned that heroic hours and a bunker atmosphere would favour the rockstars. Fiorinda went down to the floor, her presence cutting a path through the crowd, to where the steps of the sanctuary would have been, when these moots were held in the mediaeval Chapel of St Stephen.

'I feel as if I should have quartered oranges, and brought fresh towels.'

'You're not supposed to be here,' said Ax, sternly. 'You're supposed to be in Liverpool, protector of the poor.'

'How could I resist?' Fiorinda smiled for the cameras, of which there were plenty. 'This little place may not be much, but we're fond of it, we English. It's nice to see it functional again.' She put her arm around Sage, an unusual public gesture that made him grin at her and murmur, *nice;* but she felt his weariness—

'You were *great*, Jack. Terrific stuff, all those *references*. Well played, sir.'

The Few left the scene in a body, a little crowd of beautiful people in unconsciously show-off clothes, rockstar clothes: walking away from a fight together, intact but battered, as how often before. '*Did* I tell you?' enquired big George. 'Do not fuck with them!' The boss hung his head, mortified. It was so bad, it was funny. 'I know, I know. I have learned my lesson . . . But it was fucking years ago!'

'They never forget. Hell hath no fury like a sandwich.'

'You *won't* do it again, will you?' Cack insisted, anxiously.

'He won't,' promised Ax. 'I'll see to it. I can get very jealous.'

Others were less struck by the humour of the situation. 'Werewolves!' snarled Verlaine, with uncharacteristic venom. 'How I'd love to get my teeth in that bastard's throat—'

Fiorinda tucked her arm into his. 'Cool it, son; and look happy. There's nothing to worry about. We've conceded a goal, yeah, but we've had the best of the play and it's not even half-time.'

On the second day Fiorinda turned up in the Countercultural benches beside Faud: neat and spruce in her old dove-grey trouser suit. (The green-austerity 'best clothes' of the Triumvirate made a very good impression.) She was formally spied as a stranger, and defended her position, correctly addressing Mr (Acting) Speaker, not the protestor. She was Mr President Preston's deputy and therefore at present the titular head of the CCM, with a theoretical, though never claimed, seat in the Reformed House of Lords. If she chose to use her privilege to secure a place today on the other side of the Lobby, she certainly wasn't alone! Thus began the second act, in which

Fiorinda's performance was inspired. She touched the hearts of House of Commons anoraks by her attendance to the forms, and when she didn't know, she made it up. She bounced up and down like a Jack-in-the-Box, she made elaborate use of sarcasm; she employed all the beloved jargon.

Early in the session she dropped the bombshell claim that she had not been an innocent bystander in the Lavoisier raid. If Ax and Sage were to be censured, the nation's sweetheart must suffer the same. This caused an upset. Someone from the Second Chamber back benches wanted clarification, took part in what way? Did the Right Honourable young lady handle an assault rifle? He wished he could have seen it. Or did she use her bare hands? How could she have had anything to do with the killing while she was a helpless prisoner?

'Mr Speaker,' said Fiorinda, 'we know that this is a world where time and space and material constraint, are not what they seem. I cannot tell the Honourable Lord how I took part, it is a mystery. I only know that I was there, with my rescuers, in all that they did to save me from destruction.'

The Chamber was momentarily still. The PM, on the front bench with his Cabinet cronies, arms folded, looking like a bull with a sore head, gave Jack a sign to let this pass ... Don't touch Fiorinda. Another question, from a green lady aristo of goodwill. Can the Right Honourable Ms Slater tell us, is she then also a *werewolf*?

Laughter.

Fiorinda responded (observing the forms) that she did not know. Perhaps Mr Speaker had another secret identity in mind for her, from his magical menagerie.

An elected Member of the Commons thanked Ms Slater for explaining her Houdini-like prowess so fully, and had a question about the amnesty Ax had secured for the surviving Lavoisiens. Had this life-saving negotiation gone unrecorded by the famous secret cameras? Or had it landed on the cutting-room floor due to artistic license on the part of the so-called 'martyr' behind this pitiful farrago of a crypto-neo-conservative stalking horse, sponsored not by the people of the US but by a ruthless paranational Babylonian conspiracy between the most brutal end of the entertainment industry and the weapon-mongers—

Outcry, uproar. Many voices defending the Lavoisier terrorists, yelling that it was Ax Preston who was the lackey of the evil empire. Many others shouting them down, waxing contemptuous of the Green Fat Cats' censure—

'If he was a suicide warrior,' shouted someone in the back benches, 'how come he's not dead? The Black Dragon could only be a reliable witness at a séance!'

Order! Order!

At ten-thirty the session broke up in a mill, all kinds of people trying to get next to Ax and Sage and Fiorinda: mediafolk scuffling and elbowing. The Countercultural rebels were loud in their elation. It was over, the government was creamed, the interactive-tv-vote and division tomorrow a formality. Jack had shot himself and Greg in the foot with that ill-judged, over-the-top 'werewolf' ploy. 'Tomorrow we'll finish them,' declared Faud, mopping his brow – the evening had grown sultry and close in the poorly climate-conditioned Chamber. 'We'll sink the Neurobomb without a trace, and we'll *pulverise* the bastards!'

'They said Fiorinda must not be involved,' muttered Greg Mursal to one of the elders of his Cabinet. 'She wasn't to be anywhere near the fucking House, her name never mentioned, or they wouldn't play ball. D'you think she— she *disobeyed* them? Or was it a set-up?' The veteran clapped Lord Mursal gently on the shoulder. 'You're learning, Greg. You're learning!'

Photocalls and soundbites, in the Lobby and then outside, in the airless swelter before a cloudburst. Ax and Sage were staying to socialise, magnanimous in victory: it was necessary. The Few were returning to Lambeth in a body, but they lingered too long for Fiorinda. She slipped through the meshes, avoiding both friends and enemies (it's a knack) and walked away alone in the dark, feeling depressed. So we won the field, terrific, and it wasn't even hard. But what the public will remember, what will come back to haunt us, is the werewolves smear: stand-out human interest, well, monster interest, in a waste of anoraks scoring obscure points off each other . . .

These people are not amateurs. They know what they're doing.

She was halfway to Westminster Tube when someone caught up with her. It was Joe Muldur, NME roving reporter of long ago.

'Hey, Fiorinda!'

'Hi.'

Not all journalists are insensitive prats. He fell into step beside her, and she didn't object to the company. 'How's life, Joe? I haven't seen you for a while.'

'You'll see more of me over the summer. I'll be on your fabulous trail.'

'On tour? You haven't moved on to higher things?'

'Hahaha. Like the lovely Dian? No fucking thanks.' Joe glanced at the lady, strangely alone and sad after that triumph. 'How are *they* shaping up for the season? The tiger and wolf love affair, is it in a good phase?'

'Oh, you know, as usual,' said Fiorinda gloomily. 'On again, off again. They like to keep things interesting. Well, I'm going this way.'

They'd reached the Underground. 'I'm off back to the House,' confessed Joe. 'It's an expenses party, can't turn down a free drink, it's against my religion. I just wanted to say . . . to say: You guys were *brilliant* in there.'

'Yeah. Only, unfortunately, this country hasn't been governed by Parliament since about the Napoleonic wars.'

As she headed down the steps she knew that he stood looking after her with puzzled sympathy and even pity, across the gulf that separated Fiorinda now from real life, real music, and everything that matters.

Never, never back your enemy into a corner, unless you are prepared to do one of two things: either kill him or turn him. As he sat chatting with the PM's in-crowd, Ax was acutely aware that he had offended against this law, not once but twice. He didn't see how he could have done otherwise. He'd had to get the family out of Wallingham, and he'd had to come out on top in the debate. But he could not make a friend of Greg Mursal, and he sure as fuck did not want to start a civil war—

His failsafe arrangements seemed ridiculous, now that the day was won. He had never been in that kind of danger . . . They called me back because they didn't want me running around loose, he thought. They don't want to destroy *me*, they want to destroy my power and influence, and keep my legend for their own use. But I knew that.

This is what I knew I was coming back to. I tried the alternative, arbitrary rule, and it was hateful. The country's stable, massive public works, sustainable development, in many ways this England is a success. I have to work with the gangsters, that's the only way to get the human rights back, while holding onto the success. Soon, hopefully, it'll be a better set in Westminster. I must do this.

He stuck to mineral water, slightly maliciously, knowing how this annoys alcohol-drinkers, and felt for Sage, who was downing pints for both of them, while getting coldly furious. The big cat detested playing the role of Joss Pender's son, he wasn't flattered to be accepted by this caste. Please don't get drunk, Sage . . . From another part of the bar (the big room beautifully redecorated in nouveau William Morris, and set about with planters of living flowers) Faud Hassim and his pals cast smouldering glances, like lovers betrayed. Ax would have to explain to those idiots, the President *must* schmooze with the PM, otherwise what the fuck use am I?

Thoughts of the rock and roll stage were in his mind. He had realised recently that he missed the Chosen Few very much. Playing guitar is like breathing. Jor and Shay and Mil, they were my instrument, with them I made my best music, and I'll never have that again—

A supper party was proposed, at Jack's place, no one having eaten dinner. Mr Preston and Mr Pender called Fiorinda to tell her they would be even later, and found themselves in a car alone with Lord Vries: Jack facing them in the cavernous and leather-scented rear section. They passed smoothly north and westwards and reached Hyde Park in a black downpour. Ax glimpsed the stained, crumbling tower of the derelict London Hilton, once the lair of England's first rockstar President, the monster known as Pigsty Liver. Saul Burnet. He had not thought of the Pig in years. Jack's pale eyes were watching him, and he knew he was a hostage again.

'Ain't you afraid to be alone with us?' wondered Sage.

The Wiccan scholar blinked. 'Oh, haha . . . I don't think you'll transform tonight. There is no full moon, and this is central London, not a locus of evil.'

'You don't say. Well, as long as you're happy.'

The great swathe of Park Lane was in the process of being narrowed to post-Dissolution proportions; they left the car at a landscaped garage in the midst of the deconstruction. Only emergency services and diplomat plates were allowed into Central London sidestreets. 'I won't flout the law with the king of England in my care,' said Jack, humorously. As their driver ran around to provide umbrellas a van pulled up and half-a-dozen armed, uniformed guards got down. 'I'm not usually so grand,' Jack explained, 'but tonight I can't take chances!'

The rain had almost stopped. They walked into Mayfair: three tall men wielding folded umbrellas, followed by a troop of armed bravos. Ax was disoriented, maybe because he hadn't eaten since noon, and had drunk only water. The scene seemed Victorian, Mediaeval, an amalgam of both: this could not be the present. If Sage had not been stalking dourly beside him, radiating negative energy, he'd have been sure he was dreaming.

Jack's place was in Berkeley Square, one of those flat-fronted Georgian mansions of the innermost city so prized by the new élite. A wedge of golden-white light spilled, extravagantly, from the shell-ceilinged porch to the pavement. 'I have yet to hear a nightingale,' said Jack, pointing to the shadowy masses of the gardens. It was obviously a favourite line. For once Ax caught a touch of the native Flemish in his voice, a hint of Jack's immigrant status, the naïve pleasure of someone who has fought hard to belong. 'I hope you enjoyed your Eid, by the way, Sir. The Islamic holidays are very quiet, aren't they? Inward-turned, unlike the open, public, life-affirmation of the great Pagan rites.'

'Very unlike,' agreed Ax.

They'd had time to do some probing before the debate: sufficient that Ax was now certain that Jack Vries himself had been behind what happened to Marlon. Greg would have known about it too, of course. Those tactics, supposed to be rooted out, were endemic, and if you called them on it, they just picked some scapegoat and shoved them out to take the rap ... He wondered about the personal bond between the two men; it didn't strike him as sexual. Will Jack's rehabilitation be complete? Will he get his Cabinet post? Or was that conditional on the result of the debate?

'Maybe you should install a few,' suggested Sage. 'In concealed cages.'

'Hahaha. Caged nightingales? That's against the law, Sage!'

They had reached the brightly lit steps of number 50, but the other guests had not arrived. 'Well, it was a lively performance. You play to win, Sirs, and so do I. But off the pitch I hope we're going to be good friends!'

Ax looked up. There were more lights inside. Servants. Suddenly he knew (something in Jack's tone, complacent, sly—) that this house was where Marlon had been questioned. He saw the room where it had happened. A floor of red and cream tiles, dark brocade curtains. A white woman in a severe coat and skirt, not quite uniform, her features like holes in dough, faced the boy across a small table. Jack wasn't in sight, he was listening and watching elsewhere. The woman's voice was low and menacing, too low for Ax to make out the words, but he knew what she was saying. *Has your father ever interfered with you?* Marlon answered, staring back, damning her eyes, *Only when there was nothing on the telly –*

The vision lasted no time. It vanished and he didn't know where it had come from. From his imagination, probably. Jack Vries was saying 'good friends' with a smile of comfortable superiority. A veil of thin scarlet swamped Ax's field of vision. He punched the smug puppetmaster, hard and accurately, in the throat—

It would have been better if it had been Sage who'd lost it. The former Aoxomoxoa was a seasoned public bruiser who knew how to land a smack on some annoying bastard for maximum spectacle and no serious damage. Ax had never hit anyone in his life before he went to Yorkshire, and learned to do it so as to maim or kill. Jack went down, the guards rushed up. Two of them crouched over their master.

'Mr Preston,' said one of the other men, urgently, 'you should leave, Sir.'

'What—?'

'Get out of here, I'm not kidding—'

Sage knelt, and touched Jack's face and throat. The scholar was breathing, but it didn't look good. 'Sage, you got to get Ax away,' hissed one crouching guard, and the other nodded violently ... Sir! cried the rest of them, starting to panic. Get Ax th' fuck out of this! Ax and Sage stared at each other. Dear God, what have I done? A car had entered the square: someone less scrupulous than Jack about the byelaws, maybe the Prime Minister inside. Upper caste voices and ringing footsteps approached from Bruton Street.

'I think the guys are right,' said Sage. 'We should leave. Sort the details later.'

They hurried, heads down, until the all-night streetlighting of Piccadilly made them double back: but that was their big mistake. There was no discreet escape route, no back alleys left open to intruders in this nest of privilege, and an outcry had begun. They hit voices, broken-ants-nest activity, flashlights, the affront of sirens and emergency vehicles. Sage'd had thoughts of vaulting the railings and hiding under the bushes in the gardens until the hue and cry passed, but there were police shouts, lights and movement in there. Hunting us down already, well that clarifies the situation. The rain, which had become a downpour again, was their only shelter. They ran up one street and down another, through waves of honeysuckle and jasmine scent escaped from secret gardens. *Shite*, what a fucking neighbour-hood to choose. They kept hitting the concrete defences around the arse of Grosvenor Square, where there was no resident Ambassador but the fort was still standing. Either that or some other embassy's armoured back yard, and are they sleeping, are they hell.

Try again, more dead ends, we're screwed, shit, this is a rat trap—

Crouched between the bins in a narrow basement area, Ax could feel, a heartbeat away, the moment that he needed to reach, the moment *before* he had taken that terrible action. The rain hailed on him. At the end of the area a small flight of steps led to an ivied, wrought-iron gate. The look on Fiorinda's face as she turned and walked away, in the lights of Parliament Square. Oh, Fiorinda, oh god, I'm sorry—

'Mr Preston?' whispered a shadow, seeming clad all in glimmering white.

Ax was in his office, a room where they often sat together in the new régime because the upper floor of the maisonette was mournful. Fiorinda was off somewhere. He was at his desk, knowing there was something very wrong because Silver Wing had told him so. Sage leaned by the window, in a characteristic pose. He was telling Ax, with finality, that he was leaving, it was over. 'When we were together before,' he said, 'in the dictatorship, I loved you, sure, but I didn't feel like this. It was okay in Paris, but now it gets in the way. It makes me ... It makes me not the right person to be your grand vizier, so I have to go. It's for the best, babe.'

He woke on a wave of heart-pounding horror, and lay for a moment in abject gratitude. It was a dream, *oh thank God*. He was dressed except for his suit jacket and shoes; lying on a thin mattress on the bare boards of a large, cool empty room. Sage was beside him, leaning against the wall by a window. Through a drift of muslin Ax could glimpse a courtyard, with trees and some kind of white pavilion. It seemed to be early morning, before full light. He sat up.

'Sage. I dreamed you were leaving me. *God*, that was horribly real.'

He pushed back the hair from his temples – he had a pounding headache – the dream insistent on being told. 'We were in my office, but there was something wrong with the room. You were saying that you were never in love with me before, just fuck buddies, for her sake, but now you were, and it meant you had to quit.'

Sage was looking at him strangely ... and with a hideous shock he knew that this was the room in the dream. 'Oh shit. It was a telepathy artefact, wasn't it? You were sitting there, like that, and that's just what you *are* going to tell me.'

'Ah, no!'

Sage dived back to the mattress and grabbed Ax in a fierce embrace. 'It's true, I feel differently, and it was okay in Paris, it was wonderful, but it doesn't fit back here, it makes it *fucking* hard to – to tell you what you should do. But I'm not going to quit, oh, no no no, never, never—'

They held each other like children, like babies too young to be ashamed, and other cold, shattering grey mornings gathered around, all the way back to the Hyde Park Massacre, and the allegiance forged there.

'Sage, where are we?'

'Ah—'

Where to begin, thought Ax, with sympathy. 'Don't worry, I remember what happened. I remember what I did ... It's just, I seem to have lost the last part.'

Sage kissed him on the brow and sat back, looking uneasy. Ax saw his suit jacket, in a soaked and crumpled heap, on the floor by the futon.

'Are we prisoners? Sage, *tell* me—'

'No, we're not prisoners, not s'far as I'm aware, but . . . you're not going to like this. We're inside 30 Charles Street.'

Memory returned. Maybe he was never going to remember the whole thing, only the snap of his fist connecting, and then fragments, pounded by the rain; and here's one of them, two scimitars crossed under a shock-headed palm tree—

'Ah, *shit.*'

'Hahaha. I'm glad you're still thinking like a statesman.'

Ax picked up his best suit jacket and shook it out. It was cold and clammy, water-stained and smeared with dirt. He looked around for his shoes.

'What are we going to do?'

'Well, Sah.' Sage grinned, suddenly light-hearted in this void. 'This is what I've figured out so far. We're going to say thank you nicely to Prince Al-whatsisface and his staff, leave Saudi territory as unobtrusively as possible, get ourselves back to Fiorinda, and instigate Plan B.'

Fiorinda had been at Snake Eyes in Lambeth, having an unpoisoned drink and a nice spliff among friends, when her baby went over the edge. She spent the first thirty-six hours after the Berkeley Square incident looking calm for the cameras, saying things as anodyne as the situation would bear (!), and cursing herself *furiously* for leaving them to cope with the suits alone. Sage had been okay, just dumb misery, but she had fucking known that Ax had about a quarter of a hair-trigger left before he snapped.

She knew they hadn't been caught. She wouldn't have believed anything the police told her, in their solemn voices of awed dismay, but she trusted her instincts. She set certain arrangements in motion, severed herself from contact with the Few, and waited, with a strange feeling of lightness, as if something terrible had been averted; not committed. On the second morning she went down to Brixton market, with Doug for a bodyguard, and while she was buying vegetables a woman shrouded from head to toe in black silk slipped a message into her hand.

That afternoon she was at Battersea Arts Centre, giving her rock guitar 'master class' as if nothing was wrong. The group comprised twenty-four youngsters and three mature students. Most were in b-loc: seven of them, including the boy in the wheelchair and the autistic girl with her Mentor Carer, were real South Londoners, present in the flesh. Fiorinda sat on the stage, her foot on a rest, unruly dark red curls tumbling over her face, and attempted to show them how she would take a phrase (it was from 'Stonecold') and make it the basis of a solo. *You have left the . . . babies stone cold.* 'I'm sorry, I can't help the odd terms, I was brought up very strangely: but it's those five notes, you're using the pentatonic scale, you make it fly, but you don't ever forget where you began—'

The students watched her left hand in close-up, then a single spot caught the dancing gleam of her gold-braided ring as she broke into demonstration: and the viewpoint pulled out, her fingers leaping up and down the neck of the old Martin. The armed police at the back of the hall were engrossed. Maybe she ought to suggest they bring guitars . . . She looked to the side, the music dying, and tugged the narrow screen on her headset out of the way. One of the centre staff had come quietly to the wings. She set the guitar down.

'Excuse me.'

In scuffed, utilitarian darkness she was told that someone was waiting for her at the back entrance; and spoke by radiophone to Doug Hutton. The Battersea Arts Centre woman, stiff in the face, looked scared to death: she didn't say anything. Fiorinda didn't say much either, better not; except that she asked Doug could he wait a minute or two. Doug said yes he could, just about.

She returned to the stage and looked out at her audience; sorry, class. Thirty-seven people, counting the police: seen worse. What happened to the proverbial dog? The students' curious, respectful eyes were fixed on her, all of them awed and dismayed by the current turn of events, except for Ira, the autistic girl, who didn't know anything had happened. 'I want to do something different for a moment,' said Fiorinda, with a calm little grin. 'And then I'm going to take a short break.'

She stood, hands by her sides, and sang, pure and strong.

> *As sweet Polly Oliver*
> *Lay musing in bed*
> *A sudden strange fancy*

Came into her head
Nor father nor mother
Shall make me false prove
I'll go for a soldier
And follow my love . . .

And so goodbye, Utopia. She zipped up her guitar and shrugged it onto her shoulders; collected her tapestry bag, the other guitar case and a flat oblong shoulder-bag which held Sage's visionboard. Thus laden, she walked off. The police didn't make a move to stop her: Doug was waiting just out of sight.

They met Ax and Sage in a disused trailer-café on a layby on the A24. The fugitives had managed to shed their best suits. They were dressed as inconspicuously as possible, and wearing anonymous-looking digital head-masks. They stood up as Fiorinda came in and the masks vanished. She had that feeling of lightness, a lifting of something dreadful, as she went straight to Ax and took his hands.

'I've done some of the emergency things, not the most spectacular ones. Lucy's out of the country, Doug will have told you; Hobart's Funnies are dispersed. I knew you were all right. Well, d'you think you killed him?' She'd had no reliable information on Jack Vries' status. Possibly he was dead, or in a coma. Possibly he was fine, in hospital and lying low for his own protection.

'I don't know,' said Ax. 'I know I broke his neck.'

Fiorinda nodded, with satisfaction. She hugged him, and his head went down against her shoulder, briefly. Sage's blue eyes were saying everything's all right.

That night they were on Shoreham Beach, the long shingle bank that lies alongside Shoreham Harbour on the coast of Sussex, crammed with seaside houses. It had been a fashionable address, but was falling into dereliction from fuel starvation; not many inhabitants left. They were in the kitchen of a rambling stucco pad, once the home of a music biz demi-god who was a friend of Allie Marlowe's. The demi-god lived in New Zealand now (sensible man). A slight hitch had arisen. The wind and tide were contrary. The little boat that would take them out to the bigger boat in the Channel needed liquid marine fuel, a petrol-substitute which was controlled, and involved getting the right documents stamped. This hadn't worked out. But it was okay, it was fixed, the juice was on its way. It was about two a.m. The kitchen had a lot of glass around the walls, but the blinds were tightly closed. The light was electric, one white fluorescent tube.

Doug was leaving with them. Given the part he'd played in Plan B, and his role in the Reich, it was better he shouldn't stay behind. He was a solitary fellow, serial monogamist. He'd gone through a steady girlfriend every year or so since they'd known him, had no children that he was aware of; no other ties. He'd just revealed the contents of an extra suitcase he'd been jealously lugging around. It lay open on the demi-god's kitchen table, displaying a cache of firearms and ammunition. A classic .38 automatic pistol, a big spidery modern Mauser, a smaller Dutch plastic automatic, accurate enough, okay for a lady's hands; and then in the second layer of the chocolate box the heavier, more esoteric stuff. 'I know my new career as a pacifist hasn't had a very auspicious beginning,' said Ax. 'But—'

'I'm with Ax,' said Fiorinda. 'I've never used one of those, I don't know how, so it would be stupid for me to carry it around.'

'You don't have to know much, Fio, not with modern handguns. It's just point and squeeze.' Doug looked at Sage, hoping for support. 'Tell her, Sage.'

Sage shook his head, smiling.

'Look,' pleaded Doug, 'I'm only saying, in case of *emergencies*—'

The screen of Doug's radiophone, which was lying where they could all see it, began to flash. They had left a camera trap on the single road onto the beach. There were vehicles approaching, and no chance it was anything but trouble. Time to get out. Their only exit was by sea, have to try to get offshore without the engine. Before they could move they all heard, above the sound of the wind, a rush of many footsteps. Lights flashed through the blinds. They were surrounded. Some of the *federales* had come out by boat, and must have already captured the landing stage.

It turned out, later, that it was Faud Hassim who'd set the police on their trail. Maybe his feelings had been hurt, because he hadn't been on Ax's need to know list; which he'd discovered when the video story broke. Maybe he'd found out about Ax's more secret failsafe measures, and had felt mistrusted. Or he'd been upset by the way Ax schmoozed with the bad guys. Or maybe he'd decided, rationally, that his responsibility was to the CCM, and it would be dangerous and useless to protect Ax and his partners any further . . . Anyway, he had betrayed them.

The four in the kitchen looked at each other. For a moment all of them, even Fiorinda, felt that a last stand, Ned Kelly shoot-out was an excellent idea. Out in a blaze of glory, *fuck it*, why not? The moment passed. Ax sighed. 'You'd better shut that lot and try to think of somewhere to hide it, Doug. We'll have to go quietly.'

They thought they would be taken back to London. But they weren't.

PART TWO

SIX

Insanity

The deputation came at evening, to the suite of rooms designated for the Triumvirate. It comprised Lord Mursal and his ritual consort, Lady Anne Moonshadow, which meant business. Usually the sacred partnership had a low profile, as the general public might, quite wrongly, be disturbed by its religious significance . . . Mairead Culper of Glastonbury Council, Boris Ananthaswamy, the fusion scientist from Culham (his presence alarmed the three more than anything that had happened yet); and Faud Hassim. The visitors were soberly and formally dressed; they brought an entourage of assistants, secretaries; uniformed and armed security. The Triumvirate were alone, and wearing the clothes they'd been arrested in. They'd been travelling so light they'd had no choice in this, so far. They had been offered the opportunity to elect companions for their seclusion, or detention, or whatever this was – the situation was still raw and uncertain – from a list of approved names. They had declined.

They didn't know what had happened to Doug, and this preyed on them. He had been their last responsibility, and they had screwed him up.

Somewhere outside a warm midsummer day was drawing to its close. Bees were droning as they left the flowers of the lime trees by the croquet lawn; the herbs in the Elizabethan Knot Garden shed spice and astringency into the sun-soaked air. In this receiving room, deep inside the fortress of Wallingham, there was no natural light. The walls were hung from ceiling to floor in dark blue, with a woven pattern of the crescent moon and stars, which was repeated on a splendid, though worn, Vorsey carpet. The windows behind the draperies were shuttered and locked. They hadn't seen daylight since they were on the road to Shoreham, and it seemed likely, right now, that they would never see it again.

Greg Mursal ought to be happy. He had the Triumvirate where he had wanted them: isolated and under his control, in the lovely nouveau royal palace. But the circumstances were not auspicious. The Moon and Stars suite was not among the show-off rooms. It had been hastily prepared, and there were signs of dust and neglect, which added to the embarrassment.

Greetings were exchanged. The deputation treated President Ax in particular with a sorrowful, knowing deference that set Fiorinda's nerves crisping. She sat in a dark-blue armchair, and idly counted the woven stars (though a whisper of intuition told her she ought to save this small pleasure). They were told that Jack Vries was not dead but he might not live, there were no further details for the moment. As to Mr Preston's request for a personal call to President Fred Eiffrich—

Sometimes you have to lay that useless high card down. Ax's friends and associates would have been reasonably safe if he'd been free: they were in grave danger now. He'd had to try calling on the leader of the free world, he had no other recourse left.

'We've spoken to Mr McCall, and I'm afraid it's not going to be possible for you to speak with the President, Ax.'

Ax frowned. 'McCall?' He did not know the name. He had hoped they'd get to Hana Rosen, Fred's redoubtable Chief of Staff: a decent woman, no big fan of rockstars in politics, but someone who knew about the situation in England.

Greg nodded, exuding suppressed satisfaction. 'Yes. Denton McCall, acting deputy assistant Secretary of State. Apparently there's been a touch of palace politics going on in Washington that's been kept completely under wraps. It's amazing what you can do, this digital age, if no one breaks ranks. We're getting the real picture again now. It's not for you three to worry about.'

'I see,' said Ax.

The room, lined with stars and shadowed like midnight, rang with the silence that follows a shock you can't hide. So it was true. The forces of unreason had dispensed with electoral process. What's become of Fred? What about his niece, Kathryn Adams? Harry Lopez, the golden boy with the hot White House connections, did he get caught up in this? It was as if they'd heard of a shipwreck, far off on black, icebound seas. Did the unsinkable, beautiful monster really go down this time? Did our friends get to the lifeboats?

Boris Anathaswamy cleared his throat.

'We'd like to proceed to the matter in hand,' said the Prime Minister. 'The matter in hand ... Well, I don't have my Wiccan Consultant, but Boris is standing in, as our chief neurophysicist. We're lucky to have such an authority on call.'

Fiorinda's wandering attention was caught. She looked straight at Boris with a sudden, warm and dazzling smile. The scientist flinched, cleared his throat again, covering his mouth, and casting a longing glance at the double doors of the room. The guards stared woodenly back: no escape there. The Prime Minister and his consort looked expectant, and gravely resolute.

'Ahm, the condition is incurable.'

'Condition?' snapped Sage. 'What *condition*?'

'Commonly known as lycanthropy, the condition is a, not strictly a regression, but a, resurgence of the primitive, best recorded in Europe in the *berserkers*, naked outlaws, of Scandinavia. Men who are recognised as having become rabid animals; neurological outcasts ... Physical effects of neglected grooming, overgrown nails and hair, are the first heralds of actual transformation, often periodic. Allegedly linked to the lunar cycle, which we know to be potent in human psychic affairs. We also see cases like the Maréchal de Letz, public fame coupled with a secret reign of terror; where self-control is unimpaired, and witchcraft supports a façade of normalcy for years ... Compare the psychology of conscript war veterans, African child soldiers, any young males thrust suddenly into extreme violence: supernatural heroism and berserker feats followed by sociopathy, psychosis, moral and mental degeneration. Recent Crisis in Europe has brought a resurgence, well-attested cases. Final fugue indicates the condition has become irreversible. Damage will be found to the amyglyda, seat of emotional roots of humanity, and typically more than twenty-five per cent loss of brainstem tissue—'

'Yeah, we remember Jack's presentation,' Sage cut the babbling off: it was a kindness. Anathaswamy might have come here thinking he could keep a straight face, but he wasn't up to it. Sweat was standing on his face. 'Yer neuro isn't up to yer physics, Boris. Lose a quarter of the brainstem, you wouldn't get a berserker, you'd get a stroke victim struggling to breathe unaided—'

'Except where lycanthropy is involved,' said Lady Moonshadow, with a smile. 'An unbiased neurological scan will swiftly establish the facts, should you so wish.'

The three didn't look at each other. They took her smooth assurance, which told them – had they needed to be told – that they were beyond all legal process, that there would be no unbiased evidence, nor even the pretence of a trial, and dealt with it together, without a betraying glance. If anything disconcerted the deputation it was this eerie unity between the prisoners, this sense that the three were scripting everything, live. But a little unease was not going to deflect them from their course.

'The situation is this,' said Faud Hassim, in a low voice, eyes on the dusky carpet at his feet. 'The President, Mr Preston, is not guilty of assault, or attempted murder, nor manslaughter, nor of causing grievous bodily harm. He is very, very sick, he is becoming like a ravening animal—'

'He is guilty of witchcraft,' said Mairead, sternly. 'A capital crime.'

Anne Moonshadow spoke again. 'We offer, if preferred, a painless assisted suicide by lethal injection. Should Ax wish, or should his wise partners so advise him, we can provide expiatory rites, in the manner of his death, to restore his human nature. In either case the Countercultural Movement will be freed from the taint of guilt by association, and there will be no further repercussions.'

Ah. Nice work if you can trust them, Faz—

'What happens to my partners?' said Ax.

The old lady shook her head. 'That's not for you to know, Mr Preston.'

'There wouldn't be any ugly publicity,' offered Greg, elbows on his knees: eager and blunt. 'No more show trials, eh? It would be quiet and dignified, very private. Close family with you, if you like.'

The deputation waited, gazing at these fallen idols. The two men in their mid-thirties, both tall, one a gangling blue-eyed giant; both looking older than their years, worn, unshaven, a little grubby ... And the young woman a decade their junior, her mixed-race frizzy curls tangled, the unconventional beauty quenched. How quickly the physical splendour of power departs when the mandate has passed on.

Ax drew a breath, leaned back in his chair, and said something, evenly and almost cheerfully. Nobody on the PM's side recognised the language: for a moment they all looked pretty scared.

'Don't worry, it's not a spell. It's Greek. I said, "the appropriate penalty would be to pay me a stipend for the rest of my life, to support me in the criticism of individual citizens of Athens . . ." It's what Socrates suggested to his judges, in the blasphemy trial, 399 BCE. Death was the proposed sentence then, too.'

'He'll be right,' said the President's Minister, helpfully. 'Check it out. He knows his Classics. He had a stack of Ancient Greek and Latin stuff on his chip, the one the Mexican kidnappers took out of his head. If you have one of those implants for a while, a lot of the information gets transferred to the grey matter.'

'The Athenian judges expected you to bid high for your punishment,' supplied Fiorinda. 'To show a proper feeling. Socrates made them an offer, instead.'

'Will you two please stop talking about me as if I'm not here?' Ax smiled at the Prime Minister. 'Well Greg, in English, that's my offer and it's a good one. What do you say?'

They didn't say anything.

Fiorinda glanced once from Greg to Lady Moonshadow, her eyes grey stones, the pupils almost invisible (a strange response to this dim light): and resumed counting stars. The Zen Self champion, long legs folded into a spiky half-lotus in his chair, tipped his head back and gazed at the ceiling.

Lady Moonshadow rose to her feet. 'We shall of course give you time to think it over.' The others rose. The deputation departed, taking their entourage and guards along with them. The three stayed where they were, wondering if that was all. Very shortly they heard returning footsteps. Faud Hassim slipped into the room and stood there, his back to the doors, rather wild-eyed.

'I'm sorry, Faz,' said Ax, without rancour. 'If you're supposed to soften me up, don't bother: I am not going to top myself. You'll thank us some day. I'm sure you did what you thought best, but you made a bum choice. Do you really think you can trust those buggers to stick by a deal?'

'It's not that.' Faz swallowed, and spoke in a muttering undertone. 'I have a word for you, from Babylon. I don't know what it means, it's *Iphigenia*.'

'Okay,' said Ax. 'Thanks.'

The former Assassin stared at them, maybe in horror; maybe in pity. 'I will stay beside your mother, Ax,' he blurted. And he was gone.

They left the receiving room and went into the red bedchamber. They had three bedchambers, and bathrooms, besides a dining room, a small library, and the blue receiving room. This was their favourite, because it was the biggest. It was hung in dark red (with heavily shuttered windows behind the arras). The pattern of interlocked golden briars, repeated everywhere, had a disturbing resemblance to the bio-hazard sign; but that was appropriate enough for a werewolves' lair. They hadn't tried to nail the surveillance cameras, there was no point. Be thankful for great mercies, there were no guards inside the suite with them. There was no natural light, but there was plenty of space, and the ATP battery-lamps were under their control.

'I am shocked at Boris,' said Fiorinda, rubbing her arms. It was cold in the red room; the air was musty but tomb-like. 'How could he fall so far, so fast?'

'I expect he's hoping to stay alive,' said Sage. 'He was screwed the moment he accepted the invite to the Neurobomb Working Party, and now he has no way out. We have been there. We know how it happens ... How shocked, my brat?'

A flash of sharp, blue enquiry: which Fiorinda avoided. 'Oh, just shocked. I bet they copied that idiot idea about the brainstem, that they made him say, from what I told them about forest-fire schizophrenia. The tea-leafs. I'm sorry, Ax—'

But relief was evident in both of Ax's lovers, their worst fear averted, and his own spirits rose, into the strange lightness that still possessed them all.

'Don't beat yourself up, little cat. It's where they've been heading for years, Druidic pseudoscience. I expect the camps are full of neurological outcasts.'

They had been in these rooms two days and a night, no food or drink provided. Fiorinda and Ax's phones had been taken, and the digital mask disguises. Sage's eyesocket button had been confiscated, his wrist implant had been zapped to death. But that was all the depredations so far (what it is to be a royal prisoner). Fiorinda and Sage walked around, surveying their domain. The red chamber didn't have much furniture: a curtained four-poster bed, an Arts and Crafts armoire, slightly damaged; a couple of chairs. There were pictures on the walls, but none of those Wallingham table displays of priceless *objets*. The chimney in the gothic hearth was wide enough for a full-grown sweep to climb, but there was an iron grille cemented inside it. Ax sat on the floor by the bags and decided to make an inventory.

'Lady Anne is a hereditary aristo, isn't she? I mean, she's Lady Anne something or other, besides the Moonshadow bullshit—'

'Lady Anne Stanley,' agreed Fiorinda, looking at pictures. 'She's personally connected with this place, maybe she's a great-great-great niece of the millionaire, not sure how many "greats". But I don't know. I've tried never to talk to her, because I'm afraid she knows – knew – my Gran—'

'Well ladidah,' said Sage. 'D'you think she fucks Greg at Beltane?'

'Aargh. Thanks for the charming image. She's *eighty*.'

'And Lord Mursal has the chemistry of a brick with acne,' countered the babe. 'I don't envy her. You are being ageist, Ax, and anyway, the Great Marriage is not supposed to be fun.'

'What does *Iphigenia* mean?' asked Sage. 'Do you know?'

'She was Agamemnon's daughter,' said Ax. 'He was supposed to sacrifice her, to get the Greeks a fair wind for the Trojan Wars.'

'And there was hell to pay.' Fiorinda stared at a murky cottage, set about with dirt-blurred haystacks. Is that a Corot under there? 'Oh yes, I remember, "*Mourning Becomes Electra*" and all that. What d'you think it means as a message?'

Sage folded himself into the red armchair by the hearth; dust rose from the upholstery. Fiorinda drifted over to join him.

'I imagine it's some kind of *sorry, can't help you*, from Fred.'

'So that means—'

'Fred can't chat, but he's in a position to be handing out obscure Euripidean apologies,' said Ax. 'Which I call good news, far as it goes: could be worse.' There was nothing to eat in the bags. He'd been hoping for an overlooked biscuit or something. 'I am *so* fucking hungry.'

'Everything could be worse. I bet there are rats in these walls,' Fiorinda settled herself on Sage's knees and laid her cheek against his chest. 'I have my tinderbox, and there's wood all over. We can have rat au vin. If we had any vin.'

Sage took her chin and lifted her face. 'Did you curse him?' he whispered, his mouth against her lips.

'Did not!' Ax came to sit at their feet, bringing an untouched litre of water and his smokes tin. Dust rose from the gold-briared carpet, and now they did not seem to be prisoners. They were travellers on a lonely road who had stopped for the night in Dracula's Castle, daring the sinister shadows of their own free will. Fiorinda and Sage were kissing and whispering, Ax's cock was standing. He had not felt so horny in weeks; the afterburn of peril will do that, sometimes.

'I say we don't ration water, we drink the stuff in the bathroom taps. What are you two muttering about, hm?'

'Nothing,' said Fiorinda. 'Babytalk.'

'Shush,' Sage grinned at the bad brat, and bent his head to her breast, ah, it's a fine thing to have hands that will unfasten her clothes. 'I say we live for the moment.'

'I am doing.' Ax filled his lungs with gentle smoke and got up on the arm of the chair to pour it into her mouth. A three-way snog developed, rich and intense. Ax was lost in it, getting near the point when he must have more, when he realised he'd lost them both—

'What is it?'

No answer. The big cat and the little cat had raised their heads, and were tracking something he couldn't see: something moving across the lamplight. There wasn't a sound in the room, apart from their breath. Not a rat scratch from the panelling behind the red curtains, no blustering wind in the chimney. If it had been as quiet as this two nights ago, maybe they'd be in Paris now.

'All right. I'll buy it . . . What the fuck's up? What can you see?'

The Bodhisattva and the magician's daughter exchanged a cautious glance.

'C'mon. What is it? Don't tell me there's a ghost.'

'Could be,' said Sage, on a speculative note. 'You could call it that.'

'Maybe,' agreed Fiorinda. 'There's something in here with us, anyway.'

'What's it look like?'

'A black shape. Like something, not there, only moving.'

'Terrific.' Ax stared hard, and shook his head. 'Well, I don't get it. What kind of a ghost? Is it, like, a person . . . of some kind? Could we turn it?'

'I dunno.' Sage shook his head. 'I suppose we could try.'

'Better let it get used to us for a while,' said Fiorinda. 'I think it's nervous.'

They moved to the bed and enclosed themselves in the curtains, in a cloud of dust (good job none of us gets asthma). Were they still watched? They put the question out of their minds with ease, got naked and pursued the heady bliss of this void, this freedom: no regrets, no obligations, only the threefold knot, their whole world. 'My angels,' mumbled Fiorinda, clambering between the cold damp sheets to sleep.

'Fee, hey, you have to be in the middle.'

Fiorinda claimed she found sleeping in the middle demeaning, it made her feel like a disputed soft toy; also suffocated. But she didn't put up much of a fight.

'I'm going to turn off the lamps,' said Ax. 'Is it okay if I open the bed curtains?' Mumbles of consent. He made the expedition, mildly wondering what it would feel like if he bumped into that moving black shape: returned safely and found their warm bodies again, in the startling pitch darkness.

'Oh,' said Fiorinda, shortly. 'The ghost's gone.'

Ax was plunging towards sleep. 'Yeah, figures, we probably scared it. Remember, Elsie would never stay in the room when we fucked—'

Elsie had been the original *little cat*, Ax's pet, who had lived with them on Brixton Hill. She'd been killed, an ugly story, in the green nazi time. Ax mourned her still, poor Ax, he falls in love so easily, and never forgets . . . Sage and Fiorinda were touched to hear her invoked; it seemed like a good omen.

Maybe the ghost came back and watched over them. Maybe they were in shock: and fear for their friends, terror for the way they might die here, locked in these rooms, had yet to reach them. They slept well, anyway.

The next morning breakfast was brought to them by servants in black and white. Their luggage arrived. There were no concealed messages, but they felt that Allie had chosen the books, the jewellery and toiletries, had folded the clothes: and though all their friends should have been busy getting the hell out of England by now, they were comforted. Later Greg and Lady Anne appeared to hammer out the details of the contract. Ax's offer had been accepted.

Rick's Place

What happens when you take a nation of hard-wired hedonists, deep in debt and sodden with alcohol, first you knock them down with a massive economic crash, then you feed them for years on a diet of wild green violence and joyous rock; and then you give them license to believe in fairytale monsters? What you get is the England of the Fifth Revolution, the headless chicken on the edge of the map, where the ripe craziness of Crisis Europe is distilled to the nth degree. The epitome of it all is the Palace of Wallingham, eighty kilometres from London in the beautiful country of Kent, where I found Ax Preston and his Triumvirate partner's holding court. Ax's government tried to sentence him to assisted suicide a few weeks ago, after an incident involving a high-ranking official. When he refused to co-operate, they gave him a palace to live in and a tv show of his own, on which he'll continue to criticise government policy. International protest at Ax's arrest was muted, maybe because the "Lavoisier video" had left people feeling there's no smoke without fire.

Rick's Place on Net and Cable, Freetc yungbingliu/g/royalintern.eng/s86730 Star Nippon Oita and Phoenix, also mTm Oz and Asia, & US 'mtv'

The Revolutions
Number One: The Deconstruction Tour (also the Hilton regime, from the first Popstar President Saul Burnett's HQ in the London Hilton)
Number Two: Ax Preston's Dictatorship (the Rock and Roll Reich)
Number Three: the Green Nazi occupation (Extreme Celtics)
Number Four: Ax Preston' shortlived Presidency
Number Five: The Wallingham House Arrest

Want to be on Rick's Place? Buy your ticket when you buy your permit t leave the capital, there are a varying number of places available in the liv audience. The club is recorded as live, in the Yellow Drawing Room, Thursday Friday and Saturday, Ax n' Sage n' Fiorinda arrive at seven and leave at midnight. Don't promise your Mum she'll see you, because the televised show is an amalgam, but expect to hear the hottest new bands ar the established greats of English music, besides the Triumvirate and the supergroup known as the Band of Gypsies, Ax's rock and roll Cabinet. And rub shoulders with the green and pleasant land's new high society. Wallingham House is a trip in itself, but at the moment it's closed to the publi Keep off the subject of politics, but toreign tourists are in no danger. Priva hire cars are only for those who enjoy dealing with hostile bureaucracy, b trains from Victoria are frequent; take a shared taxi from Ashurst and agree price before you get in! DON'T miss the last train back to London. Overnig accomodation in Kent is rare as hen's teeth, blindingly expensive & you cou end up in labour camp if you're picked up and can't prove you have a place sleep.

Maybe no one knows WHAT to make of the situation now. But one thing's for sure: the Ax Preston charisma remains strong as ever. It was my privilege to meet Ax for the first time, at this strange juncture in his extraordinary life: and to interview the three most fascinating, controversial figures in World music . . .

Fiorinda read through the copy. She held out her hand for a pen, removed one errant apostrophe and corrected 'country' to 'county'. The journalist, a wizened, middle-aged Australian rock expert called Keith Utamore, watched her. Around them, chaos reigned. The Yellow Drawing Room was being set up for Rick's Place. This had to happen every week, because Lady Anne insisted it be returned, as far as possible, to its pristine state between shows. Artists were drinking and socialising while high tech, medium, and no-tech worked around them. The dancefloor crew were manoeuvring the big turntable onto its bearings, a tricky job; the sound engineers were testing their ability to focus on any conversation, at any table. The set for The Gintrap was being cabled-up for their trademark retro kit.

'Will there really be Oz tourists clamouring for tickets to the show?' Not unless they make the trip by b-loc, she thought. Which wouldn't happen, because the Great Peace frowned on that kind of technology.

'Huh?' Keith looked puzzled, then he laughed. 'Oh, no, no, that's just style. Armchair travel, kind of gallows humour? The Rough Guide to places you'll never see again. I do that a lot, on the World Music Round Up.'

She smiled and nodded. World Music, ah: that puts us in our place.

She had never heard of Keith Utamore, but this just proved her ignorance. He was a friend of Joe Muldur's, a highly respected figure, the interview was for a huge Australasian radio/net show. The Yellow Drawing Room roared like the sea in a shell, tv studio dark and bright, although it would be summer daylight outdoors. She always looked first at the terrace windows, when they came down, but there was never a chink in the heavy curtains. Never a glimpse of sky or lawns or trees. The ON AIR signs were getting tested now, flashing red, and alternating to CASH CROPS KILL in green.

Very little of what happened here would get onto the actual show. Fiorinda hadn't seen it (she wasn't sorry); they didn't have a television in the suite, but reports made that clear. Even the guest bands' numbers were faked elsewhere. But the screws liked the make-believe to be thorough ... There was something sinisterly childish about the whole deal. We had the Insanitude, so *they* have to have a hot nightclub venue, only theirs is better because it's on tv, the old holy of holies, politicians' Mecca. Which proves they won and we lost. The journo was looking at his slaughtered apostrophe.

'It's a first draft. You'll have full approval of the whole thing before we broadcast. Are we ready to go?'

She looked at her glass. Keith refilled it with the local vodka, yellow and warm as piss; and viciously strong. There was no bar at Rick's Place, only a stingy ration of wine and water on each table, and a press pass won you no extra. But the servants would bring liquor, for a price. A snake of cable wandered by, crawling over Keith's feet; shouts of panic came from the struggling dancefloor crew. At the next table a man in an evening jacket that he wore with easy elegance, with slick, jaw-length dark hair and skin the colour of milky tea, had joined the Scottish party: two bands and hangers-on, who were touring together but didn't seem to be mates—

The rock and roll princess of Crisis Europe knocked back a healthy slug. Fiorinda could put that stuff away.

'Sure, but we should move from here.'

Keith looked at Mr Preston. 'Er, this seems a good quiet spot.'

'You'll talk to Ax later. Trust me, any time you see blokes wearing skirts over their trews, I mean strides, like that, it's best to give them space . . . Especially this lot. The unnaturally white guy with the very black hair and, strangely, no tattoos, is Phil MacLean, and the Sikh woman at the end of the table, her name's Campbell, although she may not look it. They're re-enactment nuts, they have a grudge going back at least three hundred years and every time the bands run into each other, it gets physical. They're regulars, so I know. They had a real barney last time.'

Fiorinda snagged the vodka and the glasses. Keith Utamore perforce followed, looking over his shoulder. 'Then why do they go and sit together—?'

'They're Scottish.' She signalled to a couple of burly waiters and had them carry a table to a spot in the outer regions of the universe. 'There. Now we'll be fine.'

'Could we clear up a couple of things first, so I don't fall over myself? "Rick's Place", that isn't the real name of the show, is it? In

176

the English tv listings, I noticed, your show is called "Merry We Meet".'

'Mm,' agreed Fiorinda, screwing up her face.

'"Rick's Place" is better, yeah.' They laughed. 'Is that a reference to the classic movie, *Casablanca*? The *Café American*, Play it again Sam—?'

'Romance, plots and counterplots on the sidelines of a global war,' agreed Fiorinda. 'Haha, yes, of course.'

Mr Utamore nodded, still curious. 'Okay, who is "Rick"? There's nobody called "Richard" among the Few.'

'Ax is Richard. It's a convoluted English joke about incarcerated monarchs.'

'Ah! The Mediaeval Richard II! Let us sit upon the ground, and tell sad stories of the death of kings—!' Keith caught himself, consternated.

'Gallows humour,' said Fiorinda, with a charming grin. 'We do it too.'

'Shall we begin?'

KEITH UTAMORE: Fiorinda, may I say how wonderful it is to be speaking to you, after having followed your meteoric career, and played so much of your music for the audiences of the Pacrim and the southern oceans . . . 'Stonecold', 'Sparrowchild', 'Wholesale' . . . Great songs, many great songs, the anthems of an era. And then '*Yellow Girl*', one of the top female singer songwriter albums of the decade. You have the music in you, princess . . . And for the soundists out there, anyone without a picture, let me tell you, I'm a lucky man, sitting beside a very beautiful, gracious lady, in the most amazing English stately home, which is being transformed into a tv studio nightclub, as we speak . . .

FIORINDA: As we speak, portable dancefloors are suffering disasters.

KEITH UTAMORE: Cables are strangling each other. Well, it's beauty before age, because I've managed to snag the lady first . . . Do you ever do interviews in trio?

FIORINDA: Not often. There's too many strands, with three active musicians.

KEITH UTAMORE: And recently, another strand. Could we talk about the new supergroup, that debuted in the US last summer at the Hollywood Bowl, the Few and the Triumvirate combo? The Band of Gypsys, or is it G Y P S I E S?

FIORINDA: Er, I think it's G Y P S Y S. Apparently that's the way Hendrix spelled it, and then later it was corrected to "Gypsies": I am too young to know these things. We didn't call ourselves that, by the way. Some West Coast magazine labelled us.

KEITH UTAMORE: (Laughs) That was an amazing set, a real tour de force, both concerts. But is this going to be a recording phenonmenon, or was it only—?

FIORINDA: (dryly) Too soon to tell, Keith. We aren't making long term plans.

KEITH UTAMORE I'd love to see the Band of Gypsys on tour.

FIORINDA Me too ... But we've always played together, mix and match. I think we'll keep our separate identities, maybe the evolved 'supergroup' title should be all of our band names, combined. Like one of those very long chemicals.

KEITH UTAMORE: I was hoping to see this very long chemical tonight, and tape them, but apparently that's not to be.

FIORINDA: Maybe later in the series. But we have The Gintrap for you, and Sovra Campbell, and the Phil MacLean Band, back for a second visit, and very welcome ... Ah, there you go, you see, the Scots don't have band names. It's a trend. Except for Gintrap, but they're very retro lads.

KEITH UTAMORE: I've been hearing a lot about Gintrap.

FIORINDA: And the Chosen too, all five of them, which is quite an occasion.

Sage had waylaid the Preston family in the Green Room while Fiorinda entertained the man from Oz, and mine host was occupied with the Scots. It was a perfunctory gathering place, a closet-sized room by Wallingham standards, that nobody else was using. Sheet-steel maidens in fluted draperies paraded, lifesize, appliquéd to the peacock-blue walls; adding style without warmth. There were hard chairs, refugees from some government waiting room, set in rows. On a side table stood pitchers of beer and cheap English wine, with paper cups and a few plates of snacks.

Sage was in evening dress, like Ax: it was their uniform for Rick's

Place. The Chosen wore expensive versions of the nothing-special jeans and jumpers look they'd always favoured. They didn't often find themselves alone with Aoxomoxoa, and they were wary. A very tall, weirdly good-looking intellectual geek, dressed like a waiter, throws himself on the mercy of four suspicious, down-to-earth West Country rock musicians—

'He's scaring me,' said Sage. 'I know where we are, I know what's happened, but there's something else. This is not a joke: I don't like his state of mind.'

Ax's siblings looked at each other. Milly Kettle rolled her eyes.

'Everything he ever did was wrong,' suggested Jordan, mordantly. 'He hates himself. Everything stinks. Don't argue, trash the fucking lot, NOW.'

'Despair and die,' said Milly.

'You *are* kidding us?' demanded Maya. 'Did you really only now notice?'

'We've had that fucking everyone better despair and die mood laid on us every fucking album,' Jordan enlarged, eyes kindling. 'He's a perfectionist, a control freak. He turns it on himself, hardest, and this is supposed to make it all right. Would you say he can be difficult to live with? Possibly? Eh?'

'Oh God,' said Milly. 'D'you remember "Put Out The Fire"? It was HELL.'

The Chosen specialised in terrible, hopeless names for their songs and albums.

'Every album? Every fucking gig.' Shane shook his head, grinning. 'We do it all wrong, he has to rip up the set and start again. It's *his fault*, of course, but—'

'Always *his fault*, he's to blame, but somehow we're getting yelled at.'

'Because, yes, he's fucking demanding. Someone has to be.'

'Because compared with Ax, everyone else is taking the piss.'

Not what I meant, thought Sage, not at all: but he took the comfort he was offered, gratefully. 'Okay,' he said, mugging relief. 'Yeah. Thanks. You're right.'

Then The Chosen and Ax's Minister didn't know where to go with this, and looked at each other helplessly. 'So why do you guys put up with him?' said Sage, at last. Immediately he wished he hadn't said that, because their demanding, impossible big brother was in the trap he'd hauled them out of. There was nothing they could do, and their distress was suddenly open, written on their faces—

'Because if you let him do it,' said Jordan, dead straight, 'if you let him take you in hand, the way he wants, what he does with you is *fucking brilliant*.'

Strange words to hear from your lover's brother. But why not? Why shouldn't Jordan know how it feels to be with Ax? Love is love.

'Can we lurk in here until our set?' asked Milly, changing gear.

The band looked hopeful. In the Drawing Room they'd be surrounded by Wallingham black and whites, and they were afraid.

'No,' said Sage. 'That's not safe. I want you to stay where a lot of people can see you. There's a well-known Oz radio journalist in there. Make sure you say hi.'

The nightclub took shape. The VIP audience arrived, plus humbler members of the privileged classes who'd queued, schemed and paid large sums in whatever currency they used (barter, favours; wheelbarrows of Swedish euros) for their 'invitations'. Mr Preston and Mr Pender moved around, bestowing their company, obedient to the conceit that these were welcome guests, 'at home' with the royal rockstars. Random fragments of interaction were recorded, with the eager co-operation of the lucky targets. Far away on the edge of things the journalist continued to monopolise Fiorinda, which was fine by Fiorinda.

KEITH UTAMORE: Speaking of life as an icon, what about those Starborn portraits? He's said he rarely thinks about anything else, and he'll go on 'painting' you all his life. Is that uncomfortable, or is it thrilling?

FIORINDA: (off-guard) Toby Starborn is a stalker! LAUGHS. No, I don't mean that. Toby's very devout, and he sees me as some kind of magical sign—

KEITH UTAMORE: Er, I'm afraid I'm still a rational materialist.

FIORINDA: Hahaha. So am I, Keith, but we're living in the past. Look at it as just another way of cutting up the world, that gives new insights, and access to new technologies. Try the term neurophysics, it's easier to say than magic.

KEITH UTAMORE: Another way of cutting up the world ... For a rockstar, you're something of a philosopher, aren't you, Fiorinda—?

Across the room Ax Preston (who had long deserted the Scots) took an acoustic guitar from a waiter. Keith snapped to attention. 'Excuse me, Fio—'
'Oh, sure.'
She watched as he switched his tablet over to the Drawing Room's superb sound desk and made adjustments. The questions stopped: Ax played and sang 'Long Black Veil', a current favourite, for an enthusiastic little crowd.

> There were few at the scene, but they all agreed
> That the man who ran looked a lot like me...

Gallows humour.
'Maybe you shouldn't have run,' said Keith Utamore softly.
'Oh, we should have run,' said Fiorinda, smiling, eyes on her prince. 'We shouldn't have got caught.' She glanced at the tablet, which was not recording spoken word on this table. 'How are you planning to get home, Keith?'
'I don't know.'
That startled her. She'd been assuming Mr Utamore was some kind of master of the universe, free to return to his own world at any time.
'I came to Europe eighteen months ago. Your, er, unrest problems seemed to be settled, there was a window when SIA was doing scheduled flights into Paris. I wanted to have a context for all the terrific music I'd been playing. Now I don't know what to do. I'm afraid of the airship accident rate, and crossing the Pacific by sea, it's a bloody dangerous trip. I'd island-hop from Singapore to Perth via Guinea, they say that's the safest route, but you'll have noticed I'm Japanese ethnic? I could get pulled over and wake up in Guangdong, in a re-education camp—'
She'd have thought anyone oriental-looking risked the same fate in Melbourne: maybe he had influential friends there, or knew the right people to bribe. But what did Fiorinda know? The so-called Great Peace was probably the same as Crisis Europe: looks monolithic from

the outside, lot of variation on the ground. Hey, compadre, are you trapped like us?

A touch on her bare shoulder. It was Ax, looking cheerful and relaxed.

'Mind if I join you? I have some time now, Keith.'

Gintrap, with their 'deliberately crude' (Bless. Like they had an option) tunes and daft lyrics went down well, as did a couple of – shall we say unremarkable – bands with the right kind of politics. The return of Phil MacLean's Gaelic Country outfit was greeted with rapturous applause. About equal with the reception for Sovra Campbell's folk/classic violin set; thank God. Between guest spots Fiorinda played the piano, her gold and green party-frock skirts rustling around her, while Bill Trevor and Sage leaned on the grand to sing ... musical royals, enjoying their neo-feudal soirée, happy to show off and just as good as the professionals. Ax was off in the outer regions getting interviewed, she was glad he was getting a long break ... Fiorinda had a moment of what Allie called reverse déjà vu. What is this weird place, where did the real world go, how did I get here, is this a nightmare? She pulled herself back from vertigo to hear Bill Trevor's beautiful tenor rising unearthly: *Is my team ploughing, that I was used to drive, and hear the harness jingle, when I was man alive?* And the Boss replied, deep and sweet, with an edge of cruelty that sent a shiver to every woman's core, and plenty of the men. Oh yes, the world goes on fine without you, *my dead friend.* It was a Benjamin Britten arrangement of a Housman poem, a fuck-you party piece of theirs from long ago: first released as an extra track on the most terrifying of Heads albums, *Arbeit Macht Frei* ...

Her fingers almost stumbled on the keys, because she remembered that Fred Eiffrich had loved Housman.

The Chosen's set was recorded last. It was big and emotional, and featured their new huge hit, 'Straight From Green': which the establishment loved because the tune was catchy and they never listened to the words of pop songs; and the opposition (none of whom you would ever see in here) loved because they did ... But it was okay, it was safe to write lyrics like that, no censorship was the deal.

'Now we're going to do a Chip Desmond and Kevin Verlaine song,' announced Ax. 'It's called "Dupes of Babylon". We may be gone for some time.'

'If we don't come back, send out search parties!' shouted Milly Kettle from behind her drums.

The high life laughed and clapped, delighted with themselves for getting the joke. Of course, Chip and Ver (the Adjuvants) were notorious for their convoluted, no-exit, marathon tracks. Keith Utamore came to find Fiorinda, and leaned down beside her. 'Just wanted to say it's been terrific, you three have all been wonderful in, er, not ideal circumstances. Thank you so much. I have to leave, my car is waiting.' He stared at the band. 'Tell me one thing,' he murmured. 'Ax and Sage. Can they really transform into animals?'

She saw that he was serious, maybe surprised at himself but perfectly serious. Unbelievable. 'Can human beings turn into monsters?' Fiorinda smiled. 'You're asking *me* that? Oh yes, Keith. Teeth and hair, I've often seen it.'

Sage had suspected her of cursing Boris Ananthaswamy. He was wrong. Fiorinda would not even use the mild formula she had known since childhood, *all the harm that's good for you*. She would not dare to touch this situation; not by a breath. She felt it shivering, fearfully balanced, on the edge of destruction, on the edge of escape—

Sadly, Mr Utamore missed the last encore, which was one for the annals. Sage Pender had returned from the interview table. He and Ax, guitar unshipped, stood up together in front of the Prestons and sang 'Liquid Gold' in close harmony, dreamy and slow, with The Chosen for a backing band.

Of infinity
Figure of eight
Has that swing, up and round
In the sweet swaying plane,
up and down, on the wave
and again, and some more
come and go, let me soar
float and fly
as I ride,

as I ride
And seals our trinity

How much how much how much how much of sweet(ness) can one heart
    hold?
My baby my baby my baby my baby my baby my baby is liquid gold

The 'waiters' were calling time. Ax and Jordan looked at each other,
thought about it, decided to go ahead, and gruffly embraced. 'You're
not coming back,' said Ax, holding the hug for a moment. 'It's not
safe, you're to stay away from now on, all of you. See you when I get
out of this.' The Triumvirate were searched, scanned, escorted
through the house and locked into their suite. The red bedchamber
welcomed them, with its cool, dank and enclosed air.

They'd been imprisoned for nearly two months, and *oh God to see
the sun again.* They hated the rest of the suite, especially the moon
and stars where they met their tormentors, but to an extent the red
bedchamber had become home. The nervous ghost, something
between a pet and a bad dream, had seen them playing games and
having silly spats in here, reading poetry and the classics of English
literature aloud to each other: acting out scenes from plays. It
overheard all their conversations, but that was okay, as long as you
remember you're not alone.

Sage flopped into the red armchair, tugged loose his black tie and
sang softly, reprising that perfect encore: *How much, how much, how
much . . .* Ax sat on the floor: laid his head on the big cat's knee and
picked up the harmony, with his eyes closed. *Of sweet can one heart
hold, my baby my baby my baby . . .* When you know you did a good
performance it soothes your soul, no matter what.

Fiorinda drank water to ward off a hangover, lined up the three
refills she'd snagged while necking Keith Utamore's vodka, and
thought of a night at Brixton Hill, when they had serenaded her with
her own music . . . *I was pain, then I was meat, then I was water in the
desert. Then I believe I was oxygen, fire in the air. Now I'm molten
metal.* Hm. Is this progress? They weren't supposed to take anything
from the Drawing Room: but Fiorinda carried a shoulder-bag with
her evening shawl in it, and the screws on the way back, though by

no means friendly, often didn't bother to hassle her. The bottles they'd had with them when they were arrested had begun to deform, bio-degrading slowly in this sunless world. This frightened her. It would be bad when they were gone: an epoch.

Little did Keith Utamore know he'd had to interview them separately because they were suspected of telepathic powers when they were together. Little did he know that they'd had to be interviewed, awkwardly, in the middle of a tv show recording, because that was the only time they were allowed out of the cells. Self-censorship, like abused children, we don't tell, we know the things we're not supposed to say. But she corrected herself. Oh, he knew. He had a good enough idea, he's a professional journalist, he had a rare opportunity and he handled the situation—

The legendary Wallingham interview with the Triumvirate gains poignancy: we know that a few days later Ax 'n' Sage ' n' Fiorinda were shot, and their bodies buried somewhere in that house.

'Liquid Gold' drifted into silence. Sage stroked Ax's hair.

'How did you get on with the Scots?' asked Fiorinda.

'Fine,' mumbled Ax.

'I dunno why you encourage them,' said Sage. 'They're nothing but trouble.'

'Reasons of state,' explained Ax, still with his eyes closed. 'You have to be aware, Mr Minister, Scotland is our main trading partner. Cultural entente greases the wheels. It's part of my job as President to entertain the approaches.'

'Oh yeah, and what about Wales?'

'Bring me a Welsh band, I'll sit at their table. They can be regulars too.'

There would be no Welsh bands at Rick's Place. The Welsh didn't like what had been done to Ax. As so often in these situations, the neighbours knew more than the English public did. They knew about Lord Vries, and the ruthless extent of his role in government; they felt he'd had it coming. The Scots also knew the score, but they were more hardheaded. Phil MacLean and Sovra Campbell were secret agents. They had come to England on tour and penetrated Wallingham, with instructions to talk to Ax about a new job. The offer laid on the table, undercover of nightclub conversation, might be genuine; or it might not.

It was like Paris, except it wasn't funny. Everybody thinks they can headhunt the disaffected President. Was it possible that the Second Chamber didn't know about MacLean? He'd been known to the Reich for years . . . But these suits had often proved amazingly ignorant about recent history. Maybe they'd never figured out that when you can have a rockstar warlord, when rockstar revolutionaries are making the fur fly all over Europe, inevitably other rockstars are going to be recruited as spies . . . Ax had no intention of incriminating himself. But he was letting the Scots talk, at the back of his mind the knowledge that one day he might be desperate enough to take any risk.

'What about Joe's backpacker, Fiorinda?' asked Sage, suspiciously. 'You seemed to be making an impression there.'

Fiorinda's boyfriends were hostile to anything remotely connected with Joe Muldur, she couldn't imagine why. She shrugged, unmoved by a kingfisher flash of reproach. 'Why ask me? You talked to him as much as I did. Hey, did you get that he's an A-team refugee? He sends his famous interviews and his very respected prog down the line, but he doesn't know how to get home himself . . . He hasn't a clue.'

'Oh,' said Ax. 'Poor guy.'

They'd had a faint hope Keith Utamore might be an emissary from Pan-Asian Utopia, but Fiorinda had tried him, without raising a flicker. Ah well, can't expect everyone who walks into the gin-joint to add to the hectic romance.

'He can't go by sea, because the South Pacific is full of sharks and pirates. Or is it the Indian Ocean? I'm not good at geography; maybe it's both. And he's scared to go by air, because of hydrogen accidents.'

'Hahaha . . . Has he used our intercity railway system at all?'

'I didn't ask. I thought it would be unkind.'

Ax had surrendered under terms, and his terms had been accepted. He could criticise the government all he liked from behind the bars of his gilded cage: no one censored his lyrics, he was trusted to talk to foreign journalists. But he was still under a death sentence, and the Triumvirate were still prisoners. How long could this state of affairs continue? The last time Greg Mursal had come down to Wallingham, a week or so ago, he had told them Sage was to be allowed out on parole, 'if all goes well'. He would be able to talk to Allie Marlowe, and to his father: Greg had mentioned those two, specifically, which meant something, they weren't sure what. Ax had been hustling for his partners' release, and a lot of other changes, ever since they knew they weren't going to be walled up and left to starve. But now they were scared. The red room was safety. Sage on parole would have wandered far, and Ax and Fiorinda would be afraid for him.

Sage and Ax vacated the armchair and walked around, restless. Fiorinda arranged her water bottles. They talked about their hopes. Could this parole be the first step to a negotiated plea? Sage must speak to lawyers, must try to get sight of any statements that had been made. What had become of those security guards? The prisoners had been told that there were 'unimpeachable witnesses' to 'a scuffle', 'apparently between Lord Vries and Mr Preston'. As if there was room for doubt as to what had actually happened ... And yet, at the same time, this was the event that had proved Ax was a monster. No one had asked Sage for a statement, and he didn't think he should volunteer ... Suppose (admitting nothing) the werewolf idiocy were dropped. Suppose Ax were accused of the unpremeditated thumping of the Wiccan scholar? How would that go? Compensation, wouldn't that be the Celtic way? We could do compensation ... we could talk about that. It was a puzzle, with hopeful touches. Everyone's being cautious, it's *sub judice*.

But there could be a way through. We may be able to put this behind us.

Coded comments, unfinished sentences, motormouths: it always took them a while to recover from Rick's Place. A spliff would have been helpful, but they'd finished their supplies long since and no more were forthcoming. No smoking allowed; which caused Ax suffering. No alcohol, except what they could cadge from the punters ... At last the dead silence of the shuttered room returned, like the darkness that flows back, underground, when you switch off a torch. Fiorinda curled up in the red chair. Sage and Ax sat with their backs to the bed: black jackets discarded, bowties untied. Could we saw through the locks on the shutters behind the arras with a nailfile? Could we suborn our guards, or find a secret passage? But they never spoke of escape. They did not plan to escape; escape would be defeat. They planned to win this difficult and delicate game. We've seen worse, we've been in rougher spots than this and turned things round.

Fiorinda watched the two men. 'I think you are being galley slaves.'

They grinned at each other. 'Hahaha, yes we are,' said Ax.

'What do you do when you're being galley slaves?'

'We're on the bench,' said Sage. 'Chained together, hauling on our oar—'

'Blisters rubbed raw, and we have to keep going, boom crash, boom crash—'

'And then you have sex.'

'Er, no,' said Sage.

'Not really . . . We get whipped all the time,' Ax went on, with enthusiasm, 'and it's dark, and we have heavy manacles that gall our wrists horribly, ankles too and—'

'Sometimes, rarely, we're allowed to sleep under our bench.'

'And *then* you have sex—?'

They shook their heads. 'You don't understand, Fee. It's not like that. It's very sexual, but not directly about fucking. That's the very, very sexy thing about it.'

'I want to be a galley slave.'

'You're too small,' said Sage, quickly. 'You couldn't handle the oar.'

'Bastards. I don't care. You are just idiots. What's the use of a sexual fantasy where you don't even have sex?'

'All right, okay,' said Ax. 'You'll be pissed off, but you may as well know, when we are galley slaves we keep you under the bench, folded up very small.'

'To keep you *safe*,' explained Sage, with a naked look. 'Because we're all right, as long as you're safe—'

Fiorinda had thought of a way that she could join them on their bench and haul that massive oar. In her mind, as if looking into a mirror, she saw a big chestnut-skinned man in flamboyant middle-age, with a curling mouth, offensive eyes, and shining, black ringlets to his shoulders. It was her father, Rufus O'Niall. She kept him on a leash in a sealed compartment in her mind . . . Ax and Sage knew this. But she wasn't going to remind them of it, not now, not in this place.

'Sage, if you do get out, will you bring me some Volvic water?'

'Yep, er, if I can. Any other brand that would do?'

'N-no. Volvic. I like the picture. *Maybe* Buxton, if you can't be bothered to hunt around—'

'Gimme a break, Fiorinda. I'll do my best. You got any orders, Ax?'

'Liquorice and wine gums.'

'Oooh, tha's not very healthy Mr President. Organic liquorice, of course?'

'No. I don't want to chew a fucking root, I want sweeties.'

Not a word of the mortal dread of parting. Not a word, never, of how it really felt to be trapped in here. A palace is a place where people never speak their minds. How different from that night two months ago when they had faced death together, so happily, with such sensual abandon. But the doom passes, you find that you are still in the fight, so you keep fighting. What else can you do?

'Hey,' said Ax. 'Is the ghost with us?'

Fiorinda looked into the dark, empty quarter beyond the armoire: ghost territory. 'It's here. It's prowling around over there, being a black shape.'

'Why don't you try turning it?'

'I don't believe it's turnable,' said Sage. 'It's been locked up in here too long, it's been driven stupid. I'm tired, let's go to bed.'

Sage had hoped to walk out of the prison gates and make his own way to the station, but not a chance. He was driven to London, and only achieved the minuscule victory of getting dropped off at Grosvenor Place; rather than have a Wallingham car inside the walls of the Insanitude. There was a placard on the door of the nightclub venue in the State Apartments saying it was *closed for refurbishment*. Ah yes. He remembered that euphemism from the Crash years, shop-door notices, slowly acquiring a mature patina of grime, yeah, we're closed for refurbishment ... Across the Courtyard the decorators were noisily at work.

Allie's new office was on the ground floor of the South Wing. She had seen him coming: as he walked in she held up a neatly rolled spliff. 'Ah!' Sage collapsed onto a chair, dragged over another for his feet, sparked up and leaned back.

'*Thank you!*'

'My pleasure,' said Allie. 'Hey, you're looking buff!'

Sage grinned . . . Allie's trying to cheer me up, I'm touched, but whoo, I must be dying. 'Well, there's a gym, and not much else to do. You want some of this?'

'No, I'm working. How are they?'

He looked around. The décor was grey and cream and cocoa-brown: very Allie, feminine, elegant, and a little narrow. A moving frieze of festival scenes, artisan digital art, East Midlands school, pretty good, circled the walls. The projector, futuristic magic-lantern, made a dainty piece of furniture in itself. Nice look.

It was hard to adjust to the idea that he was not on camera.

'Fiorinda's good. Very good. She's in a bad temper with the VIP punters, which they love, they love her cut-crystal put-downs. An' getting most of her calories from vodka, I'm afraid . . . but she's wonderful. Ax, hm.'

Allie and the Few's superhunk had been enemies once, and he could still provoke her; but they had been partners for a long time on the intensely important issue of Ax and Fiorinda's wellbeing.

'Ax is not fine.'

'Nah, don't take on: he's okay. If it had been me that downed the bastard, I'd prob'ly be feelin' a lot more shit than I do. It's just a very wearing situation.'

'I'm *glad* he did it,' said Allie, passionately.

'I wouldn't go that far.'

None of Ax's friends and neither of his lovers had ever had a word of blame for Mr Preston, and they never would. He was *well* entitled to make one slip, after everything he'd carried on his shoulders all these years; and it had just been fate. The fact remained that the Rock and Roll Reich's situation had taken a dive from difficult to impossible. The noise of the decorators crept through Allie's soundproofing, along with the tinny, nagging shadow of their execrable taste in music.

Allie shrugged, and grimaced ruefully. 'Okay, maybe not that far.'

Sage tapped the spliff carefully in the ashtray provided.

'Well. What's the situation look like from out here?'

'Impressively weird,' began Allie, vehemently. 'The President is definitely a werewolf and he has to kill himself—'

Ouch. They had been really hoping the werewolf charge was on the fade.

'But he has to go willingly, to prove the mandate has passed on. No one talks about it, not even the gutter press, but everyone knows that the so-called Moderate Celtics are trying everything. Wiccan power-sex, skyclad prayer meetings, voluntary blood-letting, illegal sacrifice, you name it. The one thing they can't do is execute Ax unilaterally, because that would be a disaster. Cows would die.'

'Is Lord Vries still alive?'

'Hey! What are you implying? This is a civilised country, we don't have the death penalty for murder, it doesn't matter if he's alive or not, the issue is witchcraft!' She changed her tone, deflated. 'We don't know, Sage. We think he must be, but we can't find out, and nothing has leaked . . . So, Ax is a werewolf and he has to die. On the other hand, at the same time, you three are happily settled at Wallingham, "Rick's Place" is a big success, people will start calling it "Merry We Meet" as soon as they've seen the rebranding campaign, and all's right with the world. Oh, and they say we can't visit you privately, for security reasons. But we get sent stacks of "Merry We Meet" invitations, and implored to use them.'

'But you won't.'

Allie gave him a wry look. 'Yeah. We got the message. Fiorinda tells us it's over, in a voicemail. Then you three get a tv show and refuse to put us on the guest list. Somehow we knew we weren't supposed to turn up.'

Sage's brother Heads, Bill Trevor and George Merrick, had defied the clear message from their leaders, arriving at the club's doors with tickets of their own; which they had acquired some nefarious way. The management had been delighted, of course: having Bill and George along looked great. The prisoners had been weak enough to accept the *fait accompli* . . . But no one else better fucking imagine they'd be welcome. No one else must fall into the pit—

'Strictly speaking,' said Allie, only slightly intimidated (she'd used to hate the way Sage could frighten her), 'we're supposed to have fled the country and denounced the Reich, I know, I know. But it's lucky we stayed, isn't it? Because Ax did rescue something, and if we'd run out, there'd be much less chance of getting back to normal. There really is a chance, Sage. People recover from horrific scandals all the time . . . He can be President again, we can get back on track. But we have to make something move soon, or it's going to go long term. It's going to be an Aung San Suu Kyi thing, with Ax under house arrest for thirty years—'

'Thanks for the charming image.'

'Sorry.' Allie sighed. 'Oh well, to continue the news update, Mr Eiffrich is back, and looking good for a second term. Italy has disintegrated, officially, it's now er, eight countries? And China has invaded Uzbekistan, sorry, liberated the Uzbeks from the brutal rapists who were destroying their rich heritage, did you get that?'

Sage grimaced. 'Yeah, don't bother, we get all that stuff. An' I promise to pay attention, as soon as I have less on my mind.'

As far as you can believe anything, Fred Eiffrich had survived. He'd emerged from the Washington 'coup' with new staff in significant posts, no more problem over the 'Lavoisier scandal'; and a commitment to review the Neurobomb research. US voters were getting used to the word 'occult' and they liked the idea of a new superweapon ... All the global news stories came to Rick's Place. Sage and Fiorinda ignored them, Ax went round collecting the stuff, avidly ... Sage wondered how it felt to be an Uzbek? What's it like to be liberated by the Chinese? Could it be all bad?

Fucking hope the EU doesn't get dragged in—

'Oh, and Alain wants to talk to you. I told him I couldn't be sure when you'd get here: he said he'd stay by the phone.'

'What's he want to talk about?'

'Lavoisier and Violence double bill. The soundtrack, I think.'

Alain de Corlay was producing a remastered version of the famous video, coupled with highlights of the Commons debate. Plus a terrific soundtrack, of course. He'd invented a claim that French techno-green expertise had stripped out the vicious tampering, and these were the original images ... So it goes, people have to try and undo the damage to the cause; and you have to be grateful.

He sighed. 'Oh well, okay ...'

'Ah, bonjour Sage, how's life in the Conciergerie?'

'Not so bad, hahaha. We're getting the better quality straw now, thanks—'

The landline connection between the Insanitude and the Île St Louis was standalone, as secure as it gets: he struggled to believe he did not have to censor himself ... The conversation shifted into

French, Allie sat back, and didn't try to follow it, but she saw him frown. Sage put the handset down, looking thoughtful.

'What is it? Oh God—'

'No, it's all good. Except he says they're going to close "Rick's Place".'

Allie stared, professionally stung, hey, you don't cancel the Triumvirate!

'But you only just opened! The ratings are terrific! How does he know?'

'Rumour mill, I dunno.' Sage shrugged. 'I doubt if it's true, the bastards love their tv show, but it might not be a bad sign. It might mean we're getting out.'

'We hear fifty rumours a day,' agreed Allie. 'Good, bad, plain weird.'

Briefly, their eyes met. More bad news? Don't dwell on it.

Sage hauled up the bag he'd dumped when he took the spliff and thumped it onto her desk. 'It's probably nothing. Anyway, here's the correspondence.'

Ax had resumed some of his Presidential workload. His hand-written and typed letters were usually taken from the suite in a sealed bag, which was presumably then opened and the contents examined. This time Sage had walked out with the bag untouched. Bizarre. But who could figure the Second Chamber's priorities?

'Nobody's around,' she said, apologetically. 'Not 'til this evening. Everyone's in Hyde Park, doing Party In The Park.'

The summer season crowds had taken their lead from the Reich's calm demeanour, and were not allowing the Triumvirate's imprison-ment to spoil the fun. Sage could not join the Party in the Park. It was a condition of his parole that he stay away from any place of public entertainment. No meetings with the Countercultural Rebels either. He nodded. He wasn't too cut-up about these restrictions.

'But at seven you're to meet your dad, at the restaurant where he's taking you for dinner, with some highly useful and important people.'

'Aargh.'

She handed him an e-reader. 'He'll talk to you before the big guns arrive, but here's a briefing. You have to be very confident, but please don't pick up the bill. You can't, it will be huge. Really.'

'Those days are gone.'

'Well, *try* not to pick up the bill,' said Allie, resignedly.

'Hahaha, I'll do my best.'

'Then there's this.' She gave him a clear envelope that held a minute gleam of metal. 'It's your mask button: you can have it back.'

The eyesocket button that carried the living skull mask had been taken from him – not by force, but very clear that there could be force – when they were arrested. He tipped it out and held it on a fingertip.

'Are you going to put it in?'

'Not straight off, sorry. I know you're a fan. I'll interrogate it a little first.'

'And this, which is from Ammy for Fiorinda.'

He took the parcel, which wasn't sealed, and peered inside. Packets of herbs, little dropper bottles. A closer look, and his heart turned over. He pushed the parcel back across the desk, shaking his head.

'Nah, no good. That's not going to get in.'

'Huh? Ammy left it open, so they could see it's all organic magical stuff.'

'Ah, tha's where she was wrong. They don't give a flying fuck if we smuggle a truckload of mouldering Russian tactical nukes into Wallingham, but anything organic an' magical, that's another story. Tell Ammy thanks anyway.'

The lo-tech craftwork noise of the decorators rose again. Crash, bang, saw, saw . . . Is someone chopping down a cherry orchard out there?

'Well,' said Allie. 'There's a lot to discuss.'

'Yeah. Tomorrow, okay? After I talk to my dad, and do this dinner party. I'm gonna head off to Battersea now. I'll call you in the morning.'

'Is that where you're staying, not Brixton?'

He shook his head. 'I don't fancy Brixton.'

'I'll send a car to take you to the restaurant,' said Allie, staunchly. 'A *nice* car. About seven at yours, okay? You don't want to be early.'

'Fine. Hey, have you any idea where I could find some Volvic spring water? I mean, don't care about the analysis, a bottle with the nice label?'

'Made in France, by volcanoes?' said Allie, immediately.

'Shit. Is this a big *thing*? Ancient girl-tradition, that I ought to have known about?'

'Sage, it doesn't exist. Not for years. You won't even get a good fake: she's winding you up. Get the princess some Buxton.'

'Oooh, no. I don't take that kind of risk.' He stood, unfolding to his full, improbable height. 'I learned my lesson one day in Dissolution Summer. The *one time* in my life I wasn't there to drive the princess home, thought I had better things to do, and what happens? She takes off for Lambeth, fucks Ax Preston, an' the rest, as they say, is history. God knows what she might bring home next.'

He's such a bloke, thought Allie. Ax is incredible and unique, and Fiorinda would be different from anyone else in the world, even if her father hadn't been Rufus O'Niall. But once you get past how weirdly clever he is, and what he looks like, and the Zen Self, Sage is such an ordinary *bloke,* underneath it all . . .

He'd hoped Allie would take pity on him. He had often been told he didn't know how to shop, he only knew how to impulse-buy like a five-year-old. He secured liquorice and wine gums, hunted inefficiently for Volvic water around Belgravia: decided he might have better luck on familiar territory, and headed down the King's Road. The August sun was white in a hot dull sky, making him wish he'd been taking sunscreen. Yeah, there's a gym. It's a box, with no natural light. Guards walk you there, lock you in, let you out, walk you back. No, I don't think we're in immediate danger, not even if Rick's Place closes. But if I thought this was going to go on for years, with my Ax going crazy with remorse and Fiorinda withering into bitterness; I don't know, Allie, I might welcome a swift way out. He was institutionalised. The King's Road was unreal, all he could think about was the red room. All he wanted was to be back there. There was a tune going through his head, very familiar, what's that?

Never a frown, with golden brown . . .

Hm. Maybe not.

He had forgotten to ask about Doug. Allie would have told him if there was news, but he must remember to ask.

At Battersea Reach he found Cack, skull-masked, waiting in the hall.

'I thought you'd be at the Park.'

'Didn't fancy it, George and Bill said they'd be okay without me.'

Other reclusives gathered and Sage gave them what he could, the reassurance of seeing their sacred idol alive and well. Then he dismissed them and retired with Cack to the glade-room, a favourite haunt of theirs, with the singing, ringing trees. 'There was some barmies here earlier,' offered Cack, 'wanting to talk to you.'

'What, in uniform? The fuckers. They know they're not supposed.'

'Not uniform, but they said they were ISB Crew. I took this off one of them.'

'This' was a Yap Moss button, a circlet of moorland rushes on a cream ground, campaign medal for the ugly final battle of the Islamic Campaign. Sage turned it over. Every genuine Yap Moss button was engraved on the reverse with the soldier's name or tag; and numbered, because the artist-enamellers, Lacey and Wear of Gloucester, numbered all their works. This had neither mark. He shook his head. 'The Insane Stupid Behaviour Crew' were good enough lads, famous for their ridiculous exploits, but none of them had been at the bloodiest battle.

'Pitiful.'

'You couldn't call it a fake, hardly, could you? The greens are way off.'

Sage agreed, and the collaborators fell into a discussion, which seemed to both of them perfectly natural, of the minute deficiencies in the dark and olive greens to be found in the enamelled crown of rushes: the cracked creams were equally poor. They moved on to a more general discussion of Lacey and Wear's work, how the chemical changes of firing the enamel affected different colours, and how this related to shifts in a different kind of firing, and partial-firing of individual neurons, in the visual cortex. But colour is only symbolism. Light is God, if you want to create synthetic percepts, and soon they were talking about light, edge and line, an endlessly absorbing topic. Perfect pitch for luminance is far rarer than perfect pitch for tones of sound: Sage and Cack Stannen were equally matched, equally obsessive—

At last they returned to the barmies themselves.

'They were scared of our spooks, stupid buggers: spooks never hurt anyone. They said, they'll be upstairs at that pub on Battersea High Street all afternoon, and they know something. It's about Ax, and some security guards.'

Oooh, is that so? Sage had found himself a pack of Anandas. He lit up.

'Which pub was it?'

'The one that's been shut a long time.'

If you hurry Cack he loses the thread. They established, unhurriedly, that this pub was not the Castle, nor the Woodsman, nor that strange fancy one from which Aoxomoxoa got banned; nor the ill-fated one that keeps trying to be a restaurant and never makes it. It was Dwyers, the defunct Irish bar with the chocolate-maroon glazed tiles (a digression to nail the hue code for various angles) on the outside.

'Are you going to go?' asked Cack. It was a long time since they'd taken a walk out together, just seeing the world and discussing how to code it.

'I might. Want to come along?'

They left by the water frontage. Their giant shed on pillars, a little upstream from Chelsea Wharf on the other side, was the last stand of post-industrial disorder on the Wandsworth bank. The government spooks occupied a flat in the first of the low-rise housing blocks that lined the water beyond, all the way to Battersea Bridge; but there was no sign of them today, not a wink of a lens. Spooks never do any harm, do they? said Cack. Never, said Sage. It was the Heads' policy to tell Cack this so he didn't get anxious.

Riverside Walk, despite inundations and stinks, and much-disputed flood proofing, preserved its ancient charm. Everyone was living a floor higher up, that's all. Sage and Cack remembered fondly the evacuees, who had come to stay for a year, and lively Borough of Wandsworth Council meetings, when George and Bill were councillors: when the battle for ground clearance to make a flood sink was won, the year inner London gained some new wetland, and all the dictatorship prefabs went up. But today the river was docile, slipping by, glassy smooth in its old bed. There's a fishing cormorant, making great ripples; and an interesting post. Here's the modest beauty of St John's on its patch of green; the sandbag bunkers and the ancient school. No kids of course, it's harvest time. *Better Death Than False Of Faith* . . .

Sage noticed at last how sweet it was to be outdoors, and the black mood left him, can't afford them, those days are gone. What a great place Battersea is, and how infinitely superior to Brixton. The toytown yellow-brick houses, the funky, endearing psychological landscape that hasn't changed, just a few variant details, in a decade of violent upheaval. It was an oft-noted phenomenon. The inner cities had thrived on green revolution (except for the small matter of being unable to feed themselves), while the rural hinterland fell into the abyss. Ironic, but there were factors that made it inevitable.

It takes one *idiot savant* to ignore another. They'd covered half the tiny winding High Street, Sage adapting his stride to Cack's shorter legs, before he noticed that Cack was still wearing the skull. Etiquette said that Sage should therefore also be skulled-up, but he didn't have his button in place. Belatedly he wondered why Cack was masked at all. They didn't do that any more, not among themselves.

'Hey, Cack, why the mask?'

Cack's Hallowe'en head grinned, without expression.

'I thought I should.'

Sage kept walking. Asperger's is a catch-all label. Even sufferers with the same deficits have their own quirks. Not to dwell on the past, but Peter 'Cack' Stannen could have his pants on fire, and he wouldn't say a word (this has been proved) until you asked him the right direct question. On topic he's unbeatable. Off topic he often thinks you know things when you don't. He thinks he's told you things when he hasn't. He wears the mask when he's upset.

'Cack, why did you take the button off those barmies?'

'I thought I should. They didn't know I took it.'

'Okay. Was there anything else about those barmies?'

'I don't think they were really Crew,' said Cack, in his serious little voice.

The defunct Irish bar was coming up. Sage had a momentary glimpse of a figure moving in one of the grey windows on the upper floor.

Cack looked at the once-bright lettering above the door. 'That's a *very* nasty green,' he said, severely. 'I don't know what gets into people.'

'Nor me. Peter, my dear, I think we should take an elementary precaution. You're to walk on until you get in range of the public callpoint at Clapham Junction. Then you call George, and you tell him where I am and why. Don't call him before, make sure you use the public callpoint. Lose yourself in traffic. You got that?'

'Elementary precaution,' said the death's head. 'I got you.'

The door on the corner was open, the bar inside was dark, and stank of defeated years. Sage walked in, very relieved that he'd realised he shouldn't bring Cack with him. In the old days he wouldn't have thought twice: Cack was little, but he was useful. But none of them had really sympathised with Peter's strangeness, back then; although they'd loved him dearly . . . He had noticed, of course, that he'd been allowed out for the nights of a full moon (fer fuck's sake). But he was forewarned, and George would know where he was. He was also in very good shape, if not the Aoxomoxoa of old, and this had a visceral effect. All his thoughts were focused on the red room, back in Wallingham.

Let's see what these fake barmies want to sell me—

He went up the stairs, he opened a door, and grasped immediately that he'd better retreat. But if you sup with the devil you should take a long spoon, every pitcher goes once too often to the well, and if he keeps on trying, sooner or later the king of the lads is going to put his fist through the wrong window.

Cack reached the junction of Falcon Road and St John's Hill. Here there were streams of people, after the friendly quiet of Battersea Village. Crowds in a familiar street didn't bother him, but the 'boss in jail' idea had hit him very hard, and having Sage home 'for two days' wasn't easier. How glad is two days' worth? When do you reach the cut-off point on the curve, the downhill slide to 'boss in jail again'? It sounds simple but it isn't. The crowd didn't get to him, but the gum stains did. There were gum stains all over the dirty pavement. Bane of my life, muttered Cack, and started counting.

It was many hours before the search parties found him.

Hungry Ghosts

Sage remembered that before the fatal debate his son had been taken from a police station, with the knowledge and consent of some of the officers involved, for a vicious illegal interrogation. And he had been powerless to pursue the culprits . . . He had ignored this warning. They had ignored all the many warnings that should have told them it was time to quit. They'd come back to England to reprise the dictatorship the way Ax had originally intended. Charm offensive, softly softly: but you can't do that. You can't return to the same fucking poor situation you held in check with an army, and say let's play nicely. They don't know how to be nice, they're institutionalised.

He thought he understood the depth of Ax's distress now, that staring-into-nothing mood. We took on the bad guys, and we did not SEE their priorities, we only saw our own. That's our unforgivable worst crime.

The chief of England's nameless, unaccountable secret police entered the room in a motor chair. A rigid plastic collar, swathed in white silk, held Lord Vries's chin at a haughty angle, making him look like a nineteenth century dandy: ineffably sleek, blond and pink, a true blond, hardly a shade of vulgar yellow in it.

Sage grinned. 'Is the collar permanent?'

The chair glided to the desk. Jack flicked a switch. 'We are now recording. You have consented to this procedure, Mr Pender?'

'I've consented.'

Jack rose and came over, using the cane that had been balanced on his knees. Walking didn't come easily. Got a body brace under his clothes, Sage guessed. 'We believe that two realtime cognitive scanners were stored in the building on Battersea Reach. We searched the premises some weeks ago, including the rooms under the basement, and found nothing. The residents, including your, er, colleagues, Mr Merrick, Mr Trevor and Mr Stannen, denied all knowledge of the controlled neurological equipment.'

'Yeah, I know.'

'You may not have realised this, but it is illegal to possess, or have in your possession, the precursors of weaponised magic ... I don't want to bring the Heads in for questioning, Sage. Or any of your employees. They aren't criminals. That's why it's best if you tell me where the scanners are.'

'I can't tell you what I don't know. But you're welcome to try.'

He wanted to ask what was being done to Ax and Fiorinda. If I am here ... But it would be bad to show anxiety. Keep things simple. Humiliate someone, he will humiliate you back if he can, and they had humiliated Jack Vries cruelly, in a very public way. It's a fundamental law: bastards have feelings too. Forget that at your peril. So I take my licks, Jack will feel better, and maybe I'll survive.

The white tiled walls of the room gleamed. What happened to Peter?

'Do you know what day it is?' said Jack, leaning on his cane.

'Er, Thursday? Evening?'

Dad is at the restaurant, thinking how fucking unreliable I am.

'It is the sixteenth of August, and the night of the full moon of the seventh month of the Chinese year. The Chinese call this the moon of the hungry ghosts. We call it *Lúnasa*. You know the story of Lugh? The god of cunning and of light, the woman made for him out of flowers by the elder magician? It adds up to a time of great power. If you can't help us to locate the scanners, then we may precipitate the transformation, which would be another answer to our enquiries.'

'You've got to be kidding.'

'As long as you understand that you may involuntarily incriminate both yourself and the President; and you still consent to the procedure.'

Sage laughed. 'Jack, listen to me. I'm not Superman, and I'm not a werewolf. The rules have not changed. I took part in a very high-tech neurological experiment, the A-team took part in another, and outside of those conditions "magic" is as futile as it was a thousand years ago. An' you can't make the Chinese and the so-called "Celtic" calendars add up, because they don't. None of it adds up.'

Oh, fuck. Supposed to be humouring him.

The dandy moved his poised head carefully from side to side. 'You're the one who doesn't understand. In all my studies I never had one single unequivocal proof that I could move the world, and yet I believed. I am a believer, I am a practitioner of sacred truth, and you have proved my faith, and the faith of millions like me.'

Fiorinda had told Sage that if there were an A-team built in England, Jack Vries would be a prime candidate. He stared up at the ineffable dandy, pitiless secret policeman, with this deadly knowledge running through him.

'You don't want Olwen's scanners. They'd be useless to you.'

The Wiccan scholar took a long slow breath, and set out on the difficult journey back to the desk. Sage watched with a terrible shrinking in his throat and belly, a tremor in all his limbs that he could feel through the chemical paralysis.

'The interview was halted for a call of nature.'

Jack turned around, and spoke frankly, off the record. 'You'd better understand that nobody is going to stop this, and if you think I'm afraid to touch Joss Pender's son you're mistaken. The lord and the lady are sacrosanct, you are not. If you're bluffing, I suggest you stop bluffing now.'

'I don't know where the scanners are. I consent to the procedure.'

The equipment was Pacrim, Indonesian: he guessed it was about ten or fifteen years old. And this is how the British government was spending my tax money when I was a filthy-rich bad boy, back before Dissolution. So remember, this is not new bad news ... The mask came down, the stiff gag was pressed between his teeth, his eyelids were mechanically drawn back. Was Lord Vries still in the room? He didn't know. Fine, flexible needles slid around his eyeballs and probed deep. He had been told the nerves would suffer no damage, unless this went on for a long time. He was afraid it could not be true.

He was back at the Insanitude, in Allie's new office. He said to her, 'You never did get your eyes lasered, did you?' Allie said, 'I'm fine with contact lenses, thanks.' He was afraid for her, because she would be in trouble when there were no more contact lenses in the shops. She would be helpless. 'You should do it, get it done, stop pissing around. Eyes are important. Go to Cardiff, take DK with you. Once you're there, don't come back.' If he made it plausible, she would leave. He returned to other scenes, and told other people. Get out now. It's over. Go! But Sage must not get out from the house of pain. Don't start meditating, or you will die. Die, hear that? So DON'T.

The Stranglers alternated with Schubert, first movement of the B flat piano sonata D960. Both good, neither of them cutting the pain.

He thought of the muscles of his face, the cascade of tiny spasms that added up to the word agony: which would not be written, because the anaesthetist who was standing by had upped the dose and he was completely paralysed. He heard them murmuring about what they saw on their screen, the voices neutral, unintelligible. The Expression of Emotion in Man and Animals, Charles Darwin, ancient photographs pored over by the teenager who had become Aoxomoxoa.

Those images had fascinated him. He had found them a very useful resource when he was thinking out how to build the avatar mask; how to map the muscle-fibre contractions by mental reverse engineering. Are all artists part-butcher? Yes. We cut open the world. I am a vivisectionist, no wonder I have bad dreams. Surprisingly, he could still think. How hard am I? He wished he could black out. The immense vitality that was his birthright, that had carried him to the Zen, was not his friend now.

The sessions ran together, the spaces between them were pauses of calm clarity, and he was not aware that he was losing track of time, of place. He saw the world the way the bad guys had seen it, with COGNITIVE SCANNERS all huge, and everything else dwindled, two-dimensional. A couple of times he thought of saying why don't you ask my dad? But he was in uncharted territory. Ax's failsafe precautions had assumed Joss Pender was safe from reprisals: can't assume that now. For once in my life I would have screamed for you, please help me Daddy. But I daren't.

Illuminations. A clear glass, standing on a red-gold velvet tablecloth. At first he thought it was a remembered detail from an old picture: Chardin? No, more modern. Eventually he realised the painter was himself. The glass was Ax, and the velvet was Fiorinda. But where am I? He was worried, he was afraid he had disappeared from the relationship, something he was always afraid of because they are locked in process, I am just the catalyst, the medium; whatever. Then he knew: I am the picture, of course. The picture of the world that the mind makes is the I that sees the picture, it's a paradox. He began to code himself.

SEVEN

The Walls

On the first night they were alone something unprecedented happened. It was about an hour after they'd been escorted back from Rick's Place; they were still in the wired, after-the-show phase, cruelly compounded by Sage's absence. Ax was building card houses, Fiorinda was pretending to read, but turning few pages. The bell that summoned them to the receiving room rang. They stared at the row of antique chimes above the door of the red chamber . . . Ax moved first. He went to her, took her hands and kissed them. 'I'll get it. You stay here.'

He passed through the suite preparing himself, a reflex long established. Allah Akbar, be ready to die, do it well, be glad it will be beside her. God is good.

The Moon and Stars room was empty, likewise the antechamber, with its doors to the outside world. Someone knocked, a discreet, respectful tap, and he felt a change, a shift deep in the murky entrails of this impossible situation. A manservant in black and white stood in the lamp lit corridor, guards behind him with parade-ground faces. He proffered a silver tray, in white-gloved hands. On the tray lay a mobile phone of venerable design.

'A call for you, Sir.'

'Is that you, Ax?'

Ax frowned at the servant, stepped back into the antechamber and closed the door. 'Who's this?' He knew he should know the voice, but he didn't.

'It's Joss, Joss Pender. Listen, Sage has gone missing.'

'What? Can you talk—?'

'I can talk, a little, not much. He was supposed to meet me at a restaurant, he didn't turn up. We know he reached London, he was

205

with Allie at the Insanitude, then he went to Battersea, probably on foot. He went out with Cack Stannen; George and Bill were at the Party in the Park. Then we don't know what happened. They found Cack about ten, wandering around Clapham Junction. George and Bill are talking to him, but it's difficult to interrogate Peter. Sage didn't have a hand phone, no chance of a trace. There may have been some ex-barmies at the warehouse, earlier today. They may have been offering some kind of information.'

'Have you—? Who else knows about this?'

'Yes,' said Joss, dryly. 'We've involved the police. No news yet.'

'Joss,' said Ax, thunder in his head, a fury of helplessness. 'Be careful.'

'I'll be careful. I'll find him, Ax, don't worry. I have my resources.' The older man's voice sounded calm, resolute, fatherly. 'May I speak to Fiorinda?'

He sprinted to the red room. Before he reached her the phone was dead.

Greg Mursal came down from London for meetings, and went away again. Lady Anne, the governor of this royal prison, had her own apartment. They did not hear her comings or goings, buried alive as they were, but she would send her respects to the Moon and Stars suite, punctiliously, announcing her presence. The next morning a handwritten note arrived, on a silver salver. It said she would be remaining at Wallingham, at their disposal, 'during this distressing time'. A gracious turn of phrase. They wrote back, asking to be informed of any news at once; and prayed for another phonecall from Joss. It didn't come.

At Rick's Place Bill and George didn't turn up. The Scots were absent too; they had tour dates on the other side of the country. The crowd knew not to expect Sage, he had 'business in town' (euphemism: everyone knew the real situation, of course). As far as they could tell no one, punters, guests or tv, was aware that he'd disappeared. The habit of performance saved them. They worked the crowd, brought up against the fact that they had no friends here, not one person they would dare to trust among the VIPs, the hopeful bands, the social climbers. They told themselves that if the disappearance hadn't been acknowledged, maybe it was all right. Maybe the enemy had decided that the parole meetings couldn't happen; but Sage was okay and coming back. He should have returned on Sunday morning. He didn't, and Lady Anne regretted to inform them that there was no news.

The royal prisoners sat at either end of the dining table, a manservant behind Mr Preston's chair, a womanservant behind Miss Slater's. Mr Pender's place was not laid. Courses were presented, in elaborate sequence: a selection of cold cuts, as it was Sunday. An asparagus soup; followed by a superb round of beef, with several dishes of plainly cooked vegetables. Traditional English cooking was the rule. It was like being the living dolls in a doll's house, and the Wallingham servants callous children who insisted on keeping up the dreadful game. Fiorinda couldn't eat these meals; she had lost too much weight in two months and it scared Ax. But she did not look weak on it. She looked electric, her pale skin burning from the inside: she was live-wire.

'I found out about the ghost,' she announced, signalling for her entrée to be removed untouched. 'The ghost in our red room? It was in a memoir in our library.'

'Oh yeah?'

'It's the ghost of a young woman who lived here in the nineteen fifties. She was playing with a ouija board, although she'd been warned not to, and she conjured up something that evil that withered her soul. So then she died and she's been trapped in that room ever since, getting more and more crazy.'

'Rough.'

The staff who worked inside the Moon and Stars suite were carefully chosen. Their loyalty was to Lady Anne, Wallingham, and possibly the Prime Minister. If they'd been given their choice of living dolls they'd have liked to have kept Jordan and Milly Preston: such a handsome, docile couple. They considered Ax and Fiorinda ungrateful, cold, and too intelligent, which isn't what people want in their royals. But they believed in the ghost, and they didn't like it. They'd been overheard telling each other that the red chamber had always been haunted, by the legendary Black Shape, and you mustn't let it touch you ... Ax saw the eyes shifting, felt the *frisson* passing him, and grinned malignly. No peace for the wicked. Stick it to them, Fio.

'D'you think we should change bedrooms?'

Fiorinda shrugged. 'Can't be bothered.'

'You don't think it will harm us?'

She raised her hollow grey eyes and smiled like ice at the girl presenting another dish. 'No, thank you ... Nah, not us, we're untouchable. Think who we are.'

A card game, on Monday night. Ax and Fiorinda cross-legged on the floor of the red chamber, two lonely royal children locked up and forgotten in the haunted room.

'D'you remember the Armada Concert?'

'What about it?'

'It was the end of the Rock the Boat tour, and we were giving the concert in a derelict kiddies' theme park in Cleethorpes ... Are sevens transparent?'

'Yeah.'

'Then you're picking up again, sorry.'

'Fuck.' Ax arranged a massive influx of pasteboard. 'These cards are getting old ... Pleasure Island, yeah, I remember that. Horrible dangerous dump.'

'Oh? I liked it. It was so odd, colourful and dreamlike, and the rides the hippies got working were insane. Tom had just been killed, but that's not what I'm remembering. I'm remembering a moment when I met you, on a falling-apart theme-park "Mediaeval" street. I was ... I had armed guards round me. For the first time. Just like a big celebrity eh? But it wasn't like that.'

'No,' said Ax. 'Your turn, babe. It was more serious.'

Fiorinda picked up. 'You had the armed guards too, but *you*, you fucking looked armed yourself, although you weren't. I looked at you ... Hahaha, but I can put them all straight down again, sorry. Anyone could see you had killed people, well, of course, everyone knew you had, up in Yorkshire.'

'Thanks. I love it when people look at me and see a murderer. I looked at you, you looked at me, an' the backstage crowd looked at us. Yeah, I know the moment.'

'And we saw that *this* would happen,' said Fiorinda.

A hush of awe, that closes like a fist over the young man of twenty-eight and the eighteen-year-old girl, in the nervous hour before they face the crowd. Any one of those big, violent concerts in Boat People summer could have been the same. They had been the iconic celebrity couple, when a nation was tearing itself apart. They had chosen not to be celebrity-cattle, they had chosen to make a stand, to hold things together, to protect the poor. And that choice had brought them, inexorably, to this dank room, the smell of dust, the dim lamp, the deathly silence. You can't call those moments seeing the future, it's not the future.

When we were there, we were also here.

Fiorinda uncovered her three concealed cards for the end game. Ax sighed, he was losing badly. 'Sage wasn't with us, was he?'

'No, he came and found us later, in that storm shelter.'

'Oh yeah, I remember.' He looked up from his sorry hand and smiled at her. 'You know, I *know* there was a time when we were together and he wasn't our lover. He was your big brother, best friend, and—'

'Your best mate, who used to be your big NME feud enemy.'

'Not *enemy*, Fiorinda—'

'Hohoho. You just hated his-a steenking crowd-pulling guts, Ax Preston.'

'Anyway, I was saying ... I can't remember it. Literally. My memory plays tricks. I think of us, Sage is there. If I think of us in the past, he must have been there. In bed, whatever, and if he wasn't, he must have just popped out for—'

Fiorinda put down her cards, face-up. 'I've won, let's stop. Please.'

They held each other's hands: desolate and terrified, crouched on the dusty golden briars, in a slew of worn, greasy playing cards.

Suffering in public is a hell only for pride. Celebrity-cattle will scream and flail for the cameras, and feel no extra pain. Ax watched Fiorinda's contained agony for as long as he could bear it, which wasn't long. On Tuesday he requested an interview with Lady Anne. The request was granted immediately; a startling change. He was escorted – it was strange to see new parts of the house, to have glimpses of the outdoors through unshuttered windows – to a fine set of rooms, though not one of the great public apartments, with leaded windows over the south lawns.

The old lady had favoured female-type business suits whenever he'd met her before. In her private study she wore a floor-length gown in pillar-box red with blue slashed sleeves; her meagre hair was covered with a close-fitting red cap. She was standing when Ax walked in, her hands clasped over a big chatelaine of decorative keys. He thought of Rox, grown old and shrunken and withered, but Lady Anne somehow made sure you knew she was female . . . She curtsied, and then remained standing when Ax sat down.

'Please.' He released her with a gesture, thinking of the Mediaevalists in Paris, and the fatal conviction you get that these people are so far out they're laughable. Oh, they dissociate, but they're sharp enough. She was a parched little mummy inside the lobster carapace: he could have broken her in half. But that's the werewolf talking.

Lady Anne took a chair. There were no attendants in sight, he'd asked for a private interview and this seemed to have been respected. She embarked on a speech of greeting, before he could forestall her; he sat it out politely and asked if she had any news. A wary look flickered over her face and was gone: no, there was no news. As soon as there was anything to report it would be with Lady Anne at once, and she would relay it without delay.

'I'm surprised Bill Trevor and George Merrick didn't turn up at the Drawing Room on Friday or Saturday,' said Ax, 'to update us. It was from Battersea Reach that he disappeared. I'd like to speak to them. Could you get hold of them for me?'

Lady Anne looked as vague as was possible for the tough old bitch. 'I believe it's been decided that Mr Trevor and Mr Merrick should not visit or communicate with Wallingham for the moment. For security reasons.'

'I see.' Oh, fuck. What's happened to the Heads?

'We don't know *why* Mr Pender disappeared, you see, and that makes, well—'

She hesitated, with the vague smile and wary eyes. He realised that she was afraid he knew the truth, by telepathy. Wolfman here could be playing games with her, knowing all along just what was happening to his boyfriend. I did not know for sure, thought Ax. Not absolutely sure. But I do now. I know enough, God help me. He stood up, walked across to the windows and looked out over the drowsy gardens, the tank-trap; the tree-dotted park.

Allah Akbar.

'These "expiatory rites" that were mentioned at the beginning of our stay here? I'd like to know more about that.'

He knew the painless lethal injection wouldn't cut it. If the king's going to die you want some *TA-DA!* about it; some wicked fancywork. But he could taste the fanaticism in this woman, and she wasn't alone. If he offered them a king to be executed as a werewolf, in trade for a living superweapon (who was refusing to co-operate, obviously), he knew where Lady Anne's vote would be, no fucking question. He could divide the bastards, at least. What will they do to me? Late summer sunshine on the lime trees by the croquet lawn, and a shocked silence behind him.

'Your Majesty.'

Ax turned, feeling that his face was a mask and he was looking through the eyeholes. Lady Anne was on her feet, totally disconcerted. Were those *tears*, brimming in her sunken old eyes?

'Your Majesty. In ... in advance of the formal announcement, which Lord Mursal plans to make very soon, I intend to order new arrangements in Your Majesty's household, very gladly. By many signs, we are now aware that there was not the slightest hint of lycanthropy. Whatever happened that night – we may never know – no blame attaches to Your Majesty! The blow, if there was a blow, was within a king's perquisite, your outrage was just, and Lord Vries will beg your forgiveness for the—'

Ax was bathed in a craven wash of relief: this animal does not want to die in extended agony. But now he had nothing to trade. All he could do was stare her down, recalibrating, trying to figure out the new position.

'Lord Vries is alive!' He affected surprise. 'I'm glad to hear it. Where is he?'

'Lord Vries has recovered sufficiently to return to his duties. He is hesitant, maybe *unduly* hesitant, to seek an audience with Your Majesty.' Lady Anne drew a breath, having revealed this whacking fault line. Her old face glowed. 'But soon everything will be as it should be. The Lord and Lady will rule, from Wallingham, under my watch and ward. Mr Pender will serve his country in his ... his own way. All will be well in England, all manner of thing will be well.'

She went down again, foundering in her heavy skirts like a ship hitting rocks, into a deep reverence, her old back ramrod straight, her eyes fixed on Ax's face in exaltation. Yep: tears. Tears of actual joy, he thought. His skin crept.

'Well, this is a great day,' he said, coolly, when he thought the pause was long enough (fucking hope that stunt murders her sciatica). 'I hope the salving of my reputation is a good omen, and that we'll be hearing from Mr Pender soon. I'd like to call Joss and give him the good news; could you arrange that? You know, our lack of private telecoms is a problem.'

Lady Anne rose up, unembarrassed. 'Any news will be relayed to Your Majesty at once.' She didn't seem to have heard the part about private telecoms.

In the red room Fiorinda was working at her embroidery. She'd requested the materials some time ago, to make a change from reading. It would have frightened him to see her like that, once. He'd have been sure he was going to catch hell for throwing her back into a world where women could do little else, because of course the whole Crisis was his fault entirely. But she was a long way from using handicrafts as satire now. You have to do something: preferably something painstaking, that helps you to give nothing away.

'What did Lady Anne say?'

He felt immeasurably shaken, where was I just now? On the brink of what horrors? 'I'm not sure . . . I mean, I know what she said, but I don't know how much I'm reading into it. I think Sage is okay. I feel as if I have reason to hope.'

Fiorinda paid attention to her careful petal stitch, frowning a little. 'And in words?'

'As soon as she has news, we will have it. Bill and George won't be coming to the club for the moment, for security reasons . . . And I'm not a werewolf any more. I'm not suspected of being a werewolf, I've been cleared, don't ask me how. Lady Anne was about to inform us; my request for an interview forestalled her.'

It was a turning-point in their affairs. Lady Anne came to see them, with ceremony. She repeated the joyful tidings, and when asked about Sage spoke in veiled terms about high security matters, which might be resolved soon. They were presented (another silver tray, offered by Lady Anne's favourite senior womanservant) with the internal keys of the fortress.

The keys were ceremonial. They unlocked the outer door to the Moon and Stars suite, which was always guarded, and bolted and barred on the outside every night; and public rooms that were never locked during the day. The freedom to roam was genuine. They went out into the gardens; with an escort. They felt the sun, they saw daylight and growing things, they breathed fresh air. When they returned to the suite they found servants bustling over it, beating the hangings and opening shutters; replacing their worn bedlinen and towels with far superior articles.

They were shown to a drawing room, on the same floor but in a different world. The inevitable guards waiting there saluted them with reverence. The black and whites who served afternoon tea behaved nothing like the screws in the Moon and Stars. Later they were escorted back to rooms that had been scrubbed and burnished; the rich colours of the hangings and carpets revealed, the air scented with bergamot and vanilla. At around midnight the antique mobile phone was brought to their door, same routine as before. Ax thought it would be Joss, and it still might be bad news, so he made sure he took the call.

'Hi, Ax.'

'*Sage!*'

Fiorinda was beside him. Her eyes shone, he gave her the phone.

'Sage! It's good to hear your voice, where are you, are you okay?'

'I'm fine, my brat, relax, everything's all right. Look, I'm sorry you've been anxious, but I couldn't help it. I can't come back, not yet, I've something to do, it'll be a while longer. Is Ax still there?'

'I'm here, I'm still here—'

'Are things better for you in Wallingham by now? They should be.'

They clung to the handset together, their cheeks touching. Sage's voice was tired, calm, cheerful: obscurely more convincing because they couldn't see his face. 'Yes,' said Fiorinda. 'Things are better, I wouldn't say they're good, but m-materially improved: and you? How about you? Can you talk?'

'Yeah, yeah, I can talk. Don't worry, I'm going to get you out. Got to go now.'

'Can we talk to you again? Sage!'

'Soon, so just relax, stick with it. This is good, not bad, everything's okay.'

The phone was dead.

'He didn't mention you not being a werewolf,' said Fiorinda.

'Maybe he doesn't know.'

On Thursday night they found that Rick's Place had been reprogrammed too. The transformation was subtle, presumably because as yet there had been no official announcement. But the guards who escorted them through the house had a different attitude, and the burly 'waiters' who had followed them around the nightclub floor, officiously close, had been stepped back. Gilded young men of the new élite moved into the take-the-bullet space. They didn't introduce themselves, but they acted very respectful. Ax and Fiorinda might have imagined newsflash headlines PRESIDENT AX EXONERATED! TO BE CROWNED KING!

On Saturday night the Scots were back. Ax spoke to them briefly, joking about their persistence. Did they think the 'invitations' went into a prize draw, were they trying to make sure of the jackpot?

'Do they not?' Sovra's tone expressed disbelief. 'That wad be a grave disappointment. Not to say you don't have a wee fanbase here, but we're counting up the scores and verra hopeful we have the odds.'

'Well, that's *good*,' said Ax, smiling with his eyes. 'You keep wishing.' He laughed and moved on, shaking his head, followed by his respectful shadow.

George and Bill had not appeared, they hadn't heard from Joss Pender again, and there'd been no second call from Sage. They were still prisoners. They'd have been fools not to realise that in essence they were more helpless; more isolated than they had ever been.

Fiorinda cultivated the female staff. She did not speak to them, she made them speak to her, in the simplest way. She sought out places where the cleaners were working (it took an army of them to keep Wallingham in perfect order), and *touched* things. The women could not scream at her, or attack her, while she was holding some fragile gewgaw. They had to ask her politely to desist, and then they discovered that Fiorinda was very interested. She would like to know what she was touching, where it came from; how do you look after it? Plenty of the women would not play, but some of them would . . .

She didn't know if this would ever be useful. A space had opened around her and she was moving into it, as in a game of Go; that was all. And it was something to do that kept her out of Ax's way. Such is life. Shared terror for their darling had made them cling to each other when they were locked up alone in the haunted room, but now everything jarred.

Endless corridors. Staircases for every rank, miles of attics, odd little doors opening onto a planetary landscape of roofs and parapets. Endless show-off rooms at the front of the pile, opening into each other, larded with decorative plasterwork, thick with gold-bordered, rose-pink carpeting (it was a Wallingham colourway); always cold because of the north aspect, and the huge fountains at the head of the carriage sweep. This house is built backwards, it belongs in New Zealand.

Sage had been gone for thirteen days, and a dull afternoon was hazing into evening outdoors. Fiorinda helped a Wallingham lady called Hazel to dust porcelain in the Reynolds Passage, their progress surveilled by a gallery that starred a pair of fake-pensive eighteenth century debutantes with huge fluffy fake grey hair.

'It's been a *lovely* summer,' sighed Hazel, a sandy, scrawny little woman with pebble glasses, an aimless smile and the authority of her passionate dedication.

'Gorgeous.'

A fat pair of blue urns, finned in gold like exotic fishes, flanked a gilded nymph and shepherd group on a pedestal. Two by two by two by two. Nothing goes by threes. Did these things ever mean anything to anyone? Try to imagine Wallingham as a family home, generations of the tat a home accrues, presents and prizes and souvenirs, all laid out in immaculate manic order. Look, inside these urns there will be hairgrips, buttons, hairy Blu-tac, plecs, stubs of pencil—

'And very, very special for us, because of having you and His Majesty here. Both hands on the piece at all times, ma'am.'

'Sorry.'

'I don't know where the time goes. It seems as if Lammas is hardly over, and you start to think about Samhain. I do hope we'll still have you then.'

'Were you brought up a Christian, Hazel?'

The woman must be sixty. Obviously she loved her job, maybe she wasn't very smart, but she must remember the normal world, before Dissolution—

'Oh goodness, yes, ma'am. I only came to the Old Religion in my teens, in the seventies, what a long, long time ago it seems now. So many changes. That's when I started working here, for the National Trust, and met Lady Anne, who took a real interest in all of us. She's such a wonderful person—'

Damn. Cross *you* off my turning list.

'I was wondering if it was at Samhain that His Majesty meant to undergo the rites, such a noble thing for him to do.' Hazel sighed sentimentally, and her dusting slowed in contemplation. 'Though very solemn for you, ma'am, of course.'

'The rites? Why would he do that? Ax is *not* a werewolf!'

'Oh dear.' Hazel's cheeks went pink. 'I shouldn't have . . . I didn't mean anything . . . Someone said, in the housekeeping room . . . His Majesty has been discussing it with Lady Anne. Ma'am! Please! The Ch'ien-lung urn—!'

Their suite, as they had discovered when the shutters were opened, looked onto an internal courtyard. Ax sat in one of the window embrasures of the red room picking guitar and peered down at the square of pavement three floors below. There was a dry fountain in the centre of it; he could see no doors into the building. Ranks of blank windows, shuttered on the inside, walls of water-stained stone . . .

His Les Paul usually stayed in its case in the bottom of the armoire, along with Sage's visionboard, the first aid kit and Fiorinda's saltbox, in her tapestry bag. They were superstitious about touching these treasures, which had so far been ignored by the jailers. Out of sight, out of mind . . . it's a true word. But he had needed the comfort of holding this old friend in his arms . . . How closely were they watched? They didn't know. They were agreed (it was one of the things they couldn't discuss, but he thought they were agreed) that the visual surveillance might be quite poor. But you had to assume anything you said was overheard. It wasn't so terrible. Forget the invasion of privacy, who cares if they see you cry, if they see you making love: fuck 'em. Just remember to say nothing that could get you in trouble.

It's the way a lot of people live their whole lives.

His fingers moved, his mind went round in circles. If that was Sage speaking to us in real time, and intuitively, instinctively I believe it was, and I know she does too . . . then he was alive, and using one of our keywords. He is *not* okay, fuck that for a lie, but he is alive, I feel that, and who could make our Bodhisattva use a keyword against his will? What did they do to make him do that?

> Begone dull care,
> You and I shall never agree—

Ax had once told an enemy of the Reich that rockstars are like gods: dumb idols, eating well and making the priests rich. He could feel that fate closing in on him, and Fiorinda. They had powers that could tear the world apart, but they would do nothing. They would stay here, hands tied, coffined in stone, not daring to move. He looked up at the tank of sky. How much more of this can I take? What will I do if she starts losing it? She doesn't love me, she wants Sage, and I can't get him back for her.

The real meaning of the word Iphigenia was burning a hole in his heart.

Fiorinda stripped off her felt slippers and her polishing gloves and dropped to the floor, thick curls falling forward, smothering her face; arms huddled round her knees. These walls are made of glass. Every wall in this prisonhouse is a one-way mirror, and we are whores in a fish-tank, waiting to be scooped out. They took Sage. Ax won't wait to be taken, he's jumping up and down, squealing me, me, pretty please. The bastard. I hate him. I hate, hate, hate him. Torrents of silence poured through the woven stars, it's like having your mouth stitched up. Resolution almost failed her, fury almost overwhelmed her. She steeled herself and rose to her feet, stretching and sighing and holding her back. My, that stately home housework is demanding!

'Tomorrow,' said Ax, 'we could go for another walk in the gardens.'

It was late in the evening: they had dined. The shutters were locked and the hangings drawn over them, the servants had departed. They were in the scrubbed and burnished red room, bereft of their dusty refuge. Ax picked guitar: setting Fiorinda's teeth on edge, and breaching their silent agreement that the treasures should never be touched. She sat in the red armchair with her embroidery frame.

'I thought you'd decided not to play that in here.'

'It's something to do. I'm getting interested in the English idiom—'

'How fashionable of you. You should send out for a lute, I'm sure Lady Anne would be delighted.'

'Maybe I will,' said Ax, narrow-eyed. 'Right now I'm going to work on my new repertoire of Hendrixed-up English folksongs. Is that okay?'

'You do that,' Fiorinda kept her head bent, counting threads. 'Ax, is it true you've volunteered for the expiatory rites that Lady Anne and Greg talked about?'

Ax did not reply. He stared at her, dumbfounded. Are you so angry with me you've forgotten we're on camera?

Yeah, she thought. I'm so angry. 'So I take it you did . . . You are incredible. Ax, you fucking idiot, expiatory rites means they will burn you alive. They are not kidding. They had me on the bonfire, remember? Burn you alive? You'll be begging for it. They will hang you, draw you and quarter you, that's the least they have in mind. DO YOU KNOW WHAT—'

'Yes,' he said, setting the Les Paul aside. 'I know what it means. Okay, I made the offer, maybe I shouldn't have, it just came to me to do it. This is old news. Lady Anne turned me down, I'm not a werewolf.'

She applied her needle, with vicious accuracy. 'Poor Ax. They wouldn't let you immolate yourself, and it's your only trick. You bastard. You utter bastard. You didn't think you should tell me first? You always did love him best.'

'I *said*, she turned me down. Look, this is out of date, it's over—'

'I think they took Sage and tried to make him turn into Wolfman, and whatever they did gave them an excuse to decide you're clean. They were prepared to sacrifice him. They have a use for you and me. Sage doesn't fit in the picture.'

'Fiorinda, Sage is okay! For fuck's sake, we both talked to him!'

One piercing glance told him what she thought of that, and told him also she was in control. She had not cracked under the strain, she just hated Ax. She bent over her work again, her tone clipped and icy. 'So fine, Sage is on his secret government mission, we're the fucking Lord and Lady, and you'll have to settle for the slow torture of staying alive, at which I am expert. Ax, remember when I came back to the Snake Eyes house, after the Countercultural Thinktank's first meeting? Did you really seduce me that night – polite word for it – because you fancied me?'

'Huh—? What—?'

'Or was it because you had a crush on Aoxomoxoa, and you wanted to fuck something that belonged to him? I know I'm not your *type*, in the female line. I know you prefer a real woman with plenty of tits and bum, so I've wondered.'

She looked up with limpid grey eyes and a smile of contempt.

Nothing is safe with her. She's a psychopath. She'll attack something as precious and vital as the first night you spent together, *eight years ago—*

'I don't remember doing much seduction,' said Ax, curling his lip. 'I wouldn't mention it, I have never thought anything of it, but it was you brought up the idea of sex, not me. You did have that reputation, so I wasn't surprised. My memory is we both had a good time. Several good times, as I recall.'

Fiorinda went on stitching: sliced open to the bone by this misrepresentation. 'Oh yeah, I often offered to fuck blokes when I was a kid, to get it over with. Teenage girls in the music biz find it's easier. I used to have a lot of *good times* too. You're easy pleased, Ax. I was faking, of course.'

'I knew *that*,' said Ax, quickly (one of the memories on which he based his whole existence shattered). 'Fuck's sake, you were sixteen years old, with a passion for your abusive daddy and more or less oblivious to the existence of the rest of the human race. What kind of pornstar do you think you were?'

It was a knife-fight now. They were possessed. The horrible release of saying the worst thing possible, with full knowledge and intent, was irresistible.

'You self-obsessed little Hitler. Remember when you ran away, Mr Dictator, because you were convinced the threesome wasn't working, how noble of you? Was that *really* to let Sage have me all to himself?

Or was it because you finally realised you were never, ever, ever going to hear me say I loved Big Brother?'

Ax had run away because it was the king, the king's wife and the wife's lover in bed together, and he had not been able to bear it. He took full responsibility for the disasters that had followed, as she knew. But if there are no rules, then yes. YES, her scorn for what he was trying to do had been a hateful burden. Fiorinda sneering on the sidelines, refusing to take responsibility for her own choices, saying I'm a domestic animal now, that's my fate and you can't save me: saying why bother, the situation's hopeless, into the foul swamp and never get out, you can't win—

'You know, I could never understand why you didn't leave yourself. You hated what I was doing, you kept telling me I was worthless. You could have had Sage off me anytime, and enjoyed making *his* life a misery as he trailed round the jet-set world he hates, chasing your fucking pitiful grabby little ambition to be a global super-pop-star just like Daddy—'

'We're in here because of you,' yelled Fiorinda, on her feet, composure abandoned. 'YOU KNEW we should never have come back, that England was as dangerous as all hell, but when President Eiffrich says, oh please take this poisoned chalice, you know he doesn't give a fuck for us in his grand schemes, but you jump at it because he makes you feel big and Ax Preston can't resist a gamble—'

'Sorry, Fio. That won't work, you can't pin that on me. I DID NOT BRING YOU BACK. You did it yourself, it was your choice. *I'm* not your big strong Daddy-substitute. *I've* never been your boss—'

A sound, quiet but unmistakable. A door had opened, and closed.

They stood frozen, as in a game of statues, hearing nothing, knowing there had been an escalation, trying to figure out what had happened while they were screaming. The chimes were still. No bell had rung, but someone was inside the suite. This had never happened before, never. The gold briars glinted on the red wall hangings . . . A weight of menace: is this it? Are we going to die now?

Ax picked up a lamp.

'Will you stay here while I go and see?'

'No!' breathed Fiorinda.

The receiving room was a cavern of shadow, Ax's lamplight waking gleams from the stars and crescents around the walls. He thought, for some reason, that he would see two coffins lined up open on the floor. No coffins.

'Anyone there?'

Something moved. There was a tall figure sitting in one of the chairs.

It was Sage.

'*Sage?*'

'Hi there, my dears. See? I told you I'd be back.'

It was his voice, sweet and deep. It was Sage. He was dressed in a grubby white shirt and jeans: and, strangely, he seemed to be wearing dark glasses. As they came closer, he turned his face away. They realised he was avoiding the light.

'Are you all right?' whispered Fiorinda.

'Ah, I'm fine. Jus', not the light, okay?'

He seemed rooted to that chair. They looked at each other, constrained not by the surveillance but by Sage himself, something in him they dared not touch.

'Let's get you through to the other room,' said Ax.

Fiorinda took the lamp. Ax walked with Sage, guiding him. At the door of the red bedchamber he baulked, unwilling. 'They cleaned the suite,' explained Fiorinda. 'The red room doesn't smell musty any more. Part of our new privileges.'

'Oh right. Shame, I was— I was— I missed this place, I was used to this place.'

'We think so too,' said Ax. 'C'mon, you should lie down, my big cat.'

Sage lay down, obediently, on his back. Fiorinda dimmed the lamp to its lowest setting and put it on the bedstand. The other lights in the room didn't seem to bother him.

'What happened to you?' breathed Ax.

'Well, they want the cognitive scanners,' said Sage, reasonably, as if he expected Ax and Fiorinda to know all about this. 'To build an A-team. And I'm to tell them where, so they won't have to bother arresting anyone else ... They've been using memory retrieval imaging. O' course I don't know where the scanners are, so they're not having any luck, but they keep trying.' He lay very still, but kept talking, only his lips moving, motormouth. 'It's a crude machine, 'bout ten, fifteen years old. I don't know what they're seeing on their screens, but I bet it's not much. So tha's what's been happening to me. I walked into it, stupidly, but then I thought, better co-operate, does no harm to show willing. Oh yeah, and as a bonus, you and I are not werewolves any more, Ax.'

'Yeah, we know. They provoked you and you didn't bite them?'

'Somethen' like. Anyway, now I get a break. Recovery time . . . Is there, is there any way I could talk to my dad? I'd like to tell him I'm okay.'

They held his hands, staring at each other across his body.

'Will you let me take off those glasses?' asked Fiorinda, softly.

He hesitated. 'Okay . . . But not the light.'

She gently lifted the sunglasses, cheap wraparound shades she'd never seen before. They could see dark bruising from his brow to his cheekbones, some of it livid: some many days old, diffusing into his white skin.

His eyes. Oh God is good, he still has eyes, but what a mess—

'Sage. Did they damage the nerve? Baby, did they damage the nerves?'

His mouth moved, a bare whisper, trembling. 'They will if they do it again.'

'I'm going to get the first aid,' decided Fiorinda, abruptly.

'Yeah . . . please. Got some morphine, allegedly, before they dropped me off, but it's barely touching this. Uh, please. And could you move that light?'

Ax put out the lamp on the bedstand. Fiorinda darted to the armoire and came back with the white box. In deep shadow she pressed a diamorphine popper against Sage's throat, snapped it; and another. Immediately he sighed. 'Ah, thanks.' The eerily calm voice became a slurred murmur. 'Jack Vries is alive and well by the way, knew you'd be thrilled, Ax. Can I talk to my dad?'

'Not right now, sweetheart,' said Fiorinda. 'Let the drug take you away.'

'Got to keep still,' mumbled Sage. 'Lying down with m'head still, tha's all, my brat. Better tomorrow, fucking stupid, di'n't mean to scare you . . .'

They got down from the bed, closed the heavy curtains and stood, Fiorinda with her hand pressed over her mouth. The room seemed unnaturally bright, blood-red hangings, blood-red carpet; veined in wicked thorned sickles of gold.

Ax had a second interview with Lady Anne. She was rock-solid. Clearly she resented the Neurobomb agenda, but there'd been a division of the spoils and she was satisfied. She had her captive king to play with. She apologised for the charade of Mr Pender's 'disappearance' and explained to His Majesty that England must have Neurobomb technology. No other EU country was in a position to collaborate, and there was no political will for a partnership with the Welsh; who in any case denied they had access to the Zen Self company's work at Caer Siddi. Therefore the lost machines must be located—

I'll bet there's 'no political will', thought Ax. It hurt, grass cuts can sting, to know how England was rated by the neighbours. Slavery, secret police, the labour camps. Bring back the days when we were just crap at any form of competitive sport—

'I thought Zen Self scanners can't be used for weapon development?'

Lady Anne inclined her head. 'I believe all advanced technologies are open to adaptation, are they not? We think Mr Pender may have exaggerated the difficulties when speaking to Your Majesty, in the light of his religious scruples.'

'I see.'

How fucking ironic that this self-deluded apparatchik was the one who was supposed to believe in magic. He thought of Sage's information space science, in its fabulous diversity. B-loc and immix. Deciphering the os and 1s; air for Mars. And Fiorinda, ah, my living goddess . . . But mostly he thought of the people of England, the only way he could protect them now; and the flag of St George didn't matter a damn. He was disoriented, lost, stepping over the edge.

'In view of developments,' Lady Anne was saying, with respectful concern, 'Your Majesty may wish me to cancel the Yellow Drawing Room evenings?'

The name of this game is cat and mouse. When brutal pressure fails, you apply sweeteners. Make the prisoners grateful, call a halt to the torture, stop humiliating them, make them afraid the bad conditions will come back. Lady Anne's offer was amusing, in a way. But the last thing Ax wanted was to lose Rick's Place.

'Certainly not.' He took out a pack of 'Merry We Meet' cigarettes, which he'd snagged from one of the nightclub tables, last week— 'May I?' She bridled, but he lit up anyway. One of the attendants (they were not alone this time) scurried for an ashtray. 'Lady Anne, it was for times like this, great emergencies, that the Rock and Roll Reich was invented. The show must go on.'

He did not know what the fuck was happening outside these walls. All his friends could have been rounded up and shot. Japan could have sunk beneath the waves, Russia could have declared war on China, and they could both have the Neurobomb. He was not going to ask Lady Anne. He wasn't going to ask her any more questions at all ... He was only in this room because it would have looked fucking strange if his boyfriend had come back blinded and he *didn't* ask to speak to the management.

But he saw the flicker in her eyes, and stored that knowledge.

'We'll continue to entertain our guests. It's the least we can do.' He sighed. 'Mr Pender, I am sure, will be ready to continue the investigation soon.'

They left Sage sleeping with only the ghost to watch over him and went for a stroll in the grounds. It was a day of mist, the warmth of August on land colliding with a cold front from the sea. Ax told the spear-carriers, guards and servants, to keep their distance, and the two of them walked to the middle of the smoothly shaven lawns, alone. 'I know you've always blamed me,' said Fiorinda, biting her lip. 'Because you went away, and he decided he was Superman and got his liver ripped out fighting a duel with my father. *Now* you see. You can't stop him either.'

'Yeah,' said Ax. 'Plus you got yourself hatefully raped, just to save a few lives. I was always disgusted with you about that, too.'

Everything terrible thing they had said to each other was probably true, but the visceral bond was stronger. She laid her forehead against his shoulder and he held her there, for a moment, his cheek pressed against her hair. They walked on.

'I've searched the Help menu. There's nothing about people

who've been tortured by having needles stuck behind their eyes, but there's plenty about eyesocket gadget injuries. We can extrapolate.'

Medical assistance was likely to be provided, but they weren't going to trust it.

'Good,' said Ax.

'Something else you should probably know,' she added, thrusting her fists into the pockets of her drab hoodie. The royal couple were dressed very down, in contrast to the immaculate fatigues and glossy black and whites of their attendants. The Triumvirate wore drab and shabby clothes when they weren't in Rick's Place. The paparazzi of Crisis Europe (oh, there's always ways to penetrate celebrity seclusion) called this a rebel statement. They were wrong. It was taste.

He nodded, without meaning.

'I'm pregnant.'

Ax stopped walking. 'Oh, God.' He stared at her. 'How ... how long?'

'I'd missed a period just before Sage left. It never happened.'

'Oh, my God.' He had not been counting. 'I didn't think. It's never crossed my—oh, fuck— Oh God, no wonder you've been hating me.'

'Shut up. Anyway, I've been necking rotgut vodka ... You didn't ask me how I'm sure.'

'Are you sure? Have you tested?'

'Are you kidding? No I fucking have not! I'm terrified, Ax.'

'But you're sure you're pregnant?'

'It's not that I'm so sure,' she said, staring at the toes of her shoes, 'though I am ... It's like this. In less than two weeks I'm going to miss another period, and I don't think we kept it a locked-down secret before all this happened that I was trying to have a baby. This is a royal prison. You can bet your life somebody's keeping an eye on the queen's linen.'

'Fuck.'

'Well, anyway, what are we going to do now?'

They had reached the south end of the lawn, getting close to the tank-trap. A thin mist shrouded the park. They turned and headed back.

'I know what we should do,' said Ax. 'I'd already decided. We should find out if the Scots are real, which I think they are, and sell England to them.'

She thought about it. 'How do we find out?'

'Try our luck. Give them the stuff.'

Fiorinda watched her shoes for two paces, then she nodded. 'Yeah. How else?' She looked up, pale as a candleflame, her stubborn jaw set hard. 'That sounds to me like a bloody good idea. Okay, let's do it.'

Ax smiled, with the same fierce satisfaction. Then his face broke up, he began to cry, and blundered like a child into her arms. The guards and the servants were watching, a cast of Shakespearian extras, but that was okay. Good King Ax might well be distressed, considering the dilemma he was in over his boyfriend.

Phil MacLean's sympathies were impeccably Celtic, but at the time of Dissolution he'd been one of the former UK's radical rockstars, same breed as Ax Preston and the English 'Few'. He'd been vetted and approved by the management at Rick's Place, and yet he was a halfway plausible buddy for the Triumvirate. Sovra Campbell was nothing so vulgar as a rockstar! Sovra was European, a Conserva-toire-trained violinist, stooping to conquer the popular music audience with phenomenal success: no political background whatso-ever . . . They made a good team as agents; a typical, awkward, rock-tour partnership, the effect only enhanced by a few colourful fights between their followers.

Were they really empowered, by the Edinburgh Assembly and the Convocation of Elders, to offer Ax and his lovers a ticket out of jail? Ax believed it. The price was convincingly high, for one thing. No face-saving compromise: it would be sovereignty for Scotland in the new Act of Union, England as a nation state would disappear. But if Ax said yes, the Scots were ready to put their current President – an ancient celeb – aside, and take drastic action. They'd looked into it carefully, and considered that a rescue would be legally justified; and they had cleared the proposal with Dublin, and other interested parties.

Phil and Sovra had been giving Ax this pitch all summer: hiding it in plain sight, in elliptical conversations. Ax had been listening, temporising, always coming to the same sticking point. Wallingham's a fortress, wired to the nth, you don't know the details, you have no game plan, how are your reivers going to get us out? The Scots had no answer. But they knew Ax did: and they knew that when he was ready, *if* he was ever ready, he would hand over the stuff.

It had been easy to talk. It was more difficult to commit, very scary, but no other way to do it except to do it. On the Thursday night after Sage came home, Ax went beyond the point of no return, and the Scots immediately closed with him. A hard choice, but it could have been worse.

Fuck of a sight better than falling into the hands of the Irish—

He left the Scots' table and walked into the crowd: smiling, doing his job, desperately trying to read through the lies, the ignorance, the baseless gossip. Are *you* 'queer for Brussels', Mr Preston? I am not. So you think we should let Belarus go under? Ooh, it hasn't come to that, not nearly. You know, I'm just a rockstar, the decisions aren't made at Wallingham, but—

Women dressed like glittery dolls, men in sleek tailoring, jigged around on that recalcitrant dancefloor. The guest bands did their spots. Regular punters asked after Sage. 'A throat infection,' said Ax, 'he must have picked it up in London. A singer has to be careful, you know. Maybe next week.' Did they know what had happened to Sage? Nah, that's the wrong question. They know what happens: to people, even of their own rank, there's no protection for those who make trouble. They've just forgotten there was ever another way. If you told them it used to be illegal to obtain evidence by torture in this country, they'd wonder what you were on.

Fiorinda went to sit with the Scots, giving her shadows an easy time because they knew these were safe associates. She was in a teasing mood, dividing her barbs evenly between the raw home-grown MacLeans and the effete cosmopolitan Campbells. Or should that be the ragged-plaid decayed aristo MacLeans, and the forward-looking proletarian-crushing Campbells?? It was all in fun, with bursts of laughter that turned heads and brought a tv crew over. But the mediafolk were sent packing, with cat calls and showers of austerity Twiglets. You've done us to death! Go and pick on somebody else—!

At last Fiorinda and the violin diva took a turn around the room together. They made an arresting couple: the rockstar queen in her timeless party frock, a worn Kashmiri shawl in brown and gold covering her shoulders; the tall Sikh woman with the long face and strange, light eyes who bore the name of the greatest Lowland clan; arrayed in splendid and sober high fashion.

They paused to admire the Klimt hangings.

'We mustn't touch,' said Fiorinda. 'They're fabulously valuable.'

'Are they no' replicas?'

'Nope, the real thing. As is the Van Dyck over there, and the Delacroix: hung in here because they are significantly yellow. Crazy, isn't it.'

The two young women bent closer. 'I think he's class, but I don't actually like Klimt,' confided Fiorinda, absentmindedly lifting the fabric to examine a detail. She dropped it again, grabbing Sovra in pretended alarm. 'Oops, what a crime. I'll get us thrown out. I'm such a klutz about the ornaments in this treasure house.'

'A troubled man,' agreed Sovra. 'Maybe no too sure of his sexuality,' she added severely, and calmly transferred the slip of glittering crystal that had been pressed onto her bare arm to a place of greater safety: eks, not fade away.

George had smuggled the chip into Rick's Place early in July. It held the whole instruction set for the barmy army's raid on Wallingham. It had never left the Drawing Room because there was a good chance it would not have got through the punitive search and scan the Triumvirate suffered. The Klimt hangings were not touched, they were cleaned by ultrasound twice a year, so they'd been a smart hiding place, hiding in plain sight, always the best. Guests were scanned, but they didn't get taken apart, and the chip was very small, and practically inert.

This I can do for you, my prince, thought Fiorinda. You may have to tear your heart out, but you don't have to hand it over personally. So now we find out. Maybe she'll take that straight to Lady Anne, and we'll be fucked. Or maybe not. She wondered how it felt to be Sovra, and what would make someone sign up to be a secret agent, hey, be shot for sixpence, it'll do nothing for your career—

Sovra cast a thoughtful glance around her at the screaming-pitch crowd, the darkness and the hot, harsh lights. 'Are they no' afraid you three'll take advantage, mixing freely with all sorts of chancers in here?'

'The Drawing Room is comprehensively wired,' said Fiorinda, 'and protected by ritual magic. And they trust us. They know that Ax

Preston would never betray his country. Even Greg Mursal knows that.'

England and Scotland looked at each other with some respect. A hell of a bungee jump, sister. Good luck to you. They returned to the table, because Ax had begun to play. He had brought down his famous cherry-red Gibson tonight, for the first time in the history of Rick's Place. He proceeded to give them a blast of pure and hard electric ... It was an act of defiance, he didn't give a fuck how they reacted. But the crowd was smitten, wowed, ecstatic. The dip in popularity Ax and his music had suffered before the violence debate, those weeks when his star had faltered, were forgotten. As long as he was locked up in Wallingham, he could do no wrong.

'That was *way cool*!' gasped one of the courtiers at the end of the recital: pronouncing the alien jargon with gusto. 'You are such a pro, Sir!'

'Yeah,' said Ax, meeting Fiorinda's eyes across the smoke and the lights, and getting the a-okay. It's done. 'That's me. A real old pro.'

Phil and Sovra's tour ended. The last night they were at Wallingham was the last night they spent in England. Sovra had cancelled her final date to travel back with Phil: romance had blossomed. The reivers, who'd come south disguised as stage crew and roadies over the summer – their numbers augmented as the agents had grown certain they would close the deal – had gone to earth: they stayed behind. The influx, and the discrepancy in returning numbers, was not picked up in the festival season traffic. Controls were not so tight that approved tour vehicles were intensively searched, either. In Edinburgh, George's chip was deciphered, evaluated and passed on to the commanders chosen for the raid, who soon moved south to join their troops.

Ax and Fiorinda obeyed the white box's instructions and dosed their Bodhisattva with diamorphine until he refused the drug, wanting to stay clear and be with them. He often insisted he was fine, he would be fine, but he spent a lot of time clinging to them, shaken by fits of deep, helpless trembling. Fiorinda thought that one day he would tell her what had been going on in his mind, and it would be nightmares featuring Jack Vries as an appalling father, a merciless god. When the tame medic arrived to examine their patient they were openly angry, bruised and shocked, as one might expect. Lady Anne felt that Jack Vries' apology was insupportably delayed, and dreaded the moment when she would have to approve a renewed interrogation. She contemplated poison, to get rid of the unlucky third once and for all. She did not share Jack's faith in the whole desperate Neurobomb project. But it would be difficult. The Lord and Lady refused to allow the servants near Mr Pender, and would give him no medicine except of their own providing.

They'd thought of poison. They were living on Rick's Place bar snacks.

They spoke to each other with stitched-up mouths, the days passed, they went down to Rick's Place again. China's adventure in Central Asia had eclipsed the US election; which was still a sure thing for Fred. A group of rogue neurophysicists in Iran had been caught trying to build an A-team, and arrested. A mighty Russian engineering project, supposed to be the last-ditch defence against the freshening of the Baltic and the 'global-warming ice-age', had been abandoned, devastated by extreme weather. They heard no more about the official announcement that Mr Preston was not a werewolf: that deal seemed to be on hold. Otherwise, all was quiet.

They didn't know what was going on, except that Phil and Sovra had gone home; and there'd been no immediate repercussions. A couple of stragglers from the Scottish tour turned up at the club on Friday, and passed the message: it's on.

The raiders hit the Wallingham perimeter around midnight of the seventeenth of September, their arrival buried in the traffic spike when the nightclub closed. They were in a strange land, and they'd never attacked a fortress before. But Ax and Sage did plug-and-play battle orders, designed to survive hippy guerrilla idiocy or inspiration: they didn't know any other way. The first phase of the operation went smoothly. The security of the fortress had of course been reviewed after the May débâcle, but basic plant and system hardware had not been replaced. Nor had the very expensive software package that generated the alarm and security systems' frequently changed, randomised passwords. The Rick's Place traffic spike was the last genuine information Wallingham's defenders, human or machine, ever saw.

The perimeter was taken and secured in half an hour. The attack on the house itself began at about one-thirty a.m. Entry (all doors and windows were physically locked and barred, as well as being systemically alarmed), was effected through a scullery window, which was simply forced. The indoor troops were getting routine reports and visuals that looked perfectly convincing, and showed only a quiet night. They had no idea they had no alarm system, or that the perimeter was lost. They didn't know anything was wrong until the Scots were all over them.

The prisoners, waiting in the red room, were almost as poorly informed as Wallingham's garrison. Their shutters had been locked as usual, and the outer door of the suite secured, when the servants left after dinner. Their suite was so deep inside the house they would hardly have heard a rocket attack on the distant façade. They wouldn't know when the power was cut off (which should have happened early on) because their corridor had never been on the Wallingham House private renewables grid. Ax and Fiorinda sat on the bed, holding Sage's hands while he lay on his back and kept his head still. His eyes were much better, but still lightproof-bandaged most of the time. They made conversation, the real words silenced.

'It's chilly tonight,' said Fiorinda. 'Don't you get the feeling that the season turned this week, like a leaf; like a waterwheel, tipping over into autumn?'

'You feel it cos you know it's close on equinox, my brat.'

'What does an equinox do to us, Sage? Is it registered by our brains?'

'Yeah, whether you know it or not. It makes you happy, slightly.'

'It's always cold in here,' said Ax. 'I'm dreading the winter.'

Endless corridors, endless arrays of galleries and public rooms. The word had been *around midnight*, but Ax didn't know if that meant kick-off or the perimeter taken. If midnight was the perimeter they should be inside by now. How long will it take them to locate us? Better that we can't get out of the suite, he told himself. We'd be fools to try, don't want to commit prematurely. Let them come to us. If they fail we're innocent, we knew nothing.

Fat chance of getting away with that—

He listened: searching the silence until he thought he could hear the guards breathing outside the barred door of the suite. Calculating, approximating as best he could: this part of the plan had never been executed, there'd been no need for it. The ground floor window that is only directly visible to camera eyes, no other sight lines; the basement and ground floor locked down; leave a party to mop up. Send a couple of men to run a firecheck on the non-combatant servants in their quarters, and keep them quiet while the main force sweeps up and inwards. Clear up as you go, and you should never have to engage with major numbers—

You don't know where we are, that wasn't on the plan, you'll have to work it out. *Don't* head for the show-off rooms the Preston family occupied.

It's a fortress, what does that tell you, trainspotters? Make for the central keep.

find out if we can fly—

Ax's imaginary Scots were on the ground floor when there was a muffled thunder outside. They got off the bed, Sage too, nerves thrilling: is it fight or flight? A mass of armed men, must have been twenty of them, came bursting into the royal bedchamber. Oh, fuck. Never-seen-action fatigues. Not the rescue party.

'You're to come with us!' yelled the foremost man: red and blue flashes on his sleeves and shoulders, an officer of Wallingham's private army. 'Come on! Now!' He was frantic, wildly brandishing an assault rifle, lost to all respect.

Ax set the barrel of the gun aside (it had been jabbing at Fiorinda). 'Come with you?' he repeated. 'Why? It's the middle of the night. What's going on?'

'There's a helicopter waiting, Mr Preston,' cried a second man with the flashes, 'on the roof of the great library. We're here to escort you. You have to come quickly, Sir, Ma'am.' He looked at Sage, and flinched away from the Zen Self champion's bandaged blindness. 'And Mr Pender.'

'But ... but wouldn't we be safer staying in here?' said Fiorinda doubtfully. 'If there's some kind of trouble?'

I could do it, thought Ax. The guy who just called me *Mr Preston*, not that sickening *Your Majesty*, he could be turned. I could grab the wavering rifle from Mr Weak Link there, turn this whole situation around. All it takes is boldness. But what then? What then . . . ? He stared at Fiorinda, rushing on disaster, telling her, we are fucked, I won't kill and they'll call my bluff. I can't do it.

Fiorinda stared back, her grey eyes like stones in the dim light.

'Just wait a moment,' said Ax, turning to the men. 'I asked you to tell me what's going on. Is the house on fire, is this a drill? Has war been declared?

'Where are you taking us?' asked Sage, unhurriedly. 'What the fuck's up?'

The two officers were very disconcerted to be addressed by blind Sage. They glanced at each other, breathing hard, then quickly eyes front again.

'There's been a disturbance,' cried Mr Nice. 'A – possibly a break in.'

'You don't need to know what's happened,' shouted Frantic Guy, his rifle flapping again. 'It's not for you to know. You just come with us, right now!'

Their men were in a tight pack, looking nervously around the room.

'Okay, okay,' said Ax. 'We hear you. Give us a few moments to pack.'

Their essential belongings were ready, by the bed. He headed for the armoire, took down a suitcase and began to fill it with clothes they never wanted to see again; with an appearance of haste but no hurry. Fiorinda, whatever it is you're going to do, do it. Oh shit, my poor babe. One violence or another violence . . . How cold it is over here. He felt his throat close and his mouth dry, and wanted to tell her No! Don't do it to yourself, don't risk it babe, we'll find another way— when he realised he was in the grip of an overwhelming dread that was coming at him from the ghost territory.

The Haunting Of The Red Bedchamber had served its practical purpose when they'd heard it mentioned by the servants: Sage and Fiorinda'd made the fucking thing up. This had confirmed that their bedroom was bugged, and served as a good psychological tool: the ghost was always listening. Tell ourselves there are no cameras or mics inside the bedcurtains but you can't know, fucking sickening. So there's no ghost, not really, there never was a ghost, but his hands had begun to shake. Something invisible, animal and repellent was watching him, creeping closer. He kept on shovelling clothes – slow, make it look fast – this is not a small thing, this is too much, babe, don't know if I can stand up and get back to you.

Mr Frantic shouted incoherently, rushed over and took Ax by the shoulders—

Ax turned *slow, make it look fast*: raising an eyebrow.

One of the men in the pack wailed aloud, and they all backed up on each other like sheep, up against the wall by the fireplace. Mr Nice, dark-skinned, round in the face, had turned a sick shade of grey. He yelled at his partner, 'You don't touch Ax! You don't lay your hands on *Ax*!' But he was backing up himself, and so was Mr Frantic now. What did they see? It had them penned, like an invisible black dog. Ax stumbled to his feet, dread washing through him like a tugging wave. Fiorinda was staring at the invisible black dog too, and so was Sage, bandaged eyes fixed on the same spot. Ax crossed the room, couldn't have told you how. They scooped their bags, the three treasures, the first aid: and bolted through the suite, slammed the outer door and crashed the bars into their sockets.

No sign of the night guards, they must be in the red room with the others. The corridor was empty and dim, lit by infrequent ATP lamps in wall brackets. Somewhere, not far away, there was a considerable firefight going on.

'My God,' gasped Ax. 'That was strong medicine, Fiorinda.'

'Fuck!' breathed Sage. 'It was real, there was a real ghost! Hahaha!'

Fiorinda did not share the exhilaration. She was chalk-pale, her eyes huge. 'There was a ghost . . . The internal world and the external world change places. They had laid hands on the king.' She clutched at her head, as if she felt it breaking open, staring at them. 'The ghost was Wallingham . . . We're all playing with fire.'

They listened to the sounds of battle, and grew calm.

In the blind negotiations, Ax had tried to insist on non-lethals as weapons of first resort, and zero casualties as the objective: starting the bidding low to keep the final price down. Who knows if the Scots had understood, or complied: battle plans nearly always break down at some point. No regrets, but the shock of what they had done came home to them.

'We'd better get this under control,' said Ax. 'You up for that, big cat?'

'Oh yeah. Lead on. Jus' make sure I don't fall over anything.'
'I'll take care of the old lady,' said Fiorinda.

Run through the stately corridors in the dark, like hide and seek: the smell of cordite, the glue-sniffer sting of non-lethals. Hope not to hit any tear gas. Yells and flashes below as she crossed a gulf of stairwell. She found an English body, and shame gripped her. We did this. Oh, fuck. More English bodies. At least these weren't dead, just moaning and wriggling in the grip of sticky webbing—

Lady Anne had been sleeping when the attack came. Like Margaret Thatcher, she needed very little sleep, but she treasured the hours from midnight to three a.m., when she relinquished command to Tom Lacey, Wallingham's peerless steward, her ally in many skirmishes with the conniving National Trust, years ago. Usually she slept unaided, but she had taken a pill, tailored to give her a measured dose of oblivion, because she was exhausted by the stress of the Mr Pender situation. She had a guilty fondness for prescription drugs. She had known nothing of Tom Lacey's last stand, or the decision to move the prisoners. Her household officers had been unable to page her rooms, her women had been silenced.

She was roused out of bed and brought to her study in her nightgown, in lamplight, meaning the generator must have failed. The drug clouded her mind, usually so sharp and decisive. She thought they were Wallingham men, holding her up by her arms because she did indeed feel on the point of falling.

'Where are they kept, ye auld witch—'

'Let me find my glasses.' The plan of Wallingham flung down on the desk, and the confused sounds she could hear flooded her with the greatest terror. Fire.But the hands were extremely rough, and the faces unknown to her. Instead of taking out her glasses she reached under the desk and pressed the panic button, then opened a small drawer in which she kept a very powerful talisman, a gold locket that held a nub of shrivelled flesh. She thrust it into the ringleader's face.

'Begone from here!'

She was struggling, a tinder-limbed, pitiful grotesque, in the arms of her captors, when the study doors were flung open and the young queen marched in.

Fiorinda knew the raiders at once. They tended to naked ropey limbs and heads scoured of hair instead of dreads and ragged layers; and skin more luminously white than you often see in England. But they were obviously barmy army squaddies, the Scottish version of Ax's hippy guerrillas. The lunatic dregs of radical society, in other words, getting shot and not even asking for sixpence; and well over the top as usual. Her heart went out to them.

'Hey! What the fuck do you think you're doing?'

Altercation followed. The Scots were not willing to relinquish their prey, neither Lady Anne nor her elderly lady's maid, who was being roughly held still in a corner. They were righteous, stubborn, and unfavourably impressed by her ladyship's weapon of first resort, an object which Fiorinda suspected was the preserved and sanctified heart of a newborn. Abomination. Shall not suffer a witch to live, etc.

So, not Celtics then. Must be the other team.

She had to yell at them for about five minutes, handicapped by the fact that she could hardly understand a word they said, before she brought them to admit that raping politically sensitive VIP old ladies wasn't in the deal. All right, excuse me, didn't mean to insult anyone, not raping, *beating up* the old ladies—

Different, but enough like barmies for me to hold them.

'Lady Anne, you'll be able to contact Lord Mursal, or whoever else you wish, in a few hours. In the meantime you'll stay in your bedroom, under guard, and you won't be harmed. You're in the hands of a civilised nation now—' (pause to glare at the trainspotters) '—and you'll be given *civilised* treatment.'

She didn't know if it was gratitude or undying hatred that she saw rise in the mad old eyes as the PM's political consort was led away with her servant. Nor did she care. A baby's heart, how cute. Bless . . . Just don't get killed on my watch.

Someone turned the power back on. As they headed north from Lady Anne's suite the great public rooms were suddenly ablaze with light. The reivers started muttering.

'What is it now?'

The leader of the detachment said something incomprehensible.

'I'm sorry, I really don't understand. I may be a musician but I'm hopeless at languages. Is there a MacLean in the party?'

This put them on their dignity. An older man with a grizzled bullet head spoke up in English that had the same nit-picking precision as Sovra Campbell's.

'The men are just saying, they accept the ruling on summary justice against persons, but what would the *cailin rua's* opineenion be on the removal of property?'

The *cailin rua* (it means red girl) barely hesitated. 'Take small stuff,' said Fiorinda, feeling like Lady Macbeth, and *good* about it. 'Don't waste time.'

The illusion was short-lived. They left Wallingham in the bare, windowless back of a van, which they shared with a dozen or so reivers. There was one dim bulkhead light. The Triumvirate sat close together, not touching, because they didn't want to show weakness. They were no longer themselves. An hour ago they had been Ax and Sage and Fiorinda, in prison. Now their charmed lives were over. What they had been, what they had done, their whole extraordinary career was *over*. Scenes rose up, all played to music. The reckless energy of Dissolution Summer. The young Fiorinda screaming her desperate pain from Reading main stage; firelight and night. A huge crowd in summer sunlight held silent, entranced, passionately uplifted by Ax Preston's guitar. The fabulous weirdness of Aoxomoxoa's immersions, turning the world inside out in the ballroom at the Insanitude . . . It was bad to know they had sold England, but they could tell themselves the country had to be better off than it had been with Greg Mursal. There was nothing to soften their own loss of face. It was devastating.

Soon the wheels were leaping over very poorly surfaced road. Now to make this work, thought Ax, stubbornly positive. He wished they'd been able to manage their own escape, but if it had been possible, where does that get you? Ax and Fiorinda and Sage, running for their lives or fomenting a civil war . . . No, this was the right choice, statesman's choice; and now to make this work. Say it often enough, it'll come true. For England. For all those people he had served, all ages, all dresscodes, through the years of disaster. He could feel Sage's exhaustion beside him, and the big cat's fear of what this jolting journey was doing to his eyes . . .

It was a foretaste. There would be months of this. They would be taken from place to place, paraded in public. They would be interrogated, hopefully without torture, they would be taken from one captivity to another. A figure like Ax Preston is either *dux bellorum* or a piece of currency, passed from hand to hand. They saw it all stretching out ahead, and closed their eyes. We will never escape. Mouths stitched shut. Occasionally one of the Scots asked Ax a question, and he answered calmly and confidently.

After a couple of hours the van drew up. They were handed out, into cool air and a feeling of landscape emptiness, almost like the desert. They saw misty stars: a shadowy mass of trees, and a thin, sharp-angled blot rising in the foreground. Is that a house . . . ? It was a house of sorts, revealed when the Scots brought up the big lights. Two gable ends and a chimney, no roof, not much of the walls left; a stone-floored lean-to kitchen silted with rubble. Ax asked, were they stopping for the night. That got a laugh, because it was nearly dawn.

'Business,' said one of the men (if there were women, they were hard to spot).

There was no sign of the small army that had taken Wallingham, only this one van. Everyone moved into the ruined house; the Triumvirate closely surrounded. Fiorinda noticed that she could understand everything being said to her, which meant this must be a MacLean party, Highlanders. She saw that Ax and Sage had realised the same thing, and they were uneasy too. They were in the hands of the Celtics, for some private business. Fuck, that doesn't sound good . . . Everyone sat in a circle; there was an atmosphere of expectancy. The high-powered ATP battery lamps were hooded to minimise the escape of light into the sky. The men took out their Wallingham souvenirs, and showed them to each other. Gold boxes, trinkets, little rolled-up razored canvases; piece of antique jewellery. The three large items of loot felt self-conscious. One of the commanders of the raid came and sat opposite them in the open centre of the circle. His name was Neil. He greeted Ax and Sage with the respect due for what they'd done back in the house; and introduced himself to Fiorinda, with dignity.

'Now we seal the contract.'

'I'm not going to sign anything here,' said Ax firmly. 'Not until we get to Edinburgh, to the Assembly. I intend to do this by the book, no side deals.'

He was clutching at straws.

'It's no' about signing things, and it won't wait.'

Beside Neil sat a small man with a bowed back and a neck like a turkey, dressed in a white singlet and black cotton trousers, seriously tattooed around his bald, wrinkled head and down his arms. Where had he come from? He didn't look like a raider. 'It's me you've got to see,' he said. 'Don't worry, I'm an expert.'

It seemed Ax had to be tattooed. Neil agreed that this stipulation had never been on the table before; but it had always been in mind. If Ax refused, the Celtic Party, largest single political voice in Scotland, would simply withdraw support from the Edinburgh deal, and it would collapse.

'The Celtics of Scotland don't entirely trust the Assembly,' explained Neil, in a soft-spoken, reasonable tone. 'They don't entirely trust Ax Preston either, and you'll understand that, Sir. They're with you all the way in condemning extremists. But they remember the Velvet Invasion, and they have a lingering feeling in their minds that Mr Preston kills Celtics, or at least tars all Celtics with the same brush. A little knotwork will make a big difference.'

'I'll have to think it over,' said Ax, realising he'd been double-crossed.

'That's the first count,' said Neil. 'The second count is that you are known to be a wily fucker, but once you have our badge on you, you'll have a harder time wriggling out of the bargain. We'll be recording the operation, hope that's okay.'

They laid Ax on his back on a reed mat. The tattooist took out his inks and needles from a briefcase. 'My name's Billy,' he said to Ax, in his piping little voice. 'I'm not a Scot, I'm not Celtic. I'm a wanderer, maybe older than Celtic, maybe nothing. I chose this spot: I've been around here before. It's called the Wood Court, and it's holy. No shrine nor stone nor sacrifice, none of that, it's just a right place.'

Two massive reiver hands settled on Ax's skull, with a vice-like grip, and the lamps moved closer so he felt their heat.

'Keep yer head still,' advised Billy, 'and it won't take half an hour. If you can't, it's going to be longer.'

He kept his head still.

When the job was done, everyone got back in the van and they drove on. After another two hours or so the van jolted onto rough ground and stopped again. The men got out. The Triumvirate glimpsed the trunks of trees, early morning in a wood; then the doors were shut. After a while Neil appeared and reported that everything had gone according to plan. The police had been avoided. The rest of the war party was well on its way to the border. No trouble, except one of the injured men had died. Fatalities on the Scots' side now stood at three, the bodies being taken home, of course. It had been a big operation, but a smooth dismount. What about us, asked Ax. What's the delay?

We've been told to wait for dark, said Neil.

They stayed in the back of the van all day, too burned-out to sleep, or talk much, or feel much anxiety. The Scots came and went, grumbling about the boredom, and once producing sandwiches. Ax spoke when he was spoken to, expressing hopes for a smooth changeover, the swift collapse of the Second Chamber. He profoundly hoped he was right, was sickeningly aware that events had passed out of his control. He kept thinking, it's going to be tough being Ax Preston, in public, with this on my face. He had expected his eye would close up but it didn't, the needlework was just tender ... They were aware of urgent conversations, partly in Gaelic and partly in English; perhaps triggered by radio messages. No one told them what was going on, and for the moment they were beyond caring. All they really noticed was the quiet that interrupted the sound of the raiders' voices. It was very quiet that September day, in the unknown countryside about four hours' minor-road driving from Wallingham. The stillness and the dying fall of summer's end.

The van set off in the rain as soon as it was fully dark. By this stage the three were indifferent to anything: mouths stitched shut, just longing for the journey to be over, for a chance of to be alone together, and speak freely to each other, for the first time since June. They weren't thinking further than that. The van bounced along, neither faster nor slower than the night before, keeping to neglected roads and presumably heading north, though it seemed to make some strange turnings. It pulled up again. The back doors opened; Neil hopped in and spoke to the men in an undertone. Then he said, 'Take your gear, English, and get down. This is free, gratis, you are free.'

They took what they were carrying and got down onto the side of the road. It was raining, softly. Neil handed out Fiorinda's guitar-case, and the visionboard. Fiorinda had her tapestry bag, Ax had the Les Paul.

'The white box!' cried Fiorinda. 'That box, could you please hand it to me—'

One of the men in the van picked up Sage's first aid kit, and hefted it thoughtfully. Neil jumped down and slammed the doors shut. He looked at them without speaking, then he got back into the cab and the van drove away.

It drove away.

What the hell's going on?

'We're back where we were,' said Ax.

He was right. The dark mass he was pointing to was the wood behind the ruined cottage where Ax had been tattooed. They led Sage between them along the grey, ragged blacktop, through the charcoal-shaded night, between bracken-scented banks, until they reached a turn-off. This must be the track the van had taken the night before; soon they reached the ruin. The lean-to kitchen had enough of a roof, mainly a mass of brambles and ivy, to give them shelter.

Sage took Fiorinda in his arms, with a wordless sob, and reached out for Ax. They hugged each other with inexpressible relief. Then they made Sage a pillow from Fiorinda's Kashmiri shawl and he lay on the stone floor the Scots had cleared for the tattooing ceremony with his bandaged head still – which was also a great relief to them all. Ax and Fiorinda sat on either side of him, their backs to the house-wall.

'*Was* that you, on the phone,' said Ax, 'saying you were fine?'

'Yeah.'

'Why the fuck did you say "relax" when you were being tortured?'

'Because it was for the best. I was coping, an' ... Hey, this is superficial, true.'

'We're going to have to change that arrangement.'

The night was mild and faintly moonlit, though there was no definite break in the cloud. They could see the rain falling straight and fine; and hear the faintest silver whispering. 'Ax?' said Sage, after a while. 'What does Iphigenia really mean?'

'Oh, yes,' murmured Fiorinda. 'I wondered about that, too.'

'It means Poland.'

'*Poland?*'

'It's a secret codeword for Poland, used by FDR and Winston Churchill in the lead-up to the Tehran conference, during World War Two.'

'D'you know what it means, in this context?'

'I think so.'

Poland. Now that's a koan. But whatever he knew, Ax didn't seem inclined to enlighten them. Ax and Fiorinda divided the utterly mysterious, ominous and peaceful night between them. When it was Fiorinda's turn to lie down she pillowed her head on Sage's shoulder – at which he murmured without waking, freed his arm and folded it around her; and remembered that she had dreamed of this. Not a premonition but a dream of longing, when she had been trapped by Fergal Kearney, who was really dead, and his body inhabited by her father. That she might find Ax and Sage again, that they would sleep together under a hedge, in the wind and the rain, on the open road; like so many others in these Dissolution years. Without a house or a home, no direction known.

EIGHT

Wood Court

By five the rain had stopped and the starless sky had taken on a grainy transparency. He lay down beside Fiorinda and kissed her gently: the hollowed curve of her cheek, her parted lips. She opened her eyes, and smiled. A hard bed but a sweet wakening. They lay nose to nose, holding hands, no surveillance, no walls, no lies, only the air above them, the earth beneath.

'I'm going foraging,' he said. 'You'll be all right?'

She looked at him soberly. 'Ax, before I forget, I am truly sorry for all those horrible things I said, which were lies. Will you forgive me?'

He smiled, a rueful gleam in his eye. 'All of them lies?'

'Especially that one.'

'Well, same here.'

She knew she hadn't fixed the damage, blame it on stress but that had been a bad fight, and yeah, Ax's cruel perfidy would linger too . . . Sage's visionboard lay on the cleared floor with a panel removed, showing its innards.

'What've you been doing?'

He showed her the transceiver, and tucked it back into his jacket pocket. 'Cannibalising, don't worry; I can put it together again. I'm going to try and get hold of some news. And we have to eat. I won't be too long.' He bent to kiss her once more. She put up her hand, and briefly laid the palm against his chest.

Such a whirling, terrifying blank when he thought about the future, he had to quickly cauterise that whole area. Do this, only this. Bag on my shoulder, fill it with food somehow. Blackberries, if nothing else. But where am I heading? He stopped to look around. The track to the ruin skirted a valley full of trees; there was light enough for him to make out some majestically tall pines. Beyond the treetops, and ahead of him, to the south, a bare heath that seemed to stretch endlessly to a vista of wooded hills. Not a house, not a mast, not a telegraph pole. Not a sound, apart from the birdsong; and the clatter of a wood pigeon, bursting from the hedge. We left Wallingham, we drove . . . north, no, more like west? Cumulatively, take out the turns, he thought west. This was our first stop, but how far had we driven? How can there be a place like this in the crowded southeast?

Where the fuck am I?

Ax had once had a brain implant, a datastack of useful information about England, including full Ordnance Survey. Plus the works of long dead Greeks and Romans as a freebie on the side. Because of that, he *knew* his country uncannily: things came to him, like direct intuitions. But he couldn't name this landscape. He gazed for a long time, the beauty of it filling his heart and stinging his eyes, and then set off, walking softly, swiftly, alertly, to the lane: where he turned right, downhill, keeping to the shadows, an animal with a spurious air of purpose.

Half an hour later he'd found a milk halt at an unmarked crossroads. A stack of crated bottles stood on the white-rimmed concrete platform, a flowerbed planted in the bank had the name of the dairy co-op, done in seaside pebbles across the middle: WEAL-DEN AND FOREST. So that's a mystery solved. He broke into a pallet – not the one with Volunteer Initiative stamped all over it, not so low we have to steal from the Poor Box – stowed six ice-cold half-litre glass bottles in his bag and downed a seventh. It filled him with strength and courage. As he stood staring along the road, wondering if the milk would be collected, a liquid gleam appeared at vanishing point. He dropped between the platform and the bank and retreated under the hedge. Time stands still in country places. There is an England quietly going about its business. A bio-ethanol-burning milk lorry drew up, shining chrome muzzle and a little filter chimney above the cab, yellow plastic roses and a gallant, battered Barbie doll in a ballgown tucked into the radiator grille. A snatch of music as the driver and his mate got down . . . Ax felt something akin to worship: but he realised that he was a thieving tramp and he'd better move on.

From the field on the other side of the hedge he saw the roofs of a substantial farm. No barracks attached, there weren't any camps in the south: serf labour only on a domestic scale down here. Two fields further and he was watching a herd of black and white cows return to their dewy pasture after a dawn trip to the pleasures of the milking shed. A burly young man and a boy closed the gate behind the herd and ambled back to the yards, sniping at each other idly – brothers, he guessed. He followed like a ghost, hid himself among the farmyard derelicts and old tyres and stole the signal as they watched tv over their breakfast. He couldn't get a picture, must be doing something wrong, but he could read the datalines and the sound was fine. He ran through the cable channels, picking up different versions of the early news.

On the way back he had his bearings and was able to make a circuit of it: first rule of guerrilla life, never take the same route twice. The sun was nearly up as he struck across the uncultivated heath, but he felt confident that he would not meet any company. He'd found no solid food, and now there were no blackberries in sight. About half a kilometre from the wooded valley of the ruin he struck a big house with cypress hedges around the lawns and the remains of a hard tennis court. It looked as if it had been derelict for years, casualty of the Crisis, or the Crash. The cypresses cast a dank, ugly shade: but there were apple trees behind the house. He filled his bag with fruit and sat in the rank grass by a garden shed. I must take hold of myself, think. What to do now, what next?

Make a list.

Look after Sage and Fiorinda.

Stay put. Moving targets may be harder to hit but are a fuck of a sight easier to spot. (Simple unless we're being hunted, but it doesn't look like it.)

Try to find out what's going on. (Harder.)

. . .

. . .

The tattoo was stinging. He touched it, very gingerly. If that gets infected, I'm fucked . . . Déjà vu: I have been here before. The hateful, sweltering room where he'd spent a year as the hostage of a crazy drug cartel rose up around him, invoking the consolation of dangers passed, terrible ordeals safely endured. But the foetid room became Lady Anne's study, the vertigo became that moment when he knew that he must hand England over to the Scots, and he fell into a dreadful spin of shame and bewilderment in which the word *Iphigenia* rolled like thunder.

He needed to know which act had been fatal. The mad instant when he'd punched Jack Vries in the throat? Or the moment when he decided he would never again take up the blunt instrument of violence? That conversation, after dinner with the President at Camp Bellevue, in the San Gabriel Mountains, when he'd agreed to come back to England? Or the day he'd fixed, incorrigible fixer, an amnesty for the Lavoisiens, thus ensuring the Black Dragon lived to sell his video? All of that history was irrelevant now, and he didn't mourn it, but he needed to know about the turning points because he had to make a judgment. He would have given a lot for a glimpse of the white light of destiny, the utter self-conviction he had once known. A compelling sense of destiny (eventually some little Hitlers realise this) can lead you straight to hell, without telling you a word of a lie. But it would have been better than nothing. Somebody's house is burning, hellfire-red—

Oh God help me. I don't know what to do, I don't know.

He heard a faint mewling sound.

The shed had once been padlocked, but the door had been broken in long ago. He shoved his way through clinging ropes of goosegrass, and peered around. Could it be something human? There was nowhere for anything bigger than a baby to be hidden. The cry came again. He moved aside a slab of cobwebbed composite and discovered a kind of nest, hollowed in the dirt floor, occupied by an emaciated dead tabby cat and her kittens. Two of the kittens were also clearly dead. The third stood on swaying legs and mewled again, imperiously. Never say die, little scrap, but I'm afraid she can't hear you—

He picked the kitten up and held it, wondering whether the cat had been a pet, or feral, and what had killed her. Better get back.

There had been a bed of herbs outside the kitchen: lavender, rosemary and mint, blue-eyed borage, slug-eaten comfrey; eyebright, crept in from the heath, but that's a signature herb, we'll leave that one alone. Yellowed potato plants, a tangle of tomato vines that held shrunken red fruits, rock-hard runner beans, a menacing-looking marrow, straggly rocket and spinach. The gable end of the cottage was adrift on white spume that ran like a river over the trees in the valley and lost itself in an ocean of rust and wine . . . Whenever she looked up to see if Ax was coming back, she found herself washed again by a void of light and sweet air, carried out of herself into peace. Sage was still asleep. She had built a fire, using only bone-dry dead grass and broken laths, but there was no reason to light it. The ruined kitchen had a sink, and a mixer tap. Verdigrised copper plumbing pipes dangled in space, with no obvious gaps. Never know your luck . . . She attacked the tap, and managed to dislodge some flakes of rust.

Sage turned over, and lay looking at her with his bandaged eyes.

'Good morning.' The bandage frightened her: it was a dirty lie to say he was her Daddy-substitute, but she couldn't cope if Sage was helpless—

'Good morning.' He seemed to listen. 'Where's Ax gone?'

She knelt by him and gripped his hand; possibly it was true she leaned on Sage too hard . . . 'Foraging. It's okay, my baby. He's all right.'

'Oh.' Sage listened again, to the depth of silence. 'Where are we, Fee? Do we know? Did the Scots tell us?'

'They didn't tell us anything, but I think we're in the Ashdown Forest, in Sussex. In it, or on it . . . We are surrounded by a hundred acres of wild wood and a very beautiful blasted heath, and the distances would fit.'

'Is there heather?'

'Yeah. It's over, it's faded, but it's pretty nice.'

'Hm. Let's try taking the bandages off.'

She had closed her eyes, to be with him. She opened them again. 'There's quite a lot of light.'

'I know, my brat. I can see it through the dressing. I want to see you.'

He lay with his head in her lap as she unwound the layers, and looked up. There was an uncanny, fugitive awareness of *effort* (oh, fuck: what happened to Peter?) but vision getting better all the time, the blood clots at the back of his eyeballs had safely dispersed. I got away with it again, he thought. One day I won't. Fiorinda was glowing like a beacon fire.

'You're pregnant, aren't you?' he whispered.

Fuck. He had not meant to say that. But the message in Anne-

Marie's care parcel had been with him in the torture chamber, a guardian angel and a fearsome burden, oh, God, if I let that slip . . . It had been trapped inside him, speechless, all those days in the red room. He felt the shock run through her, the mingled terror and delight, and the world became new.

'Yes, I am. Ax knows because I told him, how did you—?'

'By looking at you, my brat, you are shining with it. Well, also there was a cryptic message from AM, at the Insanitude. She was onto you, somehow. I left it with Allie.' He started to sit up . . . and the memory of the white-tiled room attacked him. He went under, clinging to her, pressing his face into her belly, oh fiorinda, oh fiorinda, I was so frightened of the dandy man, he hurt me, he hurt me. *Sssh,* she whispered, *sssh, little Sage, you're safe now, I have you safe* . . . until he pulled himself together, mugging apology, and lay quietly, gazing, taking in the details.

'How is it? Don't lie.'

'Not bad. Don' think I'll try reading anything just yet.'

His yellow lashes stood out weirdly bright in the raccoon-mask of bruising; the whites of his eyes were still suffused, but not horrific. She stroked his eyebrows, what a nice texture. 'Well, there's good news and there's bad news, my hero. The good news is the Scots let us go, the bad news is we don't know why; except Ax knows something, and it's so awful he won't tell us.'

'Yeah, yeah, I was there.'

'And we lost the first aid box. I left it in their van.'

'Ah.' A stern frown. 'Now, tha's unfortunate.'

'But fear not. The good young witch remembers much of the wise lore the evil old witch once tried to teach her, although she never paid attention at the time. Got to be Hedgeschool GNVQ Herbalism equivalence. I will boil leaves and make poultices, as soon as I have fashioned a pan from something, and found some clean water.' She grinned. 'Don't get too sane, Captain Sensible. You'll find it doesn't suit the mood.'

He had not been thinking of his own need, he'd been looking ahead. She was right, better not. 'Hahaha, okay.' He sat up, stretched, and ran his fingers through his dirty hair. 'Gaagh, I need a haircut very badly. You're being unusually positive about all this, my brat. Any special reason?'

248

'You'll have to bear with me. It's the feel-good hormones.'

She dived into his arms, and yelped because her breasts were tender. Ah God, how fabulous to hold her: but he released himself and sat back on his heels. Shades of sepia and grey, sharp angles, green and earth tones, better all the time—

'What's up between you and Ax?'

'Oh . . . N-nothing.'

'Don't bullshit me. I know there was something. I haven't been on another planet, Fiorinda. Just blind and helpless and in pain—'

'All right, all right! You see, I, er, I found out he had volunteered for those expiatory rites, to stop them doing whatever they were doing to you.'

Ouch.

'Shit.'

'So I screamed at him, and I may have said things such as it was his fault we came back to England, and that we had ended up in Wallingham—'

'Oh, Fiorinda.'

'—I know, I know, the Terrible Word. Please don't *oh Fiorinda* me. He said evil things too. I wish I hadn't done it but you're out of date. I said I was sorry this morning, and we are all right . . . He didn't ask me or tell me, Sage, just unilaterally went and offered to be their fucking human sacrifice, as if it wasn't my business—'

'He doesn't. If he's going to jump off the cliff he just jumps. That's Ax.'

'God. Shit, Sage, you don't suppose he's doing something terrible now?'

'No!'

The earth bowed, the sun rose up. Veined ivy leaves shone as if waxed and polished; copper gleamed in slashed verdigris . . . 'Hey, what happened to my board?'

'It's okay. Ax took the transceiver out, that's all.'

Fuck . . . 'You didn't tell me he was foraging for information.'

With full daylight the world returned, as if a fragile spell had broken, and they were plunged into anxiety. Details that had been pushed aside by that stark episode with the Scots came crowding back, none of them good.

Sage chewed the joint of his right thumb. 'You didn't hear from my dad, after that one call?' They'd told him that Joss had been trying to trace him, that had been something they could talk about in the red room. It had been a comfort then, but now he was scared . . . She shook her head. Of course not, stupid question.

'George and Bill never turned up at the club again. You don't know anything about what happened to them?'

'I didn't see them, only Peter. I was told they'd be left alone if I co-operated.'

For what Jack Vries's word is worth. 'Mmm' She stared at the dirt on her feet. 'D'you think it was always about the scanners, from the start?'

'I think as soon as he saw the Lavoisier video – whenever that was – Greg Mursal put the same reading on it that Ax did.'

'Yes,' said Fiorinda, head down. 'That we were screwed.'

'Pretty much, yeah. No need to humour the bleeding-hearts no more, an' every reason to get hold of a Neurobomb, fast. When . . . when we had ended up under house arrest, all Jack had to do was convince his master I could safely be pulled in off the street. I don't suppose Greg took much persuading.'

'We were in much worse trouble than we realised.'

'You think?' he wondered. 'I'm not so sure. I think tha's you believing your own propaganda, my sweetheart. We knew what we were facing. The things Greg and Jack thought permissible, that culture in government, went back to before Dissolution. Remember Paul Javert? The Home Secretary who arranged the murder of – how many? Thirty? – people on Massacre Night? We'd never managed to root it out, never even tried, we just kept clear, an' made appeasement work for us, while we nurtured the young shoots of the Good State—'

'Except when my father took over.'

'Apart from that slight blip. But the fucking A-team, and then the fucking Lavoisiens, left us with no place to hide. We had to collide with the bad guys over the scanners; or just what they imagine to be my powers. An' whenever that happened, we were always going to be outgunned.'

'No,' said Fiorinda. 'Not outgunned.'

Ax came into the ruin quietly. His foraging bag clinked as he set down his bundled jacket. They jumped up and would have grabbed him: but he shook his head, recoiling from their touch. 'Hey,' he said to Sage. 'Look at you!'

'No thanks. I'm staying away from mirrors for quite a while.'

He brought the bag and they sat down together, under the ivy and bramble thatch. 'Milk and apples. Best I could do for starters. There's no sign of a search, nothing in the sky or on the ground. I think we're okay here for the moment.'

They cracked a half-litre each and drank. He watched them, saying nothing.

'Well, did you pick up the news?' asked Sage, wiping his mouth.

Ax saw where the raiders had laid him down two nights ago: the little man with his briefcase, the vivid lamplight, the darkness; it seemed like a fever dream.

'Yeah, I siphoned off the tv at a farmhouse. There's been a break-in at Wallingham. Nothing serious but the club's to be closed this week because it upset us. "Merry We Meet" will be a previously recorded programme. I suppose too many people were involved; they had to release something about the raid. But they haven't admitted we're gone, and that's good. It suggests they're hoping to cut a deal and get us back, which implies there'll be no full-scale hunt for us on the ground. Not unless the Scots have told them where to look, which I suppose is possible. The international situation is where it was, headline story still Roumanian and Belarus militias aiding the Uzbek resistance; China protests to Brussels. For what the tv news is worth.'

He spoke briskly, calmly. He might have been reporting on another disaster entirely, one of those terrible situations of the past, that they would beat, of course, because they always beat the terrible situations. But he didn't look at them.

'Why did the Scots let us go, Ax?' prompted Fiorinda. 'Will you tell us?'

'You'll think I'm insane,' said Ax, 'but all the time we were in Wallingham I meant to stay in office. I knew things were ugly. Not what Fiorinda had to face in the green nazi days, but in ways almost worse, because it was sustainable. I wanted the Few to get out, but I would have stayed, been the tame President, even if I had to live and die in that prison. To do some good in a bad situation, same as at the beginning, when Pigsty was in charge. When they had tortured you,

Sage, and when I knew Fiorinda was pregnant . . . Shit, I don't know how you can ever forgive me, either of you, for what I d-did, for getting you into—'

'Shut up.'

'Leave that out, babe.'

'Well, there was no question we had to cut and run. But right until then I would have stayed. Dig a little hole to the light and air from under the landslide. There have to be people who do that—'

'Yes,' said Fiorinda. 'That's what I thought I signed up for.'

'An' me. From when Fred asked me, would I go back with you?'

He looked at them wonderingly, as from a great distance.

'Okay, so now I have to tell you about Iphigenia. Last summer, in California, Fred talked to me about a scenario where China decides to annexe Europe, and the USA lets it happen.'

'Oh, really?' Sage grinned indignantly. 'Good of him!'

'Yeah, really. It was one of his top possibilities. I didn't. I didn't have a handle on China at all. I just knew some Pan-Asian Utopians, chat-room buddies; and the stuff everybody knows – knew. In the US they'd been watching this huge country that somehow came out of the Crash stronger than it went in: with a new leader, or leaders, hiding behind a façade of old geezers; and a mission to unite Asia . . . Fred's scenario had the US abandoning the last of the Central Asian fuel reserves in a decade or so's time, and China taking that as a cue to expand their "sphere of influence" westwards. They wouldn't meddle with the Russian Feds, they don't like the Feds, but they regard them as stable neighbours: but they'd see the crazy eco-warriors of the former European Union (Fred saw the EU dissolved, can't imagine what gave him that idea) as a threat. They'd announce that something must be done, in they would go, shock and awe, and Europe would collapse before them. I didn't believe it, and I thought it wouldn't be my affair anyway: I'd be long gone. Of course, the A-team speeded things up.'

Ax drew a deep breath. 'Before we left, Fred told me that if he had advance warning he'd get word to me, me personally, not the English government, using the codename that means, sadly, we're going to have to let the Soviets rape Poland.'

They stared at him, riveted.

'All right,' said Fiorinda, at last. 'All right, but—'

'I can see where this is heading,' said Sage. 'But, Ax, it doesn't seem possible. The Chinese were taking over Uzbekistan when I was in London, and I was having a hard time getting distressed about that ... That's a hell of a Blitzkrieg.'

'I don't know what's possible,' said Ax. 'Anything we think we know could be weeks old, or plain lies. The Chinese could have invincible post-fossil-fuel military technology. Or something. All I *know* is that about eighteen months ago a staggering new weapon was, well, detonated. And the new superpower on the block, the China nobody knows, the hidden kingdom, responded by doing nothing ... All I *know* is that the Scots were given orders to dump us last night, and somebody, probably Fred, sent me the word Iphigenia three months ago.'

He put up his hands to sweep back the wings of dark hair from his temples, a familiar gesture aborted as his fingers brushed the raw needlework—

'You think there's an embargo?' said Fiorinda, acutely.

Ax shook his head. 'I dunno, Fio. The tv and radio felt normal, what passes for normal. No strange gaps. Of course it's easier without a free press, but I know I never managed to keep a complete wall up for more than a few hours ... But I'm sure Fred never knew about my cry for help when we got arrested. Iphigenia wasn't a response, you both spotted that. It came too quickly; it was something else, and it doesn't make sense he would use that code for anything else but what we'd agreed ... I'm sorry, I should have told you about the China scenario. But it was so far-fetched, and you two get so pissed off when I try to tell you the details—'

Sage said. 'This is what was eating you all the time, in Wallingham.'

He shrugged. 'Yeah. I suppose.'

'Fuck. I knew you were in some kind of extra hell—' Sage reached out, but Ax didn't want to be touched; he flinched away, shaking his head.

'What were you supposed to do?' asked Fiorinda, who had grown very still, very concentrated. 'When you got the warning?'

'Nothing. Europe's going down, so go quietly, that's the best chance for modern civilisation. Fred says, *unfortunately I'm going to have to sacrifice you guys, to get a fair wind*, I was to keep it to myself and drop out of sight, not take the warlord route, be nobody's figurehead: lie low.' He grinned, without humour. 'What I have been doing, basically.'

Oh, those conversations with Fred Eiffrich in the godlike eyrie of Camp Bellevue, both of us knowing he was just a big puppet really, and I was a little puppet. But though we were wood and pulled by strings, still trying to get beyond that, still trying with all our might to hold up the falling sky—

'That was then,' she said. 'This is now. Fred's grand plans are gone to the winds ... Do you think we should turn ourselves in?'

Ax thought that the others ought to be here. DK and Allie, Rob and the Babes, Rox, and Chip, and Verlaine. George and Bill and Peter; Smelly and Anne-Marie too. He could see them in his mind's eye, very vividly: sitting around on the debris and the broken timbers in their rockstar streetclothes, the raffish finery of their profession, the way he'd last seen them on St Stephen's Green. The innermost circle of the Reich, listening while he told them the bad news. Terrified, tearstained, bloodsmeared faces around a table, on Massacre Night, the night the old world ended: when we were prisoners, expecting to die within the hour ... Déjà vu, they come thick and fast. He had been in this exact same ruined room before, facing the last stand with his friends around him, and, strangely, it had been a happy dream. The only person missing had been Fiorinda, oh God, where's Fiorinda?

She was with him now, rock-steady. He could feel the touch of her hand on his breast. 'There's one thing I need to know, Fio. Do the Chinese have a Neurobomb?'

'No,' she said. 'I could be wrong, but ... no, I'd say not.'

They stared at each other, long and hard. Birdsong rose in the vertiginous silence, a silence like falling into space.

'I don't have a decision,' he said. 'I have no decisions.' He tried to rub his aching temples and flinched again from the needlework. 'I don't think we should turn ourselves in. I think we should do nothing right now. Stay here, it's as good as anywhere, for a day or two. See if we can get a better idea of what's going on.'

She nodded. 'Okay. Let's do that.'

Sage thought of other times when he'd watched these two divvying up the world between them, moving the plastic armies of a game of *Risk* on the kitchen table at Tyller Pystri, in lamplight, long ago.

A boardgame has swallowed us, he thought, but I have my beautiful guitar-man and my rock and roll princess, we are together and we are out of jail. This lifted his heart, dumb and personal though the shelter might be. He noticed that Ax's bundled jacket was moving.

'What's that you got under your coat, babe? Something alive?'

'Oh . . . It's a kitten. I found this kitten.' Ax went to the jacket and brought out a scrawny tabby kitten with bat-wing ears. It sat looking very small in Ax's big hands, stared around boldly, and yawned to display a fine set of white needle-fangs. 'The mother was dead, and there were two dead kittens, but he's all right. I . . . I'd like to keep him?'

They realised that the person telling them about Iphigenia hadn't been Ax. That had been an Ax Preston automaton, saying the lines. This was the real Ax, this piteous little boy, bereft and frightened, hiding a kitten in his coat. It reminded them how shattered and bewildered they were themselves. How lost.

'Is he old enough to lap?' said Sage, keeping it steady with an effort.

'Yeah. I've already given him some milk. I'd say he's about five weeks. And he's strong, and seems pretty healthy, considering.'

'Has he got a name?' asked Fiorinda. 'May I hold him?'

'Min. I'm going to call him Min. Dunno why, it just came to me.'

Much later, records revealed that GCHQ at Cheltenham had picked up the same dramatic intelligence that had caused the Edinburgh Assembly to abort their deal (an order Neil Cameron had interpreted freely, and thereby put the Triumvirate of England forever in his debt); but it had been set aside, along with an accumulation of data that had pointed in the same unlikely direction for months. There were rumours, after the records came to light, that intelligence officers had deliberately held back the information, in despair; or because nobody dared to tell Lord Mursal his house was on fire. But that was probably complete nonsense: blunders happen all the time.

The weather continued calm and fair, unusually calm for the time of year. On the day after Ax had found his kitten, early on the morning of the twentieth of September, a domineering old man, once a Methodist Minister, was sitting in the glassed gallery at the top of a cottage on the Coastguard Path, or Southwest Path, as the tourists had called it, but it belonged to the Coastguard again now. He liked to watch the ocean from up here, and plagued his housekeeper to help him dress and work the lift for him at ungodly hours. He sat like a mummified giant, his limbs withered but hardly shrunken by age, dressed in old tweeds and a Gortex jacket, gazing at the western horizon. He was a hundred and two years old, but his eyes were bright and giving good service: glinting blue from cavernous sockets.

A swarm of little purple clouds appeared, popping up above the line between the sea and the clear, apple-green sky of dawn, in a very curious manner. The old man applied his right eye to the telescope that stood by him on a brass swivel stand. His jaw dropped. He felt no fear; he was too old to be afraid of anything: but his blood turned to ice-water in his veins from sheer astonishment.

Other witnesses of this sight were convinced the fleet was extraterrestrial; the old man wasn't fooled for a moment. He sat back, frowning, trying to remember something, ah yes: '*For I dipt into the future,*' he declaimed, with satisfaction, '*Far as human eye can see . . . Saw the vision of the world and all the wonder that would be; Saw the heavens filled with commerce, argosies of magic sails, Pilots of the purple twilight, dropping down with costly bales. Heard the heavens filled with shouting and there rained a ghastly dew from the nations' airy navies—*'

He didn't need to press any buttons. Nor did he need to shout, but he always did. 'Chesten! CHESTEN!,' he yelled, swinging his motor-chair around. 'Where is the woman, is she deaf? CHESTEN! Bring me the red phone, I need to call Joss, NOW, not next week! CHESTEN!'

He couldn't get through. The Southwest Peninsula was cut off, excised from the world: as comprehensively silenced as Western Europe had been when the Internet Commissioners had imposed their lightning-strike quarantine to contain the Ivan/Lara virus, long ago.

In the dusk before dawn Ax came face to face with a countryman, and a shotgun, on the path by the little stream in the valley. They both retreated, silently. Ax waited a while, and continued on his way. It wasn't the first time he'd been seen (he insisted on doing all the foraging), though it was the first close encounter. The very few people who were out and about kept their distance, just as Ax himself did ... But on his way back he found a brace of rabbits slung on a post by the upper path. He looked up and saw that Wood Court was just visible through the trees, though there was no sign that it was occupied. He brought the rabbits with him and laid them by the kitchen floor, which was mostly covered now with a bed of cut heather and bracken.

The invasion was forty-eight hours old. The EBC said the English forces in the southwest were 'fighting like cornered rats', but they were being rolled back at great speed: you could only hope the rats weren't dying much.

'Well, I've just heard a statement from Washington. The US government has come clean and revealed how they supported the stunt. They'd ceded Pacific and Eastern Seaboard beachheads, in secret talks, which allowed the Chinese airships to come around the world in three hops: up, beyond the atmosphere and down again.'

Ax looked at a new bundle of hazel rods, which had not been there when he left. They'd been raiding the coppice-farm again. It filled him with terror when his darlings left the den, but he couldn't stop them. He had to go out and fetch news and forage: he couldn't be on guard all the time.

Sage nodded. 'Any word on the design; or how the ships were fuelled?'

'Nope, but they had some very pretty graphics of the flight plan.'

Ax could get pictures now: Sage had fixed that.

Fiorinda had been whittling the end of a hazel pole to a point with Sage's pocketknife. She returned to this task, smoothly detaching a long shaving, which Min the kitten danced and jumped to catch.

'Are the Chinese going to take a card?'

'I dunno, maybe. The US are saying their Chinese allies have no territorial ambitions. They're taking over England and Roumania, to contain the dangerous mess that was Crisis Europe. No one else gets any trouble unless they ask for it.'

'Good of Fred to give us three months' notice,' remarked Sage.

Iphigenia. They're not blazing their way from the Caspian, they're here, and now it all makes sense. The ultimatum China had delivered to Brussels over the Uzbek resistance had expired at midnight on the nineteenth, making that stunning attack on the southwest of England a legitimate act of war. As if it mattered, but the world's powers wanted an excuse to do nothing, and they were right. Ax just wished he knew when those secret talks about the beachheads had been held . . . How long ago did you sell me out, Fred? But he bore the man no ill will, not really.

Never judge until you know the whole story; or even then.

Min approached the rabbits, quivering with excitement. Sage scooped him up, *no no no, paws off*, and dropped him in the tangle of the heather bed; fairly gently.

'Any news of the Few?'

'Nothing . . . I'm hoping they got away, out of the country.'

It was strange. When Ax came back with the latest news they struggled to think of questions; and he struggled to answer . . . Sage resumed knotting strips of birchbark into a long string: hippy guerrilla skills coming in useful again.

'Where'd you get the rabbits?' asked Fiorinda, at last.

'Oh . . . yeah. Someone saw me in the wood, a bloke with a shotgun. I thought it was okay but when I came back those were on a post. What are we going to do?'

'Eat them.'

Ouch. He was not a good forager; he must get better at it. They'd had nothing to eat in two days but the apples, some milk, a few tomatoes and the last of the bar snacks. He was afraid to make regular depredations on the milk halt, and they couldn't cook the garden vegetables because of the smoke of a fire. 'Of course,' said Ax, thinking they'd just have to risk a fire. 'But, listen, this is serious, someone knows—'

They were shaking their heads. 'It's beyond our control, Ax,' Sage told him. 'Someone knows we're here, he gives us rabbits. Let's take it as friendly.'

'What else can we do?' said Fiorinda gently. 'Ax, we have to face it baby, either we're among friends, or we are not going to last long.'

'Okay,' said Ax. 'But we could get further out of sight. I've been thinking, about that house? Where I found the apples?'

'NO,' they said together, instantly.

'No walls, I veto walls,' added Fiorinda.

'All right . . . What about cannibalising the house? There's bound to be stuff.'

'Now tha's a *good* idea.'

Ax cleaned the rabbits and spitted them, wrapped in herbs. Fiorinda lit a fire, and they devoured the meat, with tomato and marrow kebabs, and salt from the birchwood saltbox, her talisman. Later that morning, Sage decided he would start a video diary. When they raided the empty house he took the visionboard with him; then Ax and Fiorinda helped him to wire the Wood Court for sound and vision. They became *auteurs*. Different styles emerged: Fiorinda recorded the home improvements and created installations (which the kitten wrecked, but the destruction was equally valid); Ax made narratives. The maestro let the camera eye rest on details that took his fancy. His diary entries consisted of turning leaves, gossamer spider threads, the dusty, mourning flowers of summer's end, goldenrod in fallen sheaves; hardknott and purple vetch, fading by the upper path.

The stars came out in a tender depth of sky: bats flickered, a hunting owl cried. Ax sat in the fork of the sycamore tree by the west gable, touching the strings of his Les Paul, almost without a sound. He thought of Yap Moss, that gruelling winter battlefield: the empty spaces of blond grass and the clusters of scuffling men, orange darts of fire, cordite smoke. All the men had Ax's face, because who else can you really speak for? They stopped firing, they laid down their arms, and then they just stood there, hands at their sides, heads bowed. In other places, other parts of the moor, the shooting, fighting, dying, was still going on; it would go on. You can only speak for yourself, make your point and leave the stage.

The Few should have been safe. But the time to leave had been when Fiorinda told them it was over in a voicemail. After the Wallingham situation was established, no one was going to quit ... Sage's 'disappearance' had dashed their fragile hopes, but they'd been told he was okay, just back in Wallingham having violated his parole. No one believed Sage had got into a brawl with some ex-barmy army squaddies, though Peter's story (when the search parties had found him) had suggested some kind of entrapment ... But Rick's Place was still running, although Bill and George couldn't get into the club anymore, so there was hope. What else could they do but hang on? Then Allie was informed about the Wallingham break-in by a police phonecall, early on the morning of the eighteenth, and that was another crisis.

At lunchtime on the twentieth she was in her new office, doggedly calling anyone who might have been at Rick's Place, and might talk to her. Were you there on the seventeenth? Did you see Ax or Fiorinda; did you speak to them? Did you see Sage? Do you know anything about this break-in . . .? Dilip had arrived with his current squeeze, an émigrée Vietnamese ceramics artist called Nathalie Que. Chip and Verlaine had turned up on their precious bicycles and were busy trying to make a drama out of the Southwest Peninsula's lack of telecoms. Allie's assistant, a quiet young man called Charlie Middleton, was in his cubbyhole with the longer list of non-hopefuls, Rick's Place punters who certainly wouldn't talk to Allie Marlowe. He was sending them personal emails, to leave no stone unturned.

'I grasp there's no point in trying to get through to anyone in Cornwall to Somerset today,' said Allie irritably. 'Other than that, what's the difference? Wake up, Chip. Things are falling apart, it's normal. It just doesn't get reported any more.'

'Perhaps it's more significant that the European Union is technically at war this morning,' said Dilip. 'Isn't that something we should discuss, Allie?'

Allie wished they would all leave, but wanted them to stay, just for the company. 'How can that have anything to do with Wallingham? It's not that I don't care, DK, it's just there's fuck-all I can do about it—'

Verlaine groaned. 'Oh, the ultimatum? Come on, that's a *canard*, the Masters of the Universe know Brussels has no control over any of us little rogue states.'

Reflexively, he glanced out of the window: the bikes were still there, locked to the Courtyard railings. They were Giffords of Wiltshire Roadsprites, semi-AI and much loved. Chip's machine was green and Ver's was blue, with contrasting detail in mauve and acid-yellow. Their names were Cagney and Lacey.

Allie rolled her eyes and stuck her finger in her free ear.

'Allie, who are the "Masters of the Universe"?' asked Nathalie. 'I never understand what Chip and Verlaine are saying.'

Nathalie was tiny, young, beautiful, and very chic. She was timidly friendly to Allie, whose history with Dilip she knew. Allie couldn't look at her without thinking, I'll probably see you at his funeral: but she was trying to keep her bitterness to herself. DK was in reasonable health at the moment, and still off the drugs. It might be some other girlfriend who would be there by the grave.

'They mean the Chinese.'

'Oh ... I see.'

'The Uzbek Ultimatum, darling,' explained Dilip. 'It ran out at midnight.'

(When did DK start calling people 'darling', so suburban, so unlike him?)

'I appreciate you all being here, but I need to make these calls, and Charlie's busy too. We are *trying* to establish whether Ax and Fiorinda are okay.' Allie hardly dared hope she might hear anything of Sage. He had vanished from the record.

'It's a Reich issue,' Chip told Nathalie helpfully. 'Ming the Magnificent might already be attacking Roumania, and we're not queer for Brussels, but the Dacians are our ancient allies.'

'Huh? Ming?'

'The Emperor of China. Playfully identified with fictional alien despot, see.'

Wish Fiorinda was here, thought Chip. Jokes are wasted on this infant.

'It's Ming the Merciless,' corrected Allie's assistant, from his corner.

'Suit yourself, Charlie—'

'Sit up straight and pay attention, my child,' said Verlaine to Nathalie. 'If you want to join the gang, there are things you must know. The Roumanians, and we use the "u" spelling so as not to confuse them with the Roms, who are different, are in trouble because some of their guerrillas were aiding the Uzbeks. We are their allies because Ax went to Bucharest, and helped some other vampire hippies to blow up the Danube dams, which makes us responsible for their fate—'

'Ax blew up the dams! I've heard that, but it's not *true*, is it?'

'Of course it is. That's what we do, Nathalie. We are ruthless eco-warriors.'

The little Vietnamese looked terrified. Dilip hugged her. 'Ignore them.'

Chip and Ver had turned Allie's upright desk screen to face the room; it was running Channel Seven News with the sound turned down. Suddenly Chip whooped. 'Hey, this is the UFOs! It's come round again! Pay attention, this is so cool! Someone videoed them, leapt on a motorbike and zoomed out of the mystery zone at dawn, shattering records for post-Dissolution bike rides. Nothing has escaped from there since—'

'What utter bullshit. Who says?'

'Hey,' broke in Verlaine, who'd just checked the bikes again. 'Here's Rob and the Babes. Plus babies. Cool beenz! Mamba is such a great little kid—'

'If you're going to talk about UFOs, I'm *really* throwing you out—'

Rob, Felice, Dora and Cherry came rapidly into the room. Dora had Mamba in her arms. The little boy was looking sullen and tearful, a child who has been frightened by adult disarray. Ferdelice, the tall, slim four-year-old, caramel-complexioned like her mother, clung to Chez's dark hand. Felice checked the company and said urgently, 'Someone ought to call Rox.'

'Oh shit,' gasped Chip, instantly sober. 'What's happened?'

He knew at once it was the end. So they are dead. Fiorinda's dead.

On Allie's screen, a spray of purple teardrops springing up from the ocean horizon, in no formation, but surely nothing natural. Rob lunged over her shoulder and assaulted the touchpad. Liszt's 'Preludes' exploded, ear-shattering—

'Fuck, sorry, how d'you change channel?'

'I don't, I don't watch tv on my machine . . . use the number keys.'

A row of men and women in olive-green uniforms, sitting on a stage under a ribbed, shiny purple dome: they looked pleased with themselves and serious, as if posing for a school photograph. In front of them a tall, goodlooking man, in similar uniform but smarter, stood at a rostrum. A mixed crowd looked up, with blank faces.

What's wrong with this picture? The people in the audience look English, all ages, all dresscodes: some of them in military uniform. The people on the stage don't look English at all . . . Chip and Verlaine, Allie and DK, were silent in bewilderment, slowly beginning to take in the text that was running across the bottom of the screen, slowly grasping that the tall man was speaking in a language they didn't understand, except maybe a word or two; instantaneous translation following like an echo—

The invasion was by this time eight hours old. The airships had arrived in waves, each wave bringing many thousands of troops: plus political officers, support staff, and the technicians who had instantly assembled mobile fuel generators, armoured transports and armoured shelters like the purple dome. Cornwall, Devon, Dorset and Somerset were overrun, Bristol and Bath had been taken.

'Is this real?' said Allie, at last. 'Are you saying this is *real*?

'He's called Wang Xili,' said Felice grimly. 'He's the General in Command of Subduing the South West.'

'Yeah,' said Dora. 'It's real. That thing is in Castle Park, Bristol, they pulled people off the street to listen to them and this is live. England has been invaded.'

General Wang was telling the masses that they were in no danger. The Chinese Commanders would not target civilian populations, they respected non-combatants and had vowed never to deploy immoral weapons. He listed the immoral weapons, starting at the top with strategic or tactical nuclear devices. Nerve gas, biological weapons, chemical weapons other than crowd-dispersing tear gas, several of the more vicious 'non-lethals'. Neurological division. Weapons of direct cortical illusion using the forbidden 'immix' code . . .

'But how—?' demanded Allie. 'How do you mean, invaded?'

Mamba began to cry, in piercing wails.

Nathalie Que pressed white-knuckled fists to her mouth.

. . . expressed solidarity with the English people, and told them they would be freed from oppression, disorder, torture and tyranny, freed from the delusions of the Counterculture, free to worship in any of the three Monotheisms, or the five Approved Pantheisms, or to practice Principled Atheism.

'What'll we do?' cried Chip. 'What are we supposed to do?'

'Get hold of *Rox*,' repeated Felice, as if this were the vital move that would annihilate the Chinese Expeditionary Force.

'You'd better go home, Charlie,' said Allie, hearing her own words slowed down, echoey; like talking in a dream. 'Tell anyone else who's working today they should go home too. It's going to be chaos.'

'Yeah, thanks.'

Who said, but we should all stay at the San? Maybe nobody needed to say it, it was so obvious. They had to stick together. Dora and Chez took Chip and Verlaine back to Notting Hill, in the Snake Eyes people-van. They loaded up, then they drove to Lambeth, loaded up again, and said goodbye to the Big Band communards. The round trip took many hours, because anyone who had wheels in London had scrounged some kind of fuel. There was an explosion of unauthorised personal transport hypocrisy going on, with hardly any police, and the added value of a generation of drivers who'd never had to deal with traffic before. Rox wasn't answering hir phone. They swung by Queen Anne Street on the way back, but s/he wasn't there.

By the time they reached Buckingham Palace Road again it was dark. The whole area around the Victoria Monument was heaving. The permanent campground in Hyde Park had broken up, and many of the Counterculturals from there had decided to take refuge inside the Insanitude. There was a crowd of them, laden with hippy regalia, banners and bundles, besieging the Building Management Office. Further crowds had flocked to the old Reich Headquarters as if to a Big Screen, convinced that here, somehow, they would get some real news.

It was a humid, autumnal night; the air was still, noise deadened. Mounted police with lanterns appeared and disappeared like rocks emerging from the choppy human sea. More police were holding a lane open for authorised vehicles to enter the Courtyard, with great difficulty. As Dora inched through the turmoil, and the two Snake Eyes cats prowled and yowled, distressed to be uprooted, it may have crossed the party's minds that this was not the best idea they'd ever had. But once they were inside it was okay. A bunker mentality took over, they felt safe. Allie had secured a good set of rooms for Rob and the Babes and the kids and the cats. Chip and Verlaine had one room, with a window facing an inside courtyard (thinking ahead, don't want to be on an outer wall), but it was reasonable-sized and had a decent bed. They could share Allie's bathroom and kitchen. Nathalie would stay with Dilip. She lived alone, she was afraid to go back to her place. She thought the Chinese would be in London in a day. She would be picked up for re-education; and she was terrified.

Which did not bode well.

If they'd expected to be in charge they'd have been disappointed: but they'd had no thought of that. They knew they would never sit around that circle of schoolroom tables again, helping to decide the fate of the country. Other people were in charge, and the refurbished Balcony Room was an emergency shelter for homeless campers. They made Allie's new office their headquarters and spent most of their time in there, kids and cats underfoot, watching the disaster unfold. Allie moved into the general admin office on the first floor, for the Reich work she needed to do – mostly closing things down, wiping hard drives, making sure paper was shredded. No one had been able to locate Rox.

At least Allie's office had global media access, so they weren't dependent on English State tv. They watched Australian channels and the Radio Delhi webcast for an English language perspective; EBC for loony disinformation. They saw the Washington statement, they found out about the beachheads, and spluttered at President Fred's perfidy. They heard Crisis Europe described, frequently, as 'a tragic and violent backwater', which told them what to expect in the way of international support: and they saw the most momentous event of the world's recent history calmly airbrushed out of existence.

The Chinese did not believe in the 'A-team'. They had taken this line from the start. The few statements that had come out of China had cast doubt on the real nature of the catastrophe; without going into specifics. Now they had their story sorted out. The 'so-called event' was an 'absurd mystification' of the simple fact that the world's fossil fuel reserves had bottomed out, even more steeply than had been forecast. China's own reserves of poor-quality coal and natural gas, on the mainland and under the Pacific, had proved worthless, but the Chinese people saw no need to attribute this to black magic! China had made a full transition to the post-petroleum age, they had no need to shroud inertia and unpreparedness in fairy stories. US science colleagues had admitted the truth, after Chinese investigators at the Central Asia oil bases had uncovered irrefutable evidence of how the Big Lie had been perpetrated. The fake research in the US would be shelved, as Mr Eiffrich had wisely decreed. The other 'fusion event', Sage Pender's Zen Self achievement, was dismissed as unworthy of discussion. Ridiculous pseudo-spirituality!

The Rock and Roll Reich had also more or less disappeared. General Wang Xili, when asked directly about the fate of Ax Preston, seemed to have difficulty placing the name. The President? prompted the interviewer. Famous guitarist, former dictator, leader of the Rock and Roll Reich? Supposedly under house arrest?

'Mr Preston has nothing to fear from us,' said General Wang Xili. 'He will become a private citizen, before long.'

The goodlooking South West General had quickly emerged as spokesperson for the invading forces, the one you always saw on camera: which didn't mean he was in charge, but it was a start. Get an impression of the guy, thought Rob. Ax would be taking in everything. He'd have the movers and shakers down, he'd be thinking of how we could use them, turn them . . . But he felt that the task was hopeless, the Reich was nowhere, this disaster was too huge. Ax Preston, who he?

The Few had made no attempt to contact Greg Mursal, or Faud Hassim. Before the invasion was a day old you'd have had to be mad to want to be associated with the Second Chamber. For about forty-eight hours after that casual aside from Wang they really hoped the Triumvirate would be allowed to join them, released by the Chinese. Then the lightning strike reached London. Hu Qinfu, the General in Command of Subduing the Capital, made his first appearances, and in response, at last, there was a broadcast from Wallingham. It went out live (allegedly) on all four of the English State-controlled tv channels. Ax spoke to the nation, from the Yellow Drawing Room, Sage and Fiorinda silent on either side. He praised the English people for their calm, and the armed forces for their courage. Lord Mursal, who walked into the shot to join him, was warmly greeted. The two men clasped hands, and looked soulfully into each other's eyes.

Sage and Fiorinda sat and smiled.

The Few, who had gathered not knowing what to expect, moaned in horror.

'Oh, God,' whispered Allie, 'Oh *shit*. The bastards!'

'I can't look, I can't look,' wailed Chip.

The door of Allie's office burst open. A wild-eyed heavy-stubbled Boat Person type marched in, wearing battered, urban-camo 'fatigues' from a defunct fashion chain, homemade Roumanian colours, blue and yellow and red, roughly stitched onto the breast. 'You!' he yelled at Rob. 'You, you you—!' He jerked his rifle at the other males. 'Out of here. Report for duty.'

They weren't going to argue with a gunman. 'Okay, but what's going on?' Rob demanded; but politely. 'Who are you?'

'The Insanititude has become a Republic. You are citizens.'

London had fallen. The Countercultural rebel MPs had fled to Reading, where they would form an emergency government in the Palace of Rivermead. The 'ringleaders' of the Second Chamber régime were in custody. Hu Qinfu was going to accept the Mayor's surrender, in Central Hall. The former Buckingham Palace had become a magnet for every diehard partisan, and the Few were trapped.

On the fourth day of the invasion, the staff officers of the barmy army convened at their Islamic Campaign HQ for a Council of War. Easton Friars, outside Harrogate, had been a derelict country estate when it had been taken over by Ax's militarised hippies. It was still derelict: plans for its restoration and the creation of an Islamic Campaign Experience had been sidelined. The Council was held in a common room on the ground floor where Victorian ancestors looked down, pockmarked by barmy darts games, on the mildewed leather sofas and chairs nobody had troubled to remove.

Presiding was Richard Kent, the former British Army Major who had commanded Ax's army during the dictatorship: a West African by ethnicity, Midlands-born; thicker round the middle than he used to be, though he tried to keep in trim. Beside him was Cornelius Sampson, another retired soldier, his lover of many years—

There were several proposals on the table. First, that the army should go to Reading and put itself at the disposal of the emergency government. Second, that they should join the regulars. This idea received minimal support. The morale of the regular forces had disintegrated. It was well known that troops in Yorkshire and the northeast had been forced onto the transports that would take them south at gunpoint. The soldiers were convinced that the denial of the A-team event was a smokescreen, and the Chinese had horrific occult weapons ... The third option was that they should volunteer for bomb disposal, ambulance and stretcher-bearer work. That one was swiftly dismissed. The barmies had been with Ax all the way in the

House of Commons; they thought he'd done brilliantly. Of course, in the Good State, we want to reduce violence to a minimum! But nobody believed that meant Ax would not defend his country. And whatever'd happened that night in Berkeley Square (it had probably been a set-up), ten to one Ax *had* broken the evil fucker's bastard neck. Which proved that the non-violence speech was not to be taken literally.

Fourth, organise. There were Islamic militias, not yet affiliated. There was a 'Shield Ring' in Cumbria; there were other bodies, more or less shady but patriotic. The army should negotiate with them to form a combined, independent force.

Fifth, do nothing and wait for Ax.

The barmy commanders were better informed than the Few. They knew that Ax was no longer a prisoner in Wallingham, nor had the Triumvirate been secretly executed: which was the popular theory to account for their failure to appear. They had reason to believe that Ax was free, with his partners. But that was all. They didn't know where he was, and they could not account for his failure to make contact.

The discussion quickly came down to Reading as the only real option. But though no one expressed this view in so many words, they knew it was a suicide mission. They'd be joining the rats in the trap, the fish in the barrel.

'Each of us here speaks for thousands,' declared one bulky, dreadlocked veteran. 'We know what our squaddies want, they want action. But we're the last resource. We got to think about where we're gonna be most useful before we pour out our blood and guts.'

'Yeah, but we're a finely honed weapon, Marsh. Since we were disbanded, we have remained hidden but intact, like a rifle dismantled in the thatch. What's the good of throwing that away, trying to "organise" with some fuckin' ragbag of wannabes?'

The hippy war leaders had turned up arrayed for battle, which was crazy of them, in the circumstances. But Richard himself was wearing the battledress tunic he'd worn in the Campaign, with the pink triangle, and his medals. It was too tight, he looked a fool, but he couldn't have borne not to make the gesture.

He'd been taking a very small salary from the Reich as nominal 'Colonel' of the irregulars: sorting out their problems with civilian life. He hadn't liked what the Second Chamber was doing, but this young country could have survived Greg Mursal. The reforms Ax had wanted would have come. He felt blindsided, dumped on from a great height, outraged and heartbroken, bewildered and furious.

'I'm not here to give orders—'

'We don't work like that,' someone agreed, with righteous pride.

'The Chinese are an expeditionary force, far from home. Whatever their resources I can't believe there's no way to dislodge them, bring them to terms, if we can only string this out—'

But not without leadership, and where was Ax?

'All right, let's come back to it. Anybody want to tell me why the invaders don't use their incredible airships? Why no bombing raids?'

The purple fleet had not been seen in any action since the landings.

'Our distances are negligible,' suggested someone. 'A decent-size Chinese river would swallow the headless chicken, from what I've heard. They don't bomb populations, an' they've walked over our regulars. They don't need air power.'

'An air strike might take a chip out of somethen' mediaeval.'

Bitter laughter. The Chinese were ruthless with resistance, the very few times they'd met any: but they were religiously respectful of ancient monuments.

'That fake Royal Message was a desp'rate mistake,' offered a West Country voice. 'All Mursal did was convince the regulars that Ax is dead and Lord Mursal killed him. Wonderful encouraging, that was.'

Cornelius Sampson leaned back in a musty armchair and tossed the amber komboloi he favoured in place of the pipe he'd given up. 'All right. Hawk, we were a walkover. But what if Shi Huangdi had tackled Europe conventionally, from east to west? Albeit with the same overwhelming post-fossil fuels technology?'

The new China was officially ruled by the old men who held the offices of President and Vice President; Premier and Vice-Premier. Most experts believed there was a concealed junta, some kind of 'gang of four'. Cornelius, who had spent some of his career as an official Beijing watcher, favoured the 'one man' theory. He called the hidden leader Shi Huangdi, First Emperor, for obvious reasons.

The young man known as Hawk was willing to entertain the idea. 'Good question. East 2 West, you move from the dirt-poor hard cases to the big populations with the high expectations. It's going to take time, but you do your rough fighting while you're relatively close to home; the technically superior forces when they're less eager to fight ... He's a risk-taker, this guy. He plays high to win high.'

'It wasn't about ground tactics,' countered someone, repeating the received wisdom. 'They psyched the world with that stunt.'

'Like that Wang guy says,' added a much-tattooed and feathered leader, 'they don't want to fuck with *occupying* Europe. They just want to box it, pack it up. The airship stunt was probably cheap at the price.'

'I believe the goal was to establish dominance over the US,' announced Marsh, the one who wanted to join forces with the mad dogs gangs. 'Up the back passage, without a fight, by getting them to cede those beachheads.'

Cornelius tossed his worry beads. 'All good points. But Shi Huangdi has not shown himself a risk-taker in building up his Asian sphere. I believe he'd have taken the gradual east-west approach, once he'd decided that Europe must be pacified ... If it hadn't been for Rufus O' Niall, and Sage Pender.'

The war leaders frowned over this.

'You think they're shitting us? You think they have magic?' said Hawk.

'I don't think they're bullshitting,' said Cornelius. 'I think they hope there's no such thing as a "fusion event". But they're not sure, and that means England is incalculable. That's why we were targeted, and why the invading force has been so careful of life and property. I believe Ax has realised this.'

A shock of relief went through the desperate ruffians.

Gone to ground! He's gone to ground. Of course!

Silence is an answer, thought Richard. His only plan had been to hold the army back, and wait for orders. He had not known how cruelly Ax's defection (it felt like defection) had been weighing on him. Suddenly he could breathe again.

'Ax is telling us we're guerrillas,' exclaimed the muscular blonde who was the token woman in the command tent. 'Not the buggering Light Brigade!'

'Yeah! This isn't the time when we come out of our holes!'

They put it to the vote. They would wait for Ax.

The Hawk was not convinced. 'I know you, Corny,' he said, 'you talk around corners, watching us like an old tortoise. You say wait and I'll go along with it, but me and mine will go fucking kamikaze if we have to.'

Cornelius nodded. 'Fair enough.'

On the tenth day the Insanitude was under siege. The Republic of Europe had rejected the safe-conduct for non-combatants offered by General Hu and declared martial law. It was summary execution for any traitor caught trying to escape. The non-combatant 'citizens' were living in the North Wing, in refugee-camp conditions, and under guard. They had water – hard to run out of water, in the sodden London Basin – but the quality was suspect. They had sanitation, likewise. Food, cooking fuel and medicines would last for a while. Supplies were unevenly distributed, but there were reasonably fair barter markets. It was rough, not terrible.

The Few had a piece of floor in the largest of the havens. They had to occupy it all the time, or they would have lost territory instantly: but that was okay. There was nowhere much to go. Dilip was on firewatch in the State Apartments. Felice was with another couple of parents, supervising a finger-painting session under the grand piano that stood, mysterious survivor, at one end of the haven-room. The rest of them sat around on rolled-up bedding, or lay dozing on their portion of a large Turkish carpet, another random survivor. Chip and Ver, propped on their elbows, were monitoring the San's remaining external cameras on a palmtop with a virtual screen. A major assault was due this afternoon. The 'citizens' knew about things like that because they still, eerily, had access to tv and radio.

Nothing seemed to be happening outside, as yet.

Everyone missed EBC, which had died soon after London fell. It had been fun jeering at the lies, and there'd been the faint, ever-present hope that suddenly Ax would be there on the screen. The real Ax, not a stupid fake, smiling with his eyes, having the Chinese eat out of his hand, making everything come right.

The piano room was warm and dim: the tall wooden shutters were never removed from the windows. The air was stale from the exhalations of about forty bodies (not counting the children), and days of cooking smells. Rob lay on his back, staring at the ceiling. He was dead tired, nobody could sleep in here; and fear for the kids was breaking his neck. Remorse and guilt, too. Why did we walk into this trap?

'I keep thinking the next meeting will do it.'

The Few were trying to organise a surrender, preferably without getting themselves shot. 'Maybe it will,' murmured Chez; who was lying near him, equally heavy-eyed. 'I'm still sure the barmies can be turned.' She took Rob's hand, which seemed to breathe exhaustion, and kissed his blunt fingertips.

The best of the security squaddies had headed off for destinations unknown, before the 'Republic of Europe' took over. Of the remaining sixty or so, the ones who hadn't been killed had been recruited. They were basically goodwilled: but conflicted. They were with the Republic because they did not see how defending the Insanitude could be wrong.

'Yeah, maybe, but you know where that leads? A gun battle indoors.'

'I hate the firewatching,' murmured Dora, absently stroking Toots, the big fluffy black and white cat. The Babes' other cat, the notorious Ghost, who had once eaten two of her own healthy newborn kittens, had not been seen for a day or two. 'It's scary . . . But living like this is not so bad. I keep drifting off and thinking this is some other, ordinary disaster, you know?'

'Nothing's happening in the Forecourt,' reported Ver.

'The tourists *will* be disappointed,' remarked Chip. 'No Changing of the Guard. Maybe they'll go away and come back tomorrow.'

The tourists were the Chinese, so called because of their passion for historic monuments and natural beauty. They had been true to their word. They respected non-combatants and eschewed 'immoral weapons'. But what if they had to choose between Buckingham Palace and the citizens of the Republic? General Hu, as far as the Few knew anything, did not have a lot of patience with recalcitrants. None of the Chinese did. Inevitably you thought of nerve gas—

Allie sat on one of her suitcases, huddled in her beloved red Gucci jacket. She had brought all her clothes with her when forced out of her flat. This had turned out useful, good clothes fetched high prices in barter (though you wondered why); but she would never part with this jacket, it was her lover and her child. She slept with it cuddled in her arms. She looked down at little Nathalie, who was sleeping now,

272

curled in a foetal ball. So thin, brittle insect limbs . . . The Vietnamese girl had pleaded with them to kill her rather than let her be taken alive, and you start thinking, get a grip kid. How bad can re-education be?

We have no idea.

'I thought it would go on for years,' she said. 'First I couldn't believe it, then I thought the situation would linger on forever, like a normal war zone.'

'Maybe it will,' murmured Chez. 'Just not for us.'

'I know why the Republic keeps fighting, they're nuts and they can't count. But why is the Counterculture still fighting? China is huge, the odds are ridiculous.'

'Hippies,' said Dora. 'They're mad dogs.' She had compassion fatigue for the people who were prolonging this agony. She wasn't proud of it.

Rob nodded, without lifting his head. 'Thank God we're on our own. If Mursal had managed to get armed support from the Celtic nations it would've been carnage.'

'Not a chance,' put in Chip. 'Why would anyone support *him?*'

'Nothing's still happening,' reported Ver.

The other refugees lived their lives, watched the external cameras on small screens; picked guitar, played cards. Anyone who passed, crossing the floor to visit the bathrooms, the water cooler or the kitchen burners, stooped to hi-five Rob, or squatted down to say a few words. He'd become the unelected leader of the non-combatants, which made him uneasy, but he hadn't been able to stop it happening. He felt like a corporal in the trenches, promoted *faute de mieux*, and resented the women's slippery ability to dodge the draft. What became of women's lib around here? Chip and Ver lost interest in the watch on the Rhine, and rolled over.

'Pippin,' said Chip, 'd'you remember a sci-fi story called "We Who Are About To"? They're stranded on an alien planet, no skills, no hope of rescue, and the argument is, why try to stay alive, build shelters, seek for water, when—'

'It's just a question of how long, days or weeks?' finished Verlaine. '"We Who Are About To Die Salute You" from the Latin, *Morituri te salutant*, which gladiators never really said, when about to get killed in the arena.' He stroked Chip's nose. 'I think we've been playing that game since Massacre Night, young Merry. We should compose an artefact called Morituri.'

The Adjuvants composed artefacts, they did not write songs.

'It sounds like a Japanese condiment ... Hey, d'you remember when Ax and Sage had that huge, huge fight, and Sage stripped down the Heads' banner from the gates and walked off with it, stalk stalk, down Buckingham Palace Road in the dark?'

'Oh yeah. Superb. Off he went, shining like Achilles, taking his brother Heads with him. I love it when he *stalks*.'

They did not know what had happened to Rox. Cagney and Lacey had been requisitioned by the Republic, and probably boiled down for ammunition. They were almost sure their leaders were dead, because Mursal would have produced them if he could. Or the Chinese would have produced them by now. But it was comforting to reminisce, if they could get away with this forbidden topic—

'Knock that OFF,' snapped Allie. 'I swear I'll kill you if you talk about them.'

'Well, what *are* we allowed to talk about? Suggest us something.'

'I don't care. Rimbaud's Illuminations, Blackpool Illuminations, multicoloured hedgehogs, WHATEVER YOU LIKE.'

She believed that she had sent Sage to his death. She had not told the others, but she knew. He had not been taken back into custody, he had been killed. She had felt it, the whole time he was talking to her, he had been *fey* that afternoon, and she hadn't stopped him ...

Chip and Ver sat up, shocked and contrite. They got on either side of Allie and patted her shoulders awkwardly. 'Allie, hey, hey, don't cry. You're our tower of strength. You look out for everyone.'

'You know what? You're the new Aoxomoxoa, that's absolutely true.'

Rob snagged the palmtop, checked the screen, blinked; scooped out an earbead and inserted it. Gunfire exploded in his head. 'Good news. They're not in chemical suits, and I see no gas masks. We may be okay.'

In ways Dilip had missed the edge that being sero-positive had given him, and the challenge all those regular doses had presented. In ways he'd been drifting since he'd decided he was dying. High spots like the Mayday concert, and his b-loc trip to low orbit, stood out: but it was life in the departure lounge. The fate of the Triumvirate had taken him painfully by surprise: *Has anybody here seen my friend Abraham? I just looked around and he was gone ...* The Chinese invasion, not so much. How instantly, how naturally, the Few had become to the besieged palace what the Few had been to England! Unskilled paramedics at the road accident, bodies in the bucket-chain, an accidental chivalry of butterflies, and now back to where it all began. Just like yesterday, take up my guitar and play. Except that DK's instrument had always been his own body. Not the code, but the dance.

He felt he knew everything; and regretted nothing but those things one always regrets, misdeeds, words spoken out of turn. He felt he was ready: but it was sudden and strange, in the State Apartments, when the attack burst through. He passed in seconds from the frightening chore of smothering incendiaries behind the frontline, through the frontline sweeping over him, to the realisation that the siege was over, and that this was where his plane was going to take off, here, where he had been the Mixmaster General of Immix, with sea-green Fiorinda, one perfect night in the DJ's box above the whirling, shrieking, Ballroom—

He burned the books and buried the scholars

The sacking of the Insanitude brought a wave of reaction. While the survivors fled to the Tower, where they holed-up impregnably in a far more precious, far more ancient building, the people of England came out on the streets for the first time. They gathered by the millions, in protest and mourning, at the forbidden Big Screen sites: singing and playing and making passionate speeches. Up and down the country a second Deconstruction Tour broke out and raged, but this time the targets were not giant supermarkets, car lots and fast food outlets. Mobs of desolate lads attacked futuristic utopian science wherever they could find it, smashing and burning b-loc development labs and immix studios, trashing technology parks and gene-infusion clinics: all so that Ax Preston's legacy should not fall into enemy hands. The Heads' warehouse on Battersea Reach was burned out, to the annexe. The Zen Self scanners did not escape. Joss had ordered them moved them three times since his son had disappeared; he knew it was a mistake but couldn't stop himself; and the chain of command had become too long to be secure. Disks and hardware, books and documents at the hedgeschool science centres, and at Reich-friendly universities like Cambridge and Sussex, went onto bonfires heaped by heartbroken lads and ladettes in tears. In a very few days, about ninety per cent of the seedcorn Ax had guarded so faithfully was gone.

The Rebel Countercultural MPs held out at Reading, in the Palace of Rivermead, making fruitless appeals for international intervention, while the historic city that had become the Counterculture's last redoubt was taken street by street. Reading's bricks and mortar citizens had fled, with the co-operation of the Chinese. But the campground by the Thames had been allowed to fill to bursting with fugitives from places like Glastonbury; which had fallen in the first sweep across the southwest.

The wise-women and gentle-men of Reading Site had performed a great deal of ritual magic in the shock of the invasion. They'd given up about the third day, their concentration wrecked by ambivalence. They couldn't help noticing that no signs from Gaia, no wonders, were supporting the resistance: whereas the presentiments of disaster (of which there'd been plenty) had been consistently reversed. Now there was a dearth of any visions at all, except the kind easily explained by strong medicine, or the lack of it. The rumour that the Triumvirate had escaped from Wallingham and were still alive was strong: but it would have been dangerous to try and conjure their survival. Something like that comes as a free gift, it's insanely costly, otherwise. They had to conclude hope must die to be reborn.

Anne-Marie Wing set her fiddle in its case, wrapped the case in silk and laid it in the safe-hole under the floor of the bender. She arranged her other treasures around it, touching them all with love. Several bars of gold, a velvet bag of uncut gemstones, a withered wreath of traveller's joy. The children's umbilicals; an iridescent black shirt that Sage had given to Silver when she was a little girl. A cut aubergine with the name of Allah written in the seeds (given to Ammy by a Muslim wise-woman, who found it in her shopping the day of Ax's inauguration); which Ammy had sealed in Perspex. Photographs of her parents. The kids' Hedgeschool certificates, all gilt and glowing colour.

Her eldest daughter sat on the bench by the firepit, hunched over folded arms and scowling. 'They're dead,' said Paradoxa, meaning Ax, Sage and Fiorinda. 'Don't be so numb. If they weren't dead they'd be here!' She was eighteen. They'd hoped she would be a vet, but Para wanted to recover from the disease of being human. She'd been living in an extreme Gaian community in Brighton, without clothes, abandoning language; fucking like dogs. She'd come home because of the war: angry and contradictory as ever. Anne-Marie shut the hole, replaced the bacterial damp-proof membrane and smoothed down the rugs.

'They're not here because this is not the fight. The fight'll be keeping the flame of what Ax did alive. An' even that's not important, neither, because there's always another Ax. It's the cause that matters.'

Paradoxa tugged the plaited scalplock, her one vanity, which dangled from her dirty naked skull. 'Fucking hell, Mum, you're not making sense. If you believe that, why are you still here? They're going to kill us all, you know. Go into hiding!'

'I'd have to stay in hiding then, wouldn't I, love?' Anne-Marie applied her fingertips to the outer edges of her narrow black eyes. 'Or they'd send me "home" for re-education. I can't be tossed with that.'

'They hate women. The ones we see are trannys. They'll rape us with dogs before they kill us. There are no real women in China, because of the one-child policy. They grow babies in vats.'

Anne-Marie wasn't into dehumanising the enemy. It would be daft, when all she had to do was look in a mirror. She let go of her Chinky eyes and spread her hands on the bender floor. Earth and stone rose up into her veins, through the layers of bright silk and the dpm. The myriad weaving of little creatures that makes one soil different from another became one with her blood. Come England, come ... conquer the conquerors. I know you can do it. But if you're wise, my country, don't you ask anything of magic. Magic isn't to be used, it just is. You leave it alone.

'What's right for one person isn't right for another. I wish Ax was here, but I know why he isn't. This is my home, pet. That's all there is to it, reelly.'

Paradoxa took her crossbow and went off to look for her father in the town.

Anne-Marie went on straightening the bender, putting fragile ornaments out of the way as if she were preparing for a visit from her old man and his drinking buddies. At last she burned some lavender and rosemary to sweeten the air and sat watching the little flames, seeing faces there and singing softly under her breath, *I dreamed I saw Joe Hill last night, as alive as you or me . . .*

She never found out what happened to Paradoxa, except that the girl hadn't hooked up with Hugh by the last time they managed to talk on the phone.

The younger teens and the children of the campground were living in the Palace of Rivermead, where they were thought to be safe. The next day, when Rivermead burned, they had to be evacuated back to their homes in the tented township. There were no safe places. Wang Xili, the General in Command of Subduing the South West, had *warned* them. There was no such thing as a non-combatant Countercultural, old or young, it had been policy throughout the invasion. They could have reneged, they'd been given time. They knew they if they reneged they would be spared, that had been policy too. He had warned them.

Down by the river the traveller's joy was silver elflocks in the hedges, the Michaelmas daisies stood in starry lilac sheaves. The meadow where Aoxomoxoa's grey van had been a rock and a refuge for Fiorinda was trampled and bloody; littered with bodies as if a night of Dissolution revels had ended in a huge deranged brawl. Anne-Marie ran around turning up faces, looking for her second and third daughters, Silver and Pearl, who had not come back from the crèche. Now it was here she couldn't believe how she'd got into this situation, by what degrees, by what mad stubbornness? She ran all the way back up to the hospitality area, through the confusion and the smoke and the racket: took little Safire, who was howling, in her arms, and screamed at the boys to follow her. Forced to abandon Ruby, dragging Jet, the six-year-old, by the hand, she rushed to the washhouse, a substantial building of recovered brick and timber; served by a borehole and one of the biomass generators.

'Stay here!' she screamed, and ran to get Rubes.

The laundry room was seething with mothers and sobbing children, but there were islands of quiet. Jet looked around and with decision led his sister to a counter where a row of wicker baskets full of washing stood, abandoned on the last normal day. 'Sit on the floor,' he ordered. The chubby little girl, silenced and fascinated, sat, obediently. He tipped a basket over her so she was buried her under an avalanche of socks and T-shirts. 'Stay there. Don't make a sound!' He waited to see she didn't immediately crawl out. Then he took his knife, a kitchen knife he'd secretly been carrying around with him, big in his small hand, and went to help his mother.

That was the end of any organised resistance. Ax's England, the nation of Dissolution, was no more. The dream had lasted, from Massacre Night to the fall of Reading, a little less than nine years. Shocked and saddened reactions went flying around the globe. A radio newsreader in Delhi reminded listeners that this was the first successful foreign conquest of the UK since 1066, and quoted (brave man) the judgement of a Norwegian chronicler of that time: *cold heart and bloody hand, now rule fair England*. The movie called *Rivermead*, buried since the Lavoisier scandal, was put into distribution. Sales and downloads of the Reich's music rocketed. But though the tributes were generous, the protests were muted. Ax had been a romantic dictator but his Presidency had failed, his vision no match for the realities of a corrupt and brutal régime. His country was in better hands now, and it was to be hoped that Crisis Europe would accept the object lesson calmly. England's Celtic and Continental neighbours made the most conciliatory moves they could think of, and prayed that the new masters of the universe would let them be.

NINE

The Ploughshare and the Harrow

September ended. The blackberries were stripped, the hazel cobs were fattening; the horse-chestnuts had dropped their freight of spiny conker-cases and rustling, rusty-edged leaves, into quiet Sussex lanes. One misty morning in mid-October the bonded girl who worked in the dairy at Towncreep Farm and lived over the garage, glanced out of her window and saw someone in the yard. She wasn't alarmed. There were a lot of travellers about, because of the war. They were mostly harmless, just hungry; and if they thieved a bit, she tended to sympathise. But this shabby intruder was acting strangely. He was squatting on his heels by the wall, looking intently at something propped on his knees. It was after milking time. She would usually have been having breakfast with the family, but she'd come back up to her room. Her bondholders had felt they had to watch the news: the girl had felt she couldn't.

She went quietly down the wooden steps that led to her loft, through the cluttered garage where the farmer kept a vintage BMW (up on blocks; it had a petrol engine, never converted) and looked out through the open doors. He was a slim man, and quite tall. Straight, sheeny-dark hair, with a few threads of silver, fell past his jaw. He wore a brown velvet jacket; he had a ring with a red stone in it on his right hand: and now she could see it was a palmtop or pocket-tv sort of thing poised on his knees, and a fine black earphone lead disappearing under a wing of his hair; so she understood what he was doing.

She must have caught her breath, he looked up. Completely fearless. That was her first thought: as if she'd met a wild animal, a fox or a deer, in the woods, and instead of scooting, it had faced her, uncannily, look for look. His skin was milky-tea colour, he had high cheekbones, a straight nose, a fine-cut mouth and almond-shaped clear brown eyes; a graceful keel of midnight-blue knotwork was tattooed above and below the left one. She recognised him at once, of course: except for the Celtic tattoo.

Completely fearless.

He put his little tv thing away, unhurried, and stood up: smiling a little.

'Will you give me some milk?'

'Oh yes,' gasped the bonded girl. 'Oh, oh yes—'

She had to give him yesterday's milk, because everything was behind; which mortified her. 'Wait,' she said. 'Please, wait, er, sir . . .' dashed into the back kitchen and came out with a loaf of fresh bread from the crock. The family were in the big room beyond, riveted by the public executions on the telly. She thrust the loaf at him, and didn't know what else to do or say.

'Thank you,' said the fearless man. He put the loaf in his bag, jumped at the yard gate and he was gone, over it, into the wood.

'So that's him,' she whispered, staring after, her heart thumping. 'That's *him*.'

Up before dawn, shivering in the dim chill air, Sage and Fiorinda had groped their way to the summit of Camp Hill, the highest point in the Forest. Sage had the visionboard, Fiorinda carried Min: the kitten was too young to be left alone. They found a hollow close to the base of the one remaining radio mast: an antique, once belonging to the Diplomatic Corps Radio Station, code-name Aspidistra. They knew about things like that. Starved of connectivity, they'd surfed the tourist information boards in deserted car parks, feeding on scraps of nature lore and local history.

Mist dripped from the yellowed leaves of the brambles that curved overhead. Fiorinda spread a sheet of baling plastic, Sage set down the visionboard and pulled out a length of cable, looping it hand over hand. They sat with their knees drawn up. The kitten wriggled and settled, purring 'til he shook with pleasure. Silver drops ran together along the rim of Sage's hood like a string of pearls.

'One more look?'

'Yeah.'

They were about to despatch the video diary to Paris, where they'd established radio contact with Alain de Corlay. They were in love with this piece of work. It reminded them of *Bridge House*, a six-week multimedia residence created by the Few and friends in the dictatorship. But their music-video diary of the invasion (so far it had no name) was orders of power further, a leap beyond: fragmentary but coherent; hallucinatory but stripped down, nitpicking in detail; with a perfect finish. Songs come, it's a habit of mind, but the tech to dress them is another dimension, the rock and roll continuum; and they knew they'd found another level of their game. They had used the three per cent immix developed by virtual movie makers, for the arousal triggers: Sage's much stronger immersion code for the *qualia*—

'Any requests?'

'Anything, I don't mind. Oh, wait.' The rough-cut came in packets of twelve seconds, it was not, as yet, retrievable except by numbers. She closed her eyes and rattled off what she thought of as a barcode. Sage grinned to himself, of course the tech is child's play these days but damn it, she catches on fast.

'Coming up.'

A needle-thin sliver of colour opened in the air, flickered and unfolded like a Japanese paper flower. Fiorinda imagined the noughts and ones flying into her eyes, like a swarm of tiny bees, creating something in her brain that was descended all the way from finger painting on the walls of a cave. It was September, it was deep dusty sunlight, we were fixing our roof. Ax and I were on the new rooftree, Sage was pitching bundles of heather thatch up to us, which we would lash and peg in place. They had their shirts off, their arms and shoulders and breasts, all embossed with muscle like living armour, how I loved watching them, how beautiful they were—

Brief as the swallow's flight,
It's hard to realise
There are those who do not live for love
Drawn to the heated thread
Of human flesh and blood
See this
Turn all my fires on

They say it's a mark of sanity, to know people don't see the world you see

To know everyone around you, is living under stra-ange skies
I want to be insane for this, I want to see your coloured stars
Touch you when I touch you take your mind into, your body into mine

We were talking, you can hear us through the music, about that time Ax and Sage did *Liquid Gold* for the Hoorays, and my, I felt naked. You can't catch all the words, but you're getting the message. The intimacy of what we do, it's like a disease, sometimes it spooks us, that our music is music to you, that we can take you under our skies. There I am, in rags that were my red and blue chiffon print of long ago, over the remains of that plum tailored skirt, ripped off to the knees. I wear my clothes like memory, hate to see them go. I'm filthy, we're all filthy, a patina of grime over sweaty tanned skins where the sun slips; three per cent works beautifully on all that. But what you'll feel most is the dull red of the broken half-bricks in the gable; the sycamore leaf, piled with blackberries, the shaving of white birch. They'll be burned into your brain, because that's where we put the immix.

'*She needs a tambourine.*'

Clearly, then Sage laughs; and that was it, paper flower folded, gone.

'You still happy with it?'

She nodded. 'I'm extremely pleased with where my career is just now.'

'Me too,' said the maestro, equally without irony. 'This has been intense.'

Ax's 'Lay Down', the Yap Moss song (he had wanted to call it 'Untitled', but they had stopped him) would be the first single, obviously. But they didn't mind.

What did you do in the invasion, oh fallen idols? We slept with the spiders, and cut ourselves a homemade immix album, which our friend Alain will produce, without massacring it, we hope, because we can't consult him much.

Was that appropriate behaviour, when your country was in its death agony?

Don't know, it's just what happened.

Like cream poured over the back of a spoon, a layer of smooth over stinging liquor, every track is laid over pain. When your country is being invaded, and you are far from the frontline, you find yourself just *staring*, at whatever stick or stone is in front of your eyes: and that's where the bodies are buried.

'Did you know, in World War Two they used to transmit fake German Forces radio from here? Sex scandals about their High Command, to demoralise the Hun.'

'Yep, I did know that, my pilgrim. I read it on the same notice board you did.'

'Hahaha. Well, since Ax has the transceiver, I will now knock-up my fake software digital radio station again, and bare-wire it to the Aspidistra Mast.'

'How long will it take to upload the goods?'

''Bout ten minutes, if all goes well. Say twenty.'

'If we took out enough components to make a cavity, could we fix your board so it would work as a microwave oven?'

'No! Leave my fucking board alone. My board has had enough.'

'Only joking, poor Sage. We have no pizza, anyway.' She leaned against his shoulder. 'Sage, would you mind taking the kitten?'

'Yeah, sure, hand him over—'

'I want to go for a walk. Just a short walk, okay? I'll see you back.'

She disappeared quickly into the mist. Sage held the squirming kitten. 'You *don't* want to run off,' he said to it. 'You think you do, but you don't, you'd get wet feet an' Ax would fucking kill me'. He stuffed Min inside his hoodie, and bent, almost with a shrug of dismissal, to his work.

She'll come to no harm.

Camp Hill was pocked with Neolithic-looking lumps and hollows, a usefully messy digital landscape to play with, if he'd been worried about what he was doing. He was not, but he could feel the fatalistic blank of these strange days slipping from him. I'm going to be afraid, soon. I'm going to have to think about my dad, my son; all the other people in our charge whose fates we don't yet know . . . Refreshingly, the bumps were *not* Neolithic. They were the traces of an army that had camped here in 1793, to meet the threat of the French Revolution . . . Read that on a board.

Facing the wrong way, of course. In so far as those compadres, the other blood-daubed radicals, ever made it, they had landed in Cornwall and Wales. But it was an excuse you got tired of hearing.

Oh, we only got trashed because England's military might was *facing the wrong way.* The air defence region assumes an attack from the north or northeast. To avoid false alarms, the system filters out *exactly* the kind of profile, storm of hail, flock of birds, that the Chinese fleets would have most resembled ... And otherwise it would have been a different story? Do they *listen* to themselves, do they know how pathetic that sounds?

The board slung on his shoulder, Min the kitten a warm lump against his ribs, he trudged off down the hill. He was sour, irrationally so, because his own homeland had been overrun, and Sussex, so far, had not.

Ax found himself a hiding place further off and made do without a picture. He went on listening until the hard news started to break up into verbiage, and then decided to quit. The fields and woods south of the Forest were still ghostly, haunted by the *munch, munch* of looming cattle. He crossed the B-road and took the public footpath onto the heath. As he crested the rise below the Airman's Grave he saw Sage waiting for him, right out in the open, a cut-out figure on the mist. He was sitting on the wall of the little stone enclosure that marked the spot where a Wellington had crashed in 1941, on its way back from a raid on Cologne.

And this seemed right, just as it seemed right to Ax that he was out in the open himself, not skulking helpless in some cellar or attic hidey-hole: being kept like a troublesome pet, until he was found and dragged out. Fuck that. They watched each other, soberly, as Ax came up. Sage slipped down from the wall, and they turned to lean against it, side by side, looking south.

'Well,' said Ax. 'That's it, officially. Now the unofficial situation starts.'

Sage nodded.

'Where's Fiorinda? Back at the bothy?'

'Gone for a walk ... Ooh, don't panic, I have your kitten.' He unzipped his hoodie, to prove this. 'I don't want to be branded a no-good, not fit to be a father.'

'I'll take him.'

'Nah, you won't. He's keepin' me warm.'

The woods beyond Fairwarp made a crumpled, textured, dragon

shadow on the sky. The shoulder of the South Downs was a grey washed line on grey.

'What about the executions?'

'That's over too.'

'You saw them?'

'Not exactly. Either they changed their minds about the live show or they never really planned it. The executions were yesterday, at Croydon. Only the Generals and Chinese officials present, but it was recorded, that's what was on the news this morning. I watched some. I only had sound for the rest, had to move out of the yard. It seemed to be the whole list, Lady Anne included, no exceptions.'

'So Jack Vries is dead?'

'Yes.'

'Oh.'

Ax glanced at him, and saw an odd, fleeting expression cross Sage's face, almost bewilderment. There's a need to confront the person who tortured you. You feel you won't be whole again until you've faced them down. He knew about that from his experiences as a hostage. It's an illusion, nothing will ever make it so those things didn't happen ... He longed to talk about the shootings, how hurried and brusque they had been. No ceremony. A handful of people. The executioner is some menial, a shock-headed minor officer. He fires at arm's length and the body is hustled onto a stretcher, while the next in line's already being hustled, blindfold, to the mark. No, he thought. Lay off. My big cat does not need to share that.

A red admiral butterfly flew up out of the walled garden behind them. Ax watched it settle on a stone by the path, its fresh, enamelled wings folded up above its body. He wondered if it was unusual to see a butterfly in October. He knew so little about nature. The grey and brown patterns on the hind wing were like the marbling on the endpapers of an old book.

'They stopped being moderate when they got to the top.'

'Yeah. Very rational people, the Chinese.'

There'd been no moderation at Reading Site, either ... And now Faud Hassim, who had survived that holocaust: Faud, who had kept his word and protected the Preston family, at great risk to himself, and gone on to lead England's last government; he was dead. He had been dead, already hustled blindfold to that mark, when Ax got up this morning, and prayed, and went down to Towncreep to watch the Chinese do his dirty work. Ax had not even witnessed it.

Everything seemed muted and far away, under the pale, shrouded sky.

'Sage? D'you still think about the Zen Self?'

'Yes,' said Sage. 'All the time.'

'What's that like?'

'I dunno what to tell you. It was like lucid dreaming. Being *there* again, *there* again, *there* again, at different moments, myriads on myriads of them, each of them carrying a whole world, layered together, interpenetrating, all the global brainstates, past, present and future, that make me what I am. And it's fractal, so that complex four-dimensional object, my entire self, is a gateway – unless you're daring to try and resolve the unresolved shit – drawing you in, towards the point where everything turns inside out and you're here again, but totally aware of the ways, ways beyond . . . but none of it, what I just said, is strictly conscious, it's more what you come back knowing, except—' He broke off, embarrassed. 'Sorry.'

'No, don't be. Please tell me.'

Sage shook his head. 'It's not the same. Say my simultaneity levels are close to normal again. Some little thing like the Lavoisier video can make me tackle the unresolved stuff. But tha's different, jus' *fucking* hard work—'

Ax nodded. Some little thing, yes. The Lavoisier video didn't seem like much, now. 'Could anything take you all the way back to where you were? Not the peace you have, which I know about, but that bizarre brainstate?'

Sage thought, with dread, of a clear glass on a red-gold velvet tablecloth.

'Say it's latent.'

'I can't get off on your abyss of non-being,' said Ax. 'It's not for me. But I've been thinking about what I tried to do. My deluded attempt to build a better world, my great discovery that people should live a certain way: a tech culture of *re-creation*, where our purpose in life is to be ourselves, and to look after each other, like the social animals we . . . You know that thing Isaac Newton said, about the seashore?'

'Subsistence living, community service and futuristic toys.

I remember. I was sold, babe, I still am ... Yeah, I know it. Newton said he'd been like a boy playing on the seashore. "Now and then finding a smoother pebble or a prettier shell than ordinary, whilst the great ocean of truth lay all undiscovered before me."'

'That's how I feel. When I got my big chance, when England first fell apart, all I could see was my pebble, my pretty shell of a grand plan. Now I see everything that happened to us, tiny on the shore of history, and the enormous ocean of human possibility is out there untouched. It's not consolation, something else. Silence. I gaze at that ocean, it's my abyss. And he felt like that, he had reached the silence, maybe more my way than yours; and everyone knows Newton was an absolute shite. I – I find that comforting.' Tears had come to his eyes, he wiped them. 'I'm not making sense, I'm sorry. I'll shut up.'

'You're making sense.'

They stood with their heads bowed, on the shore beside vast silence, under the milk-white sky, the naked heath all around. At last, released, they turned to look over the wall, at the garden where the crew of the Wellington were remembered. Last year's wreath of weather-worn scarlet poppies lay at the foot of a white cross. Salute, compadres. You were young, you died, and it's all over now.

'I am so fucking sorry I got you into this.'

'Ax, I'm tired of that line. Allow me to know my own mind. I got myself "into this". *You* rescued me from the fuckin' miserable state I was in before Dissolution, an' I have been right by you of my own free will ever since.' He grinned. 'Well, 'cept for the slight interval when I was screwing your girlfriend.'

'You scamp.'

They checked each other over. *God is good*, Sage's eyes were clear and bright, and not a shadow left of the bruises: at least, nothing you could see through the gypsy tan and the dirt. Sage returned the compliment, smiling: looking very fine, my guitar-man. 'You're going to keep it, aren't you?'

'You mean the tattoo?' Ax touched the knotwork: it felt like nothing, like skin, but he knew it was there. 'Oh yes,' he said. 'I'll wear this as long as I live.'

Right, thought Sage, resignedly. Because you deserve to wear the badge of shame, doncha, ya' stiff-necked puritan. Ah well, that's Ax.

'You should. Wandering Billy did you proud. It's beautiful. It suits you.'

The kitten woke, and squeaked. 'C'mon. She's probably back by now.'

Fiorinda walked and walked, blindfold by the mist, until she found herself in a stand of pine trees. Between the rough-tiled red pillars, white walls on either side; starting up rabbits, her panic receded. Pine trees never look English: she thought of the Mediterranean, which she had never seen. She'd been thinking of intricate, seductive layers of code in the video-diary tracks, and the hunger tug had crawled up inside her. She had only once, since Drumbeg, played with the REAL noughts and ones; not counting the time that had left no trace in memory. Just once, when there been no other way out of a very tricky situation, that had come up out of nowhere. But once was enough to know she was a fool for it and always would be. Fuck, fuck, fuck I'm an alcoholic who has to work in a bar, and struggle with this for life because I don't WANT to work anywhere else.

She sat at the foot of a tree, fists in her pockets, shivering hard, and thought about parietal lobe damage, the world dissolving into a fitful glimmer; everything displaced, in a state of flux, it's horrible when you recognise what certified loonies attempt to describe, when you think: ah, I have been there. In ways Rufus had been luckier, he just reached out and ate the world like a, a *flatworm*. Like a megastar, no fucking theories about it. Never knew he was condemning himself to eternal torment 'til he was there—

Don't think he felt the pain; not as pain. You don't, when it's all there is.

But I will not go mad. I will walk my line, I have people who love me.

She had come to the end of her flight, and everything was still. In front of her eyes, mist dropped in dew from the fisted needles on a low bough of pine.

Sunlit dancing oakleaf shadows on the canvas roof above my head, the smell of bruised grass and paraffin. Waking in Traveller's Meadow to the blurred familiar music of the festival site, that fair field full of folk, oh is it all gone? Everything I loved, all those people I died for, when I lay down with the dead man?

Yes, it is all gone.

Ammy is dead. Dilip is dead, the Wing children are dead.

Any number of other people are dead, and I did nothing, I let it happen . . .

The mist falls from the pine-needles, I feel myself breathing. So this is where we are, and we can't pretend to be surprised. The revolution was boiling with corruption from the start, they always are, it's a crying shame. Now the clean-up crew has arrived, and the finer points about how the Reich wasn't actually *guilty*, we were just bystanders, we just tried to help, yeah, right: none of that matters anymore . . . But they came to England, these people who are planning to clean up. They've proved the A-team event was a fake, they dismiss the Zen Self. Yet they came here, like a thunderbolt; and with Fred Eiffrich's blessing, Fred who would have done anything, sacrificed anything, to kill the Neurobomb research. What are we supposed to make of that?

There was a phrase General Wang used: *awakening from delusion*. China had come to Europe to awake people from delusion, no more fairytales, no more demons, no more dancing in the streets. Ax said it was a stock expression, a cliché, don't read too much into it: just basically means (Chinese not being Mother Nature's democrats) that if the emperor doesn't like the facts he can change them . . . But the words had set something ringing in Fiorinda's soul, like the first time she'd heard Ax's techno-Utopian manifesto. Is there someone else who believes we are *not* helpless before the monstrous forces we have created? Someone else who thinks it's possible to stand in the way of destruction's tide and turn that bastard around?

How amazing, and very dangerous, people like that are so dangerous—

She was shivering hard again, teeth locked to stop them chattering. Oh, God, what if I have a miscarriage, the way I lost that pregnancy in Paris? Oh my baby, please don't leave me, dear little baby, please, please don't leave me. Shit, I must not get so frightened. They pick up on your emotional state, of course they do, we're sharing a blood supply: so calm down.

. . .

I am not going to lose this one, she thought. It's a stubborn kind, it will hang on. She sat so quietly that a young rabbit came nibbling at the grass, almost to within reach of her hand. Hey, little Shoot (she called the baby shoot, it was a small thing growing). See the baby rabbit. Maybe it will let us stroke it. She held her breath, feeling as if she were being her baby's eyes. Come here, bunny, I won't hurt you. But the young rabbit knew a hungry predator when it saw one. It gave her a dark look, a very wise little sideways look, and scooted like mad.

Fiorinda laughed.

She came through the thorns that shielded the ruined cottage, breaking its outline even now the leaves had begun to fall, and saw the bothy with fresh eyes. A structure like an upturned bird's nest stood back between the gable-ends, where the kitchen floor had been open to the wind and rain: thatched in heather, the hazel-withy walls pasted with clay and furred in moss. What a lot of work. We did this, and we wrote songs, and all that code ... When did we sleep? Well, admittedly, the tech did most of the coding, far as my stuff and Ax's was concerned: bless it.

Other shelters she had known rose around her, drawn up by nets of fire. Her bedroom in the cold house. That smoky basement in the Snake Eyes Commune, Dissolution Summer, where she'd first shared a bed with Ax Preston; first seen that rueful gleam in his pretty eyes, when the crowd left them alone together. A trailer park cabin on a cold beach in Mexico, the red bedchamber at Wallingham ... She walked through them, unperturbed: walking her line. The front door of the bird's nest, a basketwork screen you could shift aside, was open. She tugged off her boots, stowed them under the eaves and ducked inside.

'Is it over?'

'Yeah,' said Sage. 'All over.'

'Good ... Any more for the casualty list?'

'No,' said Ax, quickly: he knew she meant their personal casualty list, he wasn't going to talk about the executions. 'One to take off. I saw Rox on the tv.'

'You didn't tell me that!' exclaimed Sage.

'It went out of my mind, sorry. It was only a glimpse, but s/he seemed fine. Getting out of a taxi in Queen Anne Street, straight indoors, through the Press pack, declining to comment.'

'How . . . how normal.'

'Yeah, it was strange.'

They made room, she sat between them on the heather bed; enhanced now by blankets from the empty house. Everything looked different. The water-still, their single blackened cooking pan, the equally blackened kettle. No fireplace; they made their fires outdoors, she remembered that. The generous body and taut-strung throat of Ax's Les Paul, glowing in shadow, her tapestry bag; the coloured rags, formerly clothes, stuffed into the basketweave. Rabbit skins, bones, feathers, ogre debris like a fox's den. She felt that she had woken from an eerie, compelling dream. *Where was I just now? What day is this? The Scots dumped us by the side of the road, and then . . . ?* She looked at Ax, she looked at Sage, and saw that they were feeling the same. They had fallen asleep, they had been in another world, but they were awake now.

'There's bread and milk,' said Ax. 'Let's eat.'

They shared the milk, tore up the bread and devoured it. Min dragged his share off, killed it elaborately and wolfed it down with gusto. He ate anything, and he had weird bower-bird tendencies: brought pebbles and sticks indoors, hid them in a secret cache and went bananas if anyone touched them . . . Outside the mist turned to rain, and they spoke of the ramped-up weatherproofing they'd need if they were going to stay here much longer. It was time to talk about the choice they'd made a month ago, and what they should do about it now. But not just yet, not right away. Fiorinda tried to convince Sage to let her at his hair.

'I'll do you cane rows, I've got a good comb.'

'You don't know how.'

'I do! Well, I've seen it done. How hard could a few little plaits be? All right, let me cut it. I have nail scissors. C'mon, whatever I do, it'll be an improvement on the greasy yellow afro.'

'Fuck off, evil brat. I am nurturing dreadlocks.'

Ax lay beside them with the kitten on his chest. He felt hollow and exhausted, and for a moment wondered why. *Memory cuts out, you live in the present. For in my day I have had many bitter and shattering experiences, in war and on the stormy seas.* He had a glimpse that this, the way he felt here and now, was what it would be like to reach the Zen Self. The world is a terrible place, and that's not going to go away, it's still got to be there, all of it, in the sweetness of the brimful cup.

We have to discuss what to do next, my cats.

Someone coughed.

The light at the doorway was blocked by a stooping figure, and a face was peering in. 'Morning all. I was passing, thought I'd drop by, er—?'

It was the poacher, one of those friendly locals they'd had to depend on.

'No problem,' said Ax.

'Good to see you, mister,' added Sage

'It's Dave, name's Dave, Mr Pender.'

'Come in,' said Fiorinda. 'Have a seat. We're not doing anything.'

'I brought you some tea,' said Dave the Poacher. He ducked indoors, like someone well used to living in a bender, and handed over a paper twist: looked like about a hundred grams, a substantial present. This was the man who had left the rabbits on the post, back in September: who had made Mr Preston effortlessly at that first encounter, because he had once been in the barmy army, been within an arm's length of you, Sir . . . He had served in the Velvet Invasion; since when he'd taken to living rough and found he liked it.

'It's raining a bit.' He drew out a packet of biscuits from an inner pocket, doubtfully, as if afraid he was overdoing it. 'Thought I'd say hallo, how are you?'

'We'll brew up then,' said Fiorinda. 'We were just going to.'

The poacher had spoken to Ax, in the dusk of dawn or nightfall, and left his gifts of game on the post, but he had never let himself be seen near the bothy; certainly never come to their door. Nobody referred to the novelty of the visit, or hazarded a guess at the reason for it. Sage boiled a kettle out in the ruins and they shared a brew.

The pain and pins and needles of returning life

The gingernuts didn't go far. More visitors arrived, by ones and twos, until the headcount passed thirty: which was a shock. They'd known they had protectors, who might become betrayers; or pay a heavy price for staying loyal. They'd accepted this as fate, but you wondered just how far the whisper had spread. Ah well, too bad, we more or less knew what we were doing . . . Most came for a few minutes, bringing gifts of food, as is traditional. Others stayed longer;

some made a session of it. No one stated what was happening, or why. Conversation was mainly about the Forest, the habits of wildlife, local affairs: a little, at last, about the events this morning in London, and yesterday in the prison yard in Croydon.

The hosts kept the teakettle going. Milk and sugar arrived with the company. Cups and mugs were shared, which caused good-humoured problems over differing tastes. Later, the poacher offered to top up the brew with 'something'. He meant vodka, but finding Fiorinda and Ax demurred he just passed the bottle round. Ax took down his guitar and started picking. Nobody took any notice. The visitors behaved as if it was perfectly natural to have Ax Preston playing guitar like that. Sage and Fiorinda acted like it happened all the time; which indeed it did. People spoke more boldly, about the astonishing speed of the invasion; how far away it all seemed.

Degrees of separation. I could have been in London that week, but I wasn't. My wife's cousin was killed in Cornwall. My grandad saw them coming in. What about those amazing semi-orbital ships? What d'you think they use for fuel? Somebody had heard that the rocket fuel was made out seawater. The Chinese run everything on seawater and shit.

'I think that's a joke,' said the younger of the two boys from Stanger's dairy farm, one of the places where Ax went to siphon news. 'Hu was making a joke, and he meant brackish water, worthless water, only he didn't know the word.'

'Oh yeah,' countered his brother. 'And how many Chinese words do you know, smartarse?'

'I know the name for England. It's Yingguoren, it means "brave country".'

That cracked everybody up.

'They'll have to think of something else,' said Mrs Brown from the Anchor at Hartfield, where Ax had gone begging, basically, at the kitchen door; and been treated like a king. Which had impressed him very much, until it dawned on him (duh) that she knew who he was.

Mrs Brown's teenage daughter, Alison, was doing a hedgeschool maths and physics intranet course. 'If you had the exact flight plan,' she offered, trying her best, 'you could work out some parameters for the fuel, couldn't you?'

'If I had the exact flight plan,' said the eggman, going red in the

295

face, 'I'd beat you over the head with it. Callous little bugger!' he exclaimed, in general. 'It's not a pub quiz! It's people's lives, it's—'

The Forest Ranger, the one who'd caught Sage and Fiorinda nicking hazel poles, nudged him sharply; and he shut up. Apart from that outburst no one showed any distress except the railway linesman, who was a little weepy. But there were long pauses, as there had been all day: in which Ax's guitar came up singing.

At nightfall Fiorinda lingered over putting her fire to bed. The chimney in the west gable had proved functional once they'd removed the starling nests. They had even *cleaned* it, by dragging bunches of heather through the flue. Just leave us alone, she thought. Let us mend our house in peace, we don't care where the government lives. The rain had stopped; a few stars were coming out. Sage and Ax emerged from the bothy with the poacher; the last of their guests.

The three men stood gazing at the sky.

'I'd better be going,' said Dave. Then he looked so solemn and daring that Ax wondered what the fuck was coming: but he just thrust out his earth-coloured right hand. Ax shook it. '*Thank you,*' he said, very chuffed. 'Well, now they'll find out.'

Ax grinned, and nodded. 'Yeah. Now we have to win the peace.'

The poacher was a sharp man, probably no older than Ax and Sage, but one of those people who moves quickly to a permanent ageless state. He looked at Ax as if calculating the behaviour of something wild, and maybe dangerous.

'Ah. Is that what we've got to do, Sir?'

'It's the only way.'

The three stood looking after him, 'til he'd vanished between the thorns. They were adapted to this time, the half-light that animals live in. 'I didn't think I'd spend today celebrating a wake,' said Ax.

'I had no idea I knew how to do it,' said Sage.

'The awkward silences and everything,' agreed Fiorinda. 'We did well on the food.'

Ax had not realised how much he'd missed this state of mind, the cream poured over the bitter shot of liquor, you think you remember but you forget; until you get back into the same situation. I have found the white light again, he thought. I'm going to find a way out of this snare, and I don't give a damn, right now, if believing I can do that is dangerous medicine.

'One more Shakespearian moment,' he said. They nodded: yeah. The King and the Queen, and their lover, the great Minister, standing in the castle courtyard, at the nadir of their fortunes. Now out of this nettle, danger, we will pluck the flower, safety.

> Let the sun come up tomorrow
> Let the sun go down tonight
> Let the ploughshare and the harrow.
> Work and rest, work and rest.